ISAAC ASIMOV'S
ROBOTS AND ALIENS
VOLUME TWO

ROBERT THURSTON

ROBERT THURSTON has been writing science fiction and fantasy since the early 1970s, after attending the second and third Clarion SF Writing Workshops. When the first collection of stories from Clarion was published, his story "Wheels" was awarded first prize; the story later became the basis for his novel *A Set of Wheels*. He has written over a dozen novelizations and original novels, including *Alicia II, Q Colony, Battletech, Robot Jox,* and nine *Battlestar Galactica* books. He lives in New Jersey with his wife, Rosemary.

JERRY OLTION

JERRY OLTION is the Nebula Award-winning author of "Abandon in Place," which won its award for Best Novella in 1997; a novel based on it was published in 2000 by Tor Books. Another story, "The Astronaut from Wyoming," co-written with Adam-Troy Castro, was also nominated for both the Nebula and Hugo awards in 2000. He has been a gardener, stone mason, carpenter, oilfield worker, forester, land surveyor, rock 'n' roll deejay, printer, proofreader, editor, publisher, computer, consultant, movie extra, and garbage truck driver. For the last 20 years he has also found time to write twelve novels and over 100 stories, including four *Star Trek* books: *Twilight's End, Mudd in Your Eye, Where Sea Meets Sky,* and *The Flaming Arrow*—the last a collaboration with his wife, Kathy. The Oltions live in Eugene, Oregon, with the obligatory writer's cat, Ginger.

ISAAC ASIMOV'S
ROBOTS AND ALIENS

VOLUME TWO

INTRUDER by
ROBERT THURSTON

ALLIANCE by
JERRY OLTION

ibooks
new york
www.ibooksinc.com

DISTRIBUTED BY SIMON & SCHUSTER, INC

An Original Publication of ibooks, inc.

Copyright © 1990, 2002 by Byron Preiss Visual Publications, Inc.

Introductions copyright © 1990 by Nightfall, Inc.
ALL RIGHTS RESERVED

An ibooks, inc. Book

ibooks, inc.
24 West 25th Street
New York, NY 10010

The ibooks World Wide Web Site Address is:
http://www.ibooksinc.com

ISBN 0-7434-3513-3
First ibooks, inc. printing March 2002
10 9 8 7 6 5 4 3 2 1

Cover art by Paul Rivoche
Cover design by j. vita

Printed in the U.S.A.

ISAAC ASIMOV'S
ROBOTS AND ALIENS

BOOK THREE
INTRUDER

ROBERT THURSTON

WHAT IS A HUMAN BEING?

ISAAC ASIMOV

It sounds like a simple question. Biologically, a human being is a member of the species *Homo sapiens*. If we agree that one particular organism (say, a male) is a human being, then any female with which he can breed is also a human being. And any males with whom any of these females can breed are also human beings. This instantly marks up billions of organisms on Earth as human beings.

It may be that there are organisms that are too old to breed, or too young, or too imperfect in one way or another, but who resemble human beings more than they resemble any other species. They, too, are human beings.

We thus end up with something over 5 billion human beings on Earth right now, and perhaps 60 billion who have lived on Earth since *Homo sapiens* evolved.

That's simple, isn't it? From the biological standpoint, we are all human beings, whether we speak English, Turkish, or Japanese; whether we have pale skin or dark; red hair or black; blue eyes or brown; flat noses or beaky ones; and so on.

That, however, is a biological definition, a sophisticated one. Now suppose that you are a member of a primitive tribe, homogeneous in appearance, language and culture, and you suddenly encounter someone who looks superficially like you but has red hair, where you've seen only black; fair skin where you've seen only dark; and, worst of all, who cannot understand "people language" but makes odd sounds, which he seems to understand, but which clearly make no sense whatever.

Are these strangers human beings in the sense that you yourself are? I'm afraid the consensus would be that they are not. Nor is it entirely a matter of lack of sophistication. The ancient Greeks, who were certainly among the most sophisticated human beings who ever lived, divided all human beings into two groups: Greeks and barbarians.

By barbarians, they didn't mean people who were un-civilized or bestial. They recognized that some barbarians, like the Egyptians and Babylonians and Persians were highly cultivated. It was just that non-Greeks didn't speak Greek; they made sounds that made no more sense (to a Greek encountering other languages for the first time) than a silly sound like "bar-bar-bar."

You might feel that Greeks may have made that division as a matter of convenience, but that they didn't go so far as to think that barbarians weren't human.

Oh, didn't they? Aristotle, one of the most sophisticated of all the ancient Greeks, was quite certain that barbarians were slave-material by nature, while Greeks were free men by nature. Clearly, he felt that there was something sub-human about barbarians.

But they were ancients, however sophisticated they might have been. They had limited experience, knew only a small portion of the world. Nowadays, we have learned so much we don't come to those foolish conclusions. We *know* that all human-like creatures are a single species.

Yes? Was it so long ago that most White Americans were quite certain that African Blacks were *not* human in the sense that they themselves were; that the Blacks were inferior and that to enslave them and let them live on the outskirts of a White society was doing them a great favor? I wouldn't be surprised if some Americans believe that right now.

It was not so long ago that Germans maintained loudly that Slavs and Jews were sub-human, so that they were right to do their best to rid "true" human beings of such vermin. And I wouldn't be in the least surprised if there were lots of people right now who harbor similar notions.

Almost everyone thinks of other groups as "inferior," although often they do not care to say so out loud. They tend to divide humanity into groups of which only a small part (a part which invariably includes themselves) are "true" human beings.

The Bible, of course, teaches universality (at least, in places). Thus, consider one of my own favorite passages in the New Testament, the parable of the "good Samaritan" (Luke 10:25–37). Someone tells Jesus that one of the beliefs one must have if one is to go to Heaven is "to love . . . thy neighbour as thyself." Jesus says he is correct and the man asks, "And who is my neighbor?" (In other words, does he love only his friends and people he likes, or is he supposed to love all sorts of bums and rotters?)

And here comes the parable of the good Samaritan. To put it briefly, a man needs help, and both a Priest and a Levite (professional do-gooders, who are highly esteemed by pious people) ignore the whole matter, but a Samaritan offers a great deal of help.

Now we talk so much about a "good" Samaritan because of this parable, that we think of the Samaritans as all good and are not surprised at the help he offers. However, to the pious Jews of Jesus' time, Samaritans were heretics, things of evil, objects of hatred—and here we have a despised Samaritan doing good when Priests and Levites do not.

And then Jesus asks, "Which now of these three, thinkest thou, was neighbour unto him that fell among the thieves?" And the man is forced to say, "He that shewed mercy on him."

This is as much to say that all good people are neighbors even when they are the kind of beneath-contempt individuals as Samaritans are. And it follows, since all human beings have the capacity to be good, all people are neighbors and love should extend to all.

St. Paul says in Galatians 3:28: "There is neither Jew nor Greek; there is neither bond nor free; there is neither male nor female: for ye are all one in Christ Jesus."

That is a flat statement of universality.

I know that there are many pious people who know these passages and who nevertheless maintain racist views of one sort or another. Such is the desire to be part of a superior group that nothing can wipe out the tendency to picture others as inferior; to divide human beings into a) human, b)semi-human, and c)sub-human, being careful always to put yourself into the first class.

And if we have such trouble in getting human beings to define what a human being is, imagine the problem a robot would have. How does a robot define a human being?

In the old days, when I was first beginning to write my robot stories, John W. Campbell (my editor and mentor) challenged me on several occasions to write a story that hinged on the difficulty of defining a human being. I always backed off. I did not have to try writing such a story to know that it would be a particularly difficult one to write and that I couldn't do it. At least, not then.

In 1976, however, I finally tackled the job and wrote "The Bicentennial Man." It dealt essentially with a robot that became more and more human, without ever being accepted as a human being. He became physically like a human being, mentally like a human being, and yet he never crossed the line. Finally, he did, by crossing the last barrier. He made himself mortal, and as he was dying, he was finally accepted as a human being.

It made a good story (winning both the Hugo and the Nebula) but it didn't offer a *practical* way of distinguishing between robot and human being, because a robot couldn't wait for years to see if a possible human being died and thus proved itself to be a human being.

Suppose you are a robot and you have to decide whether something that looks like a human being is *really* a human being, and you have to do it reasonably quickly.

If the only robots that exist are primitive, there is no problem. If an object looks like a human being but is made of metal, it is a robot. If it talks in a mechanical kind of voice, moves with awkward jerky motions, and so on and so on, it is a robot.

But what if the robot looks, superficially, exactly like a human being (like my robot, Daneel Olivaw). How can you tell that he's a robot? Well, in my later robot novels, you can't, really. Daneel Olivaw is a human being in all respects except that he's a lot more intelligent than most human beings, a lot more ethical, a lot kinder and more decent, a lot *more* human. That makes for a good story, too, but it doesn't help identify a robot in any practical sense. You can't follow a robot around to see if it is better than a human being, for you then have to ask yourself—is he (she) a robot or just an unusually good human being?

There's this—

A robot is bound by the Three Laws of Robotics, and a human being is not. That means, for instance, that if you are a human being and you punch someone you think may be a robot and he punches you back, then he is *not* a robot. If you yourself are a robot, then if you punch him and he punches you back, he may nevertheless be a robot, since he may know that *you* are a robot, and First Law does not prevent him from hitting you. (That was a key point in my early story, "Evidence.") In that case, though, you must ask a human being to punch the suspected robot, and if he punches back he is no robot.

However, it doesn't work the other way around. If you are a human being and you hit a suspected robot, and he *doesn't* hit you back, that doesn't mean he *is* a robot. He may be a human being, but a coward. He may be a human being but an idealist, who believes in turning the other cheek.

In fact, if you are a human being and you punch a suspected robot and he punches you back, then he may *still* be a robot, nevertheless.

After all, the First Law says, "A robot may not harm a human being or, through inaction, allow a human being to come to harm." That, however, begs the question, for it assumes that a robot knows what a human being is in the first place.

Suppose a robot is manufactured to be no better than a human being. Human beings often suppose other people are inferior, and not fully human, if they simply don't speak your language, or speak it with an odd accent. (That's the whole point of George Bernard Shaw's *Pygmalion*.) In that case, it should be simple to build a robot within whom the definition of a human being includes the speaking of a specific language with a specific accent. Any failure in that respect makes a person the robot must deal with *not* a human being and the robot can harm or even kill him without breaking the First Law.

In fact, I have a robot in my book *Robots and Empire* for which a human being is defined as speaking with a Solarian accent, and my hero is in danger of death for that very reason.

So you see it is not easy to differentiate between a robot and a human being.

We can make the matter even more difficult, if we suppose a world of robots that have never seen human beings. (This would be like our early unsophisticated human beings who have never met anyone outside their own tribe.) They might still have the First Law and might still know that they must not harm a human being—but what is this human being they must not harm?

They might well think that a human being is superior to a robot in some ways, since that would be one reason why he must not be harmed. You ought not to offer violence to someone worthier than yourself.

On the other hand, if someone were superior to you, wouldn't it be sensible to suppose that you *couldn't* harm him? If you could, wouldn't that make him inferior to you? The fallacy there ought to be obvious. A robot is certainly superior to an unthinking rock, yet a falling rock might easily harm or even destroy a robot. Therefore the inferior *can* harm the superior, but in a well-run Universe it should *not* do so.

In that case, a robot beginning only with the Laws of

Robotics might well conclude that human beings were superior to robots.

But then, suppose that in this world of robots, one robot is superior to all the rest. Is it possible, in that case, that this superior robot, who has never seen a human being, might conclude that he himself is a human being?

If he can persuade the other robots that this is so then the Laws of Robotics will govern their behavior toward him and he may well establish a despotism over them. But will it differ from a human despotism in any way? Will this robot-human still be governed and limited by the Three Laws in certain respects, or will it be totally free of them?

In that case, if it has the appearance and mentality and behavior of a human being, and if it lacks the Three Laws, in what way is it not a human being? Has it not become a human being in actuality?

And what happens if, then, *real* human beings appear on the scene? Do the Three Laws suddenly begin to function again in the robot-human, or does he persist in considering himself human? In my very first published robot story, "Reason," come to think of it, I described a robot that considered himself to be superior to human beings and could not be argued out of it.

So what with one thing or another, the problem of defining a human being is enormously complex, and while in my various stories I've dealt with different aspects of it, I am glad to leave the further consideration of that problem to Robert Thurston in this third book of the Robots and Aliens series.

CHAPTER 1

ROBOT CITY DREAMS

Derec knew he was dreaming. The street he now ambled down wasn't real. There had never been a street anywhere in Robot City like this distorted thoroughfare. Still, too much *was* familiar about it, and that really scared him.

The Compass Tower, now too far in the distance, had changed, too. There seemed to be lumps all over its surfaces, but that was impossible. In a city where buildings could appear and disappear overnight, the Compass Tower was the only permanent, unchangeable structure.

It was possible this strange street was newly created, but he doubted that. It was a dream-street, plain and simple, and this had to be a dream. Anyway, where were the robots? Nobody could travel this far along a Robot City street without encountering at least a utility robot scurrying along, on its way to some regular task; or a courier robot, its claws clutching tools; or a witness robot, checking the movements of the humans. During a stroll like this, Derec should have encountered a robot every few steps.

No, it was absolutely certain this was a dream. What he

was doing was sleeping in his ship somewhere in space between the blackbody planet and Robot City. He had just come off duty after dealing with the Silversides for hours, a task that would tire a saint.

At one time, just after his father had injected chemfets into his bloodstream, he had regularly dreamed of Robot City, but it turned out that his harrowing nightmares had all been induced by a monitor that his father had implanted in his brain. The monitor had been trying to establish contact so he could be aware of the nature of the chemfets, which were tiny circuit boards that grew in much the same manner as the city itself had. Replicating in his bloodstream and programmed by his father, they were a tiny robot city in his body, one that gave him psycho-electronic control over the city's core computer and therefore all its robots. After he had known this and the chemfets' replication process had stabilized, he had had no more nightmares of a distorted Robot City.

Until now.

Since he was so aware he was dreaming, perhaps this was what Ariel had explained to him as a "lucid dream." In the lucid dream state, she said, the dreamer could control the events of the dream. He wanted to control this dream, but at the moment he couldn't think of anything particular to do.

He looked around him. The immediate streetscape seemed composed of bits and pieces from several stages of the city's development, a weird composite of what Derec had observed during his several stays there.

But where were the robots?

If this was a lucid dream, maybe the reason he hadn't seen any yet was that he hadn't guided any into the scene. Maybe they were waiting inside the buildings to be summoned. Maybe he should do so, before he panicked. But which one could he bring onstage? How about Lucius, the robot who had created the city's one authentic artistic masterpiece, the breathtaking tetragonal, pyramidal building-sculpture entitled "Circuit Breaker"? He'd be a good choice since, as the victim of a bizarre roboticide, he no longer existed. It certainly would be pleasant to see old Lucius again, his body so unrobotically stooped, if only to chat with him about art. There hadn't been much art in his life lately, especially if you didn't count the rather breathtaking spectacle of a thousand blackbodies spread across the sky. That was pretty, but it wasn't art.

He wondered why his thoughts were rambling so. Had the Silversides disturbed his mind's equilibrium that much? Forget them. Forget them now. Get a normal robot into the dream. One of the most unforgettable robots he had known. Avernus, say. Let's see his stern visage again, his jet-black metallic skin, his interchangeable hands. He concentrated on Avernus, but the robot didn't appear. How about Euler and his glowing photocell eyes? Nope, no deal. Let's try for Wohler, then, *before* he went nonfunctional trying to save Ariel on the outer wall of the Compass Tower. Golden and impressive, Wohler would be a wonderful choice. But no Wohler responded to his summons. He would have to talk to Ariel about this. As a lucid dream, it was shaping up as one hell of a failure.

Ariel, in her compartment aboard the ship, was also dreaming. Hers was not, however, a lucid dream. Deeper than that, it was a clearcut nightmare.

Jacob Winterson, the humaniform robot who had been her servant, existed again. Jacob had been destroyed by Neuronius, one of the flying aliens called blackbodies. He had blown up and mangled most of Jacob (and himself in the bargain). The few charred pieces that remained were now buried in some unmarked area of the agricultural community she had initiated as a political compromise with the blackbodies. The compromise had worked. They had been about to destroy their planet's new robot city entirely because it was a threat to their weather systems; however, an agricultural community was acceptable to all sides.

She missed Jacob. Very much. In that comfortable, detached way a human could love a robot, she had loved him. Not that it could ever have been real love. She was too much in love with Derec to be unfaithful to him except in dreams. On the other hand, she could not deny that she had not sometimes been romantically attracted toward the handsome and imperturbable humaniform robot.

In the dream, Jacob sat in front of a computer terminal, his humanlike fingers flying over the keyboard, pressing keys as if he wanted to push them all the way through, making the screen shake with the ferocity of his entries.

She asked him what he was doing. He said he was searching for the formula that would transform a humaniform robot into a human being. There was no such formula, she told him. When he turned toward her, his eyes seemed filled with a frightening human anger. He protested that there were at least a hundred Earth and Spacer legends in which creatures changed into human beings. Statues, puppets, fish, trees, all became human in such myths. He was certain, he said with an un-Jacobian shrillness, that there had to be a formula by which he, too, could be transmogrified.

Why did the Compass Tower look so diseased? Derec asked himself. Was it possible for him, as a lucid dreamer, to change that? He concentrated on the building's shape, trying to restore it to its architecturally magnificent pyramidal form. But nothing happened. If anything, the tower became uglier, and he had to look away from it.

In the distance something came toward him, traveling down the street at a high speed. As it passed by buildings, the buildings changed. When it neared, he saw it was a vehicle, but one quite unlike any Robot City mode of transportation. It ran on three thick wheels, making it vaguely resemble a jitney, the smaller, lighter utility type of vehicle used for taxiing around the city. The vehicle's body was misshapen, as if a lot of ungeometric chunks had been welded together on a long central stem. It was colored black and gray in an illogical and splotchy fashion.

Still certain he was in the midst of a lucid dream, Derec stood defiantly in the center of the roadway—daring the vehicle to come to a screeching stop at his feet. Which it did. *Good,* he thought, *I'm in control of the dream at last. Just watch me now.*

A large hatch at the top of the vehicle sprang open with an explosive sound, and Dr. Avery, his father, pulled himself through the opening. What kind of a lucid dream was this? The last person he wanted to see was his megalomaniacal father, interfering in a dream in just the way he'd interfered with Derec's life, injecting him with chemfets and transforming him into a walking computer. Half-computer, anyway.

Avery was looking more demented than usual. His eyes, usually intense, now glowed with an overdramatic madness. In fact, Avery looked so exaggerated that Derec felt he could relax. No reason to be afraid, after all, just a dream. A dream he would seize control of at any moment.

• • •

Ariel placed her hand upon Jacob's. His hand, she noted, felt soft, more like human than humaniform. She told him to stop. There was no need for him to become human. Even if he found a formula, it would be foolish to use it. As a humaniform robot, Jacob had all the virtues of human existence without all the miseries, without human physical and emotional pains.

Jacob turned away from the computer and looked at Ariel, for a moment a humanlike sadness in his eyes.

"Don't you see?" he said, "I *want* the misery. I want to feel what a human feels. Pain, happiness, love. I want to love you, Mistress Ariel."

She put a finger on his lips. In contrast to his hand, they felt robotic, hard metal lips that could, if she pressed hard enough, make her fingertip bleed. She almost wanted to test that out. If she tried to cut her hand, would Jacob be able to invoke the First Law of Robotics—the part stating that a robot could not allow a human to come to harm—fast enough to prevent her from succeeding?

"You can't love me, Jacob," she said tenderly. "I love Derec, so there's no point in your loving me. It would be—what do they call it in romances—unrequited."

"That wouldn't matter. I would be happy with that, too. I could respond to it, as in your great literary works. I could, like one of your legendary lovers, die falling off a bridge or swimming a river or with a vial of poison and a great dagger plunging in—"

"Hush, Jacob. Please stop. I wouldn't want you to die for me."

"I am already dead."

"No, don't say that. You're here. You're—"

"In a grave."

"Jacob—"

"A rotting scrap pile of metal, spare parts covered by soil."

His words were so fiercely spoken they frightened her. She backed away from him.

Dr. Avery was dressed in a black-and-gray silver-buttoned uniform that seemed too militaristic for a scientist.

"You look bemused," he said, then added almost contemptuously: ". . . my son. What is bothering you?"

"It's well, it's that this is my dream, and I'm supposed to be in control, and you're not welcome in it."

Avery smiled sinisterly. "You can't get me out of it. I am everywhere. In the city, in your dreams, in your hat."

"My hat? I don't even wear a—"

"Just an old Earth expression. I am an expert in old Earth expressions. Can it, flip out, you're the bee's knees, life is hard and then you die. I know Earth expressions from all parts of its history."

"But I wouldn't know any, and this is my dream, and you come out of my mind."

"Are you sure?"

"I know you're nowhere near. I am on a ship heading for Robot City. You may be in the city, muddling things up as usual, but you're not on this ship."

"Maybe I am. I am, after all, omniscient and omnipotent."

"I know, I know. Always a god in your own mind."

"Yes."

If this was a lucid dream, Derec thought, then he should be able to flee from the old bastard. He whirled around and started running down the street. On both sides of him buildings seemed to slip into the ground while new ones popped out.

Many buildings were oddly shaped, not at all like any existing Robot City ones. Some were tilted at odd angles, with several leaning into others while others leaned away. In the distance a tall edifice swayed from side to side as if caught in a violent wind. But there was a rhythm to its swaying, reminding him of a dance. What dance? Something intruding from his past, a vague memory that would not get focused. His past had a way of doing that, with some memory fragment flashing into his mind and going right out again before he could make any connection with it. There were so many parts of his past life that were still blocked from his mind by the amnesia that had once been total.

Ariel suddenly found herself in an underground corridor on Earth, but it looked nothing like any of the tunnels she had seen during her actual visit there. For one thing, it was deserted. You never saw an empty passageway on Earth. Human bodies were visible everywhere, except in private quarters.

Her steps echoed hollowly through the corridor, with a hundred echoes of echoes. She felt as if she were being hounded by a mob of people all walking at her exact pace. Each time she turned around to confront her trackers, there was no one in sight.

She came to a Section Kitchen, the kind of public eating area she'd come to despise. Plenty of food steamed on cafeteria-style trays, but no people sat at the many numbered tables or worked behind the counters. The room looked as if there had been a sudden alarm and everyone had scurried out.

She felt hungry, and, taking a spoon and wiping it thoroughly on a paper napkin (she was an Auroran, after all, who was repelled by Earth's poor hygienic habits), she scooped out a biteful of something soft and white. However, when she put it in her mouth, it seemed to flame up and singe her tongue and the roof of her mouth. She spit it out.

"Are you poisoned, Mistress Ariel?" It was Jacob again, appearing at her side as if by magic.

"No. But it is good of you to ask."

"I must. First Law."

"Oh, of course. If you decide to become human, Jacob, you won't have to obey the Laws of Robotics any more. I'll miss the advantage of having you protect me."

"I would protect you, mistress, whether I were human or robot."

There was something so touching, something so sad and vulnerable about this dream version of her dead robot companion, that Ariel began to cry. She cried in her dream, and she was still crying when she woke up.

Derec looked back. Avery and his strange vehicle had vanished from the center of the street. Good, at least something in this lucid dream had worked out right.

Ahead of him there was a park. Derec could see tall trees, thick with branches, heavy with green leaves. Brightly colored flowers lined cobblestone paths. Metal umbrellas shaded soft lights that were spaced evenly along the pathways. At the top of a slight rise, he could see swings, slides, see-saws, monkey bars, all the equipment of a playground.

He raced toward the park, picking up his pace. The street seemed to speed beneath him as if he were powering a treadmill. Before he reached the park, the buildings lining the street grew larger, towering over the thoroughfare, bending toward it, shading the light and making everything darker.

His last step from the city street onto the park's cobbled path was an impressive leap, one longer than he could normally accomplish. Landing, he stumbled forward for several steps.

He started walking toward the playground. The pathway was soft, resilient. He decided to trot, and the bounciness of the path added a spring to his steps. He attained such a speed that he nearly skidded past the playground entrance.

A closed gate blocked the way into the playground. Above the gate was a gilded sign that read; AVERY PARK. The old reprobate, he'd named a park after himself. What gall! Playgrounds were supposed to represent happiness and joy. In no way did they suggest the doctor's monstrous cynicism.

Underneath the large sign was a smaller one that read, STAND ON SOAP, ALL GEEKS WHO MENTOR HERE. What did Avery mean by that? And how could he, after all, mean anything? He was merely a figure in Derec's dream. The real question was how could Derec's mind have formed this unusual scene, these strange words. He would have to discuss all this with Ariel, the expert on such matters.

When he opened the gate, there was a sonorous beep as the gate-latch separated from its fastening. A deep voice that seemed to come from above said, "Welcome. Enjoy."

"Enjoy what?" Derec asked. There was no reply, no doubt because the voice was a recording cued by the opening of the gate.

Tentatively he took a couple of steps into the playground. To his immediate right was a high slide. Even though he didn't remember his childhood, he knew it was a slide. It even looked like a familiar one. Walking up to it, he discovered it was incomplete. No ladder led up to the platform from which a child would start his downward plunge. The slide appeared to stand without any support.

An overwhelming urge to try out the slide came over him. Although he could have climbed from the bottom edge of the slide up to the platform at its top, he knew he *had* to start from the platform itself. This was *his* lucid dream and he could do anything he wanted to, including jump higher than was physically possible. Crouching down as close to the ground as he could get, he jumped up. He reached for the edge of the platform, but just missed. Back on the ground, he scrunched down again and made a second, magnificent leap that took him higher than the level of the platform. Reaching out, he grabbed its rim. Struggling and grunting, he pulled himself onto the small platform. It bounced up and down like a diving board, nearly flinging him back to the ground.

The slide seemed even taller than it had from ground level, or else he had become very small, a child again. Looking down at his hands, he saw they'd shrunk. They *were* child's hands. Not only that, his clothing had been magically transformed. He was now dressed in one of those silver jumpers that were once all the rage for toddlers. (How did he know about silver jumpers?) Before he could even speculate on this mystery, a voice from down below called to him: "C'mon down the slide, honey. I'll catch you."

There was a woman standing at the foot of the slide. She seemed tall and thin, but he could not make out the details of her face, even though it was turned upward at him. Her voice was soft and wonderfully friendly. He felt ready to slide down to her. But, even as he stared at her, her shape changed. Now she was a short, rather plump lady in odd, out-of-date clothes, but the face was still not discernible. Was this some trick of one of the Silversides? Were they experimenting with human shapes, using pictures they extracted from the ship computer?

"Don't be afraid, honey," the woman said. Was he mistaken, or was that Eve Silverside's voice? "You won't fall off the slide. It'll be all right."

If it was a Silverside, he or she just might make him fall to the ground by pulling her hands away just as he reached the bottom edge. He shrunk back, no longer wanting to slide down.

The woman was now medium height, medium build, wearing a pristinely white lab smock. No matter what shape she took, what clothes she wore, he still saw no face. He knew there was a face there. It just wouldn't come into focus for him in spite of the vivid details of the rest of her.

"Let go of those bars, dear, and come down. Don't worry. Mommy'll catch you."

Mommy! This was his mother? No, it *must* be a Silverside, playing a joke. He didn't know his mother and, in fact, knew very little about her. His father had provided no informaton. How could a Silverside even hope to duplicate her? Wait. This was a dream. The woman below was neither Silverside nor his mother. It was an apparition from his own mind.

One thing he did know now. He didn't want to go down the slide, not even to his mother's eagerly awaiting arms. He started to scream. His screams sounded childlike, shrill, high-pitched, tremulous.

"No, I'm not coming down. I'm not! I'm not!"

"It's all right, David. Mommy's right here."

David: his real name, or at least the one that Ariel and his father had said was the right one. Perhaps this was no dream and this was really his mother. If he slid down, he could see her better. But her arms might turn into knives, fire, pain. He was suddenly very afraid of her.

"Leave me alone!" he screamed. "Leave me alone!"

Suddenly the bars he was clutching became red-hot, and so did the metal beneath him. It felt the way a slide did when it had been standing in the sun at high noon on the hottest day of the year. (How did he know that?)

He could not hold on.

He had to let go.

He slid down, screaming.

His mother's face seemed to come up at him, but there were still no recognizable features on it.

He saw her reach out toward him.

And woke up.

He could feel the sweat on his face as he stared up into the lovely face of Ariel Welsh. She stood beside his bunk, her arms reaching out to him just like his dream-mother's had.

CHAPTER 2

DEALING WITH THE SILVERSIDES

Ariel rubbed Derec's forehead gently. The way she touched him was now one of his favorite things in life. It seemed to him that her fingertips did not actually make contact with his skin but merely gave off comforting rays as they passed above it. Ariel had told him that there were people who appeared to heal the sick because of the comforting warm emanations that came from their hands. The warmth had actually been measured and was sometimes burning hot. On the planet Solaria, she told him, such affection or healing was rare. Solarians obeyed taboos against touching others, and that seemed sad to her.

"You're positively drenched in sweat, Derec. That must have been one whale of a dream."

"It was. Awful."

"I know how you feel. I just had a lulu of a nightmare myself."

"What was your dream about?"

She didn't want to tell him that it concerned Jacob Winterson or that she had awakened crying. He'd been somewhat jealous of Jacob, so the subject was best ignored right now.

"Nothing special. Tell me yours."

"There was the city, Robot City, and it was all strange, mixed up. And my father in a car that looked like a disease. And . . . and . . . my mother . . ."

"Hush, hush. Take it easy. When you're ready, tell me all about it, calmly and in order."

He nodded. Getting up from the bunk, he brushed past her. As he paced, he concentrated on stretching the sleep out of his muscles and lowering his breathing to an acceptable rhythm. "I thought I was having a lucid dream, but, you know, I was never able to control it, not even for a second."

As he related the dream, Ariel noted that his face and voice were childlike. Sometimes she forgot how young they actually were. All the responsibility and strain of their lives since they had first come to Robot City had seemed to age them incredibly. Sometimes her mental image of herself was of a much older woman, one who'd been coping with adversity for so long that the experience registered in deep lines on her face. However, a look into any mirror showed her the same young, almost adolescent, mien: the baby fat of her cheeks, the brightness of her eyes, the radiance of her long black hair, the youthful sheen of her skin. Her figure, once fairly gaunt, had filled out well, too—as Derec so often reminded her.

Looking into his tired eyes, realizing he had not slept well for some time, she wondered how a couple of kids like them had stumbled into a life filled with so much tension and danger. Why couldn't they go back to Aurora (they had been there, excited with their love, for too brief a time) and romp without care through one of its lovely forests or swim in a placid lake? If not Aurora, the strictly regimented, uncomfortably overpopulated Earth might even do. Anywhere where they could be suitably young for a while.

"What do you make of it, Ariel? The dream?"

She wondered how much analysis he could take right now. His face pale beneath his damp, sandy hair, he looked vulnerable.

"Well, I don't really know. Maybe all the worries you've had, what with the strange messages you've been getting from Robot City, maybe they're just coming out in your dreams."

Derec's chemfets had gone haywire when he had tried to contact Robot City. Normally he could easily check on operations there from vast distances across space, but all he could sense these days was some vague activity and some nonsense he could not interpret. The last time he'd tried, he could swear the central computer was too occupied with transmitting a medley of unusual songs to bother responding to him. That wasn't the way the chemfet system was supposed to work. The computer was the conduit between Derec's chemfets and Robot City, allowing him to run the place and, since the responsibility was so awesome, to delegate authority properly to the appropriate robots. In a way, Robot City had become an extension of Derec, or at least of him and his wishes, his orders, his plans and dreams for the city's future. He had previously been able to take charge of any part of the city's operations in an instant, without having to accept musical digressions from a computer. Now a good part of the city's activities seemed shut off from him.

He felt isolated, as if the chemfets, unable to sustain normal contact with the city, were idly traveling through his bloodstream to no useful purpose. It was a nerve-wracking feeling that may have been something like the detachment and distortion of reality that a disturbed person must feel, and he didn't like it. His father was, Derec believed, insane, and he sometimes worried that genetics would win out, and he'd wind up in a loony bin himself.

Dr. Avery could very well be behind the present looniness in Robot City. Whenever there was trouble there, he was always the first logical suspect. Since he was the creator of the city, no one would know better than he how to disrupt it.

Ariel now smiled at him. What must she be thinking as his mind drifted off like this?

"Frost," he said, "it all seems pretty warped when I think of it. Maybe it's just worry about Robot City. But that part where I can't see my mother's face, that really scares me."

"Take it easy, darling. Maybe you dream about her because you want to see her—"

"I never think of her! I don't want to think of her!"

She hadn't expected him to be so vehement on the subject of his mother, a woman whose name neither she nor Derec knew. Ariel had conducted an extensive computer search of genetic records on Robot City and Aurora, but had not been able to locate a single fact about Derec except the skimpy details accumulated since their arrival in Robot City. She had no idea why so few records of him existed. She thought his father might have blocked or erased any file on Derec, or that even her mother, Juliana Welsh, who had financed Dr. Avery's work, had pulled some strings to suppress any bureaucratic documentation on Derec's earlier life. Derec himself remembered enough to know that he was, indeed, a Spacer, that he had some training as a roboticist, and that his memory had been deliberately erased. None of the memory that his father had restored had provided any solutions to the other mysteries surrounding his existence.

She put her arms around him and hugged him. "Forget it, Derec. I'm just psychologizing, and I'm not really good at it. It was just a dream, only a dream. Nothing to worry about. *Really.*"

"You're right, probably." His voice was calmer. "What I need is some real rest. I never could sleep in one of those tubelike contraptions." He gestured toward the bunk, which did, indeed, look like half a tube. "Maybe there'll be some time to relax in Robot City, especially if everything's okay there. *And* if we can get the Silversides straightened away."

"Adam and Eve. You'd seem friendlier to them if you'd use their first names. Old human custom."

Ariel was happy to see a smile briefly cross Derec's face. "Sorry, just can't get used to those names, especially since they tend to look like us when they're in the mood to look human. Anyway, it's a wonder I didn't dream of *them*!"

"I think they've invaded some of my dreams. And I'd much rather dream about you, darling."

She kissed him and said, "I think I'll check in with Wolruf. She's with Adam and Eve right now. You know their new game?"

"I don't think so."

"Adam's taught Eve a version of the wolf-state."

Adam had arrived on the planet of the kin, intelligent wolf-creatures, in an egglike vehicle. Because he had not yet encountered sentient life, he had been shapeless. When he joined the kin, he transformed himself into kin-shape. He had a tendency even now to return to that form regularly. The kin had dubbed him SilverSide because, even when he changed his overall appearance, he still retained the metallic, silvery surface of a robot.

"Now the two of them become wolves and start nipping at each other while barking out that strange language. It's weird, really. They go around in a circle and growl, go after each other's tail. Wolruf says they're imitating some wolf-pup behavior Adam observed at what he calls the Pack Home. Lately, they've been transforming from shape to shape too much, and just to annoy us. Adam says they have too few forms to imprint on. I guess he means they need practice. You know, if we let them use the Key to Perihelion and flash them to Earth, they'd probably go insane trying to copy all the life forms there."

The Keys to Perihelion were transport devices that took the user first to Perihelion, the place said to be nearest to all other places in the universe, and then to other specific, preset destinations.

"They do seem different lately," Derec said. "A little bored, I think. Remember how Adam was so intent on imprinting on everything—us, the kin, the blackbodies, robots? There was something desperate about it, something to do with his quest to define what, exactly, a human was. All the present changes are playful rather than purposeful. They seem less curious somehow."

"Maybe it's us. Adam's so intent on defining 'human' as the highest order of being, and he doesn't seem quite convinced yet that we're *it*. He needs a greater variety of humans to study. Anyway, get yourself some rest. I'll get you up again according to schedule, and that's coming around soon enough, sonny boy."

Blowing him a kiss at the door, Ariel left the sleeping compartment.

Derec glanced at his bunk, unsure whether he wanted to return there. Why welcome the dreams that awaited him, stalking him like the kind of wolf Adam had been when they first met? He put one foot on the edge of his bunk and began to vigorously massage the skin of his face, trying to make himself feel more awake and alert.

Adam was so unpredictable, he thought, meddlesome. He had admired the blackbodies, taking them, with their high intellectual abilities and impressive appearances, as probably the truest example of the humans he was programmed to seek. His experiments in imprinting on them had nearly wrecked Ariel's establishment of a new farming community. Then, when Adam had discovered the embryo form of Eve in the forest, Derec and Ariel's problems had doubled. Adam brought Ariel to the "egg" in which Eve had arrived. Since Ariel was the first living creature she saw, Eve's first shape, and the one she returned to most often, was as a silver-toned image of Ariel.

Despite all the knowledge the Silversides had accumulated from contact with humans, kin, and blackbodies, they frequently acted like children. They were fascinated by new information and sometimes flaunted an idea with repetitiveness and ferocity.

Derec recalled the day before they had all left the blackbodies' planet. He had been in a lab working on an adaptation of a remote control device designed to make it easier for the robots in the field to communicate with their central computer. Ariel's transformation of the settlement from a Robot City to an agricultural setup had necessarily expanded the geographical area in which the robots had to function, often removing them too far from the computer for effective comlink communication. Derec had designed a powerful modemlike wireless remote that could be operated easily at such distances. It was itself a miniature computer with limited-access memory. Attached to the chest of a robot, it could be activated when the robot placed its hand over the middle of the device. Without otherwise interrupting its task in the field, the possessor could transmit or receive data easily without having to travel to a computer terminal.

Adam and Eve had come into the room while he was busily attaching the experimental devices to a pair of utility robots who had been reprogrammed to be field foremen. He had switched off the robots so that he could more easily attach the remotes to them.

At the moment of their entrance, Adam had looked like a slightly distorted version of Derec molded in silver, with a touch of Ariel added, while Eve merely resembled Ariel alone. Derec had firmly wished that the Silversides would encounter other humans, so they would at least look different. Of course, there was no telling how much mischief they could cause if they met up with the wrong human.

Derec had always been a bit uncomfortable around Eve in her Ariel mode. Now that the robot was getting better at the mimicry, he had often wondered if, in a dark place where the silver exterior of Eve would not be so obvious, he could mistake her for Ariel and gather her into an embrace.

With Adam, the effect was less disturbing but equally annoying. For Derec, looking at Adam was like seeing an avantgarde artist's rendition of himself.

"Why have you disconnected this robot?" Adam had asked, his busy fingers touching the robot in several places. The hand was vaguely caninoid, Derec had noticed, suggesting that Adam had just come from a session with the caninoid alien Wolruf.

"Because there is less chance of damage to already existing circuits when modifications are made during the disconnected state. And, Adam, this is delicate work and I have to concentrate so please don't ask any more questions. I won't answer them."

"Why have you become so hostile to us?" Adam had asked.

"Because you're pests, both of you, and you test my patience. Anyway, I'm busy now."

"But how can we absorb new information and learn about humans if you refuse to deal with us?"

"Right now I don't care whether you absorb beetle oil off a dirty floor."

"Is there a beetle here?" Adam said eagerly. He was already scanning the floor for an insect to study and perhaps, in part, become. Derec had shuddered at the picture of a Silverside taking on the image of a giant bug. At least there had so far been nothing derived from insects in any of their shapes. Human, wolf, robot, and winged alien, yes, but nothing even vaguely entomological.

"The floor isn't dirty," Eve had observed. "What would beetle oil look like? Is it transparent? Would it blend in with the dirt of the floor, if there were any?"

Derec had always had difficulty coping with the literalness of robots, but with the Silversides the wordplay had become excessively ridiculous and irksome.

"There is no beetle, no beetle oil, no such thing as beetle oil as far as I know."

"Would you lie to us then?" Eve had asked. There had been an Ariel-like sweetness in her voice. He had wished she would use a different sort of voice.

"Gladly, especially if it would get rid of you."

He had spoken to Eve while still attaching the remote to the robot and had not observed Adam pick up the other remote from the table. At first he had held it in his hand, then had held it to his head for a moment. When Derec had finally noticed Adam's meddling, the silver humanoid robot was pressing it against his leg. Finally, he had observed where Derec was attaching the other one, which had led him to press the device against his chest.

"How is it attached?" he had asked.

"That doesn't matter," Derec had said irritably, "since they're not going to be put on either one of you. Put it back on the table."

"But we crave knowledge even when it has no practical function for us," Eve had remarked.

"And I find this device aesthetically pleasing," Adam had said as he replaced it on the table.

Derec had returned to his work and so didn't notice the slow changing of Adam from humanlike to robotlike. When he did look up, he had seen that Adam was now what he had originally termed a WalkingStone, a humanoid robot. However, there was one major difference. He now had a duplicate of the remote upon his chest, as if welded there.

Passing his hand over its front, a band of light in the center had gone on, and, across the room, the computer screen had seemed to go haywire with flashing data as it transmitted information to Adam's remote. This had been a new one for Derec. Adam could copy a device like this, attach it properly to his mimicry of a robot body, and *make it work.* His imprinting abilities were improving by leaps and bounds. How could they possibly control him?

Instead of letting Adam know he had achieved something interesting, he had hollered at him. "Stop that!"

"Why?"

"Because I say so. You are putting this place into jeopardy."

"I am only receiving geographical information. What harm could that do, Master Derec?"

"With you there must be something!"

"You don't seem to approve of us, Master Derec," Eve had said. Derec had taken note of how the two of them had suddenly invoked the polite form of address for a robot to a human.

"Does my approval really matter to you, Eve?"

"Yes, it does. You and Ariel are the only humans we know. If you are indeed the high intelligence we are programmed to seek, if you are indeed the humans you claim you are, then we will be in your image. And, in your image, we must be acceptable to you. Is that a part of First Law?"

"No, it isn't."

"Well, it should be."

Derec had given up. There had seemed to be no sensible way to control them. The more traits and features they copied, the more their chameleonic abilities were a threat—and the more power they could attain. The First Law should protect humans against them, but they were so clever, they could become the first robots to circumvent the law without destroying the letter of it, simply by denying people their status as humans. If they achieved power and could manufacture more of themselves, there was no telling what they might do. If they could add to their fund of human knowledge with imprints from every alien they encountered, they could eventually become the sort of world-conquering monsters, conglomerations of aspects and traits from many creatures, that robotics experts had always thought impossible.

Derec had clenched his fists tightly for a moment, to try to get rid of his ridiculous thoughts. This was the kind of thinking that had probably driven his father insane. Releasing the tension in his hands, he had returned to his work, ignoring the Silversides who grew bored, changed back to their human shapes and left the lab.

Later, Derec had discussed their charges with Wolruf, who had managed the best lines of communication to the Silversides. He was not sure why she was so successful with Adam and Eve. It was perhaps because Adam, when he had first emerged from his own metal egg, had encountered the kin. He had molded himself into kin shape and stayed in that form until he began to encounter other intelligent forms of life. Wolruf's appearance (actually more doglike than wolflike) reminded Adam of the kin, perhaps making him comfortable with her.

"I'm confused," he had said to Wolruf without a word of greeting to her. She stroked the side of her jaw with the backs of the sausagelike fingers of her left hand, a gesture he recognized as indicating concern or even worry.

"What botherss 'u, frriend Derec." Just as Wolruf's s's had the faint sound of a hiss in them, her r's tended to be a bit extended too, reminding Derec of a whispered growl. The lupine structure of Wolruf's mouth did not allow her to enunciate his language easily, although she had certainly improved her linguistic skills. The s's and r's used to be more pronounced and the 1 nonexistent. Once he had had to concentrate fiercely to understand, but now he never had much difficulty.

"Adam and Eve. They're driving me crazy. How can we let them loose on any world?"

"Do otherrss have rreason to fearr them, 'u think?"

"Darn right. Most human societies certainly. Look, many of us are quite superstitious. Back on Earth, a simple-function robot is looked upon with dread, and most robots are kept out of the way, and on the Settlers' planets they've tried to ban robots altogether. I think there's some of that kind of fear in all humans, even though the Spacers have managed to accommodate themselves to the situation by using robots as a servant class."

"I wonderr: Should the Silverrsidess be trreated different from otherr rrobots?"

"It's the shape-changing. Look, my people have a history of superstition toward what they perceive as unnatural. In our imagination we see monsters in closets, believe illogically in the possibility of blood-sucking vampires, werewolves who—"

"Excusse me, I know not the terrm werrewolvess."

"Can't tell you much. Evidently, at the time of the full moon on Earth (a time when, superstition has it, people tend to grow madder), certain humans get transformed into wolf-shape and run about the countryside killing and ravaging until the moon sets."

The brown and gold hair on the sides of Wolruf's face had begun to stiffen and rise slightly. Derec recognized this as a physical sign that the alien was disturbed. And then he had recognized why.

"I'm sorry, my friend. I was thoughtless. It happens that, like robots, wolves are regarded with some fear."

"And, to 'umanss, would I be some kind of wolf?"

"Maybe, to some. Hey, old superstitions are hard to cope with. To most, you'd be more like a dog, and we humans have a bizarre fascination and love for dogs. Back on your home planet, don't your people have some fears, some superstitions?"

"Don't know what 'u—well, perrhapss. A kind of inssect, verry tiny, that—"

"See? All I'm saying is that we're a superstitious lot, we humans. Give us a robot who can look like anything he wants to and molds himself into a different shape right in front of our eyes, and we're liable to back off in a hysterical fit. The Silversides change shape as regularly as most of us change clothes. And they are trouble. Wolruf, my friend, they're two whirlwinds looking for villages to wreck."

She had stared at Derec for a moment, her dark deepset eyes searching his face in a way that might have seemed sinister had he not known her so well. "Well," she had finally said, "seems to me that the besst place forr them might be a worrld wherre they could not causse the harm you suggesst, and wherre itss inhabitantss wouldn't even rreact to their shape-changing. Be good forr uss, too. We then study them furrther with the proper facilities, try to rrid them of their—what would 'u call them?—inconsistenciess."

"Yes, exorcise them of their demons. That's a wonderful idea, Wolruf, but where is this perfect world?"

"Robot City."

"Robot City? But I don't want to take them to—wait, you're right. Adam's really bored with robots and there're only robots there. He says he receives little satisfaction from imprinting on robots. I think he's somehow relegated them to a lower order of species."

"I don't underrsstand. If manmade, can they be a sspeciess?"

"They're not. But Adam perceives them that way, and has dismissed them. He's searching for the highest order of being on which to imprint, and he sees no future in being a robot. Apparently his programming is to imprint on humans, but he still resists the idea that Ariel and I are the answer. And in Robot City she and I would be the only humans, unless my father showed up. It's good. With us, and you, as the only nonrobots there, we might be able to keep them in check. If we couldn't affect their programming, maybe we could bore them to death."

"Oh, but I don't ssuggesst they sshould die, Derrec. Oh, no."

Derec had smiled. Sometimes Wolruf could be just as literal as a robot.

"I didn't mean it that way. I mean a boredom so intense that it'd render them relatively inactive."

The plan had been easy to put into operation. The Silversides were curious to see the Robot City they had heard so much about and had given Derec no opposition to the idea. They had been relatively quiet on the trip out so far, and he had begun to wonder if they were being devious, planning some massive Silverside trick. However, as they neared Robot City and the chemfets in his bloodstream began to cause havoc within him, Derec had worried less and less about his robotic charges. In fact, he was tired of thinking of them now. He wanted no worries at all. If only he could relax with Ariel, make love with her, rest in her arms.

For now he might as well settle for his uncomfortable bunk.

He did fall asleep. But more dreams came. In one of them a Supervisor robot changed its face to resemble Dr. Avery, then announced that the Laws of Robotics had been repealed and he would derive infinite pleasure from purposely mutilating a human.

CHAPTER 3

SOMETHING IS ROTTEN IN THE CITY OF ROBOTS

Derec's apprehension grew as his ship, piloted by the robot Mandelbrot, settled down onto a landing platform at the Robot City spaceport. His chemfets seemed to be in turmoil, as if they were struggling to process information that had been deliberately scrambled. At the same time his emotions were becoming scrambled, too. He snapped at Mandelbrot even while he was struggling to control his temper. Before the landing, Mandelbrot made a routine request for orders, and Derec responded testily, "We'll land when I feel it's right and not before."

Of course Ariel, at that moment, had to be standing nearby, examining the cubes, spires, and blocks of the city from a view-portal, and of course she had to throw her two credits in.

"Whatever's wrong with you, you don't have to take it out on Mandelbrot," she muttered.

He could have merely acknowledged the truth of what she said, but he had to top her two credits with a pair of his own.

"I'm not taking anything out on Mandelbrot, Ariel. You know as well as I do that it doesn't make any difference to him what I say or how I say it, so long as he doesn't have to remove me from harm or save my life. First Law and all that. I know I can be a real bandersnatch, call him every name in the dictionary of insults, foam at the mouth and jump up and down—and it all won't make any difference to him. Only humans brood over other humans' words."

"How epigrammatic."

He didn't want to tell her he didn't know what epigrammatic meant. It was already clear she had more general knowledge in her brain than he, and he didn't want to give her the satisfaction of supplying a definition.

The anger in her face softened, and she moved toward him, patting him on his arm. "Honey, there's no reason to be a grouch, even with a robot. Anyway, how can you be sure he's not aware of your irritation?"

Derec glanced at Mandelbrot, who calmly sat at the controls.

"Oh, he's aware all right. He has to be. Again, the ever-present Laws. He has to know what mood I'm in, what my nuances might mean, what my attitude is toward him—it's all information which he processes in his positronic brain, and it helps him to judge how to react when the laws need to be applied. A robot can simulate emotion for a human being's comfort or pleasure, but a robot's emotion is only specific positronic activity. Aware, yes, but insulted, no."

Ariel sighed. Derec hated that sigh. It clearly indicated she didn't agree with him but was finding the argument too tiresome to continue with. The sigh dismissed the argument along with him and his moods. Yet, when *she* was moody, they had to play by different rules. Ariel could achieve a righteousness that would make a moral philosopher blush.

She walked back to the view-portal, muttering, "Well, when do you expect us to land, then?"

"Soon enough. I just have to look, make sure everything is all right down there."

"I don't understand, what could be wrong?"

"With what we've been through, you can ask that?"

"Frost, you really are in a blue funk today. I'm not going to put up with it. Summon me when you need me, master."

After she had stalked out, Derec said under his breath, "Oh, Ariel."

Apparently Mandelbrot heard him, for he asked, "Is there something wrong, Friend Derec?"

"Nothing that need involve you, Mandelbrot."

If the robot was at all bothered by Derec's irritability there was no way for him to show it in his face or body. Derec wondered if Ariel was right about robots having feelings. Certainly the humaniform robots like R. Daneel Olivaw or Ariel's precious Jacob Winterson appeared to have emotions. They seemed so human, it was hard for observers not to apply an emotional overlay to them.

"We are closing in on the Compass Tower," Mandelbrot said.

The large view-screen in front of the pilot seat displayed the tower, the first Robot City structure Derec had ever known. He and Ariel (then known as Katherine) had arrived there from the gray misty spot known as Perihelion, when they had pressed the corners of a Key to Perihelion. That particular key had been set for Robot City, and they found they could travel nowhere else, except back to Perihelion, with it. The tower was a pyramidal building that was larger and higher than any other building in the city. Inside it was the office in which Dr. Avery had secreted himself to observe Robot City. Derec wondered if his father were in there now, messing up the workings of the place just so he could mess up the workings of his son's chemfets and, for that matter, his mind.

"Hover here for a while, Mandelbrot."

Derec stared down at the city, his city now and not Avery's, uncertain of what looked strange about it at this moment. The Compass Tower was the same tiered structure it had always been. There were none of the odd lumps upon its surface that he had seen in his nightmare. The city itself, as it always had, stretched from horizon to horizon, except for some parkland to the south. New buildings had sprung up while old ones had been disassembled by the robots, whose job it was to continually refine the city, making it even fitter and more luxurious for human habitation. Someday, human colonists would actually be admitted into the place. Normally Derec would not have been aware of such architectural alterations, but his chemfets kept him up-to-date on all of the city's transformations.

The robots in the streets below moved busily enough and appeared to be concerned with their usual goals. Yet, even their movement didn't look right to him, didn't feel right. And many of the usually busy thoroughfares seemed deserted. Perhaps Robot City had indeed turned into the city of his nightmare.

It was probably his imagination. The Silversides, Ariel, all his responsibilities were making it work overtime. He was just plain exhausted, frustrated—that was probably the answer. He would have to make himself human again, rebuild his own personality the way the figures below rebuilt the city.

Lately Derec had had the sense that since his awakening in an amnesiac state, he had become a robot himself. He was increasingly concerned with his duties (one crisis after another, it seemed) and, like the robots below, rushing to goals that were usually shadowy and mysterious.

Sometimes he felt he was divided inside between the human and robot sides of his personality. Certainly, because of the chemfets, he was at least part robot. At times the human side ruled his life and emotions; at other times the robot part took over. He was human at the height of a crisis, when a battle had to be fought or a decision made; human when he was with Ariel, at least in the loving and tender times, or even the angry ones; human when he had to instruct and guide the robots or intellectually confront Avery. On the other hand, in between these active human periods, there were times when he allowed the robot inside him to take over. The robot was in charge when he had to do the dirty work, the menial activities that occupied so much of his duties. He was also robot when he felt nothing but an emptiness inside toward Ariel or Wolruf or Mandelbrot, the trio who meant so much to him now. There were times when he suddenly realized that time had passed and he had only the vaguest idea of what he had done during it, and in his mind that became the robot's time rather than the human's. He wondered if a robot, along some pathway of his positronic brain, was ever conscious of everyday routine.

After landing, Derec was surprised to find the spaceport deserted. Usually a few maintenance robots were in evidence, searching for rarely found trash, shining up already shiny surfaces. The spaceport seemed to Derec like an enormous white elephant, an area that functioned only when he or Ariel used it. Of course, much of Robot City was like this—structures designed for thousands or even millions of human immigrants, magnificent living quarters for people-to-come, commercial setups for invisible shoppers, workplaces used now only by programmed robots who mainly made tests of equipment.

As they passed through the deserted terminal, Adam and Eve looked about, their heads snapping from side to side as they tried to absorb all the new information. To Derec it looked as if the two chameleonic robots were searching for someone or something to copy. He smiled. There'd be no new beings to change into in Robot City. The robots they'd encounter were so much like ones they'd already seen, they would, as Wolruf predicted, grow bored and become more malleable to human manipulation. Then perhaps Derec could straighten the two little buggers out.

"Shouldn't someone be welcoming us or something?" Ariel asked.

"I'm not sure," Derec answered. "I'm not up on spaceport protocol. It just seems that we should be seeing a few robots behind a few counters or something."

Outside the terminal, at the proper station, they found a floater, so called because it went down Robot City roadways without actually touching pavement. It was a two-seater, so Derec told Wolruf and Mandelbrot to locate a larger vehicle and follow him and Ariel into the city. "Keep a lookout for anything that looks out of sync," he said to them. "We'll rendezvous at the Compass Tower and compare notes."

On the ride down the long access road to the city, Ariel said, "Now that you're here, what do you feel, Derec?"

"I still can't make any sense out of the chemfets. But I don't know what's wrong. Something has changed here, but I can't see it yet."

"If you don't see something, how do you know it exists?"

"That sounds faintly philosophical."

"My habit. Sorry."

The floater was small, so small that their shoulders, hips, and legs were pressed together. Normally he liked being this close to her, but today there was a stiffness in the way she held herself. It made him uncomfortable to be touching her at all.

He smiled at her. She stubbornly refused to smile back. Although she tried to look relaxed, her tension was apparent in her eyes.

Touching the bar that controlled the vehicle, Derec brought it to a stop at the first block of buildings after they crossed into the city proper. He got out before the floater had settled down onto the pavement.

"Where're you going?" Ariel asked, as she, too, squeezed out of the vehicle.

"Just a look around."

He approached the side of a cube-shaped building and stared at it. "Look at this."

Standing beside him, she tried to see what he saw.

"What is it?"

"That seam there." She had to squint to see it. "The city is assembled from five-meter-square slabs that come out of an extruder in a sort of ribbon. The material forms and re-forms, following some sort of predetermined programming. It becomes windows, walls, rooms, entire storeys of build-ings, structuring itself. It's done so flawlessly there should be no seams, cracks, openings, except where architecturally logical. This seam isn't logical."

Looking closer, she could see that there was indeed a tiny separation. Only a very thin coin could get through it, but it was certainly a flaw.

He strode away from her, running his hand along the wall and around a corner. When he was out of sight, she

heard him yelp. She ran around the corner to find him staring down at his little finger.

"Look," he said, holding out the finger to her. There was
a tiny cut at its tip and a minuscule drop of blood had oozed
out. She was always surprised by how much darker than
hers his blood was.

"What happened?"

"The damn thing cut me, that sliver there."

"Sliver? But that's impossible. You once told me the
building material is programmed with the First Law. It can't
allow you to get hurt, especially on it."

"That's right. By all rights, I shouldn't be bleeding. Well,
take a gander."

The sliver was even more minuscule than the split seam,
but it was there, all right. A tiny bit of red at its tip made
it slightly more visible.

"What's happened?"

Derec did not stand around long enough to respond to
her question. He was several steps farther on, his eyes nervously inspecting another building, a small sloping structure that thrust upward into the sky, ending in a spire.

"Look up there!" he cried.

He meant the spire. As she peered at it, she realized that
there *was* something just slightly out of kilter about it.

"It's tilted a bit," she said.

"Right," he said. There was an offensive tone in his
voice, as if he were condemning her for verifying the obvious.

"No Supervisor robot would allow such a deviation from
the norm."

"I don't know. I seem to remember something I read
about Earth and a leaning tower there. It was quite a tourist
attraction."

"Well, I'll refer your observation to our Tourist Board."

"Don't be sarcastic. I'm trying to help."

Again he didn't respond. He was now running, eager to examine another building. Ariel clapped her hands twice as a signal to the floater. The pair of claps made the vehicle rise from the ground and follow her as she walked to Derec.

He stood in front of the building's entrance and stared at it.

"Anything wrong with this one?" she asked.

"Nothing I can see. I'm sorry I snapped at you. I just feel at—"

"Forget it, buddy. I ragged you pretty hard back on Aranimas's ship when we first met. We'll just consider your present mood a paying back."

"Thanks."

As his eyes scanned the wall in front of him, his concentration was broken by a loud thumping sound.

"What was that?" Ariel asked.

"I don't know. Let's go in and find out."

"Every time I turn around, you're being brave. Okay, you lead."

The building's entrance was situated in a corner of the street facade. Next to the door was a handplate that could identify both human and robot personnel. This meant it was considered a security area, and only registered individuals would be allowed into the building. That didn't worry Derec. His handprint was automatically registered with all Robot City identity systems, so he placed his hand against the handplate confidently and casually, expecting the door to pop open immediately. It did not. He pressed his hand harder against the plate. Again nothing happened.

"What's wrong?" Ariel asked.

"I don't know. Maybe it hasn't been connected yet."

"Here. Let me try."

Brushing past him, she placed her hand on the plate. Derec was again impressed by the thin angular look of her fingers and would have been willing at that moment to take her hand and lead her to someplace dark, comfortable, and quiet where they could concentrate on kissing and making up.

The door wouldn't open for her, either. Irritated, she slammed her fist against the door itself, and it slowly, creakily, came open. The sound was especially disconcerting. It was another anomaly. No door in this Robot City should squeak.

"Well, fancy that," Ariel said, "it was already open. Shall we?"

She gestured toward the dark interior.

When they entered the building, they should have triggered a force field that would immediately switch on the lighting. But after a few steps, they still stood in what seemed like absolute darkness, broken only by the light streaming in from the doorway. That light was soon lost as the door slowly swung shut. The air seemed stale, and Derec wondered if the circulation systems had broken down, too. Instinctively, he reached for Ariel in time to feel a shudder go through her body.

"You're right," she muttered. "Something's wrong here." She hugged him tightly. "Derec, let's inspect some other building."

"I'm with you on that. The doorway should be—"

She suddenly screamed, not a scream of fear so much as of startlement. With her head so close to his, the sound of it nearly deafened him.

"What happened?"

"Something brushed against my leg."

"What?"

"I couldn't tell. Felt like an animal. Like a rat or something."

"What kind of animal could it possibly be? You're imagining things. There're no aminals in Robot City. They—"

"There it is again! It just slammed into my calf."

"Maybe it's a robot. A delivery or cargo—"

"Didn't feel like a robot. Too soft, too—"

Derec felt a forceful nudge against his ankle. Ariel was right. It did feel like an animal. Must be the power of suggestion.

"Ariel, everything is all right. We'll just make our way to the door and get out of—"

To his left there was a faint animal-like noise. It sounded like a subdued cackle. An elf or tiny demon pleased with his or her work. There was another small cackle on the other side of him. A third behind Ariel. In a moment there were cackles all around them, and they had become louder. Whatever was inside this building seemed to like chattering to each other.

Taking Ariel's hand, Derec fled backward toward the door that was faintly outlined from outside daylight. Near the door, before the two of them had flung it open and fled from the building, he nearly tripped over something, something that screeched back angrily at him.

CHAPTER 4

THE WATCHFUL EYE

There was no such thing as an all-seeing eye in Robot City, but the Watchful Eye believed it must come close. Even though it usually sat safe in its haven, its rudimentary body drawn snugly inside, it could observe and examine whatever happened in the city.

Since the time it had arrived in the city through an underground tunnel that had originally been meant for human sewage (of which there had so far been so little that the sewer's walls were brightly pristine and its clear water smelled fresh and pleasant), it had gradually taken over all Robot City systems.

The Watchful Eye had no idea how it had arrived on the planet. After coming suddenly to awareness in a field outside the city, it had molded itself into simple but functional form. Searching the countryside, it located the sewer tunnel. At first it had transported itself by the kind of carts used for supply and passenger transport through the intricate network of tunnels, and eventually found its way to the lair of the central computer. It had taken a while to learn that the computer was merely a machine and not a living being. It took some more time to discover how to operate it. For one period it roamed at will around the inside of the computer and absorbed random bits of knowledge. Now it had collected a considerable amount of the computer's information, much of which it was not certain how to use. The only way to find out, it had discovered, was to practice.

First it practiced on the numerous robots that roamed the huge city's streets. Although it had not yet seen a robot up close, it knew about them from studying the viewscreens set up in the underground computer center. As it became more computerlike itself, it began using the computer to communicate with the robots. It convinced the robots that it was human and, according to Second Law, should be obeyed as a human. (As long as they could not see it, the Watchful Eye was able to carry off the illusion convincingly. It had forbidden the highest ranking robots to come into its presence or have any sight of it.)

Although it had accessed much information about humans—visual data, anthropological studies, physiological and anatomical maps, psychological data—it believed it hadn't yet reached an understanding of what a human really was. It yearned to see one.

There had been no problem in making working models of humans, no difficulty in creating thousands of computer visualizations of human beings. Where it had failed, however, was in really *knowing* what a human was. All the information files had been entered by humans who already knew what they were. Essential things had been left out, and the Watchful Eye needed to fill in those blanks.

The next step on its agenda had been to study and then obtain control of the city itself. From computer files the Watchful Eye evolved an extensive, albeit distorted, view of the place. Since it had no previous knowledge of humans or robots, it couldn't always interpret the data it collected. But that didn't matter. Knowing bits and pieces was enough for the time being. After all, it had learned something about quests and felt that if it continued its Robot City experiments, it could eventually control the place completely. It did not know what it would do when it became that powerful, but it believed that life must, if nothing else, be a learning process. The computer's philosophical files reinforced that conclusion. When it had power, it would know what to do with it. Once it had not known what a computer was; now it had completely subjugated one. Domination of the city would present little difficulty.

It liked to think of itself as the Watchful Eye because it could keep track of so many parts of the city without moving from its haven. The screens displayed any place it wanted to view, and it could keep track of several points at once. Not that there was much need to oversee the robots. They accepted orders readily and acted upon them with dispatch and without further questions. That was good, because it did not have time to keep specific attention on the individual robots. There was so much to do, so many experiments to conduct, so much to think about. . . .

Eve Silverside walked behind the others, pleased that Wolruf had decided they should walk into the city rather than search out a proper-sized vehicle. Her head often turned to examine the city's immensity. She had previously seen only the pastoral landscapes of the blackbody planet, with its natural wonders and its robot-made agricultural community. Adam, who had seen a robot city, had described it to her, but she had not been prepared for the overpowering qualities of the real thing. She was now in human form, resembling a chunkier and silver-colored Ariel, and her startlingly human-like eyes were open wide in amazement.

Even though she had been told about Robot City's incredible mass of architectural wonders, she had not been prepared for its dazzling array of colors, its intricate walkways, the geometric perfection of its buildings. Although she tended to examine the scene around her with a robotic objectivity, she was impressed and thought Robot City was indeed a splendid place.

Ahead of Eve, Wolruf hunkered down, peered at the edge of a curb, and picked up something.

"What is it, Wolruf?" Mandelbrot asked.

She held up a crumpled piece of paper. Adam took it out of her hand and examined it. "It seems ordinary, not unlike paper I have already seen," he commented.

"Not that it'ss paperr," Wolruf said, "it'ss strrange it'ss here at all."

"I do not understand."

When Adam talked with Wolruf, his face seemed to change slightly, its human aspects taking on a suggestion of Wolruf's caninoid features. Adam's nose seemed to lengthen and his face became flatter, like Wolruf's.

"Paperr shouldn't be here, that'ss all. Here on thiss street it iss litterr. Small robotss take care of litterr wheneverr it occurss, which iss rare. Robotss, afterr all, do not use paperr. The small robotss detect litterr, 'u see, then collect it, then dispose of it."

"I see no utility robots in this area," Mandelbrot said. There were, in fact, no robots of any kind to be seen. "Perhaps one will come soon."

"Maybe," Wolruf said, then loped a few steps farther and pointed at the pavement. "Thiss iss slidewalk," she said.

"Yes," Mandelbrot said.

"Shouldn't it move? We stand on it, it remainss still when ourr body weight should make it move."

"That is truly puzzling. Perhaps it is inoperative."

"If so, where are Slidewalk Maintenance Robotss? When something in city breakss down, maintenance robotss are ssupposed to appearr immediately."

"Perhaps they are busy elsewhere with a different slide-walk."

"Maybe. But thingss don't break down in Robot City at such rate. Two areass of slidewalk down at same time in same sector iss unusual, 'u see."

"Yes. I should inform you also of another matter."

"What, Mandelbrot?"

"Since you have been observing these flaws, I have been trying to contact other robots through my comlink to obtain answers for your questions, and so far none have responded. Based on data from my previous visits to this city, such a phenomenon, even on the outskirts here, is highly anomalous."

" 'U believe ssomething iss wrrong here, Mandelbrot?"

"Yes, I do."

"Let'ss go on then."

Eve wasn't sure what to make of the conversation between the caninoid and the robot with the strange arm, itself something of an anomaly. The arm, which had once belonged to a robot of a different class than Mandelbrot, was shaped differently and, because it was thicker and longer than his other arm, looked awkward on his body. It was malleable and Mandelbrot could change its shape, although, unlike the Silversides, he could not transform any other part of his body.

Thinking of her shape-changing ability seemed to start

up a mechanism in her body. She looked around for something to change into. Adam had explained to her that there seemed to be an urge inside them to seek out new beings and imprint upon them. It was very humanlike, he said, or at least Derec had informed him so. "Derec says that humans love to seek out new experience. A new experience for us is a previously unseen kind of being whose shape we can take. Although we are not supposed to have emotions about it, I think the mechanisms inside our bodies are engaged when we think about changing ourselves or when we see a being on which we can imprint." Whatever it was, a simple mechanism or a genuine yearning for new experience, Eve now felt a strong urge to form herself into a new shape.

But what shape could she choose? She had been human like Ariel, caninoid like Wolruf, a robot like Mandelbrot.

There must be some different kind of life here, she thought. She walked closer to a building, a strange structure, narrow and tall. Staring up at its top, she saw a row of ugly birdlike creatures staring down at her from under the building's eaves. They were still, impassive, although she thought she perceived a meanness in their eyes. Stepping back to try to see them better, she pointed upward and asked Mandelbrot, "What are those, please?"

Mandelbrot glanced up at them. "They are not alive," he said. "They are some kind of ornament placed along the upper rim of the building. I think they are called gargoyles. These are made of Robot City material, but in the past they have often been sculpted from stone."

"They are interesting. Adam? Do you think we could become like that?"

Adam had adopted a quite humanlike shrug, copied accurately from Derec. "We could become statues, yes, but I see no point in it. There is little for us to learn from representations of life, Eve, unless we actually encounter the creatures that were the models for these statues."

"I doubt that that would be a pleasant experience," Eve said. She looked away from the gargoyles and walked a few steps farther, then she turned and went back.

There was something here, inside this building, and it was not gargoyles. She sensed there was something on the other side of the wall, just standing still but perhaps with life inside it.

"Mandelbrot?"

"Yes, Eve?"

"How does one gain entrance to such a building as this?"

Mandelbrot had been instructed by Derec to cooperate with the Silversides as much as possible unless he sensed danger for them. There did not seem to be any threats hereabout, so he replied, "I believe the door for this building is located on the north side. Up those steps."

Eve immediately went up the steps. Climbing was one of the few activities that made her appear more robotlike than humanlike. There was a certain mechanical awkwardness to the way she proceeded from stair to stair.

At the top of the stairs, there was indeed a door, and it was slightly ajar. From below, Mandelbrot saw the door hanging open and cautioned, "The open door. That is another anomaly. Do not go in there, Eve."

One thing that Eve had "inherited" from copying Ariel was stubbornness. Once she had a goal set in her mind, she would not easily veer from it. She pushed the door open and went inside.

With a faint crackle, some light came on. To Eve it was clear that the illumination was not full power. That didn't matter to her; she increased the power of her optical sensors.

The room was dim, and there were many shadowy areas. She increased her olfactory sensors and observed that the hint of an unpleasant odor in the room was more than just a hint. There was a heavy pervading sense of decay in it. Something might be dead in here.

The room was cluttered. Broken glass littered the floor (she recalled what Wolruf had said about utility robots keeping things clean); some furniture had been heaped in one corner, most of it with missing pieces or chunks; metal debris was all over the room in piles of varying sizes; everything was laden with dust.

She walked through the room boldly, scrutinizing its contents. Behind her, Mandelbrot came through the doorway.

"Eve, Derec has instructed me to keep you and Adam away from harm. We don't know anything about this building, so please come with—"

"What is this, Mandelbrot?" She held up what appeared to be a long jointed tube made of metal wires and strips, plus some electronic wiring.

"I would say part of the skeleton of a robotic limb. Well-articulated if complete. Now, Eve—"

"There's something over here."

As she neared a shadowy niche, she saw that there was someone in it. However, she could detect no life coming from the figure. Even though it was standing, its legs were crossed unnaturally. There were shreds of cloth remaining from an outfit that was not definable. Its torso seemed ravaged and scarred. Its eyes were so deepset that at first she wasn't sure there were any. There were black circles around them. Its arms hung at odd angles.

"Mandelbrot, this looks like a—"

As she came close, the figure's head moved slightly as

if about to slide onto its left shoulder, and it reached out its left arm toward Eve. She was tempted to ignore Mandelbrot's warnings to back away from it and instead take the hand.

The Watchful Eye had detected Robot City's new arrivals and was quite gleefully keeping track of them. They might be human, it thought. The first two it saw on its viewscreens answered many of the requirements it had deduced for humans, requirements that it had laboriously formulated from the visual and technical information in the many computer files. Still, its uncertainty as to what actually constituted a human made it want to continue observation at a distance.

The Watchful Eye had a need to know about humans. So far it had been frustrated in its studies and experiments by the lack of any genuine humans to observe. Now perhaps they had returned to the city apparently built for them.

Listening in on their conversation, it detected that the new arrivals' names were Ariel and Derec. There was a lot of data about a Derec in the files. This might be he. Derec had been so important he had one of the access codes to the computer. It had been extremely difficult for the Watchful Eye to bypass and then cancel it.

After Derec and Ariel had entered the warehouse where some of the Watchful Eye's failures (Series B, Batch 29) were housed and had been attacked by the cackling monstrosities, it became confused. The humans, if they were indeed humans, just ran away, out to the street. Why did they run? What kind of emotional weakness could cause such cowardice? Maybe they were not humans, then; maybe they were failed entities, just like its own creations.

It didn't have much time to consider their behavior because it detected another set of intruders. First he saw the small furry being who was so assiduously examining whatever she found in her path. Her intelligence was clear, and she was observant. It listened in on her comments about the litter she had found. That was perceptive of her, observing that discarded paper was a rare thing in the city and that utility robots should have removed it long ago. It was not sure where the paper had originated, but it suspected that it came from one of its experimental creations in the building that Eve had inspected. It recalled that the place was a warehouse for some more of its abandoned experiments. There had been some ritual among these creations that had involved paper. It had not liked the ritual, in which strange-looking marks were made on paper, and so had forgotten it. As far as the litter problem went, perhaps it would re-activate the robots that had once had that job.

Next in line was clearly a robot, but even the robot was a variation on what it was used to. Mandelbrot, as it heard the robot called by the fur-creature, whose name was apparently Wolruf, had an arm that did not seem to belong on his body.

The figures following Mandelbrot confused the Watchful Eye, who was not easily disturbed. It recognized right away that they resembled the two humans it had seen earlier. They had similar faces and bodies, but their skin was a sort of silvery blue as compared with the faint pink tone of the earlier arrivals, and there was a bit more rigidity in their movements. Otherwise, they could have been twins of the pink beings. Further, there was assurance in their walks and the way their arms swung calmly at their sides.

It had a new problem to consider now, one that increased its interest. Both sets of intruders resembled humans as described in computer files. The first set seemed more awkward and not as self-assured as the second set. However, the second duo, who had the proper bearing and look of intelligence, were, in coloring, more like the city's robots. Its first impression was that while both sets could be human, the second might be an advanced version of the species.

When Eve entered the warehouse, it was very pleased. It found that a circuit inside one of its creations there was still operable (though very weak), and it was able to make it move by remote control. It liked Eve's cool response to the event. She seemed much more in command of her emotions than the skittish pair who had entered the other warehouse then scampered out of it at their first opportunity. If the Watchful Eye could have smiled (and it could have but had never bothered to learn the manipulation for the physical display of amusement), it would have smiled with satisfaction at what it now perceived as the superior human, Eve Silverside.

CHAPTER 5

TIMESTEP AND BOGIE

As the warehouse door slowly and creakily shut, Derec thought he saw many eyes looking back at him from the closing sliver illuminated by daylight. Even after the door was closed, he still felt there was a good chance he would see the eyes again in his next nightmare.

Ariel, now relaxed in his arms, snuggled her head against the side of his neck. Since she was a bit taller than he, she had to slouch awkwardly in order to perform the act.

"What *was* that?" she said, her words muffled.

"I don't know. Whatever they are, they shouldn't be there. There are no animals indigenous to Robot City, and I know I've made no allowance for any kind of animal life here. I'm not sure I even like animals, especially small ones."

"Maybe they weren't on the planet when the robots arrived. Maybe they were underground. Maybe they've come to the surface from the bowels of the planet. They might have gotten, I don't know, stirred up while the robots were building the city and have been slipping out under those construction slabs." The slabs Ariel referred to were the five-meter-square pieces of iron/plastic alloy that emerged from a machine called the Extruder. "Maybe they were already—"

"Calm down. I've examined all preliminary studies of this planet, the ones done before the city-forming project began. The place was barren, no animal life evident anywhere. So they're not likely to have come up from the underground or—"

"How about from space then? They landed in a spaceship while we were gone, and now they're hiding out until they know what to do about us."

Derec frowned and broke from the embrace. "You might have something there. I'll have to check records. Even better, we can interrogate robots. After all, they can't lie to us."

As if in response to his comment, a robot came whirling around a nearby corner. Both Derec and Ariel were astonished by this figure, since whirling was indeed the correct word for its current maneuver. It moved as if on roller skates, balletically spinning with its arms outspread. Before reaching them, it executed a lovely twirl on its left leg alone, with its right leg pointing elegantly backward.

"Stop!" Derec ordered it. It had brought its right leg down and seemed ready for another move, but Derec's order brought it to a halt. Its body appeared to collapse a bit, and it slumped ungracefully. "Come here!"

When the robot stood in front of him, Derec asked, "Your name?"

There was no response, which irritated Derec. "Come on, every robot has a name."

"Except during a name-changing period," the robot said. "I have not chosen my new name yet, and so am without a name for the moment. I was considering renaming myself Timestep."

"Timestep? What kind of name is that? Does it indicate a function or role? As a name it is against regulations."

"There are regulations about names?"

Derec didn't know the answer to that, so he said, "Never mind. Tell me, you said *new* name. That means you must have an old one. What is it?"

"Line Foreman 43."

"Have we met before, Line Foreman 43?" The robot did not respond, but merely stood with the blank face and relaxed body that was the look of robots when they conversed with humans. "Why don't you answer me, Line Foreman 43?"

"Are you talking to me, sir?"

"Didn't I call you Line Foreman 43?"

"You may have indeed. But that is not my name."

"You said it was."

"It was, once. It is not now. I do not respond to it."

"All right then. You, there, the robot standing in front of me, have we ever met before?"

"Not formally, but I know you are Derec. This is the first time you have ever spoken to me."

"Why were you dancing just now?"

"I don't know. It just felt good."

"You have a *feeling* about dancing?"

"I think perhaps. It is also perhaps a positronic anomaly."

"There are enough anomalies around here without me having to worry about positronic ones. Robot, you might be in some way programmed, or reprogrammed, to dance, but I doubt you have a feeling for it."

"My partner says I do. My partner says I am a very smooth dancer."

"I'll bet you are."

Derec felt as if he wanted to yell uncontrollably at this too-clever, evasive robot. Ariel squeezed his hand and said softly, "Let me talk to him for a moment. Robot, have you no duties at this moment?"

"Duties? Yes, I suppose so."

"You suppose so? A robot doesn't suppose when it comes to duty. You either have one or you don't."

"Well, yes, I have a job that I do."

"Why aren't you doing it then?"

"I had not realized I had stopped doing the job."

"You had not—"

Ariel's anger was clear, so Derec, calmer now, took over again.

"You mentioned a partner. Where is your partner now?"

"I don't know. We agreed it was time for me to go solo. Want to see my soft shoe?"

"No. I give up. Ariel, this is worse than arguing with a robot about one of those odd hypothetical cases where a Law of Robotics can't be easily invoked."

"I know what you mean," she said, nodding. "Let's try another tack. Robot, there are some terribly strange beings in that building over there. Do you know anything about them?"

The robot's head jerked toward the warehouse. "I know nothing of any strange beings," he said.

Ariel shrugged.

"Wait," Derec said, "it might be the word strange not registering with him. They might not be strange to him. Let me try. Robot, are there any beings at all in there?"

"I could not say for certain, for I have never entered that building."

"Let me put it this way. Have any new beings of any

kind, humans, robots, aliens, entered the environs of Robot City?"

"Yes, besides you, three new robots and an alien came today. The alien and two of the robots have been here before."

"He must mean Wolruf and the others," Ariel commented.

"Besides them, and us, has anyone new come to Robot City at any recent time?"

"That sounds properly phrased, all right," Ariel whispered.

"Yes," the robot said.

Derec stared at the robot for a long while, expecting him to say more. Frustrated, he finally asked, "Well? Tell me about our newcomer."

"I may not."

"What?"

"I am not allowed to. A block has been entered for that particular information."

"A block! How could there be a block for me? I am Derec Avery!"

Derec realized that he was sounding overbearing, but he couldn't help it. This robot got on his nerves.

"While it is true that you are Derec Avery, and I owe you the kind of loyalty that would remove such a block, I cannot. There is a further block upon the first block."

Derec shook his head vigorously, trying to clear it. "What do you mean, blocks on blocks?"

"If the first block is removed, the one preventing me from revealing the information you request—and Second Law tells me such blocks may be removed by you or, for that matter, Ariel Welsh or Dr. Avery—a second block wipes out the information before I can voice it. Therefore, if I obey you now and attempt to tell you what I know, then I will not know it anymore. Consequently, I will not be able to tell you. Because Third Law requires me to protect myself, and by extension any vital information I hold, I have to try my best not to allow such a situation to come to pass, and must respectfully request that you interrogate me no further on this matter."

As the robot awaited Derec's response, he executed a few mild soft-shoe steps. His arms appeared to throw imaginary sand onto the ground.

Derec wondered if what the dancing robot said was true. He had often told robots to forget specific information but had often wondered if they really did. Perhaps the data would not be erased but instead skillfully diverted from one positronic pathway to another, leaving it hidden rather than eliminated. It was possible he could find a way of getting such data out.

"I will *interrogate* you as long as I wish," Derec said coolly. "In fact, I am so angry I don't give a hoot what happens to you or your information. Robot, I—"

"Timestep. I have decided on that as my name. It has a nice ring, don't you think?"

As if to prove how wonderful a name it was for him, Timestep tapped out a quick and intricate hard-tap routine with his feet. Since the feet were made of metal, their taps were louder and more resonant than the average human tap dancer could achieve. There was an inappropriate look to it all, especially since he waved his arms like a clumsy man falling.

"Timestep, I order you now to tell me the answer to the question I asked before. Inform me of any newcomers to Robot City whose identity has been previously blocked."

The dancing stopped, but Timestep said nothing.

"Well?" Derec asked.

"Well, what, sir?"

"Give me the answer."

"The answer to what?"

"My question."

"I don't know the answer to your question."

"The information has been destroyed then?"

"I don't know the answer to your question."

"Timestep, do you recall once having the answer in your memory banks?"

"No, I do not. I know nothing about any newcomers to the city except for yourselves and your companions."

Derec made a quick gesture with his hand, the dismissive one that most humans used for robots. "You may go, Timestep."

"Thank you, Master Derec. And, please, look for the silver lining."

"What do you mean by that?"

"I don't really know, sir."

Timestep danced off. When he was going forward, his movements and dance steps were more precise and graceful. Before he rounded a corner, he twirled around a high pole with a round old-fashioned lamp at the top. Derec did not recall the pole being there when they had arrived at the corner moments ago. He had to admit that the height at which Timestep twirled around it was quite impressive.

"What are you smiling about?" he asked Ariel.

"I'm not sure. I liked that robot, I guess. I hadn't realized how much I missed some entertainment. When we first arrived here, we watched entertainment tapes, and they were pretty sad. I knew they couldn't take me away from my worries then, but, to tell the truth, I wouldn't mind viewing some of them again now. I mean, we've been so busy lately,

I haven't had much time to relax. You know, just relax and watch something, no matter how trivial. I'd really like to see Timestep's whole act."

Derec wondered if he could just curl up someplace and concentrate on a book or a hyperwave program. His mind always seemed to be stuffed with responsibility, work, research—all the problems that came with the territory in Robot City, any Robot City.

"I think Timestep could use a dance teacher," was his only comment.

"Really? I thought his moves were pretty good, especially for a robot. Maybe we could arrange a little recital for him."

"Ariel—"

"Sorry, sorry. Only trying to cheer you up."

"Can't work up much cheer when the place seems to be falling apart."

"Best time for it. Anyway, it's not all that bad here. A dancing robot, some pests in a warehouse, a few things out of order, your strange intuitive feelings . . ."

"That's just it, you know? My intuitions. They're one of the side-effects of the chemfets. I *know* when something's wrong here. And something is definitely wrong."

"Like something is wrong in Denmark, wherever that was."

" 'Something is rotten in the state of Denmark,' " Derec corrected. The line came from the fairly rotten production of *Hamlet* that he had staged (while playing the leading role to Ariel's Ophelia) with an all-robot supporting cast.

"What's really rotten is your mood," Ariel said. "I thought you were going to lighten up."

Her words, spoken so softly, soothed him. Ariel could be the cleverest, most sarcastic person in the universe, especially when she got her dander up, but she often knew the moment when a quietly spoken phrase was the right tactic. He took her into his arms.

"Oh, Ariel, it's just—just that I'm never sure. I still remember so little of my life that I feel like I'm Hamlet."

"Isn't that just a carryover from having played the role?"

"Maybe. But I do relate to the character. I'm alone—"

"Hey, you've got me."

"I didn't mean it that way. I mean that I have to be in charge of this city."

"There's a saying somewhere about its being lonely at the top."

"Something like that. I'm never sure what I do is right. My father didn't really tell me how to take care of things. Just made me leader and took off. I don't know who my mother is. I don't really know what my mission is. Stuff like that. They're not the same as Hamlet's, but they're similar uncertainties."

"Maybe what destroyed Hamlet is he thought too much about what he was doing. Like you're doing now. Snap out of it, my love. You're *not* Hamlet. If anything, you're a hero, a man of action rather than a procrastinator. These, what you call uncertainties, are only human reactions to, well, the *uncertainty* of existence."

Derec laughed. "Now *you're* getting too heavy."

"I have been putting on a bit of weight. Ever since falling in love with you, my love. So let's get moving. I need the exercise, and you need some work to get the glooms out of your head."

"It's a deal. You know what we have to do? Find Avernus, Dante, Rydberg, Euler, all the other Supervisor robots who link up to the computer. They must know what's going on around here. And we can hack through the computer itself, see if we can come up with something."

"Okay, buddy."

Holding hands, they started in the direction of the Compass Tower. After they'd walked a few steps, two humanoid robots came running by. They were tossing around a large metal sphere, perhaps an oversized ball bearing from somewhere. The sphere went back and forth between them. From their speaker grilles came a continuous outpouring of satisfied sounds.

"What was that?" Derec said after they had passed. He would have stopped to interview them, but he had been too amazed at the sight to think of any logical action.

"They seem to be playing some sort of game."

"Game? Robots playing games?"

"Odd, I agree. Kinda cute, though. I never thought much about robots having fun."

"I'm not sure robots are supposed to have fun."

"Don't be a spoilsport."

"Maybe I'm jealous. I wouldn't mind having the time to throw a ball around."

"Well, we could join in. But, from the size and apparent weight of that ball, I think one catch'd flatten either one of us. I know what you mean, though. I'd like to return to Aurora and hike across a few fields, or just lie about and enjoy a rigorously enforced lethargy."

"Still, that game there is just another anomaly for us to consider. Why aren't they occupied with their duties? Who could have told all these robots to take time off to dance and play ball?"

"Maybe we're just not used to them having time off."

"No, it's more than that. Robots don't have time off. Whenever they're not doing something, they just stand there. On Aurora, you people store them in those wall-niches. And why in blazes would any robots ever play games? And, if a robot is playing a game like that and making happy sounds, does that mean it's having fun? Is there any way it could feel the sensation of—"

"Stop! I'm not up to one those positronic conundrums right now. You can be terribly single-minded, darling."

"And you love me for it."

"Only when I'm what you're single-minded about."

They stopped walking for a moment to kiss. A robot passing by whistled. Unused to such rude behavior from a robot, Derec angrily broke from the embrace and ran up to the whistler, ordering it to halt. It stood, awaiting Derec's words.

"Did you whistle just now?"

"Yes. You know how to whistle, don't you? You just pucker up your lips and blow."

"I *know* how to whistle. But how do you know? You don't even have lips to pucker up."

"A technicality. I can reproduce any human sound using my mimicry integrals."

"You have mimicry integrals?"

"I do now."

"You didn't once?"

"Until recently, I didn't."

"And you can copy human sounds?"

"Name one, kid. Please."

"You shouldn't call me kid."

"I was not aware of that. I call everyone kid."

"Well, not me. And why aren't you answering my questions?"

"I don't cotton to the third degree, copper."

"Kid, cotton, copper? You're using slang, aren't you?"

"You ain't just a kiddin', kid."

"Where did you learn slang?"

"Same place I learned whistling."

"And you never told me that. Okay, start back at the beginning. Where did you learn to whistle?"

"I saw it in a movie."

"A movie? You watch movies? How is that possible?"

"There are many stored in the Compass Tower, pal. They are for research. We must study humans to understand them, kiddo. And there ain't been many o' you fellas around Robot City, so how else can we study you? We obtain the movies from the computer's entertainment system."

"Is that what's going on here then? You robots'v been watching old movies?"

"Some of us."

Ariel stepped forward to address the new robot. She talked quietly, in contrast to Derec's nervous and energetic tone. "When do you have time for that? What about your duties?"

The robot swiveled its head toward her. "Oh, I get it. I like it. You're doing one of those copper tricks. The good-guy-bad-guy routine, I think it's called."

"It's no routine. Answer my question. You have to obey Second Law."

"Sorry. All right. I am not aware that the fulfillment of my duties is in any way impaired by the time I spend with hyperwave and prehyperwave movies and shows."

"What is your job?"

"I am a perimeter-observation and intruder-inspection specialist."

"A what? That doesn't—wait, do you mean a border guard?"

"That is the vulgar term, Mistress Ariel."

"We don't need border guards. Robot City's all over the planet. There aren't any borders."

The robot made a move with his shoulders that, in a human, would have been a shrug. "I was misinformed," it said.

Now Derec took over the questioning. "You do a job for which there is no need?"

"It seems so."

"Was border guard always your job?"

"No. I was once an Analyst."

"You would have to be reprogrammed to change your role here."

"Yes."

"And you were?"

"Yes."

"Who did the reprogramming?"

"I am not allowed to say."

"Yes, you can. You are allowed to tell me."

"Nope. I realize you are Derec, but this is not a matter of Robotic Law protocol. I really cannot. There is a block upon the information which, if I attempt to reveal it to—"

"I know, I know. The information self-destructs. You forget it before you can say it."

"That is so."

Derec, looking worried, turned his back on the robot. "Heads up," he said to Ariel, then reared back his fist, as if to smash her in the face.

The robot's hand was quick. He had Derec's arm in between pincers in a split second. Derec relaxed in his grasp.

"It's all right, robot. I would never hurt her. I was just testing you."

"Testing me?"

"I wanted to make sure you would still obey the First Law and keep me from harming Ariel."

"I would. I must."

Derec sighed. "At least something in this place is working according to Hoyle."

"Excuse me," the robot said. "I missed a beat there somewhere, pal. Is there someone named Hoyle I should know about?"

Derec laughed, pleased that at least this robot, with its skills at slang, could still be crossed up enough to take a statement literally. "It's nothing," he said. "Just a figure of speech."

"I will look it up. Thanks a bunch, kid."

"Stop calling me kid. It's not only inaccurate, it's disrespectful."

"It's not so inaccurate," Ariel muttered. "I mean, you're still a teenager."

"I don't feel like one any more."

"I apologize, Master Derec. I thought kid was a respectful term. It is in the movies, I think."

"I give up. Get on your way."

"As you wish. Here's looking at you, k—Master Derec."

The robot began to glide away.

"Wait, what's your name?" Derec called after it.

"Bogie."

"That's your new name, one you chose?"

"Yes."

"Do you see many movies?"

"I have studied a certain period of the cinema, yes."

"Why? Why a certain period?"

"It was my assignment."

"Who made the assignment?"

"I am not allowed to say."

"Okay, okay. I get the message. I won't ask any more questions. You may go now, Bogie."

"Yes, Master Derec."

Bogie disappeared around another corner. Derec might have been mistaken, but the robot's hand, extended in front of him, looked like it was flipping an invisible coin.

"What do you make of that, Ariel?"

"When I was a child, my mother had me watch a lot of movies from old Earth. They were shadowy, and dark, and in shades of gray they liked to call black and white. Very hard to watch, quite unreal. They were usually about crime and murder and private detectives. Bogie's like a character in one of them. The slang seems about the same, far as I can remember. Maybe we can watch a few."

"Might help in figuring out what Bogie is talking about. For right now, though, I think we better get to the Compass Tower before any more of these wise-guy robots show up."

"Wise-guy? And you were complaining about Bogie's slang?"

"It gets to you after a while."

"What about your respect for language?"

"Not sure I have any. C'mon, I want to find the Supervisors and work with the computer."

"Unless it thinks it's a movie character, too."

"Don't even think that."

As they headed toward the Compass Tower, the Watchful Eye studied the situation. If these were the superior humans, they certainly were tentative, but also a bit aggressive. Derec nearly hit Ariel, after all.

It was hard to examine them as long as it stayed put in its haven, yet it could not move now. It must remain at the core of the city. Perhaps it would be useful to have Derec and Ariel spied upon. Spies could signal it when there was

any danger of being discovered. It decided to assign Timestep and Bogie to that job. They had already proved their
efficiency with the successful way they had absorbed the
research materials assigned to them.

Through the comlink system it contacted both robots,
who, with nothing better to do, changed direction and met
at the Compass Tower, just after the humans had entered
the immense pyramidal structure.

CHAPTER 6

MUMBLING ROBOTS AND SASSY COMPUTERS

Bemused by the actions of Derec and Ariel, the Watchful Eye turned its attention to the other set of newcomers in time to observe Eve and Mandelbrot leaving the building where she had discovered the residue from some of its early genetic experiments. Eve's conduct in the old building seemed worth the Watchful Eye's admiration. It certainly preferred her cool reactions to the cowardly and brutal responses of Ariel and Derec.

Its admiration increased when it eavesdropped on Adam's questioning of Eve. His queries were much more analytical and logical than those of Derec and Ariel in their interrogation of the two robots. The Watchful Eye was, however, puzzled by certain aspects of the Adam-Eve relationship. It had detected a warmth and shared emotion between Derec and Ariel, even when they had been arguing with each other. Their silvery counterparts seemed close only when they shared information. And they did not touch each other gently the way Ariel and Derec did. The Watchful Eye placed no importance on emotion, but it had noticed that

emotion seemed to play a key part in many of the descriptions of humanity contained in the computer files.

There was, as *Hamlet*-obsessed Derec might have put it, a method to the Watchful Eye's madness. It was confused by some aspects of Robot City, and it believed it needed help. Whichever of the two pairs appeared superior, it would enlist in its cause, as advisors, helping it to run the city.

Up to now, it had only had the assistance of robots because there was no one else available. Robots did good work when properly instructed, but, if any of their Laws of Robotics were involved in the task, they could ask many time-wasting questions. If one of the Watchful Eye's orders seemed to put a robot in danger, it would initiate long discussions about the task until the Watchful Eye finally revised the job to eliminate Third Law obstacles. Now that the newcomers had arrived on the planet, it was beginning to hear First Law ruminations from the robots.

Although the Watchful Eye would not have considered it in such terms, Robot City had become its own personal toy. It had not, after all, been conscious for very long, and in some ways it was still a child. That was why it had conducted so many experiments since its arrival. It was testing Robot City, rearranging the place to fit its needs, finding out what worked and what did not, reprogramming robots to store the information that was beyond its ability to assimilate. Eventually it planned to restore order to the city, a highly structured order based on theories it was formulating daily. It was determined to achieve the goal of establishing its own city.

The newcomers, with their experience and intellect, could help it. It would put them under its thumb (a colloquialism it had learned from the computer—not that it had any thumbs, or at that moment any hands) and use their

expertise to put the city also under its imaginary opposable digit.

As Eve and the others continued their journey, the Watchful Eye searched for Ariel and Derec. At first it could not locate them, but then its new spy, Timestep, informed it that they were about to enter the Compass Tower. Quickly the Watchful Eye activated the life-support systems that the pair would need inside the pyramidal structure.

"It smells musty in here," Ariel remarked as they headed down the corridor leading to the Supervisors' meeting room. "Like it's been closed up tight for a long while."

"Maybe it has," Derec responded. "It's possible that when we're not here for a long period of time, they close down the air circulation systems."

"Maybe. But I sure don't like it smelling like a tomb."

She coughed. The echoes of it seemed to swirl down many hallways in front of them.

"I don't remember it being this cold in here, either," she said. "I know, don't say it. No reason to keep heating systems in complete operation for robots alone."

They came to the meeting-room door, which was ajar. Derec placed his hand on Ariel's arm and whispered, "Wait."

She whispered back, "What's wrong?"

"That door's usually not kept open."

"So what? It's safe enough down here. No need for security."

"I know, I know. It's just disturbing. It should be closed."

"God, you're going anomaly-crazy. Let's go in."

She charged ahead of him before he could hold her back. Her sudden move didn't surprise him. Ariel had always been more impulsive than he. He ran after her.

Again, as they crossed a threshold into a dark room, the

automatic lighting did not function. At least the Compass Tower rooms had manual overrides so that, when necessary, lights could be controlled by the inhabitants. Ariel, feeling the wall next to the door with the back of her hand, found a light switch and flicked it on.

The Supervisor robots were, in typical fashion, seated around the long meeting table. She recognized Avernus, Dante, Rydberg, Euler, Arion, and particularly the first Wohler, the robot who had saved her life on the outside wall of the tower, then had lost all memory of his own heroism. Each time she saw Wohler, she felt a twinge of affection for him.

"Why were they sitting in the dark?" Ariel said. "Hey, why are you guys sitting in darkness?"

"It is not dark now," Avernus said. His voice sounded odd, a bit deeper, like a sound tape being slowed down.

"But it was. Wait a minute. You fellows don't usually play those robotic word games with us. Heck, the bunch of you together form a major computer. What's going on?"

"Nothing," Euler said. His voice sounded weird, too.

She turned to Derec. "What's going on, you think?"

"I don't know."

He walked around the table, studying the robots carefully, sometimes touching them, asking fast questions, receiving slow answers. Finally, he came back to Ariel and whispered, "They're not really functioning."

"What do you mean? They responded to your questions, they spoke."

"But their responses were meaningless, they didn't really say anything. You heard them. Whenever my questions had anything to do with possible computer malfunctions, they each said the computer is fully operational. But, when I asked any specific questions about what was wrong with the city, they said nothing was wrong. Well, we can see how much is wrong and, Ariel, part of what's wrong is *them*. Whoever's behind the sabotaging of the city has gotten control of them, too. They're just another system gone haywire. Let's try the office. Maybe we'll find the culprit there."

Before they left the room, Derec and Ariel looked back. The Supervisor robots had not appeared to move an inch. They had not sprung up, ready to serve Derec and Ariel, or provided useful information. They had seemed listless, and listless robots seemed a contradiction in terms. Before she switched off the light, Ariel said, a bit sadly, " 'Bye, fellas." Was she mistaken, or was there a faint mumbling response from them?

The office light also had to be turned on manually. The room itself looked no different from usual. Its furniture was all in place, surfaces were clean, the computer was positioned correctly on the desk. The surrounding walls, furnishing a computer display of the view from the Compass Tower roof, still functioned, although they showed an altered Robot City, now too dark and too mysterious. Derec cursed under his breath.

"What's wrong?" Ariel asked. It seemed her main question ever since they had returned to Robot City.

"The chemfets. It's as if they're getting fainter, dissolving. Whatever's affecting the city is affecting them. It *has* to. Let me at the computer."

As he activated the screen, called up access codes, made his fingers fly across the keyboard, his eyes teared up and he struggled to keep from crying. Ariel, for the first time in a long while, didn't know what to say to him or what to do for him. The chemfets had always been a mystery to her, and she didn't know how to counter their effect on him.

Finally, with an angry yowl, Derec slammed his fists on

the keyboard. A few random letters appeared on the screen followed by a question mark.

"It's like everything else around here. It won't communicate with me. Whatever I type into it, it sends back gobbledy-gook—an error message, or request for clarification, or denial of access. I asked why the lighting systems were not working properly, and it asked if I'd like a Cracked Cheeks cassette delivered to our rooms." The Cracked Cheeks were the robot jazz group that had formed during the "Circuit Breaker" incident. A fascination with creativity had captivated several robots at the time, but Avery had later programmed such "dangerous" impulses out of them. "I asked why so many systems were down, and it called up a file-management tutorial file. I asked if there had been any newcomers to the city, and it said that information was restricted. I asked it to unrestrict it, and it said it was restricted *forever*."

"How can that be?"

"I don't know. It just seemed to be toying with me, treating me like a child, not relating to the chemfets at all. There's been some kind of bypass, somebody's hacked in or something, or a computer virus, I don't know. Whatever, whoever it is, is in control. I could try to access the right information until I was blue in the face, and I'd just get nonsense from it. The computer's been taken from me, the robots are no longer in my power, the city is running down, and I can't stop it. And all I want to do is go back to the ship, lift off from this hellhole, go back to Aurora or even to Earth, and never come back."

He was close to breaking down. Ariel could see that. Gently she ran her hand through his bristly sandy-colored hair, uncertain for a moment of what to say, then she knelt down beside him. "Hey, snap out of it. These are minor setbacks, pal. We can take care of them. We've done it before."

He smiled. "You're right. What'd I do without you?"

"Probably blunder on with much less efficiency."

He sat quietly for a long while. "I wonder if *he's* behind all of it."

She did not have to ask who *he* was.

"It has the fingerprints of Dr. Avery all over it, doesn't it?"

"It has to be him."

"But," said Dr. Avery, his small form stepping out of a dark corner, "this time it is *not* me. I am, my son, just as confused by it all as you are."

CHAPTER 7

NO AVERYS NEED APPLY

"You were in that corner all this time?" Ariel asked.

Avery looked smug as he responded, "Since long before you violated my privacy by coming into the room. I've been—"

Derec suddenly screamed, "Damn you!" He vaulted out of his chair and lunged at Dr. Avery, grabbing him by the throat and shoving him against the nearest wall. The doctor's eyes remained calm, as if the way he looked when he was being murdered was the same as when he delivered a sarcastic comment.

"Derec!" Ariel shouted. "Stop! Right this minute!"

She pulled hard at his arm, breaking his grip, then she interposed her body between him and Dr. Avery. With a forceful backhand, she hit Derec on the side of his face. Derec's eyes looked momentarily dazed. Gently she began walking, edging him back toward the computer terminal.

"Now why in the name of the fifty Spacer planets did you do that?" she said.

Derec sat down again. His fingertips brushed along a

row of letters on the keyboard. "I'm sorry, Ariel."

"How about me?" Avery said, his voice a bit shaky as he tentatively touched his throat. "I think you should apologize to me."

"No! That I won't do! You spied on us."

"I wouldn't call it spying, son. I was here first, remember? Meditating in the darkness. You intruded on me. I just wasn't ready to announce it."

"He's right, Derec," Ariel said. "His spying's not important enough for an attempted murder."

"I wouldn't have killed him. You know that." Ariel was bothered by the fact that she really didn't know whether or not Derec could commit patricide. "I just wanted to hurt him."

"Well, you at least succeeded in that purpose, young man," Avery said. Now he was tugging at the cuff of his sleeve with one hand, smoothing out the cloth of his laboratory smock with the other. "You do not seem to be accomplishing much elsewhere, however. No wonder you were reduced to tears."

Derec made a small furious sound in his throat, but restrained himself from jumping up again. Instead, he said quietly, in a level voice, "What it was, Ariel, he saw me cry. I didn't want him to see that, that's all. Not him! Childish of me, I guess. I'm sorry."

Ariel hugged him. "You *are* childish, darling. And it's all right to cry. No matter who sees it."

"Not if it's him." He rubbed at his eyes with the back of his right hand, trying to wipe away any remaining evidence of his tears. "He has no right to judge me."

"I've always judged you. I am your father. I'm supposed to."

"He may be lying about being my father. How do we know?"

"You've inherited my bad temper, son. Isn't that proof enough for you? And why won't you address me directly?"

Derec refused to reply. He sat silently, staring at the computer screen's last message, a bit of gobbledygook about invalid parameters.

Avery, smoothing down his white wavy hair, then pressing down his mustache, walked forward. Ariel noticed that his eyes glowed. He had always seemed crackbrained in his words and deeds; now she saw it in his eyes. Derec whirled around in his chair and faced the scientist. A strange smile came slowly over Avery's face.

"We have a problem," he said.

"We have many problems," Derec said. "Which one are you referring to?"

Avery waved his hand in a dismissive gesture. "Not the ones between you and me, son. They are trivial. I will win you over in time. No, I mean the city. My city. Your city, too. Almost all normal functioning has stopped, as you've seen."

"And you have nothing to do with it?"

Avery shook his head no. "I understand why you suspect me. I might suspect myself. But I was away on a different project, conducting a different set of experiments at another robot city. I used a Key to Perihelion to return here yesterday, and my arrival has so far been undetected. That's no surprise, considering the way things have fallen apart here."

"What's the cause of it?" Derec asked.

"I can't find out. The changes didn't occur by themselves, I'm sure of that. Someone is behind them. But I haven't a clue whom. For a while I thought it might be you, fooling around with your domain here, trying out your wings. But I realize now it wasn't."

"Why do you think it's *someone*?" Ariel asked. "Couldn't it be a flaw in the works, something you overlooked that's making the city decay?"

A flash of furious anger came briefly into the doctor's eyes then receded as he stared at his questioner.

"No, the city cannot decay," he said. "It could choke itself to death with overproduction, as it was doing the very first time you two arrived here. It could come close to social ruin, as it nearly did when the artist Lucius created his "Circuit Breaker" sculpture. But the mechanisms themselves cannot fail, and neither can the robots. However, essentially I agree with your insight. There is decadence here. Not originating in the system but from an outside source. We must find the source."

"Stop saying *we*," Derec said angrily. "You do what you want to, but I won't work with you. Until I find out otherwise, you are my chief suspect for the state of the city."

Again the doctor smiled, and again it was a strange smile, coming over his face as if it were released by a spring mechanism. "We must work on your logic circuits, son. Why would I try to ruin Robot City, the city I created myself, then peopled with my own robots? Destroying this city would be, for me, like destroying myself."

"Excuse me, sir," Ariel said, "but your previous behavior doesn't entirely eliminate the chance you might, in a fit or tantrum, decide to get rid of your own creation. I'm sorry, but I have to agree with Derec on this."

She moved to Derec, placed her hand casually on his shoulder.

"Well, don't the two of you make a pretty pair?" Avery said. "Like dull-eyed pioneers in a tintype. All the imperfections of humanity stiffly posed on a chemically treated plate. I suppose I'd hoped for more from you two, but one thing I've learned: Humans may fail you but robots are forever."

Ariel laughed. "That's diamonds are forever, I believe."

"My robots will endure beyond the cheap glitter of geological accidents."

Derec started to stand up, but Ariel's gentle pressure on his shoulder kept him seated. "Doctor," she said, "I admire florid language as much as the next gal, but what in Frost's name do you mean?"

Avery's eyes squinted and his head tilted slightly, as if he could not comprehend how he could be misunderstood. "My dear, a robot is, although manmade, the finest stage of humanity, the ideal toward which you puny, disease-prone, uncertain beings should aspire. Instead, you don't even respect them. You order them about, treat them as servants."

"Not true," Ariel said. "We *do* respect them. Most of us."

"But not all," Avery said smugly.

"At any rate, they were created as servants," Derec said, "adjuncts to human laborers in industry, maids in private homes."

"Yes, they were enslaved at first. But I have liberated them. I have created communities for them where they can exist without the continual interference of the human race, cities more magnificent than the overcrowded hovels of Earth and the brutally isolated homes of Aurora. I've—"

"Wait, wait," Ariel said. "With due respect, sir, these robot cities are designed as relatively perfect environments for humans-to-come. Yet, you say they're really for the robots?"

"Very good, Ariel. You catch on quickly. I've had to tell my robots that they were building for humans. The Laws of

Robotics demand that. They must at least think they are here to protect humans, to follow orders from humans. Rarely, however, do they ever encounter humans. That doesn't seem to make any difference to them, so long as they think there will be humans eventually."

"But you've never intended to, say, import colonies to live here?"

"Originally I did. But I've changed my mind. I say, Robot City for robots. Why contaminate them with hordes of humans spreading their weak-minded mores and indifferent customs? Don't you see, Ariel, it would be wrong for the superior beings to continue to serve the lesser? That's why I am a liberator. The robot is the next level of existence. Humans can die out, while robots will endure."

Ariel realized that she had been holding her breath as she listened to the doctor's shouted diatribe. She turned to Derec and whispered, "He *is* mad."

"I heard that, young lady. And of course you'd perceive me that way, with your limited perception. I'd expect no more. But your antagonism only stimulates my positronic pathways."

"Your what?"

"Positronic pathways. You see, I have not only created the Avery robots in my own image, but I have recreated myself, casting away my humanity and transforming myself into a robot also."

"Ba-nanas," Ariel muttered.

Avery merely smiled. Now she could see it as a definitely robotic smile, even though she believed none of his story.

"I knew you wouldn't believe," Avery said.

"Are you trying to say, oh, that you've implanted a robot brain into your head? Is that what the positronic pathways guff is all about?"

"I see that you're patronizing me, so I think we can terminate this discussion."

For a moment Ariel wondered if this figure, identical to the Dr. Avery she had met before, might indeed be a robotic recreation. Then he swept by her, and his easily detectable body odor told her that he was still at least partly human.

After Avery slammed the door behind him, Ariel commented, "The man needs help."

"So do we," Derec said. His fingers flew across the keyboard again. Some data came up on the terminal's screen. "Look at this, Ariel."

All she saw was a bunch of figures. "What does it mean?"

"This is a report of construction activity in Robot City. The earlier figures represent the city's normal rate of new building. But lately the figures have gradually fallen off, with fewer and fewer buildings being created. Since before we arrived, there have, in fact, been no new buildings created. All construction in Robot City has stopped."

"Funny," Ariel commented.

"What's funny about it?"

"This tends to support your father's story."

"How does it do that?"

"Well, remember what he said about robots being the supreme whatever and all that, plus the city being the safest haven for them? So why would he stop that? Why would he allow the robots themselves to become, as he said, decadent? This man isn't going to be happy with listless Supervisors and robots who are tap dancers or movie buffs. After Lucius, he programmed creativity right out of his robots. No, for once Dr. Avery isn't the chief troublemaker. It's somebody else, it's got to be."

"Okay, granted. But what do we do now? I can't get anything out of the computer, the robots are uncooperative, and the city's becoming a play-village for someone whose identity we don't know. What next, my pretty?"

"Well, I've got a swell idea if you don't mind a little break in the action."

"You've got—"

"This room comes furnished with a couch-bed, and there's even a blanket on the end table there if you want privacy."

"You flip off the lights, I'll switch off the computer."

"Why the computer?"

"I don't know. I've a feeling it could spy on us."

As they embraced in darkness, the real spy outside the door, still indoctrinated with the Laws of Robotics, knew they applied in some way to this situation, and so he discreetly retreated. After all, he thought, in the best movies he had seen, the camera always discreetly retreated from this sort of scene. As he rejoined Timestep outside the Compass Tower, Bogie decided that the shadowing assignment was a fortunate one. Keeping watch on the two young humans was a bit like watching a movie—in a way, better, since it took place in three dimensions.

CHAPTER 8

CREATURE DISCOMFORTS

Each time Wolruf stumbled or bumped into something, she cursed in her own language. Eve asked her what words she was speaking, but she replied that it was merely her own private nonsense.

The Silversides and Mandelbrot had no difficulty with the darkness of the streets. Equipped with precise sensory circuitry, they could proceed easily through such darkness. Wolruf, even with the keen senses she had developed in the wilds of her homeland, couldn't detect every obstacle in her way.

"Is the lack of proper lighting bothersome to you?" Mandelbrot asked her.

"So true. I rememberr lightss coming on when walking these strreetss."

"They do not seem to be functioning now."

"Like so many other thingss here. What iss wrrong, Mandelbrrot?"

"I do not know."

"What we have seen," Eve asked, "is not necessarily like this place as you know it?"

"Verry different," Wolruf answered. "Strreetlampss alwayss lit one'ss way."

They walked a few more steps, turned a corner (with Wolruf's shoulder painfully bumping into the side of a building), and saw flickering light up ahead.

"What is that?" Eve asked.

"Not sure," Wolruf said, "but my nose tellss me approach cautiously."

"Your nose speaks to you?"

"No, that iss rrenderring of saying from my worrld into 'uman wordss. We sense dangerr, we say we sniff it out with our nosess, even when there iss no actual scent there."

Eve did not quite understand, but she chose to keep quiet, especially since Wolruf, assuming the role of scout, now sprinted ahead of the group.

"Adam?" Eve said.

"Yes?"

"Is this a strange place, this Robot City?"

"In my limited experience, where every place I have seen is strange to me, this one is, too."

The glimmering light shone from an open area in between two tall buildings. Gesturing the three robots to stay put, Wolruf edged along the front of the building until she came to its corner. Looking around it, she saw that the light came from a bonfire in the middle of a vacant lot. Gathered around the flames doing an odd, jerky dance was a crowd of small creatures. Because the fire cast distorting shadows, she could not easily focus on the figures. Yet she was sure they were shaped like humans, but much more diminutive.

At first she thought they might be a group of children.

Then a few danced into a clear patch of light. Wolruf saw that not only were they even smaller than she had thought, they were also not children. One male had a beard, a female had quite fully developed (in miniature) breasts, another had an aged, deeply lined face. Definitely not children. They were adults. Tiny, tiny adults.

The Watchful Eye no longer knew what to think about the new arrivals. Such contradictory behavior, it thought. The one called Ariel seemed all right, except when she decided to be affectionate with Derec. Derec cried and nearly murdered the new individual, Avery. Avery stomped around like a caged animal. Who *were* these creatures?

It knew from its earlier research that Avery might be the creator of Robot City, but the doctor's behavior was so erratic that the Watchful Eye did not want to make contact with him. If Avery discovered it here in its safe haven, there was no telling what he might do.

Now, to further complicate matters, the second group had come upon one of the Watchful Eye's Master Experiments. Series C, Batch 4, one of its better efforts. A failure like the rest, yes, but an interesting failure at least. Like some of the other humanic substitutes, they had developed a rudimentary society. Although none of these batches had contributed the insights about the Laws of Humanics that the Watchful Eye sought, they had, by banding together and rapidly evolving a few customs, provided an abundance of useful data about cultural tendencies.

Because there was so much for it to consider, the Watchful Eye now chose to retreat into its stasis state. In stasis, it shut off its senses so that it could concentrate exclusively on problems, this time the new and altered situations brought into its hermetic world by the intruders. It wanted to analyze how they would affect its overall existence and whether it would have to take any action against them. Before settling itself back into its safe haven, it sent out messages to its spies, Bogie and Timestep, instructing them to signal it if a new crisis developed. When that was done, it snuggled down into the haven, curled up into an embryonic state, and disconnected all sensory networks. Immediately it was welcomed into the calm comfort of nothingness, a place where it sometimes yearned to be forever.

"Well, we're on our own for a while, kid," Bogie commented after acknowledging the Watchful Eye's message. "The Big Muddy's spoke."

"Big Muddy?" Timestep said. "Is that a proper name for—"

"Let me put it this way, pal. I wouldn't speak it if the Big Muddy was looking over my shoulder."

Timestep did a little clog routine from one of the dance tapes he'd studied.

"Nice moves, Tip-tap!"

"It's Timestep."

"You say so, Tip-tap."

"What are we supposed to do now?"

"Keep tabs on Dick and Jane up there, send the Big Muddy signals if they get up to somethin' it should know about."

"What are they doing now?"

"Friend Tip-tap, we'll just draw the curtain across that little scene."

"All right. Then we should just stand here and wait for something to happen?"

" 'bout the size of it, big boy."

They stood silently for a long while, a pair of silvery

statues streaked with blue in the dim, reflected light at the foot of the Compass Tower.

"Bogie?"

"Yeah, kid?"

"Who is the Big Muddy?"

"Don't know. Just the boss, far's I know."

"Have you seen it?"

"Nope. Nobody has, far's I know."

"Why has it taken over Robot City?"

"Beats me. Place has certainly changed since it breezed in, though."

"I don't feel comfortable about that. A while ago I had a safe, normal routine. Every day I did my job. I never questioned whether or not to do it. Then the Big Muddy came, and before I knew it, I had walked off the job. That's when I found out I was a dancer. The Big Muddy told me."

"Yep. Same for me. I had a compulsion to examine old movies, came from Big Muddy. I don't mind it, though. There's a lot of truth in flickerdom, kid. I've copped much more about human life now. You don't trust society broads and you don't rat on a partner, stuff like that. The flicks've helped me to see the vast potential of the humans we serve. I'll be a better robot because of them."

"You confuse me, Bogie. I am not certain all this is right. Once we were building and maintaining Robot City; now almost everything about the city has stopped. We are the servants of the Big Muddy now."

"Maybe this burg needed a rest, kiddo. You worry too much. Dump it in a grocery cart and carry it out to the parking lot. We've got a job to do right now. Let's do it."

"Do you think the city looks the way it used to?"

"No, it don't. But, like they say, that's Chinatown, Jake."

Timestep couldn't understand half of what Bogie said,

but he chose now to keep still until something happened.

A long time passed and nothing happened.

Finally he said, "I cannot stand still this way. I've got to dance."

In the few pools of light, Timestep's dance became a silhouette of a slow tap. He moved from one lighted area to another. Bogie, who'd seen some dancing in movies, judged that a human would have probably found the robot's little routine bizarre, since it was tap dancing without music. The clunking noises as his feet made contact with the pavement echoed through the long street. They were grating sounds. Timestep should hire himself a band, Bogie thought.

Now that night had fallen, the darkness inside the Compass Tower office seemed total to Ariel. She stuck her head out from beneath the blanket and could not discern anything. After blinking her eyes a few times, however, details of the room appeared to emerge from the blackness.

"It's eerie," she whispered.

Derec, who had nearly fallen asleep, was startled awake and asked, "What did you say?"

"Eerie, the darkness in here. I mean, the room. Usually all those view-screens are on, transmitting scenes from the outside world."

"They *are* on. There's just so little light out there, you can hardly tell." He sat up. "But it *is* awfully dark. Let's take a better look."

After adjusting their clothing, Derec led Ariel to the desk that dominated one side of the room. Flicking on a small desk lamp (it had been so dark, even that flimsy light pained her eyes), he pulled out the slab of controls from its position just beneath the desk blotter. Sitting down, Derec worked the controls, searching for clearer pictures or any kind of image that would be displayed recognizably on a view-screen. Most of the screens remained shadowy. Here and there they could see the shapes of buildings, sometimes a few dim stars in the sky.

He pointed one camera downward, and it picked up the pools of light near the Compass Tower. They came, he saw, from some light bands in a building across the way. Apparently the lighting system there had not broken down.

"Look there." He pointed to the view-screen. "Something's happening down there." He zoomed in on the movement, enlarging the image until they could plainly see Timestep doing his dance. The robot, with a movement approaching grace, leaped from pool to pool. Derec turned up the volume on the sound pickup, and they could hear the hollow, plaintive, echoing, tapping sounds.

"Weird," Ariel said. "Do you think that's the dancer we met?"

"Looks like him."

Timestep stretched his arms outward and tapped to the left, then he shuffled a bit and made the same move to the right.

"It's not like human dancing," Ariel said, "but it has its own elegance, its own special grace. You know, once—when I was about twelve or thirteen—I was given an old mechanical toy, some kind of precursor to robots, perhaps, but really just a toy that was wound up and run. It was a little metal man in a harlequin costume, and it stayed in one place, a tiny pole running up its back. When it was switched on, it did this queer, floppy dance. Its legs bent in right angles at the knees, then came down and hit its pedestal a couple of times, then resumed its stance with the right-angled knees, then down again, and so forth. I was fascinated by it, played with it for hours. I liked it better than all the technologically fashionable toys that were arranged in clusters around my room. But I think my mother sneaked in when I was asleep and took it away. I don't remember who gave it to me. Look at that."

Timestep had executed an extravagantly long soft-shoe glide, coming to a stop beside another robot she hadn't previously noticed.

"Say, that's—what did he call himself?—Bogie, wasn't it? What are those two doing down there?"

"I don't know, but it seems terribly coincidental that the two of them should wind up together and right near the Compass Tower entrance, don't you think?"

"Maybe. I wish Timestep'd dance again. He couldn't possibly be tired."

"What did you get out of it? The dance, I mean. It might be a bit unusual, but it was just a robot dancing. They can do anything they're programmed to do."

"Don't be so pragmatic. There was a beauty in his dance."

"Only in your mind. A human doing the same dance with about the same ability, you'd find him awkward and minimally talented. That robot is about the same as the famous talking dog. It's that he does it at all that's amazing, but there was nothing remotely beautiful about it."

Ariel muttered, "Have it your way, Mr. Critic-at-large." She walked away a few steps, then whirled around to say, "But I liked it!"

Derec was used to Ariel being touchy on occasion, so he shrugged and said, "I'm sorry. Just my opinion. Let's go down and pay these fellows a visit."

"It's not necessary."

"C'mon. Maybe Timestep does encores."

● ● ●

The three robots and Wolruf stayed outside the perimeter of the tiny creatures' encampment. After a flurry of interest in the intruders, the small people had turned their attention back to their ritual by the bonfire. There was a definite pattern to the ritual. First they circled the fire in a line, each creature keeping a hand on the shoulder of the individual in front of it. Then they broke up into couples and performed a dance that featured a complicated but rhythmic sequence of high kicks. The kick dance was followed by a synchronized turning toward the fire, the move accompanied by a high pitched wail. Wolruf was reminded of the noises of a high-flying bird-like species from her home planet.

When the moaning had reached its loudest point, it stopped abruptly, and several of the small people dropped quickly to the ground. The ones left standing picked up their fallen comrades and dragged them away from the fire. After pulling them a short distance, they began arranging them in a number of piles. The wailing resumed, then the standing people clapped their hands three times, and the fallen bodies stirred and got to their feet. A short frenetic dance that looked like celebration followed. After that, another group took its place around the fire and executed the same ritual, step by step.

"It is strange," Eve commented.

"What does the ritual mean?" Adam asked.

"I would speculate that it has something to do with death and resurrection," Mandelbrot said.

"Why do 'u say that?" Wolruf asked.

"Some information about such rituals on other planets that I have stored in my memory banks. The rite here suggests that some of them die, the ones piled up, and then are in some way resurrected. The reason for resurrection is not clear to me. To understand, I am afraid we would have to observe their culture at length."

"I would like to do that," Eve said. "They, too, seem to be human, Adam. Perhaps they would supply some data for our quest."

"Perhaps."

"But we have to meet Derrec and Arriel at the towerr," Wolruf said.

"You two go ahead," Eve suggested. "We will follow soon."

"What will 'u do?" Wolruf asked.

"Nothing dangerous, I assure you. I just wish to study them a while."

"It would be best if you continued on with us," Mandelbrot said.

"No," Wolruf said, " 'u know these two. They get idea, 'u can't stop them."

If Mandelbrot had been a nodder, he would have nodded. He and Wolruf quickly left the lot, heading toward the Compass Tower.

A moment later, Eve crossed into the area where the tiny creatures were busy with their ritual. They didn't seem to notice her. Adam followed. They stepped carefully, putting their feet down only in clear areas. This kind of walking was easier for a robot than it would have been for a human. If there had been any danger of Eve or Adam putting their feet down upon one of the tiny creatures, they would have sensed it quickly and been able to balance on one leg for as long as it took until a safe step could be ventured.

When they were near the fire, Eve said, "They seem intelligent. Can we talk to them, do you think?"

"We can try, Eve."

She crouched down, getting her head as low as she

could without falling over. Reflected light from the bonfire seemed to move like the tiny dancers across her silvery surface.

"Hello," she said.

Some of the dancers looked at her. They stopped, stood still, and stared up at her. "Can you understand me?"

They said nothing. A tiny, prettily formed woman stepped forward. She had large bulging eyes and a swelling by her right ear. Eve expected her to say something, but she did not. She merely scrutinized her visitor, a quizzical expression on her face.

"I am Eve."

The small woman made some odd sounds in her throat and pointed up at Eve. Three others joined her, another woman and two men. They all appeared amused. The woman with the large eyes began jumping up and down, her odd raspy sounds getting louder. The trio behind her laughed merrily. One slapped his knee. Then they all began talking, if that's what the chattering sounds they emitted were.

"There seems to be a language," Adam said.

"Maybe we can learn it."

Saying hello again, Eve reached out her hand toward the small woman, who, scared, took some steps backward. Then she appeared to get control of herself. She turned her back on Eve and resumed her place in the bonfire ritual. The other three followed her. Soon none of them were paying any attention to the gigantic silver intruder who hovered above them. The ritual appeared to get fiercer each time they repeated it.

Eve stood up and walked past the fire. Many of the small people were gathered in a corner of the lot, working furiously. She had to squat down again to see what they were doing. When she saw what it was, she called out to Adam to come and view it for himself.

Gesturing for him to hunch down beside her, she indicated the group in the corner.

"What are they doing, Eve?"

"Look. There are rows and rows of these small creatures on the ground there. Beyond that, there are more of them in piles."

"Like the dance?"

"No, not like the dance. The ones in this pile are dead, Adam. The others are burying them in the ground, but there are too many dead ones and they are not able to keep up the pace. Look, over there, more are being carried here."

From all points of the lot, it seemed, surviving creatures were hauling their dead compatriots to the burial ground. There was a slow rhythm to the way they walked, as if it, too, were part of the bonfire ritual. Eve noted that there was no human emotion on their faces. They were merely burying their dead methodically.

When each corpse had been covered over, the gravediggers turned to the next tiny plot of land and dug a hole for the next in line.

"Adam, I think there's something wrong here. They are dying out, all of them. They will all be gone shortly. Yet I detect no signs of disease. No, it is more like they are just wearing out. Derec told us nothing of these creatures."

"I do not understand, Eve."

"I surmise that they did not exist a short time ago, when Derec and Ariel were first here. They have only existed for a short time, and now they are dying out. I suspect there is something sad in that."

She turned her head and saw that one of the corpses

now being conveyed to the burial ground was the small woman with the bulging eyes.

Even when he stood still, Timestep's left foot kept tapping from side to side. Bogie recalled a character in a movie who had performed the same movement at the beginning of a dance number. He could not remember specifically because he rarely watched musicals, much preferring the mystery and action films that were so well represented in the Robot City Film and Tape Archives.

He was about to suggest that one of them should again station himself in the hallway outside the office when he heard the last few soft treads of Ariel and Derec as they came to the outer door of the Compass Tower. As Bogie glanced toward the tower, he saw the door beginning to form itself before letting them exit.

"Run," he said to Timestep, "they're coming out."

They both started clanking up the street, but the Second Law of Robotics, that they must obey an order coming from a human being, made them stop running when Derec yelled for them to stop. As Derec and Ariel walked up to them, Timestep's foot resumed its slow tapping movement.

"You two, you're spying on us," Derec said. His voice has assumed the firmness that humans often used when addressing robots. "Why?"

"We are not allowed to tell that," Bogie said. "It is a confidential order."

"From whom?"

"We are not allowed to tell you that."

"Another one of your infernal blocks?"

"Yes."

"It's my father," Derec said angrily. "Only he would think up tricks like this."

"I still disagree," Ariel said. "His tricks would be even more diabolical."

"And there's no way I can remove these blocks right now?"

"Only the one who put them there may remove them."

"Did a human put them there?"

"I cannot say."

"You cannot say because you don't know or because my father put in those blocks?"

"I cannot say because I am prevented from saying."

"Nice try," Ariel whispered, "trying to trick him into admitting your father's the perpetrator."

"Well, tricks like that sometimes work, Ariel."

"I know, you've been around the block a few times."

Derec was about to continue his interrogation of Bogie when Mandelbrot and Wolruf rounded a corner and headed toward them at a fast pace. Wolruf was loping on all fours, as she sometimes did when she was tired. Since she stayed beside Mandelbrot, keeping at his pace, they looked like a man and his dog out for a stroll—if you didn't look too closely.

"Where're our two mischief-makers?" Derec asked when they reached him.

"A good question," Wolruf said. She explained how they had left the Silversides behind to study the creatures they'd discovered, and she was surprised to see Derec's eyes light up with interest. He turned to Ariel and said excitedly, "These may be more of the same pests that attacked us in that building. Let's go see."

"Good idea. Anyway, it's never wise to leave Adam and Eve alone anywhere they could cause trouble."

They started down the street, the way Mandelbrot and Wolruf had come. The alien and the ever-loyal robot walked right behind them. After a few steps, Derec glanced back at Bogie and Timestep.

"Hey," he called back to them, "you're going to follow us and spy on us anyway, you two. You might just as well come along with us."

It was probably his imagination, but it seemed to Derec as if the two spies began their walk toward him with some eagerness in their stride.

CHAPTER 9

TROUBLE RIGHT HERE IN ROBOT CITY

Even though Wolruf had described the vacant lot's strange colony to him, Derec was unprepared for what they found there.

First, the bonfire had gone out. It now smoldered pathetically, a few wisps of smoke rising from what proved to be some type of synthetic wood. The wood, now a jumbled pile of charred curls, gave off a strong chemical odor that reminded Ariel of a broken-down food synthesizer, never one of her favorite smells.

Next, Derec saw the dancers. They were still a circle, but no longer moving. They were on the ground, some face down, some face up, their hands still joined, but clearly dead. Their bodies had not been moved because the carriers and the gravediggers had died out now. As he walked around the yard, he had to step over more than a hundred undersized corpses.

Finally, he saw Adam and Eve at the half-completed graveyard. Eve was delicately picking up the creatures' bodies, one by one, and placing them in a row of graves she had quickly dug with her hands. It was an odd action, Derec thought, one that seemed to indicate compassion on her part. While she could have some understanding of human feelings, he thought it doubtful she could feel such compassion herself.

Still, Adam and Eve were a new breed of robot, one that had appeared as if by magic on two planets now (Adam having found Eve on the blackbodies' planet after himself coming into sudden existence on the planet of the wolflike creatures, the kin), and so anything was possible. The way the Silversides kept surprising him, he might never get a fix on them. Perhaps they were indeed the prototypes for emotional robots, a concept that did not correspond with Derec's present knowledge of robotics.

"Where did they come from?" Ariel said, looking down at the many bodies.

"I don't know. They seem to be one more thing that's gone wrong with the city."

"Are they the same ones who attacked us in the warehouse?"

"Maybe. Or that might have been another bunch."

Ariel shuddered. "You mean they may be all over the city, living in open spaces or dark places like rodents?"

"Rodent may not be the proper analogy. They do seem to have been human or humanlike. What do you think, Adam? Eve?"

Adam was holding one of the little corpses in his left hand while he poked at it with a finger of his right. The figure appeared to be a gaunt young man with a short beard. His body was extremely thin.

Adam, while still strongly resembling Derec, had taken on some of the corpse's appearance. His face had thinned and there was a hint of metallic bristles on his chin. He

seemed to have grown taller and slimmer, also.

"They seem to be miniature versions of humans, inside and out," Adam observed. "I sense a musculature, a bloodstream, arteries and veins, small fragile bones."

"Bound to seem fragile. Any one of us could crush any one of them."

"Do you have to say things like that?" Ariel said.

"Sorry, thought you were tougher."

She looked ready to slug him for making that remark.

"Since when does good taste indicate weakness? Huh, Derec, huh?"

"Okay, you made your point. I'm a bit dense when my world is disrupted this violently, okay?"

She touched his cheek with the back of her hand. Her touch was so gentle, he immediately wished he could devote all his time and energies to her.

"Adam," he said, "you seem to have imprinted partially on the corpse. Have you learned anything from that?"

"Only that I cannot do it very well. Before it died, I started to study it. I found I couldn't imprint on it successfully. It was as if there was very little life in it when it was alive."

Derec nodded. "Well, it was already dying perhaps."

"Yes, but it was more than that, Master Derec. There was simply very little awareness inside here." He held out the corpse. Derec flinched a bit. The corpse's tiny, delicate face was twisted in pain. "The impression I had was similar to what I have received from small animals. What I concluded was that they resembled humans but were not human."

"I do not agree," Eve said. Adam looked toward her. Derec wondered if Adam could possibly feel the discomfort that he always felt when Ariel challenged his opinion. There

was a sense of competitiveness between him and Ariel that sometimes interfered with their ability to communicate. But Adam and Eve should not, as robots, have that kind of communication difficulty, and there was no reason for them to compete with each other.

"We saw very little of them," Eve explained, "but there was a definite society here. They interacted with each other, joined in a complex ritual together, did indeed combine together into a sort of colony. They had a need to dispose of their dead. Are not these proofs that they had at least a rudimentary society?"

"She's got a point there," Ariel observed.

Derec glanced at Eve. Her face seemed to alter slightly, becoming even more like Ariel's whenever Ariel talked.

"What matters right now," he said, "is not what they were, but why they were here."

"Do you have any answers?" Ariel asked.

"Not many. Only my father. These creatures may be the result of some lousy experiment he's done down in his mysterious underground laboratory. He's let them loose to—to do I don't know what. With him how can you—"

"Let's not give you too much rope to hang yourself with," Avery said, as he strolled into the lot, again emerging from some dark place. "Yes, don't say it, son—your old dad was eavesdropping again. I would have remained hidden, but I'm tired of your trying to hang the blame on me for everything that goes wrong here. After all, you're the one in charge, Derec. Try considering it could be you who's to blame."

"I haven't even been here since—"

"I know, I know. And of course you're not at fault. But I was away, too, remember." He sauntered around the lot, examining the ugly scene. "This place was once a small park

as I recall. I remember programming these for the city, soil and all. I never expected the dirt to be used for burials." He wrinkled his nose. "They're decaying at an above-normal rate, these corpses." He reached down, picked up one of the bodies. "Interesting workmanship," he muttered.

Ariel charged forward, angry. "Workmanship! How can you—"

"How can I analyze this dead thing so coldly? Objectivity. I am a scientist, my dear. It's my mind-set, if you will. Anyhow, this was not a true living being. Although realistic and cleverly designed, with a great deal of genetic accuracy, I suspect this is merely an android, a kind of dime-story copy of a humaniform robot, with admirably realistic detail."

Ariel thought of Jacob Winterson and how he was just as "dead" as the tiny body Avery held so casually in his hand. "I don't believe you," she said, although to herself she admitted the doctor might be right.

"Well, my dear, of course I can't be sure. I admit I can detect no mechanisms in this particular miniature. But a well-crafted miniature has to be what this is. Do you know about miniatures in art? They're quite wonderful. On a small surface, sometimes made of vellum, sometimes ivory or copper, the artist would render exquisitely detailed little landscapes or portraits or whatever. Often the painting was done with the patient strokes of a single-strand brush. The details might astound you. You'd swear that you were looking at an intricate painting that had been mechanically reduced or done with microsopic brushes."

"What was the point of them? I mean, why choose a small area when you could have a whole canvas?"

"Perhaps the challenge, perhaps the artistry of working on a small scale, or perhaps commercial motives. You see, miniatures were often encased in jewelry—lockets and such—and so a pretty penny could also be earned from such a specialized craft. When photography came in, and you could place a small photo in a locket, the need for miniatures diminished and painters had to look elsewhere for places to cash in on their talents"

"You sound bitter, Dr. Avery," Ariel said. "As if you were an artist yourself."

"I am, in a way. I started out as an architect, and architecture, when done right, is an art form, too. Robot City was my masterpiece—until my son allowed it to get out of hand."

"Don't say that!" Derec shouted. "It wasn't my fault, what happened to the city."

"I didn't mean to say it was. All I meant is that it is your responsibility. Please excuse me now. I want to get this specimen to a laboratory to examine it before it is fully decayed."

Holding the tiny figure aloft, the way he might have held a beaker with volatile contents, Avery rushed off the lot. Derec, his eyes glowering, stared after him.

"Don't let him get to you," Ariel said.

"He hasn't gotten to me," Derec said sullenly.

"Sure, and this place doesn't stink. Let's get out of here."

Derec and Ariel led an entourage that included Wolruf, Mandelbrot, Adam, Bogie and Timestep out of the lot. Eve insisted on staying behind to finish the burials. Although Derec found her behavior peculiar, especially for a robot, he did not argue with her. There were, after all, more important problems to occupy his mind, and anyway, the task would keep her out of trouble for a while.

When he looked back at her, she was gently placing a

body into a minuscule grave in the delicate way a child might put a doll into a toy crib.

Bogie and Timestep took up the rear of the bizarre little march through the dark city streets.

"Hey, kid," Bogie said, "whattaya make o' that scene back there?"

"I did not know I was supposed to interpret it," Timestep said. "None of the humans made that request of me."

"Yeah, I know. But I just wanna know about these little people so we can figure out our duties if we ever meet any live ones. Are they human and covered by the Laws, or what? After all, these guys don't seem to know what they are. If they're human, they're our concern, too, right?"

"It would seem so."

"On the other hand, if their fate is inevitable, as Derec and the others seem to be saying, there's not much we can actually do for them. If they live a very short time then pop off, no interference or help on our part is going to stave off their destiny. Then we may not have to help, except perhaps to protect them from immediate dangers."

"That may be true."

"So what do we do?"

"I don't know."

"Me neither. We'll have to wait and see, just chug on up the river and hope the leeches don't suck us dry."

"Well, one good thing," Ariel said, "the city is more peaceful this way. Remember how there used to be a hum of activity even in the dead of night? All these anomalies may be beneficial."

"Ariel, the city is decaying, and fast, just like those corpses. It'll be—"

"Hey, lighten up. I wasn't serious." They walked almost a block in sullen silence before she spoke again. "Don't take everything on your shoulders, Derec. The city is important to me, too—as are our lives, as you are."

Without breaking stride, he took her hand and held it. In response, she squeezed his.

"Your father's not looking too well," she said a few steps later.

"An understatement if I ever heard one."

"He's your father. I'm a bit hesitant to come right out and say he's bonkers. But he is. Somebody should talk to him, try to help him."

Derec stopped walking and smiled, slyly. "Would you like that job?"

She wasn't prepared for the question or the challenge contained in it, but after a moment of consideration she said, "Yes. Yes, I would."

"It's yours then. Catch him if you can."

"I'll find a way."

"I bet you will."

After they had proceeded a little farther, their steps clicking hollowly on the pavement and the city seeming to envelop them from above, Derec said, "I've been thinking. The taming of Adam and Eve is the main reason we returned to Robot City, and we've lost sight of it. But I've *got* to work out what's wrong here." He stopped walking again, took both her hands in his. "Ariel, will you take charge of the Silversides, see what you can do to, well, civilize them? With your psychological expertise, perhaps you can figure out how to get into the minds of these new-styled robots. I know they're a mystery to me."

"Sure, I'll do it. You knew I would. Any other miracles you'd like me to perform today?"

He smiled. "That'll be sufficient for now, thank you very much."

"What are you going to do in the meantime?"

"I'm not sure. Seems to me the clue to the anomalies has to be in the computer somewhere. I think Mandelbrot and I will take a trip down to the central core, see if we can detect anything. I'll take these two with me, too."

He gestured toward Bogie and Timestep, both of whom had also stopped walking, while staying a precise two steps behind. If he had looked closely, Derec might have noticed that Bogie stood oddly, the slightly tilted stance that robots sometimes adopted when they were in communication with each other.

"Do you think a tap-dancer and a wise-cracker can help? I mean, as robots go, they're weird. Talk about your anomalies . . ."

"By the same token, I don't particularly want them out of my sight."

"Gotcha, hot-shot."

"Your language is deteriorating. If you don't watch out, you'll sink to Bogie's level."

"Hope not, kiddo."

"Stop."

They agreed to keep each other informed on the progress of their tasks. Ariel told Wolruf and Adam to come with her, and Derec continued on, the silent Mandelbrot at his side, and Bogie and Timestep trailing after.

As soon as Bogie heard that Derec intended to travel down to computer level, where he knew the Watchful Eye was, he obeyed its instructions to rouse it if there were any danger. The signal ("This is your wake-up call, pal.") was sent, and the Watchful Eye came abruptly to consciousness.

CHAPTER 10

THE WANDERING EVE

It took some time for the Watchful Eye to catch up on the events that had transpired while it was in stasis. Bogie's report, transmitted over the robot comlink, was more confusing than helpful, what with all the ancient slang the robot had copied from movies.

The Watchful Eye had only itself to blame for Bogie's movie obsession. When it had first arrived in Robot City and obtained control of all systems, it had decided to form a network of knowledge. It wanted so much to find out about humanity that it had been unwilling to take the time to penetrate the computer each time it needed a particular item of information. So it had delegated certain groups of robots to research and store information in certain peripheral fields. Bogie was part of the Popular Culture Through the Universe team, while Timestep had belonged to the group studying performance arts. Other groups had specialized in such areas as sociology, psychology, and economics, all fields that the Watchful Eye rarely needed now for its running of the city, but might require in the future. Whenever it did need an item of knowledge from one of these teams, it requested it via comlink, and the robot who had specialized in the requested category would respond with a useful precis of the topic.

Some of the robots, like Bogie and Timestep, had immersed themselves so thoroughly in their areas of expertise that they had developed very peculiar characteristics related to their new-found knowledge. Bogie had adopted certain attitudes and in some cases actual dialogue from the old Earth movies he had been assigned, while a similar robotic pathology had affected Timestep in a more physical way. Although Timestep was less obsessional than Bogie, he had nevertheless acquired a need to perform the dances he researched. Perhaps he had watched too many recordings in hyperwave and old-style technologies of dancing through the ages. Part of his research had included a precise examination of the anatomical requirements for good dancing, and he had soon begun to try out the terpsichorean movements themselves. At one time or another he had executed steps for various types of ballet and popular dancing. Lately he had centered his interest on tap dancing. Whatever movements he attempted, the Watchful Eye knew, would appear terribly awkward when compared to the recordings of old dancers, but there was at least a kind of achievement in the clunkily graceful and more or less accurate way he danced.

Timestep was dancing now, as he followed Derec down city streets. Mostly he was doing something called the soft shoe, with an occasional foray into buck and wing.

Bogie's message had stated that Derec intended to inspect the central core computer. The Watchful Eye would have to seal itself in its hiding place. To throw the intruder off-guard, it would also supply some other surprises.

• • •

Eve was not certain what to look for. She wanted to know more about the tiny creatures, and so she searched for signs of their existence the way a hunter sought the spoor of the animal he was tracking.

There *were* traces. The more she looked, the more she refined her own tracking abilities, seeing clues that might have been ordinarily overlooked. Near a gutter, where—in a normally functioning city—it would have been swept away into the sewer system, she found a coat, so small she could barely hold it between her fingertips. There was a barely discernible piping around the coat's collar in delicate golden stitches. Short-lived or not, these creatures picked up some skills along the way.

In a corner of a doorway, she discovered some food crumbs. Derec or Ariel would never have perceived them, because they looked so much like dust that had been neglected by the now-inefficient sanitation robots.

Eve went through a half-open doorway into the building, where she saw that a colony of the creatures had indeed once inhabited the place. They had apparently moved on, leaving behind many clues, artifacts of their existence. She was particularly taken with a small metal unit evidently used for cooking. There was a tiny pile of ash beneath its lower grating that indicated some substance was burned there to give off cooking heat.

Leaving the building, she walked a long way before encountering any more clues. She passed several of the city's robots, many of whom seemed to be, like her, wandering aimlessly. When she tried to address them to ask them about the tiny creatures, they kept babbling about blocked information. Some of the robots passed by her without even responding to her.

Dawn came to Robot City, and the place quickly got lighter. Bright rays reflected off the metal sides of buildings. Eve was dazzled by the sudden intensity of the light. It must be different here, she thought, from ordinary human cities, where there might not be so many clear bright surfaces for sunlight to bounce off.

As she passed by a spherical building, she heard a mournful noise that reminded her of the wailing in the vacant lot. She stopped and listened at the building's door. There were more sounds, faint and muffled, that seemed like the voices of the tiny creatures. She pushed the door open. It stuck less than halfway, but she managed to push herself through the narrow opening.

She entered a lobby that, like most Robot City rooms, was decorated with some hope of eventual human habitation. An ornate desk was strategically placed in its center and there were many pictures on the walls. She inspected the pictures, but they meant nothing to her. There was so little in her experience that she could apply to the viewing of *any* scene. A couple of the pictures presented recognizable activity, but in the main they were unusual colors set in unusual patterns.

Walking across a deep-piled rug whose configurations were mazelike but colorful, she approached the desk. She noticed that the legs of the desk were shaped like claws, making her think for a moment that the desk had feet that clutched the rug. Strange, she thought, why would anyone want to carve an animal's foot on a piece of furniture? Further, no line of the desk was straight, another design feature that seemed unnecessary to her. There were curves, inset grooves, knot-holes, many shapes she did not even recognize.

But it was the top surface of the desk that really caught

her attention. Kneeling on it, in a circle, was a group of the tiny creatures, all facing inward. They held hands and made soft, moaning sounds. In the circle's center, a delicately formed young female swayed, her movements apparently guided by tone changes in the group's moaning. When their sound increased, her body began to jerk violently. When they became softer, grace returned to her gestures.

Eve put her hands on the desk so that she could lean down and look closer, but her quick movement alerted the group to her presence. The ones facing her looked up at her, while the others twisted around to see her.

Breaking handholds, they started scattering to all sides of the desktop. Directly opposite her, Eve saw the top of a small ladder, that apparently led down to the seat of a plain chair behind the desk. None of the group went to the ladder, however. When they had gone as far as they could, standing with their heels right on the edge of the desktop, they stood tensely. They trembled, as if willing to jump off should Eve get any nearer to them. Only the young female who had been in the circle's center remained in place. She stared up at Eve with curiosity.

"Who are you?" Eve asked. Her words seemed unnaturally loud as they traveled around the room and discovered echoes of themselves.

There was no response. A skinny little male on one side made a broad hand gesture to a female across the way, but Eve could not discern what it meant. She decided they could not understand her words.

A better idea, she thought, would be to make a sign of peace. Moving her hand slowly, she laid it in an open area of the desktop, palm up, fingers open. There was another flurry of fear among the creatures at the desk's fringes, but the leader, after a moment of consideration, strode confidently forward and, climbing into Eve's palm between her thumb and index finger, walked slowly around the center of her hand. Once she knelt down and felt Eve's malleable metal skin. The female stroked it several times, as if concerned with its texture, then studied her own skin, clearly comparing it to Eve's and perhaps wondering why hers was so much softer and more pliable.

When she was through with her inspection, the tiny female sat down in the center of Eve's palm and looked calmly up at her. Eve interpreted this as a signal that it was all right to lift her hand off the desk and hold the female aloft.

Bringing her hand close to her eyes, Eve examined the little creature. She was quite slim, with delicate limbs and very small hands and feet. Her clothing was colorful, with an intricate design, leaves interweaving. There were buttons going down the back of her one-piece garment, and she wore a cloth belt at a slight tilt at her waist. Her round face was as delicate as the rest of her. A bit of a nose, a narrow line of a mouth, eyes like little dots. Her hair was long and wavy. She obviously spent some time grooming it. How could these people not be intelligent, Eve wondered, especially if they could make themselves clothing and take such care of their appearance?

Down below, the ones who had scattered now came close together again. They stood in a group and looked up in awe at Eve's scrutinization of one of their own. She noted that they, too, were carefully dressed and groomed.

"Now I'm going to put you down," Eve said, modulating her voice so that it was quite low. Again she put her hand on the desktop and held it there while the female slowly, almost casually, got off. She went back to her group that had not stirred this time when Eve rested her hand on the desktop.

Eve was not sure what to do next. As the tiny figures gazed up at her, and she down at them, they seemed in a standoff.

"Eve," Adam said. He had entered the room and now stood a few meters behind her. "What is this?"

She explained about her search and how she had found this small band moaning in their odd circle.

"It could be a religious ceremony," he commented. "The group were at prayer, perhaps."

"You might be right. They seemed to be imploring, or perhaps mourning."

"You're interested in them, I see."

"As a study, yes. They are strange to me."

"Are you sure, a study? There seems to be something more to it."

"What?"

"You seem to care about them."

"Are we capable of caring?"

"I'm not sure."

"Neither am I."

"Ariel sent me to find you. She has set up headquarters at a place they call the Human Medical Facility. She dismissed the robots who were stationed there because they did not respond properly. Now she is trying to extract information from a computer devoted to medical data. She is cursing often because it is malfunctioning or has been tampered with. I am to bring you back there with me."

"Why?"

"My opinion is that she wants to keep track of us. Derec has put her in charge while he tackles the problems of the city's systems."

"What if we do not choose to be in her charge? Should she necessarily have dominion over us?"

"Mistress Ariel appeared to believe you should be kept out of trouble."

"She is so sure I will get into trouble?"

"It seems so."

"What is the logic of that?"

"It is not necessary to analyze it."

"I would like to."

Eve glanced down at the desktop. The little creatures there were conferring among themselves. Their chattering sounds could barely be heard, but they seemed to contain more agitation than meaning.

"Adam?"

"Yes?"

"Let's bring them with us."

"That is unnec—"

"It is for research, Adam. We need to discover more in our quest to define humanity. They may help."

She reached her hand toward the group, intending to pick up a couple of its members as delicately as she could. But the fear returned to their eyes, and they began to scatter.

"No," she said, carefully modulating her voice so that it took on a humanlike, soothing gentleness. "I will not harm you. Adam, is there something here we can carry them in?"

He scanned the room. "I see no container of any kind."

"Then we will carry them on this desk."

"Eve, they could fall off."

"We will walk slowly."

Only Avery saw them carry the desk slowly through the city streets. He hadn't usually paid much attention to furniture-moving robots on Spacer planets. With their strength and meticulous sense of caution, they were expert at it, able to keep their load level, never bumping the item against anything, and delivering it undamaged.

It seemed to him that robots regularly performed miracles, as a matter of course. In fact, he thought, *only* robots could perform miracles nowadays. Whatever capacity humans may have had for such feats was long gone.

The more he watched robots in general, the more he knew he needed to become one. And he would. He could feel himself transform more and more into a robot as the days went by. He had convinced himself there were microprocessors in all his limbs and that his senses were now controlled by sensory circuits. All he needed was the positronic brain. That would come, he was sure. He would find a way to turn the inefficient lump in his head to a perfectly functioning, spongelike, positronic entity.

In a dim back part of his mind, he recalled an old Earth story where a primitive robot had wanted a human heart put inside his body so he could be more human. Of course, he really wanted human emotion, a useless prize if there ever was one, Avery thought. The story was so vague in his memory that he could not remember whether the robot had gotten a heart. Probably it had. Earth stories could be dreadfully sentimental about such things. (He did not, of course, know it, but Timestep could dance a musical number from a film adaptation of that story. And Bogie could have told him how the tale came out.)

As Avery moved closer to the desk-toting robots, he noticed the living creatures cowering at the center of the desktop. They seemed puzzled by the city, as if they thought they had passed over into another dimension.

His excitement grew as he saw how nicely formed these tiny humans or androids were. They might be just the experimental rats he needed. The body he'd taken from the vacant lot had been too decayed by the time he'd carried it to his laboratory several levels beneath the city.

He had been able to put it through only a few tests before discarding it. Under a microscope-scanner he saw that a simple microchip had been implanted in its brain and that there appeared to be patterns of circuitry that might control the body's movements, the way a puppetmaster gave false life to the wooden figures attached to strings.

However, nothing was conclusive. The creatures did not appear all that robotic, either. He suspected they had been genetically engineered, then activated by the implanted technology. At any rate, he was certain they were not actual laboratory-grown humans. No, they were more like dolls, formed from genetic materials but given a kind of life through robotic means. It was even possible they had a minimal awareness.

He had to find more specimens and had been seeking them out when he saw Derec's odd robots taking that desk down a Robot City street. The runty creatures on the desktop were the specimens he needed.

The robots were of special interest to him, also. He had recognized immediately, when he saw them back at the vacant lot, that they had not been constructed from his own designs. They were definitely not Avery robots. Where had they come from, and whose design were they?

Avery nearly laughed from happiness. (Derec would certainly have been surprised to know that his father could actually laugh.) There was much to study here, and he was never happier than when he was engaged in theorizing or conducting experiments.

Watching Avery watch the robots (who, in this chain of spying, were keeping a close watch on their diminutive charges), the Watchful Eye was puzzled by the new turn of events. How, it wondered, did Avery keep appearing from out of nowhere? He seemed to have an uncommon knowledge of the labyrinthine routes through the city and particularly of the hiding places that removed him from the Watchful Eye's surveillance.

And why were the new arrivals carrying a desk? And what were the experimental subjects (from Series C, Batch 21) doing on top of the desk?

Too many mysteries, too much disorder.

It seemed as if Derec and his cohorts had, since their arrival in Robot City, thrown much of what the Watchful Eye had done into confusion. They had, in fact, become a serious threat to his domain. It believed it should just eliminate them—but it could not. That was also a mystery to it. What was it that held it back from simply disposing of the intruders?

It sometimes appeared that it, too, had to respond to the demands of First Law, just the way a robot might. But it could not be a robot, it was sure of that. Robots could not do what it could do. Also, it knew it was different from the so-called humans who were now interfering with his design. It could not be a human, either.

There was a sound outside the computer chamber. It reassembled itself and waited for Derec to enter.

CHAPTER 11

COUNTERPOINTS

Ariel slammed her fist against the keyboard, making it bounce and slide backward. "There's no help in this Frosted computer," she yelled. "It isn't functioning any better than anything else around here."

Wolruf, who had been reacquainting herself with the layout of the medical facility, studying scanning systems and trays of medical instruments, came to Ariel and asked, "Iss something wrrong?"

Her gentle tone and phrasing calmed Ariel down. Wolruf's kindness, as well as her directness, would always make her a good friend.

"Something's wrong, all right. I ask this computer for suggestions on how to treat Avery, and it tells me to give him two aspirins and put him to bed."

Wolruf squinted at the screen. "Doess it rreally rrecommend that? Perhapss—"

"No, Wolruf, it didn't say that in so many words. It's just that no matter how hard I try to track a hypothesis, the computer leads me to a dead end or loops me back to some sector I've already seen. All of its essential information has apparently been cached away somewhere in inaccessible data banks."

Ariel was about to turn back to the computer and fight the damned machine again when an abrupt sound from outside the room startled her. Wolruf's head turned toward the noise.

"What was that?" Ariel said, standing up, looking around for a weapon to use to repel invasion.

"Someone iss outside," Wolruf said, wrinkling her nose.

The noises on the other side of the door did sound something like footsteps, Ariel thought, but of someone moving very slowly and with a very heavy tread. She nodded to Wolruf, signalling her to open the door while Ariel moved to the other side, ready to react to an attack if it came.

When the door opened, it revealed a somewhat bent Adam Silverside, his back to the room, his arms clutching his end of a desk that would have sold for a pretty penny back on Aurora. Ariel had seen one like it in her mother's home, and Juliana Welsh bought only the most expensive items. Her money went into self-indulgent luxuries or to finance fanatics with crazy schemes, like Dr. Avery and his grand city-forming experiment.

As Ariel went to the doorway, she saw Eve on the other end of the desk, standing straight on a lower stair and holding her end of the piece of furniture aloft. They smoothly eased the desk into the room and gently set it on the floor. For the first time Ariel saw the group of tiny people on the desk's surface.

"Where'd you find these?" she asked. Eve told her about her adventures in exploring the city.

"Are they the same as the ones in the vacant lot?" she asked Eve.

"We cannot be certain," Eve replied. "Perhaps you could help us figure that out."

Ariel smiled. "God," she said, "just what I need. Another impossible problem dumped in my lap." She saw that Eve was about to speak and anticipated her. "No, I know that you have dumped nothing in my lap. We humans have some outlandish ways of phrasing our thoughts, especially when we are miserable. No, Eve, I am not miserable; I am just exaggerating. And I'll explain the virtues of exaggeration to you some other time, thank you very much."

On the desktop the tiny figures were surveying the room. There was a strange sadness in their eyes, as if they saw at once that there was no easy escape.

Derec had not been near the central core of the computer for some time. It had changed in some way, but he was not sure how. Still encased in thick transparent plastic, the intricate mechanisms inside looked like the work of several abstract expressionists painting in a number of styles. It definitely did not look like the workings of a computer.

He walked to the side of the shell and put his fingertips against its surface. They came away with a thin layer of dust on them. He scowled, puzzled but—with everything else that had been going wrong—not surprised. Before, this environment had always been kept pristine. There had been robots housed here whose only job was maintenance. Where were they now?

Walking around the enormous chamber, he found several small floor-level robot niches meant for the kind of function-robots that computer room janitors were. Some of them still had maintenance robots snuggled inside, but clearly they were now inoperative. If he had had time, he would have scheduled them for repair, but the repair shops were no doubt just as inoperative at present. Functionless cleaning robots would have to wait their turn in the line of the many anomalies to be dealt with.

Returning to Mandelbrot, he held up his dirty fingertips without speaking. Behind Mandelbrot, Bogie and Timestep stood silently. Well, not completely silent. Timestep's toes beat out a soft slow tap rhythm on the metal flooring.

Pointing toward the computer, Derec said, "Well, guys, I'm going inside. You wait here, but if you sense me in any trouble, remember the First Law."

"You need not remind me," Mandelbrot said.

"I know, I know. Sorry if I hurt you."

"How could you hurt me? That is outside the—"

"I spoke out of turn. Just give me good backup, hear?"

Without waiting for any of the robots to question his colloquially expressed order, Derec walked up the steps to the platform that led to the computer chamber entrance and pushed a red button set in the door. Fortunately, the button still worked, and the door slid open.

The button was the only mechanism that did work, however. After he went through the doorway, the heat lamps did not come on, the sprayers did not send a full body spray of compressed air over his body to remove dust. He would have to enter the chamber in a contaminated state. That probably didn't matter, since from all evidence the chamber was probably contaminated already.

In order for him to enter farther, the wall in front of him should slide open. With nothing working right, it of course did not. He recalled, however, that there was a manual override located just beside the outer door. He had to fumble around in the dark for a moment to find out. When he did, it at least worked. The wall slid open.

Now he entered what to him seemed like a shadowy

world. In the dimness the computer's shapes (he recalled circuitry, microprocessors, tubing, synapse wiring and other electronic marvels from his first visit here) seemed ghostly, unreal. He needed light. The manual override for the inner-room functions was nearby, he knew, and he groped for it. Before he found it, his hand briefly brushed against the outside of the Watchful Eye's haven, which it had reshaped into an innocent-looking storage cabinet, a good disguise as long as the human did not decide to inspect its contents. Although detecting the touch, it felt no danger yet from Derec and remained still.

Derec's manipulation of the override produced only partial light, but enough to see that not only was the main computer malfunctioning, it appeared to be covered with a strange kind of dark green moss.

The Watchful Eye perceived the bitterness in Derec's whispered curse. It had known the moss, even if it had been conceived on the spur of the moment, had been a good idea.

Bogie wished he could discuss his dilemma with Timestep but they could not converse privately, either out loud or by comlink, because of the presence of Mandelbrot. He had no way of knowing whether or not Mandelbrot could eavesdrop in either way, but there was no point in taking a chance.

The problem that Bogie felt just now had to do with allegiance. He sensed that the Watchful Eye was close by, somewhere inside the transparent shell, perhaps near Derec. If one of them were to attack the other, what would be his duty? he wondered. His allegiance had been to the Watchful Eye until the arrival of Derec and the others. The First Law said to protect the human, but would that interfere with his loyalty to the Watchful Eye? It would help if Bogie had actually seen the Watchful Eye, who said it was human, yet did not act especially human and never referred to itself as of masculine or feminine gender. If it were human, had it displaced Derec in Robot City's ruling hierarchy? Could he allow Derec to harm the Watchful Eye? Must he come to Derec's defense if the Watchful Eye attacked him?

Considering orders did not help. Derec's order to come in an emergency was recent, while the Watchful Eye's command for dutiful obedience had been in effect for some time now.

The only thing to do, Bogie decided, was to hope that real life was not like the movies, where so often violent activity preceded the peaceful finale. He had no desire at this moment to cut to the chase.

The creatures had seemed to calm down after Ariel had approached them. She had drawn a chair up to the desk, keeping her hands safely out of sight, and talked to them. Her words didn't matter, she had known that. What language they had was their own. Whoever had created them had neglected to program any known language into them, perhaps on purpose.

Now they sat in a semicircle facing Ariel, seeming to listen to and understand her gently told version of Cinderella, a tale she embellished with some ancient Auroran variations. Cinderella became relegated to the management of the household robots (since no Auroran performed menial scullery tasks), and the glass slipper was replaced by a personal robot left behind at the ball. The prince's emissary had been instructed to examine how the robot reacted to the maidens of the land. When it came to the mysterious, pretty woman who had danced with the prince, the emissary would be able to tell by the robot's response that this was she. One of the ugly stepsisters nearly fooled the emissary (the robot, having been part of the household, did respond efficiently to others in it), but then Cinderella swept in and the emissary could tell by the promptness with which it went to her that the pretty maiden dressed so much more plainly than her stepsisters was indeed the beautiful woman in the lavish gown of the previous night.

Standing on the other side of the desk, the Silversides and Wolruf were also entranced by Ariel's version of the tale, although Eve had to ask frequent questions of Adam that he could not answer. She decided that the fairy godmother must be, like them, a shape-changer, and that was why she could do such marvelous things with pumpkins and farm animals.

Ariel came to the end of her story and was about to say that the prince and Cinderella lived happily ever after, but she thought of the questions that the Silversides might ask her, especially about how a human pair could possibly live forever, even if they were long-lived Aurorans, and she swallowed the phrase and merely said that everything went nicely for the happy couple for the next few decades.

When she stopped speaking, the tiny people looked eagerly at her, as if they wanted more. However, now that she had settled their anxieties, it was time to find out something more about them. But what? She had in front of her a bunch of minuscule human beings, apparently sentient, possibly (if Avery was right) android in nature, essentially a sophisticated version of the kind of mechanical toys she had played with as a child. Should she see if they could play a tin drum or walk stiff-legged like tin soldiers? Eve had said she had observed dancing in the ones at the vacant lot, and that this group had been performing some kind of ceremony.

Ceremony, that was the key. Whatever life they had,

whatever "civilization" they could develop in their short lives, it seemed that it all was tied in with ceremony.

Carefully putting her hand down on the desk at a sufficient distance from where the group was gathered, Ariel began to trace out a small circle with the tip of her index finger. She hummed an old melody, a song about a woman whose lover kept going off to war, was eventually killed, then returned to her as a ghost. It had a plaintive sound, she knew, even when sung in her slightly out-of-tune voice.

At first the group merely watched Ariel's finger move around, then the leader stood up and made authoritative gestures to her followers. Joining her, they clasped hands, formed a circle, and began to dance around, slowly, to the rhythm of Ariel's tune. Tears came to Ariel's eyes as she watched them dance gracefully and with more than a touch of elegance. It was beautiful, both the dance itself and the fact that they had understood her so quickly and easily.

She stopped tracing the circle and lifted her hand from the desktop. A moment later the dancers halted, too, looking up expectantly at Ariel, who nodded and returned her hand to the desk, this time tracing out a figure-eight with her finger. She moved her finger faster, and hummed a quicker-tempoed song, one about the happiness of frolicking in Auroran woods. (The Auroran songs made her feel nostalgic for her home, and briefly she wondered when she would ever return there. The way things were going, she might live the rest of her life confronting danger with Derec and desiring a more peaceful time with him.)

The dancers reformed themselves into a line. With the leader in front, they began a quite lovely quickstep dance following the figure-eight with more precision than Ariel could with her finger. Tears now fell from her eyes, and Eve noticed them.

"What is it, Mistress Ariel? Are you injured?"

Ariel was touched by Eve's First Law reaction. "No, I'm fine. I've always done this—bawled like a baby when I see anything done with any artistry. I mean, this is almost like dancing, ballet even, the way they move so delicately. Sometimes people think I'm reacting with sentimentality, but that's not it at all. It's just the way I respond to the beauty of it, even more the fact that such beauty is possible. Maybe it's a kind of sentimentality, but it comes from admiration and not from tender feelings. You don't understand very much of this, do you, Eve?"

"No, I do not."

"Nor do I," Dr. Avery said, stepping out—as usual—without warning from a hiding place. He had stepped through the doorway, which had been left open after the Silversides brought the desk through it. Ariel was so startled she didn't know what to say, although she was already calculating how to make him stay so she could, as ordered, try to cure him.

"If there is anything to your theories of art, Ariel, or to *anybody*'s theories, for that matter, it is not in intakes of breath at seeing something well-performed or sighs of admiration at a work well-executed. But that is unimportant to me, actually, since I don't believe there is anything to theories of art. I believe imagination is a curse, unless it is used for applied science. Works of art are garbage unless they demonstrate a useful theorem."

Ariel, recalling Lucius's sculpture called "Circuit Breaker," the one authentic piece of art produced by a Robot City robot, and the doctor's hatred of it, knew that Avery was speaking the truth. He truly despised artistic creations.

"Was not that idea once called utilitarianism?" Eve asked.

Avery seemed impressed. "My, she does look amazingly like you, Ariel, doesn't she? And is, perhaps, smarter. At any rate, that ancient philosophy, utilitarianism, does perhaps vaguely resemble the assumptions behind what I said."

He walked to the edge of the desk and stared down at the tiny figures. When he had started speaking and Ariel had stopped singing, they had ended their dancing. Now, they looked up at Avery. Fear had returned to their faces.

"I can see why playing with them made you feel like God, my dear," he said.

"I never said it did."

"Oh, but I could see a godlike look in your face. You were looking for ways to send down tablets from the mountain or part a body of water for them, were you not?"

"No, I was not!"

"I wasn't speaking literally. But I think you're trying to establish a relationship with them that is godlike, studying them and finding ways to improve their meager existence."

"I requested Mistress Ariel to study them," Eve said.

"Is that so? You continue to amaze me, what's your name, Eve? You are quite a feat of robotics. While we're on the subject of gods, who made you?"

"I do not know that."

"Some fancy piece of programming blocking out the information?"

"No," Adam interjected. "We do not know our makers. Each of us appeared on a planet in an egglike, embryonic form with no awareness of where we came from."

"Embryonic? How did you come to look as you do now? Derec and Ariel did not cause you to be formed in, as it were, their own images."

"We imprinted on them and thus resemble them. I have been many other forms."

Avery was impressed. "Hmmm, I must pursue all this with you soon, but one experiment at a time. I try not to divide my concentration. It's destructive to my work. And my work at present is these well-made little toys. I need one to take apart and find out what makes it tick."

"Don't be callous," Ariel said angrily. "You can't just take one of these and kill it."

"That's exactly what I plan to do. How are we to discover anything about them otherwise?" He looked around the room. "And this place is ideal, with all the right tools for dissection. I won't waste time by returning to—"

"No!" Ariel shouted. "You can't do it. I won't let you."

"My dear, your tears were sentimental enough. Forget any gallant defenses of these things. They are merely mechanical devices. Fairly sophisticated ones, yes, but—"

"Can't you see? Look at them. They are sentient human beings."

Ariel's dislike of Avery had made her choose one side of the issue when, only moments ago, she had been contemplating just the point of view that the doctor was now suggesting.

"Not at all. They are, I am certain, genetically engineered experimental figures. Some miniaturized human cells have been grown to form an incredibly accurate framework but they are not alive."

"They danced. They communicated with me."

"I am sure they make decent substitutes for pets, but what you saw was the result of some impulses of cybernetic origin."

"I don't care what the hell is inside them or even if they were made in a lab. They are real people with a genuine culture."

"Just some anthropological factors put into the design."

Moving quickly, Avery reached down and picked up one of the figures, a chubby man with puffy cheeks. It began squirming in his hand, while the others scattered across the desktop.

Derec wondered why, at a time like this, he so often felt a need to use a Personal. There were none here at the computer center. There was no need for one, since humans did not generally come here. He would have to ascend to the surface to find one (they were in almost all Robot City buildings), but when he got there he no doubt would find out that all the Personals were, like the rest of the city's systems, out of order. And he dreaded even imagining what a nonworking Personal would be like.

Tentatively he touched a shard of the hanging moss. He was surprised to find it smooth instead of slimy, dry and not wet. *It's fake*, he thought, *but why would anyone make fake moss and hang it on a computer in big bunches like this?*

"This part's definitely out," he said out loud. "Maybe I can juice it up."

He looked around for a typer, the kind of keyboard designed to communicate with the core computer. There was a bank of view-screens along one wall, but all the keyboards had been removed.

"It would take somebody to disconnect them," he said. "No computer could do this to itself. Somebody's monkeying with things. But who? If not my father, who? There's got to be somebody I don't know about."

As he said this, he leaned against the hiding place of the Watchful Eye, who might have been amused by the irony of Derec's words if it had comprehended irony. It studied Derec closely (the haven did not block out sensory information), discovering much about him that it had not perceived when observing him through the city's spy systems. There was apparently a musky odor to his body, perhaps caused by the fact that he had not had time to bathe since arriving on the planet. Since none of the spray-bathers worked, the chances were that Derec would get muskier.

And there was a surprising heft to the young man. He was thicker than he'd appeared, and inside the thickness, there was much more concentrated weight. Derec's outer shell, what they called skin, was more softly textured than had been expected, at least by the Watchful Eye, who up till now had been knowledgeable only about the hard surfaces of robots.

It was tempted to reveal itself but was taken aback by Derec's sudden curse. The man ran to the center of the room and looked up—where the Watchful Eye had hung the keyboards in clumps around cables. There were three clumps, all looking like some odd kind of fruit.

Derec, swinging around, appeared to address his words to the ceiling. "What's going on around here? Who are you, you filthy Frosted bag of sewage waste?" The Watchful Eye wondered why Derec's words made no sense. There had been nothing filthy in the sewer he had traveled through, and sewage waste might indeed be a compliment. "Why are you doing this? Why are you turning my city into a pesthole?"

It was amazed by Derec's anger. While that was supposed to be a human characteristic, Derec nevertheless had not seemed the type to lose his composure. Now his face was quite red, and his body was trembling.

It longed for Derec to leave so that it could restore its haven to its normal shape, slip it into the compartment fashioned behind the wall, where he normally kept it, and shut out Robot City for a while. It had to calculate its next moves, and whether they'd be directed against Derec or elsewhere. It could not harm Derec or any of his companions, nor could it, under most circumstances, injure any of the city's robots. But it could destroy the city, it thought. It only needed a rationale to begin the process.

As soon as Avery picked up the tiny creature, Ariel leaped toward him. But she was not quick enough. Eve got to Avery first. She grabbed him from behind and forced his arm slowly down until he released his captive. When the small man had run back to his companions, Eve let Avery go.

He whirled upon her, fury in his eyes.

"How dare you attack me?"

"First Law," she replied. "Your actions were going to result in the death of the human in your hand."

"But that is not a human being! It is an android, a robot like yourself."

"That may be true, but it has not been proven. I see a human being. I must not allow him to come to harm. And, sir, wouldn't Third Law also be applicable to these circumstances?"

"How?"

"If the being is, like us, a robot, then shouldn't we protect our own from harm as we would ourselves?"

Ariel might have been mistaken, but she thought that Dr. Avery nearly choked with rage at Eve's question. At any rate, he did not respond immediately. He merely stared at Eve, the way he might have if a peer had asked the question.

"Where in blazes did you get that idea?" he finally asked.

"It seems natural to me."

Avery seemed stumped for a moment, then he addressed

Eve slowly and methodically, "Eve, you and Adam are expensive pieces of merchandise. There is no need for you to endanger yourself when a human's safety is not involved. That is what the Third Law is about. It is not about a community of robots evolving a set of ethics based on this law. You do not, I repeat, *do not*, have a duty to protect your own as you would yourselves."

"I am not certain about that," Adam said, coming forward. "Especially since many robotic matters are different for us, for Eve and I. To our knowledge, we are the only beings like us. When a function-robot is deactivated, there are many other function-robots to take its place. If the very existence of either of us is threatened, I believe it the responsibility of the other to perform any act that would protect us."

Avery smiled. "That's almost theological, Adam. You seem to see yourself almost as a separate species, committed to preserve your kind as well as yourself."

"Perhaps," Adam said. "I believe you may be right, but as yet I don't know why."

"We don't really know who we are, what we are," Eve said. "It may be that the Three Laws are not the only ones that apply to us, or that our existence may depend on a different way of interpreting them."

Avery shook his head several times in confusion. At the same time, Ariel noted, there was some admiration for the Silversides in his eyes.

"You're verging on existentialism, Eve," he said. "But I think you're dead wrong. Look, humans have a history to preserve, science and philosophy to transmit through generations. They *have* to be concerned with protecting other humans from harm. They have vital reasons to, even if many of them, perhaps a majority, show no inclination to-

ward such selfless activity. As robots, Adam and Eve, your only real duty is to protect the investment. No sense in letting yourselves be destroyed unnecessarily. *But* you have no reason to identify yourselves with anything more than that, not a higher calling or some set of philosophical speculations, especially some sort of ethical idea about being the protectors of each other. The important matter is that you harmed *me* when you should not have."

"You were in no harm, and the little man was," Eve said.

"All right, all right. I vow to you then: I intend no harm to this tiny creature you fancy so much. The Laws do not apply to this situation, understand?"

Eve and Adam were not sure what to do. It seemed that the doctor's vow prevented them from moving against him. Yet . . . even if he handled the tiny creature gently now, would the future harm he might cause it in his laboratory be sufficient reason to intervene?

As Avery made another move toward the table, Ariel stepped forward, a surgical knife in her hand. "But I, because there are no effective Laws of Humanics, may stop you, Dr. Avery."

"And I," Wolruf said, "can act without rrestrrictionss, since I am neitherr, rrobot nor 'uman, and there are no Lawss of Caninoidss."

Avery looked from Ariel to Wolruf, then to the two robots. A smile flashed briefly across his face. It was a clue to a smile rather than a smile itself. Then he pulled a straight chair away from the nearest wall and sat down hard.

"Why am I even arguing with you?" he said in a soft, troubled voice. "I'm not a human. I've transformed myself into a robot."

Ariel started to say that that was just his madness, then

an idea came to her. "It's worked, has it? You've got a positronic brain and all the rest?"

"Of course," he muttered.

"Then, as a robot, you must obey me, a human. Correct?"

"What are you—I'll never—I can't—"

All the anger seemed to go out of his eyes, and he slumped in his chair. "Yes," he muttered. "I must obey you. Second Law. I will obey you . . . Mistress Ariel."

Ariel rubbed her hands together. She didn't know how long she could work this new ploy, but it gave her an opportunity to use the doctor for both her projects. His great intelligence could help her to study the tiny creatures, and toying with his delusions might be the answer to curing them.

"Sit straight, doc—wait, what is your name now?"

He looked up at her with sad eyes and said weakly, "Name?"

"Do you have a robot name? Have you chosen one yet?"

He seemed momentarily puzzled by her questions.

"Yes, I have," he said. "Just now."

"And what is it?"

"Ozymandias."

"Very good. That's the name of a poem, isn't it?"

"Yes. It's about a once-mighty king, a 'king of kings.' On the pedestal of its statue are inscribed the words, 'Look on my works, ye Mighty, and despair!' "

"How nice. You don't mean them ironically, I hope. Well, I haven't despaired yet, and neither should you. That, by the way, is an order, Ozymandias."

"Yes, Mistress Ariel."

"Okay, let's get to work. I'm not sure where to start."

• • •

Derec came out of the computer chamber with a hang-dog look on his face. "The computer's been severely tampered with, Mandelbrot," he said. "We've got a pack of work to do."

"Yes, sir. I will help."

"Thank you. Let's go."

After Derec had taken a few steps, Bogie called to him, "What about us, Master Derec? What should we do?"

Derec resisted an offensive answer and said instead, "Do you have anything to do at this moment?"

The Watchful Eye had given the two robots no further orders, so Bogie could truthfully say, "No."

"Well, then, I guess the two of you have danced and wise-cracked yourselves right into my heart. Why don't you tag along? That is, come with us."

"I know what 'tag along' means," Bogie said, and Derec wondered if there wasn't a suggestion of huffiness in the robot's reply.

CHAPTER 12

FRUSTRATIONS

Avery itched to grab one of the tiny creatures, whom Ariel was now calling "the dancers," and take it apart under a microscopic scanner with a selection of the fine surgical instruments available in the medical facility. However, since Ariel forbade that any harm should come to the dancers, the dissection would be a violation of Second Law, and he must not violate Second Law. She still claimed it would also be a violation of First Law because of the essential humanity of the dancers, but he rejected that preposterous idea out of hand.

(Sometimes, in the back of his mind, he almost remembered he was really human and not subject to Ariel's orders. At those moments his hands automatically reached toward the nearest dancer, and his fingers trembled.)

On her part Ariel felt as if she were swimming from one whirlpool to another. Each whirlpool was a different task, a different goal. At the center of one was Avery, who was acting crazier by the minute. The dancers (occupying her dreams as well as her daily routine) swirled in the middle of another. The third contained Adam and Eve, who, although themselves quite fascinated by the dancers, were still unpredictable and often disobedient. The previous day she had caught them trying to teach the dancers acrobatics. Eve picked up one, a male, and, keeping him firmly but gently between her fingers, tried to show him how to execute a series of midair flips. The little creature was obviously frightened, even though he did not struggle. The dancers, Avery suggested, treated their captors as gods and cooperated with any foolish things a god might try, no matter how dangerous.

It seemed that the Silversides would do anything to sidestep an order from Ariel. They had apparently never resolved the dilemma of whether or not Derec and Ariel were humans or if they were the proper kinds of humans, those for whom their mysterious and vague programming had been set. They knew they were supposed to serve humans and imprint themselves upon them, but had been given no guidelines about what a human was and how to recognize one. They were frequently puzzled by the behavior of Derec and Ariel (and, for that matter, the insanely contradictory actions of Avery), and had trouble convincing themselves to accept these particular humans as representative of the highest order of being in the universe.

Earlier in his existence, Adam had believed the blackbodies to be more intelligent than the humans he had encountered up to that time, and Eve had accepted the word of a demented blackbody that it was the only human in the galaxy. Their mistakes were just as responsible for making them cautious as were their doubts about Derec, Avery, and Ariel.

In a way, they were searching for some higher kind of human, dismissing Derec and Ariel as, like the dancers, some primitive and unworthy form of the species, not worthy of their loyalty and obedience. As a result, sometimes they responded like any robots to the requirements of the Laws of Robotics, but at other times, questioned every word of an order, or analyzed a First Law situation so interminably that Ariel or Derec would have died before the Silversides had stopped them from coming to harm. And sometimes they were just plain ornery, rejecting orders without rhyme or reason, as if they just meant to taunt her.

Ariel had decided to treat them as if they were human and subject to human weaknesses. If they were being obedient, she gave them orders. If they were not, she ignored them.

There was enough to do without pampering them.

Today Adam and Eve were relatively docile. Eve, especially, tended to be cooperative when Ariel was working with the dancers. She would stand beside the desk and study them with the same intensity that Ariel showed (and often looking exactly like her, a state that Ariel found unnerving). When the dancers needed to be fed, Eve even volunteered to do it. She would take a dancer and hold it in her hand, then put some food on the fingers of her other hand while each dancer picked the crumbs off her fingertip and ate them with evident enjoyment. The dancers always ate in a specific order, the leader first, an urge for order that Ariel believed proved their essential humanity.

She had worked out a proper diet for the dancers through the use of the chemical food processor, trying out various dishes until she found some they would accept. She was glad that Derec had chosen to fix the foodmaking machines early in his repairing of the city's systems. It had come second, right after getting the Personals operative again.

"Can we make them play the game again?" Eve asked Ariel, after the last dancer had taken the last crumb from her fingertip.

"You bet. It represents about all the progress I've made with them."

Avery, who had been sulking in a corner (guarded by Wolruf because he had already made four tries to escape), came forward to speak to Ariel's back.

"Of course you've made no progress. There's so little to be made. If you would only let me at them . . ."

"Swallow the words, Ozymandias. I won't permit you to murder these—"

"But it wouldn't be *murder*. They are no more than toys. They are not even miniature Frankenstein monsters or golems; they are merely mechanical devices. Mistress Ariel, way back in Earth history there were many manmade contraptions that fooled others into believing they were actual living beings or even miracles. There was a mechanical duck that would not only appear to eat and quack but would even excrete materials from its nether end. There was a chess-playing robot that convincingly won games from masters. A small figure with a quill pen that could laboriously but correctly write a letter; a companion piece that could draw kings and ships. There were figures whose movements were lifelike, who even appeared to breathe. Milkmaids swinging pails and mountaineers in alpenstock hats emerged from clocks, appearing very real. In more sophisticated times, people found the early robots, machines that couldn't really do very much, quite amazing and lifelike. So you see, Ariel, your desktop figures are just extensions of a long tradition. They are partially grown from cells, and partially controlled by technological means, but they are not the small-scale humans you are so protective of."

Ariel sighed. She had heard variations of this diatribe so often since they'd captured Avery that she wanted to wrap her hands around the doctor's throat and strangle him, or at least remove his tongue so that she would not have to hear his whining maniacal voice again. Fortunately, as long as there were robots around, First Law prevented her from taking such drastic measures. That was why she could day-dream about them without guilt. Come to think of it, she said to herself, she could not rely on either Eve or Adam to come to Avery's rescue. If they were not in the mood for First Law that day, they might be willing to be a detached and curious audience to an actual act of murder.

Maybe strangling Avery wasn't such a bad idea.

"Do you have anything constructive to offer, Ozyman-dias?"

"Wasn't that constructive?"

"Not by a long shot. You know what really frosts me? That you consider yourself a robot and yet appear to hold robots in such low esteem."

He shook his head vigorously. "On the contrary, Mis-tress Ariel. Once we establish that these people are indeed manmade constructs, I will revere them as I revere all ro-bots, even the smallest function-robots that dust rooms and pick up trash. The robot is the highest order of existence, and I am proud to be one."

She couldn't dope Avery out any more. Sometimes he would talk normally—or at least in what was a normal fash-ion for a man whose eccentricity was legend—and then he'd switch over to this robot identity, praising his own effi-ciency or going on endlessly about the virtues of his posi-tronic brain. Derec continued to urge her to deal with the man, as if compassion and intelligent conversation with him would bring about a cure. It was simply too large an order. Avery's madness was beyond anything her homegrown sense of psychology could cope with.

Still, she had to try. She had promised.

While Avery and Ariel spoke, Eve moved closer to the desk. She wanted to watch the dancers play the game, which could not take place until Ariel returned her attention to them.

Or must she wait for Ariel? Indeed, why wait for her?

She placed her hand in the middle of the desk, resting it on its side, thumb up. The dancers immediately responded to the signal and began forming teams on either side of Eve's hand. When they were ready, Eve raised her hand and dropped a tiny rolled up piece of paper onto the middle of the desktop. The dancers immediately began scrambling toward it. One of them, the chubby one that Avery had tried to take, reached it first. He picked it up and began to run with it, but the opposing team quickly assembled itself. A female sprang in front of the male carrying the paper and gestured others to join her. In an instant, it seemed, they had surrounded the male. They were not allowed to touch each other during the game, except by accident. That had been one of Ariel's early rules, rules that she had communicated to the dancers through the use of a series of hand signs she had developed in her study of them. Once the player was surrounded, he must give up the paper, which he did. The new possessors began tossing the paper between them, while the other team, staying close together, watched, waiting for the next move, looking for their chance to surround the player carrying the paper.

Suddenly one of the females, a gaunt, thin one who had

grown gaunter and thinner since the Silversides had brought the group to the medical facility, started to rush forward with the paper tucked under her arm. The other team started to go into a formation that could easily close itself around her, but she suddenly turned and flipped the paper back to a male who was running behind her. He quickly hurled it to another male standing at the edge of the desktop. This one ran in a straight line, along the desk edge, to the other side of the desk. Nobody could catch him.

When he reached the other side, he abruptly sat down, set the paper in front of him, and did a half-bow to it. The last act established the authenticity of the score, a procedure that Ariel (who had adapted the game from an ancient Auroran sport) had not originally taught them. It seemed they were such slaves to ritual that they had to perform some rite when they succeeded at scoring.

The male stood up and left the piece of paper where he had deposited it, a signal for Eve to pick it up and again drop it in the center after the teams had re-formed. She was about to let it go, when Ariel hollered at her harshly, "Eve! I did not give you permission to start the game!"

Eve, holding the paper over the anxiously awaiting dancers, looked up. "I wanted to start it. Since you were speaking with Ozymandias, I decided to—"

"It's not up to you to decide. You haven't learned yet. You are the robot, I am the human. You wait for my orders."

"We are not sure that is correct."

Ariel threw up her hands in despair. She did not need this kind of robotic sophistry right this minute. Staring down at the desktop, she said, "Okay, who's ahead?"

Ariel didn't have the patent on despairing gestures. In another part of the city, Derec was clenching his fists and resisting the impulse to slam them down on the nearest available surface.

"Another dysfunctional session, sir?" Mandelbrot said. Derec almost laughed. A dysfunctional session? Frost, an absolute failure.

"It seems that our computer does not yet want to activate full access, Mandelbrot. This just doesn't make sense. It's like the computer is playing with me, letting me do some things, blocking me from others."

"Do not the computers obey the Laws of Robotics, too?"

Derec shrugged. "They're supposed to. Unless someone is controlling them from some outside source, overriding my requests as I make them."

"Is that possible?"

"I believe so. There is someone in the city somewhere, the same individual that the robots are blocked from telling me about, and he or she or it's the boss right now. There's something so, I don't know, *inhuman* about our intruder's actions that I suspect an alien, one as intelligent as the blackbodies and as mean as Aranimas."

Aranimas had been the alien who, before Derec came to Robot City, had trapped him on his ship and tried to make a slave out of him. The most fortunate aspects of that terrible experience were that he had met Ariel and Wolruf and constructed the wonderfully loyal Mandelbrot out of spare parts.

With an expansive hand gesture that clearly dismissed the computer, Derec stood up and began pacing the room. "Mandelbrot, I should be in charge, but the he or she or it is not allowing it. This individual doles out some information through the computer—how to activate the devices for food, Personals, the slidewalk, heat and light—but only that data that we require in order to survive. When it comes to completely activating the computer, getting the services of the city running again, and putting the robots back in their proper jobs, it keeps blocking me from accomplishing anything. Obviously it is not out to destroy us, not at present anyway. But he, she, or it is definitely hiding something from us. Its identity, of course, but maybe something more. Maybe there's something about its identity that we should not know. Or about its future plans."

"What about the chemfets?" Mandelbrot asked. "In the past they have always provided the right information about the city."

"That's what's really crazy, Mandelbrot. The chemfets aren't any more functional than the city is now. Oh, I get a sensation or two about our mysterious visitor now and then, but no real clue about who or what he, she, or it is. And I get this vague feeling that there's some kind of a solution, but it remains just outside my reach. At any rate, the chemfets are messed up, just like Robot City. There are times when I can hardly detect them. And I hate that more than I can tell you."

He stretched his arms, as if trying to stir up the chemfets. "You know," he continued, "I used to think the chemfets were a hellish thing. I thought they were controlling me, racing up and down my bloodstream, making me ill. Now that they've reached maturity and I've integrated myself with them, I can't cope with them not working like this. I want to activate them desperately, and I can't. It's like me and the city. I want to get Robot City going again. I have to. Yet I'm so darn stymied. There's got to be a way, Mandelbrot, and I'm going to find it."

The Watchful Eye eavesdropped on Derec with some satisfaction. Now, back to its natural shape but completely hidden by layers of the mosslike substance it had strewn over the computer, it considered its next moves.

The strange word that Derec had used, stymied, seemed to apply to the Watchful Eye's circumstances also. As Ariel and Avery continued their research on Series C, Batch 21, it did not feel safe in reactivating the robots who had done the original lab work that led to the creation of the various batches. It had convinced those robots that more research was needed on the Laws of Humanics, and, since there were no humans in the city, they would have to create their own. Of course the Watchful Eye knew, as Avery had perceived, that their little models were not full-fledged human beings, that they were just robotically activated biological material formed into human shapes. It could have made them into any shape, even made them look like itself, but it chose to create their appearance from pictures it called up from a computer file of historical figures.

Because the intruders had to occupy so much of its time, the Watchful Eye could conduct none of its other experiments, either. It had been about to begin a stress-test to see how the iron/plastic alloy that the city was made of could hold up under many different circumstances. It had intended to fully explore the many facets of Robot City and then, when finished, restructure and refashion it to suit its needs.

It was concerned with the Laws of Humanics because it wanted to find out just what a human was. Something just beneath the level of its consciousness compelled it to discover humans and emulate them. There were times when it hoped that Derec and Ariel, or Adam and Eve, would finally prove to be the real humans, so that the matter would be settled and it could go on to its future, whatever its future was meant to be. It was certain it had a destiny that would eventually be revealed.

More than anything else, however, the Watchful Eye missed the freedom to work on the biggest question it faced: who or what it was. It had to be *something*, fit some category of existence. For it did exist.

It could be human, although—if the intruders were humans (and which ones? Derec and Ariel? Adam and Eve? The dreadful Avery?)—it did not physically resemble them. But then, in its natural state, or at least the state it had been in when it came to awareness, it had resembled nothing more than a blob of matter. Later it had discovered that it had the ability to change its shape. Right now it could change itself into the *shape* of a human, but would it *be* human? Did these humans start out in the same puttylike shape it had? Had they originally hidden in their havens until they had chosen what they must look like?

It wondered if it could be some kind of animal. There did not appear to be any kind of animal native to Robot City, so it could only judge that subject from information extracted from computer files. The files only confused it further, since it felt no link with any animal in any picture it called up. In addition, it noted that many of the so-called animals resembled the so-called humans in many respects. Were they also kinds of humans?

It could be a robot, but it resisted that idea most. It had studied the robots and found them to be too subservient, too easily programmed. Admirable pieces of construction though they were, they simply did not seem complex enough for the Watchful Eye to belong to their class of being. It could not convince itself that there were any resemblances between a robot and it. If anything, it felt more like a computer than a robot. But it had a sentient life that the Robot City computer did not. So it had concluded it could not be a computer, either.

What was it?

It intended to find out soon.

Adam Silverside wandered through the streets of Robot City, not knowing where he was going, not knowing why he had left the medical facility. He had been watching Eve concentrate so completely on Ariel and the dancers that he had come to the conclusion that he was useless to their experiments. Sometimes Ariel and Eve conversed so intently on the behavior of the dancers that it seemed they were unaware of his presence in the room.

It was not that Adam felt hurt, or even annoyed, at the way he had been ignored. A robot does not feel the pangs of rejection that trouble humans in such matters. A robot would, under normal conditions, not feel left out or even ignored. After all, a robot can even stand alone without anything happening for a long, long time.

What Adam perceived essentially, and in a logical way, was that he served no purpose in their work. It seemed to him that since Robot City was in crisis and Derec and Ariel were in turmoil about how to solve their respective problems, there should be something he could do. It would be a terribly inefficient use of his time and abilities for him to stay where he was not needed. Their maker, whoever he or she was, had evidently planned them to be special. They were compelled to serve and be useful through the direct or implicit order of humans, a Second Law imperative.

He came to the lot where they had discovered the first group of dancers. It was completely empty now, with no traces left of its former inhabitants. That was, in itself, another anomaly. Who had taken away all traces of their lives, even including the remains of the campfire around which they had danced? Who had smoothed over the ground so that even the graves could not be detected? Some of the city's robots were, it seemed, functional.

He came to a parkland, where precisely sculptured bushes were placed at even distances along a smoothly raked path. There were no footsteps on the path, and no people to sit in the benches under the park's towering trees. It seemed anomalous to Adam that a park like this, and several other Robot City areas, were so obviously built for human habitation, and there had been as yet so few humans upon the planet. The city itself seemed useless, as useless as he now believed himself to be.

He came to an area where buildings stretched in a long semicircle around a nonworking fountain. Shops with blank signs were neatly arrayed along the street level of the semicircle.

The few robots walking through the streets were intent on their own goals. None stopped at any of the buildings. (Adam wondered why he felt no sense of belonging when he saw these robots. How could he be a robot and be so separated from other robots?) There were no goods in any of the shops, no shoppers to select items in the first place. Like the park, another Robot City anomaly.

Shops and parks with definite purposes and no way to fulfill them. The problem was similar to his own, he thought. He had not only an ability to imprint upon living creatures, but to become astonishingly like them, adopting the patterns and characteristics of their lives as well as their physical appearance. He could even lead them, as he had with the kin. Was this to be his life or, if not life, the parameters of his existence within the universe? He felt *compelled* to change his shape into that of another; he *needed* to keep doing it until his dilemma of interpreting what a human was had reached a conclusion. There was no purpose for him in Robot City, no one on whom to imprint. (He did not realize that this frustrating state had been planned by Derec and Wolruf, and they in turn did not know what an astonishing success the plan had been, at least in Adam's case. It would not have occurred to Adam that he was being tamed. If it had, he would have resisted it firmly.)

As he had on the blackbodies' planet, he changed into the kin shape and began to run down the streets of Robot City; then he tried the blackbody shape and clumsily flapped his wings, knocking them against the walls of buildings; then he was a function-robot, picking up debris and depositing it in a sewer grating; then he took on Derec's shape; then Ariel's; then Avery's.

But all the transformations did not satisfy him. He had done them all before.

He needed a new creature to imprint on.

He changed back to kin shape so that he could howl at the stars spread in the sky over the city.

Then he was Derec again, walking the streets back to the medical facility, his mission in the city unfulfilled. He realized that, in a way, he was acting like the men in some legends he had read in computer files, the kind of legend where men shook their fists at the sky and castigated the universe.

He found the image odd. He could shake his fist at the sky, but, sadly perhaps, he could not really feel the emotion that inspired the gesture. The *human* emotion behind the gesture.

CHAPTER 13

AVERY AND THE SILVERSIDES

Ariel awoke with a start. She hadn't realized she'd been asleep, must have dozed off with her head on the back of the cushioned chair she'd drawn up beside the desk.

It was certainly disconcerting to come to consciousness and look down on about a half-dozen of the dancers staring up at you, while the rest played at some game that Ariel had not yet interpreted. (They showed each other their hands, palms up or down, any number of fingers extended, sometimes no fingers extended, sometimes a fist.) There was a questioning look on their faces, as if they'd been curious about why their god seemed to need sleep every once in a while. The dancers themselves never seemed to sleep. Ariel had watched them and delegated the Silversides to observe them, but no sleep had ever been detected. She sometimes wondered what it would be like to be awake for one's entire life. Would you get a lot done or go mad from being conscious without respite?

As she always did when she hadn't been studying the dancers for some time, she counted them. There were still fourteen of them. Good. Avery, then, had not somehow eluded Wolruf's vigilance and, while she was asleep, sneaked to the desk to abduct one of the tiny creatures.

She glanced toward the other side of the room, where Avery slouched in a chair, apparently dozing himself. (When he was Ozymandias, he insisted that he never slept.) Wolruf sat on the floor, keeping an eye on the doctor while thumbing through a picture book about Auroran art that Ariel had found in the small library attached to the medical facility. She was studying it for practice in reading and to learn about human customs. In the time that Ariel had known her, Wolruf's ability to read standard had improved significantly, as had her command of the language. The task of guarding Avery had given her free time to add to her education in the ways of humans and robots.

Ariel couldn't think of what to do next with the dancers. She'd been studying their customs for several days, and there didn't seem to be much more to learn. She had tried to communicate with them, but, except for the hand gestures needed either to get their attention or initiate games, most of her attempts had been unsuccessful.

All the dancers had been examined by a diagnostic scanner, the only piece of equipment in the medical facility that appeared to work successfully. She was not sure why. However, since the only systems Derec had been able to (or been allowed to) restore tended to be life-sustaining, she wondered if the scanner worked because it might be needed in an emergency. Derec was right about the presence in the city, she was sure of it. And that presence was doling out favors, stingily but with some sense. The scanner had revealed nothing new about the dancers. As Avery told her, they were anatomically consistent with full-sized humans. If there was robotic circuitry, the scanner didn't detect it.

She missed Derec so. They had not really been together since that interlude at the Compass Tower. They checked in with each other every once in a while, but at those times he was detached, more concerned with reviving the city than with reviving their passion. And she couldn't pin all the blame in that arena of life solely upon him. After all, as Derec had pointed out, her attention was just as fiercely fixed on the dancers, Avery, and the Silversides.

The two of them made a great pair, workaholics without much time for each other. But she did long for a moment alone with him, just a brief time of being held by him, kissing him, feeling his gentle touches upon her back.

Well, there was no time for romance now. *Thing to do*, she thought, *is get the jobs done, restore equilibrium, then grab each other and race to the nearest dark place.*

She raised her arms, trying to stretch weariness out of them. As always, the dancers were interested in her movement. Whatever she did, they watched her do it with absolute fascination. This time they imitated her, making ritualistic, slow stretching motions that duplicated her gestures. How, she wondered, could Avery keep saying that they were not living beings? With such grace, such skill, they could be nothing less than human.

Her mouth felt dry, and she was sure that her breath could cause an air-purification system to malfunction. There was the beginning of a headache at the back of her eyes. She needed to use the Personal.

"Eve?"

"Yes, Mistress Ariel."

"Time."

The word was all she needed to bring Eve to the desk to take over from her. Ariel stood up.

"Have you conceived a new game?" she asked Eve.

"Yes."

"Of course. I should have known. Show it to me when I get back."

When Ariel had left, Eve picked up one of the dancers, a short (for a dancer) stocky female. The female did not resist in any way (none of the dancers did, anymore) and merely sat calmly in Eve's palm.

"Adam?" Eve called.

Adam, newly returned from his wanderings, stepped out of a dark corner of the room from which he had been watching her.

"Yes, Eve."

"There seems to be something wrong with the dancers, this one and all of them."

"I have not seen it yet."

"You have to examine their faces. This one was young, like Ariel, when we first brought them here. Now look."

Adam bent down toward the stocky female in Eve's hand. He hadn't studied the dancers with the same meticulousness that Eve had and wasn't certain what she'd meant. Nevertheless, at least he was being asked to do something.

"What do you see, Adam?"

"One of the dancers, female category."

"Besides that."

"Her hair. It was once dark-colored and now it is mostly gray. Her face. Once it was unlined, now there are many lines in it. Her mouth. Once it was—"

"That is enough, Adam. It is what I see, too. Not only in this one, but in all of them. They have been here for four days, and none of them is young any more. Look at that one."

Adam looked where she pointed. A male dancer, one of the game players, had left the group and was sitting alone, his knees pulled up, his arms around his knees. His face was old, pitted, sallow.

"He appears to be unwell," Adam commented.

"I wonder what it means. Are they changing their shapes like we do?"

"Perhaps, but I do not think so."

"They are going to die," Avery said, sitting up in his chair. His movement forced Wolruf to push her book aside and tense her body.

Avery stood up and approached the desk. "I'm not sure why they have to die. I suspect that whoever created them was at least partly interested in human life cycles. Otherwise he could have made them as permanent as robots. That is, after all, one of the advantages we robots have. Their creator wanted them to die, or he messed up, I'm not certain which. When they do go, I hope to find out by examining them."

"Ariel said 'u can't touch them," Wolruf cautioned.

"Well, she must at least let me examine a corpse or two."

"No!" Eve said suddenly, unsure of why she had spoken out at all.

The doctor's eyebrows raised in surprise. "You don't wish me to, Eve?"

"That is true."

"How curious. Are you a robot with compassion then?"

"I do not know what you mean."

"If you are, and I get a shot at you, we'll have to program it right out. I don't know sometimes why things happen as they do in Robot City. First we get robots with artistic leanings (another trait I had to get rid of) and now compassionate robots. Is that a tear in your eye, Eve, or just a trick of the light? Don't respond, I was only joking."

Ariel returned from the Personal in time to hear the last of Avery's comments. She was about to speak, to tell Avery

to zip up his mouth, when she noticed what was happening
to Adam.

Adam stood at the side of the desk, just slightly behind
Avery. He was staring at the doctor and at the same time
undergoing a transformation, changing shape. It was fascinating to watch. First his body seemed to shrink as he lost
a few inches of height. (Was he trying to become a dancer?
she wondered. Could that be possible? Wouldn't his mass
have to be concentrated impossibly for him to change to
that size?) Then the shrinking stopped, and Adam's shorter
body began to expand outward, making him look rounder.
His arms became shorter and hung differently, in a sort of
apelike way. Then his face, which had been almost an exact
replica of Derec's, began to undulate slightly, with his chin
puffing out and his forehead narrowing, his chin coming to
a point, then reshaping itself to a rounder contour. At the
top of his head, his metallic version of Derec's sandy hair
lightened to white and got longer, messier. But it was not
until the next change that Ariel realized what was happening. Resembling the hair in color and texture, a silver bushy
moustache appeared to sprout under Adam's transformed
nose.

Ariel laughed abruptly, pleased at the first hint of mer-
riment in her life for some time.

Adam had changed himself from a mimicry of Derec to
a nearly exact rendition of the short, round, wavy-haired
and moustachioed Dr. Avery!

Avery didn't notice Adam's transformation until Ariel
laughed. At first he thought she was laughing at him, and
he prepared a withering comment. (Avery could not abide
being laughed at. The mockery of too many colleagues had
made him sensitive to criticism and developed in him a

lightning reflex to respond as cruelly as he could.) Then he saw where Ariel's attention was directed.

He saw Adam's robotic and (to him) nightmarish version of himself, and he screamed in anger. It was the kind of scream that rattled any loose item or emotional equilibrium in its vicinity. On the desktop the dancers scattered in fear.

Adam had not expected such a violent reaction from Avery, and it shocked as well as intrigued him. He had imprinted upon Avery several times already, but only twice in Avery's presence. Each of those times the self-centered doctor had not noticed or even looked at him.

Although Avery knew about the Silversides' shape-changing abilities, this was the first time he had observed an actual transformation.

"I won't have this!" Avery yelled. "It is mockery! You have no right to take my shape! How is it possible even? What kind of material are you made of?" He touched Adam on his arm, his chest, his face. Adam's skin was still like the synthe-skin on any robot, except the few humaniforms. "There's no human texture to your skin, no—"

Ariel stepped forward. "That's because Adam is a robot." She searched Avery's face for reactions and saw deep confusion in his eyes, so she added slyly, "Like you, Ozymandias."

Avery seemed momentarily confused. "Of course," he said. "Like me." He examined Adam more closely. "And robots are fixed, permanent. Not like humans, not like animals. Then Adam can't be a robot. He's something else in a robot's clothing."

"What am I?" Adam asked.

"I don't know what you are."

"If not human, what? If not robot, what?"

"Yes," Ariel said, moving closer to Avery, "what is Adam?"

"Some new kind of creature, but I don't know what. He is capable of changing his shape?"

"Yes, he is. He can be human, robot, animal, alien. But he is robot, Ozymandias."

"He can't be!"

"Oh, but he can. They both can. Derec's not sure how they shape-change, but he thinks it's facilitated by a kind of DNA or DNA-analog in their cells. Apparently they can gain voluntary control over their cells, even adjusting their sizes and shapes. They sort of think of the shape they'll take, and its details are worked out in their positronic brains. Mandelbrot can drastically change the shape of his arm, but these two work miracles on their entire bodies. Adam says he started as a blob and knew how to alter his shape into a practical ambulatory form in his first few moments of awareness."

"I refuse to accept that. Why did you laugh?"

"Because you are like me now. You accused me of being sentimental for believing the dancers to be human, and now you refuse to believe Adam is a robot. Nevertheless, it is true. Why does it bother you so, Ozymandias?"

"I won't discuss it."

"Of course. Because it would embarrass you. Now that you're a robot, you're annoyed when another one comes along who's greater than you are."

"That's not it at all! And it's not true! Transmogrification is no special achievement. It makes him no more than a circus freak."

"Maybe you're right. It isn't true. Good thing you're not Avery any more, Ozymandias. If you were, I'd have to say that maybe the great Dr. Avery, creator of the Avery robots, is jealous that someone else has designed and built a better model."

For a moment Avery did not speak. Instead, he merely stared at Adam, which was like looking in a mirror that slightly distorted the image. Adam's skin was silvery, and there were more sharp lines in the shape of his body than in Avery's softly curved figure. Adam's eyes had a serenity in them that Avery had not, when looking in a mirror, seen in many years. It forced him to consider a human Avery whose life had been more satisfactory, when he had been married and at the top of his profession, adored by many, certainly respected by almost everyone. Why had his eyes changed? he wondered.

Ariel saw the emotional disruption in Avery's face, and at the same time saw a way to work with the man as Derec had urged. She moved to the other side of the desk, beside Eve, who had been busy calming the dancers with gestures and a soft humming that almost had a tune to it.

"Eve," Ariel whispered.

"Yes?"

"Can you do one of those shape-changes for me?"

"Yes, into anything I know about."

"Well, do what Adam did. Imprint on Avery. Can you do that?"

"Of course."

Ariel watched with fascination as Eve went through the same transformations that Adam had. It was even stranger to view in her, since before Ariel's eyes, Eve changed from a female to a male. While she had always known that Eve could change shape, and had been told that Adam had been a female when he was a member of the kin, she was still amazed by the process. Eve's face changed earlier than Adam's had, and then she rearranged her body from the shoulders down. When finished, she was even more uncomfortably like Avery than Adam was.

"Ozymandias," Ariel said, breaking his concentration on Adam. As the man turned toward her, his jaw dropped open when he saw still another copy of himself.

"This is unfair!" he cried, furious.

"Why? Most of the time they go around looking like Derec and me, and it doesn't bother us. Why does it so upset you, Ozymandias?"

"I feel like they're taking something away from me."

"What? Your soul?"

Ariel's question came as such a shock to Avery that it made him laugh. "My soul? Hardly. What would a robot do with a soul? No, I mean my personality, all that constitutes me, my dignity."

"Dignity? Personality? What do you care about those?"

As Ariel talked, Eve had gone to Adam, and now they stood side by side, twin Averys, with the same subtle differences between them that a set of identical twins showed.

Avery, uncharacteristically speechless, whirled around and strode back to where Wolruf stood. Ariel might have been mistaken, but she thought, from the way the caninoid alien stood at a slight tilt and from the faint gargling sound coming from her throat (usually an indication of amusement for her), that Wolruf found the proceedings funny.

"Come back here!" Ariel shouted.

"I refuse."

"How can you refuse my order? You are a robot and I am human. You have to obey me. Second Law, Ozymandias." She spoke this last with a lilt in her voice, mockingly. He stood still for a moment, then spun around and returned to the desk.

Meanwhile Ariel had sidled up to the Silversides.

"Adam, Eve, I want you to do something for me." They both glanced at her, awaiting their orders. "You've been around Avery for long enough. Imitate him all the way. Talk like him, sound like him, rant like him, move like him, strut like him, whatever you have stored in your memory banks that you can use to be like him. Can you do that?"

They both responded yes. Adam, particularly, welcomed the challenge. It was a use of his shape-changing ability, after all. In a world where there was little to imprint on, any challenge would do.

"All right," Ariel said when Avery had returned to the desk. "Separate from each other, and when I give the signal, start."

Adam went to one side of the room, Eve to the other. Avery, who had not heard Ariel's command, looked back and forth from one to the other.

Then, at a gesture from Ariel, the assault began. Adam immediately launched a diatribe of Avery's that he had stored in his memory. It was an especially ripe one, filled with florid phrases and a good deal of invective. The robot's voice was a remarkable playback, catching the tones and inflections of the doctor's voice so precisely that Ariel, if she had shut her eyes, would not have known it was not the real Avery.

The target of the assault merely watched Adam disbelievingly; his eyes widened, displaying less intensity and more confusion than perhaps anyone had ever seen in him before. He chewed on his lower lip, another uncharacteristic act. His fingers tapped against the side of his legs, a gesture Ariel had seen often. Avery did it a lot when he was angry.

Making a loud cough very like the one Avery made to get another person's attention, Eve entered the fray. Avery's head turned to watch her, while Adam's diatribe continued, louder.

Eve began to mutter to herself in an Averylike way and began to pace her side of the room in a strutting fashion. As she walked her fingers, too, tapped against her legs. Once she stopped and banged her fist into the palm of her other hand, yelling, "I will not have it! This isn't the way things will be! I demand you let me have a dancer to experiment upon!"

Then she whirled around, just as Avery had earlier, and walked to the desktop to stare down sternly at the dancers. Now that she looked like the doctor, she was amazed to find that the dancers were fooled by her. They scattered just the way they did when Avery hovered over them.

Ariel saw Eve's face lose its hostility, softening into a gentler look. Because the Silversides could only form aspects of facial expression, becoming much like an artist's caricature, Eve's present look disconcerted Ariel. She did not like Avery's face appearing to be kind. Further, there was a suggestion of Ariel's face, seemingly superimposed upon the Avery mien, that annoyed her.

"Eve," she whispered, "they're all right. They just think you're him. Don't worry about it. We'll take care of them, and you can resume your familiar shape."

Eve recalled her task. Her face became hard again, and she resumed muttering. Suddenly, in a move that Ariel could not have expected, Eve slammed her fist upon the desktop (well away from any of the dancers). Even Avery flinched at the fury of the move, as if he didn't believe someone looking like him could do such a violent thing.

"What are they—" he began, but Adam came forward to stand next to Eve. They seemed an odd pair, like identical twins who had labored to differentiate themselves in any way possible, but just could not stop looking like each other.

"We should not even experiment on these," Adam said. "They are just vermin, like most humans, not like robots. We should kill them."

Eve, taken in for a moment by Adam's act, was ready to rush to defend them until she recalled her command to playact.

"That's going too far," Avery shouted. "I would never say that."

"Ozymandias," Ariel said, "what you see is just their impression of what you say, how you act. In their minds, capable as they are of processing data, you've shown your-self to be unpredictable and quite likely to perform violent acts. That you'd think of killing the dancers seems within the realm of possibility to them. And, for that matter, to me."

"You don't understand. I'm not a destroyer, I'm a cre-ator. Yes, if necessary I'd dissect an animal for scientific knowledge, but I'd never willingly kill for killing's sake."

"Now you've said it, they know it. They understand you better now. Tell them more."

Avery smiled. "I see your ploy. Make me reveal myself so you can continue this charade. Well, Ariel, it won't work."

She shrugged. "Don't know anything about charades."

"Stop them, Ariel. You're making me very nervous."

His tone had become whiny. Ariel felt they were really getting to him now. She whispered across the desk to the Silversides, "Fight, you two. Fight."

"Fight?" Adam asked. "We cannot fight each other."

"Not a real fight. Fake it."

It was a bizarre, awkward battle, especially since Adam and Eve had to use precise arm movements in order not to strike each other in any way that might hurt either—by dislodging a circuit or causing positronic damage. But Adam's voice circuit was quite capable of any imitative sound, and when they just missed with a blow, he created the sound of one. Many of the punches appeared to land with a thunderous impact. After a well-simulated blow, the victim would convincingly reel backwards from the apparent force of it.

"Stop!" Avery hollered. Then he screamed to Ariel, "They can't fight each other. It's strictly against Third Law procedure. A robot must protect its own existence. That means they can't be aggressive."

"But Second Law allows me to order them to fight to the death, if necessary."

"Well, yes, true, I guess, but consider the Laws of Humanics then. You should not give an order that endangers the preservation of robotic existence."

"That's just so much balderdash. There are no Laws of Humanics, they're just theory. Back home we call them ethics—and, Ozymandias, as anyone can tell you, Ariel Welsh is not an ethical person."

"You're lying."

"Maybe. No Law of Humanics to cover that, is there?"

Avery was momentarily bemused. Adam and Eve still struggled in their mock battle. Eve managed a skillful flip over Adam's shoulder and he staggered forward, nearly into Ariel's arms.

Ariel wished Derec could be in the room to watch the unprecedented scene of a pair of robots fighting. She almost forgot that the prodding of Avery had to be the main purpose of this theatrical display.

She whispered to Adam and Eve to quit the fray. Each

of them returned to portraying Avery, muttering and castigating, pacing and gesturing.

"Ozymandias, you're trembling," Ariel said from a point just behind his back, startling him and making him even more angry.

"I am not trembling!"

"You're shaking like a leaf."

"You are right, Ariel, you're not ethical. This whole attack on me is unethical. You're trying to drive me crazy."

"That's just paranoia, the least of your madnesses, I think. And I'm not trying to drive you crazy. I'm trying to do just the opposite—drive you sane."

"That in itself is crazy."

"You bet."

Adam came by, now doing a full-scale imitation of Avery, with the right walk, the tics, the jumpy inflections in his voice, the sarcastic tone. Avery yelled in frustration and took a swipe at Adam, landing a weak blow to his back.

"Ozymandias," Ariel said, "you just tried to hit Adam."

"That's right. I wish I could mangle him into spare parts."

"But you're a robot."

"Yes, what of it?"

"Well, you just said robots shouldn't be aggressive. You just put yourself in danger by hitting Adam. You reacted to him in a very human way. How could you possibly be a robot?"

"I am a robot."

"No, you're a human being."

"I was once, but I'm not now."

Now Ariel was frustrated. The idea that he was a robot seemed fixed in Avery's unpositronic brain. Yet she sensed that his anger over what the Silversides were doing could be used to shake him out of his delusion.

"Are 'u all rright, Arriel?" Wolruf said.

"I'm okay. I just had a foolish idea I could do something here, that's all."

"Iss there anything I may do?"

"Take me home to Aurora."

"If I could—"

"No, Wolruf, no. I didn't really mean it anyway. I'm happy here in scenic Robot City. I plan to be president of the Chamber of Commerce."

She was about to tell the Silversides that they could end their playacting, just as Eve passed her. Eve stopped in front of Avery and leaned in toward him, continuing her muttering in his voice. He pushed her away. She slid backward a few feet, then came close to him again.

"Stay away from me!" Avery cried. "That's an order. Second Law."

Ariel moved in closer, too.

"You're a robot. You can't invoke Second Law."

"What? Oh? Yes. Get her away from me."

"No. Go ahead, Eve. Stalk him. Whatever he goes, you go. You, too, Adam. Encroach."

They surrounded Avery. Whenever he broke away from them, one of them zoomed in on him again. He flailed out at them, and they sidestepped his badly thrown blows.

Finally, he broke into a run, pursued by Adam and Eve. Near the desk he spun around, and Ariel saw he had something in his hand. A moment passed before she realized what it was. She had not seen it in a long time.

The weapon was Avery's electronic disrupter, a device that emitted an ion stream that would interfere with the circuits of any advanced machine. Any machine, like the

Silversides. And he was raising it to aim at them.

Ariel, who had been standing behind the Silversides, ran between them, and roughly pushed them away. In the back of her mind, she realized that she'd just violated another of the Laws of Humanics, the one that said humans must not harm robots. Both Silversides went flying sideways.

Her move came just in time. Avery's shot went right over Ariel's head and would undoubtedly have affected circuitry in Adam or Eve.

She continued her rush to Avery, jumping at him, knocking the electronic disrupter out of his hand and throwing him to the floor.

"Some robot you are," she said, breathing heavily. "You don't even make a decent human being."

"Ariel," Avery said weakly. He struggled to his feet. "I don't—that is, I—I'm—I am—I—"

He looked sick. All the color had drained from his face. Ariel could see that it wasn't the result of the fighting. It was something else. From the look of him, he could be dying.

"You better sit down," Ariel said. "Adam?"

Adam picked up a chair and brought it to Avery, who settled heavily down upon it. Eve walked to Adam and the two took up a position behind Avery's chair. The fact they looked so much alike was disconcerting to Ariel, as if she were about to talk to a group called the Avery Trio.

"Are you all right?" Ariel asked Avery.

"I—I think so."

"Robots don't get sick, you know. They don't suffer from heart palpitations or exhaustion. They—"

"It's okay, Ariel. You don't have to speak to me as if I were a child. I know who I am. I may not like it. I may want to live forever. I may want to be a robot. But I know who I am."

"And that is—"

"Ariel, please."

"No, I'm a literalist. Are you a robot, Dr. Avery?"

"No."

"Say it out."

"I. Am. Not. A. Robot."

Ariel smiled.

"Well," she said, "that's a start."

CHAPTER 14

A DISCONNECTED DETECTIVE

Bogie stood in the corner where Derec had placed him so long ago. Timestep was across the room in another corner. While it was impossible for Bogie to be bored or to consider the possibilities of nothingness while in fact doing nothing for several consecutive days, he *was* aware that he had been in the corner for some time. It seemed to him that his position must be very much like the detectives on stakeout in several of the films he had researched. In scenes where they had waxed philosophical in tough-guy language, with plenty of wise-cracks and sentimental observations about life, they had had to pass time with only their own words to keep them company, plus a few doughnuts. Bogie would, he decided, prefer to do a stakeout for Derec than merely to stand in a corner awaiting his next order.

The order came, but not from Derec. The Watchful Eye transmitted a comlink message to Bogie over the secret channel it had created for private communications with its robots. The message told Bogie to come at once but not to allow Derec to see him go. That posed quite a dilemma for

Bogie. If he left immediately, it would be obvious. If he waited for the right time, he would be disobeying the Big Muddy's command to come at once. For a while he stood in his corner, aware that he could get mental freeze-out, a condition where a robot's positronic brain essentially stopped functioning because of an unresolvable dilemma. He was, he thought, a cybernetic goner if he could not slip away soon.

In the room Derec was speaking with Mandelbrot.

"I had another dream about my mother last night," Derec was saying.

"That is your fifth dream about her," Mandelbrot said. "The fifth that you have told me about."

"Yep. That's all of 'em. There wasn't much to this one. I was a child, and she came to give me medicine. But this time I saw her face clearly. She had blond hair and hazel eyes. She seemed very kind. We talked for a while, I don't remember about what. Then she said she loved me and left. And I woke up."

"It was a pleasant dream then?"

"I suppose. But I woke up wondering if the woman in the dream was really my mother. I mean, I've never seen her, so anyone I think up could come into my dream and say she's my mother without even looking anything like her. Do you understand, Mandelbrot?"

"Frankly, no."

"Well, I guess you don't have a mother."

"You know I do not."

Derec seemed about to explain something to Mandelbrot, but there was a soft rapping on the door.

"That sounds like Wolruf," Derec said. "I'd recognize that tap anywhere. Come in, Wolruf."

The caninoid alien came into the room.

"Messsage frrom Arriel," she said. "She ssent me. We are making progrresss with your fatherr, she told me to tell 'u."

Derec's face brightened. "That's wonderful news, Wolruf. How much progress, do you think?"

"Am not able to guesss. In my homeland iss no mental illnesss. Have not seen it before Dr. Averry."

"But he seems better."

"That may be ssaid, I think."

"Good. But she still doesn't want me to come there?"

"Afrraid you'll—"

"I know, I know. I could set him back. That's okay." (It wasn't, but he said so. He was very curious about what his father would be like as a sane man. He could not conceive of the possibility.) "How about your other project? The Silversides?"

"They help Arriel, but she feelss they are just ass unpredictable ass everr."

"I suspect so. And the dancers?"

"She ssaid to tell 'u they do not do well. They get old. One died."

"Did that upset Ariel badly?"

"No, I don't think so. Eve wass concerned. She inssissted on taking it somewhere and burrying it. Ariel ssaid that iss sstrange."

"I agree. But Adam and Eve seem full of surprises, don't they?"

"Alwayss."

"Anything more, Wolruf?"

"That'ss all she told me to tell 'u."

"Well, thank you. You make a good messenger, Wolruf. I won't have to shoot you."

"Shoot me? You would—?"

Derec laughed. "No, I wouldn't shoot you. According to some Earth legend I read about, if a king was dissatisfied with the news a messenger brought, he would order the messenger killed. But, if it were ever true, it was a custom that faded out with civilization."

"I am thankful for that."

"Stay with us, Wolruf. I'm hungry. We can eat something. I've taught Mandelbrot how to program the chemical food processor. He comes up with some awesome concoctions, and I'm sure if you state your preferences, he can devise something to your taste."

Derec rose from his chair and led the others out of the room. The food machine was located in a kitchen on the other side of the corridor.

The human need for food solved Bogie's problem. He slipped away from his corner and, checking the corridor carefully, went out into it. As he passed the kitchen, he heard Derec talking and the sounds of Mandelbrot operating the processor.

Growing again the thick legs it used to get around the computer chamber, the Watchful Eye moved out of its haven. There were no robots or intruders anywhere near the computer complex at this time, and it wanted to be ready for Bogie when he arrived. It had a plan, and it needed Bogie to make the plan work.

It was night in Robot City, Bogie's favorite time, and he noticed that the moonlight slashed off the sides of buildings like a mugger's sudden attack. As he walked quickly through the streets, he liked to think of descriptive lines like that, lines derived from the voiceovers in many of the old movies he'd viewed. He glanced around for more opportu-

nities to practice such lines. In the night sky, the stars flick-
ered on and off, like the sequins on a party girl's dress. The
tunnel he would use to go down to the computer level—and
the Watchful Eye—loomed mysteriously in front of him, like
a black hole with a welcome mat in front of it.

He wondered why his thoughts had taken such an odd
turn. Could it just be his fascination with all those movies
he'd researched, or was there some reason to be wary of
what the Watchful Eye had in store for him?

The Watchful Eye tracked Bogie on his trip through the
intricate maze that was the route to the computer chamber,
watching several view-screens so he could gain knowledge
of the robot from all angles. The more it could study Bogie
before the robot arrived, the easier it would be to duplicate
him. Further, it could store images of Bogie's movements in
its own memory banks, so that it could duplicate him with
Derec or the others.

Bogie came through the sliding wall, saying, "You
called, boss?"

"That is correct, Bogie. You are the first robot ever allowed into this sanctum by me. I hope you are honored."

"A singular honor, boss. I'll dine out on this for years.
It'll impress all the dolls. A doll in Washington Heights once
got a fox fur out of me."

The Watchful Eye hadn't the slightest idea what Bogie
was talking about, but that didn't matter. It had no more
use for Bogie anyway.

It moved out of its haven, walking on the short, rudimentary legs so adequate for the computer room. Sometimes
it had been necessary to get through interstices in the machinery, to stretch itself to an elongated shape and worm
its way, grabbing with even shorter legs (and more of them),

through an opening. At other times it had needed to puff itself out in order to roll through a chute or tunnel; at those times it retracted its legs. But now it was perched on its conventional limbs, standing in front of Bogie, who had to look down at it.

"Say, boss, you're not what I expected."

"You did not expect me to be so amorphous?"

"If you say so. What I mean, I didn't expect a blob. From the movie of the same name."

This robot had gone too far with its research, the Watchful Eye decided. Shutting him off was, in a way, a kindness.

Using Bogie as a model, supplemented with the images it had already stored, the Watchful Eye began transforming itself. Bogie watched silently as the blob began to grow in height and shrink in width. Soon its legs lengthened and it grew arms. A moment later it was in a clearly humanoid shape. Even quicker came the changes that made it clearly a robot. Last were the delicate shifts in the facial and bodily look that gave it features and characteristics. But it was not until the Watchful Eye had finished its transformation that Bogie recognized it.

"Hey," he said, "You're me now, boss. That's a nifty trick. How'd you do it?"

"That is not necessary for you to know, Bogie. I must explain to you now, because I want you to realize, that I will have to disconnect you now."

"Disconnect? You mean, rub me out?"

"That is exactly what I do mean. I need to observe our visitors up close, and so I am going to pose as you. That means I cannot take the chance of anyone discovering you here and guessing my disguise. Further, you are the only robot to be allowed into my presence, and so you have already seen too much and cannot be allowed even to carry that information in your memory banks. Also, you are no longer of any use to me. So I must disconnect you."

"It's like shooting the messenger, I guess."

"I do not understand the reference."

Bogie explained what Derec had said about messengers while the Watchful Eye opened the control panel in his back.

"Boss?"

"Yes?"

"When I am activated again, I won't remember anything? I won't even have this identity? I'll be reprogrammed?"

"*If* you are activated again, all that would be true."

"If?"

"Your existence is a threat to my safety. I must protect myself, so I must destroy you."

"Oh. I understand. Well, boss, I guess it's goodbye, huh?"

"There is no need for amenities between us."

Just before the Watchful Eye disconnected the final wire, Bogie said, "Well, we'll always have Paris."

After Bogie was shut off, the Watchful Eye, with the precision of a surgeon, broke him up into his components. He carried the parts to a recycling chute, from which they would eventually be collected and taken to a Robot Recycling Facility, where they would be used in the construction of new robots.

The Watchful Eye continued on down the corridor. It wanted to reach Derec's quarters before Bogie was missed.

CHAPTER 15

SAVE THE LAST DANCER FOR ME

Ariel was exhausted but too jittery to sleep. She had spent the better part of two days working alternately with Avery and the dancers.

Avery was, as doctors or med-bots might say, responding to treatment. Under Ariel's relentless questioning, assisted by many queries from Adam (she had briefed him on the types of questions to ask), the doctor had sunk into a depressed but much more rational state. He treated Adam politely, even though Adam had chosen to continue to look like him.

Sometimes, when Adam asked Avery a question, Ariel got confused. The question would be in Avery's old, madder voice—abrupt, condescending, sharp-dictioned—but the real Avery would respond in an un-Averylike voice; quieter, kinder, sad. Yet the technique, one never used before in psychiatric circles—a robot interrogator who could become an exact double of the patient—seemed to have good effects. Avery's responses to Adam tended to dig deeper into the man's psyche, brought out more interesting possibilities. His responses to Ariel were more evasive, cloudier. It became her task to follow up on the clues drawn out by Adam. She would zero in on any hint, any opportunity; make any remarks about any revelations; do anything, finally, to make Avery talk.

In the last two days, Avery had become more relaxed, calmer. Many of the things he said were still outrageous, and he could not get off the subject of wanting to dissect a dancer, but he no longer ranted, and his sarcasm was considerably reduced. He seemed—to Ariel at least—more rational, though hardly sane, and still not very nice.

Now Avery had concluded that he was better off as a human than he had been when he'd thought of himself as a robot.

"No real insight there," Ariel commented. "I should think that would be obvious."

"No, no. You do not understand me." When he was misunderstood, he had a tendency to pat the outside of his right thigh nervously with his right hand. "I still think of robots as the greatest entities of all. The perfect creatures, without emotion or aging; you know that old routine, I suspect?"

"I do. Schoolbook stuff back on Aurora. But I don't agree that an invention without a true inner life or without feelings is worth being, no matter how long it exists."

"Well, I did. In some ways I still do. I've always wanted a life of the mind, not of the emotions. And I've wanted to live longer than our natural lifespans."

"An Auroran lives so long, I'm surprised you'd even worry. Isn't the real issue your fear of death?"

He laughed scoffingly. "More schoolbook stuff, Ariel. If one wants to live forever, you reality-distorters automatically knee-jerk the idea of fear of death."

"Hey, I'm young and I fear death."

"That attitude is only sensible. We all have it. But I don't care about death itself. If it comes, I'll shake its hand and lead it off. No, it's the chance to watch history, to see what will happen further in science, that's the reason I want the long life of a robot. I want to see if the Settler worlds will succeed or perish from their own boorish and violent ways. I want to see if Earth can somehow survive its terrible, claustrophobic ways of life, or will decay and be destroyed from the inside, becoming a ghost planet, a worn-out memorial to what humanity once was. I want to see if Spacers—"

"Don't get carried away by your own rhetoric, Dr. Avery. I get the message. It's not fear of death, it's a need to know the future."

"Simplistically stated, but essentially correct. At any rate, I spent so much time with robots and thought so much about them that eventually I wanted to be one, *needed* to be one. I'd still like to be one. The difference is I no longer believe I am one."

She turned the care of Avery back to Adam and took a short walk across the room to confront her other problem. Eve, now restored to her Ariel form, sat beside the desk, merely staring at the dancers, the five who were left. The other nine had all died quietly or, as Avery would have it, "ceased operation."

Just looking at the remaining quintet made Ariel sad. She had hoped for great communicative advances when she had started working with the tiny creatures. So little had really been accomplished. The games were cute, and some of their behavior showed a minimal intelligence, but no language had been conveyed, only a few hand signals. The gestures were significant, but not enough for Ariel.

She had this faint sense that she had failed. And the

apparent success of her other project, Avery, somehow did not compensate for her failure with the dancers.

"Anything new, Eve?" she said as she sat down in her customary chair.

"Nothing. They merely sit, holding hands like that. They never even look up at us anymore."

"Perhaps they think that their gods are punishing them."

"I do not understand. Their gods?"

"Us, Eve."

"Would you explain?"

"Well, we—never mind. Ignore the comment."

There was something morbid about Eve's vigil over the remaining dancers. Each time one died, she insisted on taking it away, presumably to bury it. Ariel had never asked her where she went or exactly how she had performed the ritual. She did not want to know. The thought of Eve in a lonely, dark area, performing death rites for a dancer made Ariel shudder.

Avery, still demanding that one be handed over to him for study, had fussed over the first four or five deaths. Ariel's adamant support of Eve had apparently discouraged him. He had been silent on the matter for some time. Once she tried to introduce the subject, but he had dismissed it with a wave of his hand.

At times Ariel wished the dancers would finish their dying. Then she could return to Derec and help him in restoring the city. He had made some progress lately, managing to convince the computer to make all the lights of the city work again. And some utility robots had been seen picking up street debris. Water no longer tasted brackish, and the food coming out of the processors actually had flavor. But Derec wasn't satisfied, he said. There were still so many things out of whack, and the essential mystery of why the city had deteriorated in their absence remained.

Wolruf came into the room. She was returning from still another meal with Derec and Mandelbrot. Ariel didn't blame her for spending more time with them. Since Adam had begun working with Avery, there had been little for Wolruf to do here.

Coming to the desk, Wolruf glanced down at the dancers. "They look worrse, 'u think?"

"Much worse."

"What can I do?"

"Nothing much anyone can do."

"Could 'u just sset them loosse?"

"Why?"

"They could die in peace, alone. On my worrld, there iss a custom of dying alone."

"Perhaps you're right. But I think it's too late for such a compassionate act. They're too far gone."

"Yess, I ssee, I think."

When she turned her attention back to the desktop, Ariel saw one of the dancers, a once-chubby, now-emaciated male, break his grip on two of the others and fall backward.

Eve, now so used to a dancer's passing, immediately scooped up the corpse and strode out of the room. Ariel, staring after her, said, "And then there were four. Soon, none. It won't be long now."

She glanced over toward Avery. He was now looking at her with some concern in his face. How sane of him, she thought.

Timestep, in his corner, had seen Bogie leave. Then, a short time later, he witnessed his return. After Bogie had gone back to his corner, Timestep catalogued the oddities. First, if not summoned by Derec or even Mandelbrot, why had Bogie left the corner in the first place? Second, where had he gone? Third, why was his return so secretive? Fourth, an important fourth, what was it that looked so wrong about Bogie?

Derec reentered the room, followed by Mandelbrot. He was silent, his index finger tapping on his chin thoughtfully. Timestep studied the tap. It was too slow, unrhythmic. He would not have been able to use it for any dancing step he knew. (All the while he stood in his corner he called up from his memory banks the dances he had memorized and visualized how he would do them if his feet were not forbidden to move just now.)

Across the way, Bogie appeared to lean forward, which seemed odd to Timestep. But then Bogie had left the corner and returned to it on his own, so a simple bending at the waist should not seem so out of the ordinary.

"Bogie!" Derec called, and Bogie came out of his corner. Did Timestep observe a hesitation before his companion moved?

"Did you think we'd forgotten you, Bogie?" Derec asked.

Bogie hesitated before saying, "That you would forget about me would not occur to me, Master Derec."

"You seem a little sluggish. And what's this Master Derec? What happened to 'kid,' 'kiddo,' 'pal'?"

"I felt momentarily respectful, Mast—kiddo."

Derec narrowed his eyes as he stared at Bogie. "Are you functional? Should I send you to the Robot Repair Facility for a diagnostic scan or a tune-up?"

"That will not be necessary. Pal."

For a moment Derec seemed unsure. "That's okay," he finally said. "Tell me, Bogie, what do you know about our mysterious controller?"

"I know nothing of a mysterious controller, sir."

"Weren't you supposed to tell me there was a block on that information, something like that?"

Again Bogie hesitated. "The nature of the block upon information does not include such a question as the one you asked. Kid."

Derec smiled. "Very good. It was a sort of 'do you still beat your wife' question, wasn't it?"

"I do not have a wife. Kiddo."

"It'd be an idea, though. Robot husbands and wives. Robot families. I might work on it when the mess here is cleared up. Would you like a family, Bogie?"

"I cannot have a family."

"Isn't there a family feeling among robots?"

"No, sir. Pal."

"Okay, okay. You'll have to forgive me. I'm bone-weary, and my mind isn't even forming casual conversation effectively. Bogie?"

"Yes, Master—Pal."

"I need Wolruf back here. Go to the medical facility and fetch her."

"Fetch?"

"Bring her back here. In fact, since she just left, you might be able to catch up with her even before she reaches the medical facility. Well, what are you waiting for? Get a move on."

"Yes, sir."

Derec stared at the empty doorway for a long while after Bogie left. He seemed preoccupied. Then he turned suddenly and bellowed: "Timestep!"

Timestep immediately left his corner and went to Derec.

"Yes, Master Derec?"

"Is something wrong with Bogie? Anything another robot can discern?"

"I do not know, sir."

"Let me put it another way. Was that Bogie who just left here?"

"I do not know, sir."

Derec looked worried. "Well, that's some progress. You would know for certain if it *was*, wouldn't you, Timestep?"

"Yes, Master Derec."

"Then there's a possibility that something has happened to Bogie?"

"Yes, that seems possible."

"Is he malfunctioning?"

"I do not know, sir."

"Right. I have to phrase the question differently. Is there a possibility that a robot such as Bogie could malfunction?"

"It is possible, but there would have to be a reason. He would have to be forced to resolve a dilemma involving the Laws of Robotics, or he would have to be given an order he could not carry out."

"Are they the only possible reasons for him to act uncharacteristically?"

"No."

"What's another ?"

"He is no longer Bogie as we knew him. He has been reprogrammed or has reprogrammed himself."

"Mandelbrot? Do you agree with Timestep?"

"Yes. But there is another possibility. I tried to speak with him through comlink and he did not respond to his name. Also, there was a series of nicks along his right side before. They are no longer there."

"What do you think about him?"

"I think it is not Bogie. I think it is someone else."

"Our mysterious controller?"

"I cannot know that. But it is a possibility."

"Timestep, what about this? Could it not be Bogie?"

"That is possible, sir."

"Go after him, the both of you. Corner him. Bring him back to me."

The two robots left the room, and Derec began to pace. He sensed that he was going to regain his control of the city. Even the chemfets inside him seemed to be reviving.

The rest of the dancers did not survive for long. Eve disposed of the next three, then returned for a somber death watch over the last, the formerly sturdy woman who had been the leader of the dancers. She was lying in the center of the desk, looking pale and weak, with no one to hold on to anymore. Ariel had leaned down close, watching the slight breathing movements of her tiny chest.

"I wonder what she thinks," Ariel said to Wolruf.

"Iss odd to me to wonderr what such a ssmall being thinkss."

"Oh? We humans wonder about such things all the time. Part of our charm: our limitless curiosity about the universe."

"I have at timess noticed ssuch."

Avery, weary of the session with Adam, came to the desk. He stared down at the remaining dancer, whose arms rose upward for a moment in a characteristically graceful way.

"Let me have this one," he said softly, sounding quite sane about it. "She is our last chance to find out something about them."

"No," Eve said. "I must take care of her."

"Your care of them has been admirable, Eve," Avery said, "but we shouldn't waste this one on mere ritual, especially on ritual misunderstood by a robot. Ariel? It's your decision really."

"And you'll abide by it?"

He sighed theatrically, as if assuming any judgment would be against him. "I will."

Ariel looked from Eve to Avery, not certain how to say what she had been planing to say for some time.

"Eve, Dr. Avery is right. We must know about them, we—"

"But I must bury her."

In a quick move, she picked up the last dancer from the desktop and held it close to her chest.

"Eve, put her back. You can't bury her right now. She is still alive."

"Alive is not the correct word," Avery said.

"Shut up with your logic for once," Ariel said. "Eve, I order you to return the dancer to the desk. You must obey my order. That is the Second Law, and the Laws are part of you, isn't that true? You sense them inside you, don't you?"

"No. Yes. I cannot be sure. Something seems to tell me to obey you, but I am not sure that I can."

"You must. It is Second Law."

"It is not just Second Law," Adam said. He was standing behind Avery. "It is what we must do. We cannot continue if we do not discover what is wrong with the city, and the dancers are part of the mystery. Return the dancer, Eve."

Eve gently settled the dancer back onto the desktop, then resumed her customary vigil.

"Eve," Ariel said gently, "it is important to me to know whether or not these tiny creatures are living beings or merely some kind of experimental robots or even, as Dr. Avery has suggested, toys."

"They are robots," Eve said. "I have sensed no life in

them, the kind of life I have felt coming from you, Derec, Wolruf. What I detect in them is the same as what comes to me from Mandelbrot and the other robots." She pointed to the last dancer. "This, I believe, is a robot."

Ariel was shocked. "You mean, you've known this all the time and not said anything about it?"

"You did not request it from me. And no, I did not know it all the time. Or even most of the time. When I first encountered these creatures in the vacant lot, I received my first glimmerings. As Adam did at the time, I felt little life in them. But I had not experienced much of this world, or any other world, and I was not sure at the time what constituted a living being and what constituted a robot. As I watched the dancers, I understood more and more what they were. My certainty has only come recently."

"Eve, I—"

"Eve," Avery interrupted, "what do you feel coming from Adam, coming from inside yourself? Do you feel, as you say, a living being or robot?"

"I cannot say. It is different. We are different."

"That is so," Adam said. "Since I came to awareness on the kin's planet, I have not been certain what I am. I accept that we are robots, but actually, inside myself, I feel neither living being nor robot."

"Fair enough," Avery said.

"Eve," Ariel said, "If you knew the dancers were not human, why did you treat them as humans?"

"I was not aware I was."

"You cared for them, awarded them human death rituals, buried them as if they'd died. If they're robots, then they didn't really die and didn't need to be treated as such."

"They ceased to exist," Eve said. "Isn't a robot's death as significant as a human's?"

"Mistress Ariel," Adam said, "you buried the robot Jacob Winterson on the blackbodies' planet, did you not?"

"But that's—I was about to say it was different, but you're right, Adam, it's not. I cared about Jacob the way Eve apparently cared for the dancers. You did care for them, didn't you, Eve?"

"I am not sure what you mean. I performed rituals that I believed were appropriate."

"Don't go robotic on me now, Eve. You did feel compassion for them, sadness when they died."

"There was an awareness of loss. Is that sadness, Ariel?"

"I don't know, Eve. I'm not even sure I can get a sense of it."

They watched each other silently for a time, then both looked down at the last dancer. She was still breathing.

"I must still order you, Eve," Ariel said, "to allow Dr. Avery to perform his examination without interference. We need to know the facts that his work will show us."

"Yes. That now seems logical."

"Logical. Why logical *now*?"

"Enough information has been presented to me, and I understand the need. So I conclude agreement."

"No wonder you are not sure what you are. I'm not sure what you are, both of you."

When the last dancer had died, hours later, Avery gently picked it up from the desktop and went to a far corner of the room. A few minutes later he came back with a number of slides. Placing them under a microscopic scanner and transmitting images of his findings onto its large screen, he showed Ariel the infinitesimal microchips and circuit boards, miniature servo motors, linkages, wires.

"As I suspected," Avery said, but without his usual smugness, "they are cleverly designed albeit ineffective robots capable of limited humanlike behavior. The use of genetic materials was skillful, but the maker could not compensate for their rapid aging process. If he had, these might have been quite successful little humaniform robots."

Ariel stared at the screen without visible emotion. She didn't know what to feel. Relief that they were not tiny humans or sadness that, whatever they were, they had existed and only for a very short time.

Finally, she took a cloth and wiped off the desktop. "Well," she said, "that's it then. Let's go see if we can help Derec."

Before they left, Avery handed Eve a small box. When Eve asked what it was, he said it was the remains of the last dancer. He was turning it over to her for whatever disposal she chose. She carried it away.

CHAPTER 16

FLIGHT

The Watchful Eye realized as it left Derec that its disguise had not fooled him. It had come to that conclusion by analyzing the purposes of his probing questions, reading his facial expressions, and interpreting his body language. (In its studies of humans, it had called up from the computer a file on metalinguistics and paralanguage.)

As it fled, the Watchful Eye wondered just where it had gone wrong in its Bogie portrayal. Perhaps the mistake had been to try to imitate a robot in the first place. After all, it was too complicated a being, too powerful an intellectual force, to get away with posing as a mere robot. On the other hand, the flaw in its behavior may have been an error of pride. It may have felt too easily superior to Bogie, and robots in general, to pretend to be one effectively. Somewhere in the research, it had read that actors often succeeded because they immersed themselves in their roles, losing their real identity in them. It should have studied Bogie more. Oddly enough, it thought, its failure in the robot guise reinforced its belief that it was definitely not a robot itself.

Perhaps its real error had been in leaving the safety of its haven in the computer chamber. The haven was where it belonged. Perhaps it was never meant to leave it, or at least not to stray too far from it. Perhaps its existence was that of an armchair observer, participating at a distance, pulling strings like a puppetmaster.

What should it do now? it wondered. Derec had ordered it to find Wolruf, but Wolruf was too much of a threat, and the caninoid alien might be with the other humans, all of whom might be able to detect that it wasn't what it seemed to be. For a moment, as it had left the room, it had felt a compulsion to do what Derec said, treating it as a Second Law command. But if it wasn't a robot, why should it obey Derec? It couldn't even be sure Derec was a proper human, or a human at all.

At any rate, the order had been given to Bogie, and the Watchful Eye was not Bogie. If it were human, it had the power of choice; if it were robot, it did not have to follow orders given to another robot; if it were animal or alien, it could follow animal or alien instincts.

Since Derec might spread the word that it was not Bogie, there was no reason to stay out here in the streets, where the others could track it down and trap it.

As it headed toward the tunnel that led directly down to the central computer, it wondered if it could even continue its activities in Robot City. With Derec and Ariel there, it had enemies, and it could not abide enemies. Nevertheless, it didn't want to eliminate them, as sensible a solution as that might be. Something inside it prevented it from killing.

Suddenly it realized how it could give the intruders a setback, assert its power, allow itself to maintain control of the city, mold an environment that would be suitable for it instead of humans, and make it the powerful entity it had decided to be.

It would just accelerate the program it had planned all along by skipping a few steps and going directly to the main goal.

It would destroy, then rebuild, Robot City.

Wolruf had left Ariel and the others for her nocturnal roaming of the city. She had come from a place whose inhabitants traveled through the night compulsively, searching for answers to questions they had not always known they had. While she subdued the urge at most times, tonight, after watching the end of the dancers, she had known she must be alone. She climbed over the smaller buildings, raced down dark streets in long loping strides, crouched at the edges of roofs.

Rounding a corner, she collided with a robot she recognized as Bogie.

"Bogie! What arre 'u doing here?"

But the robot did not answer. It merely leaped over Wolruf and raced on, around the corner from which Wolruf had come.

"Stop!" said a voice. It was Mandelbrot, coming toward Wolruf so fast he would have run her down if she had not jumped adeptly out of the way. The robot Timestep tapped along behind Mandelbrot.

"There iss something wrrong, Mandelbrot, I can ssee," Wolruf said. " 'U only rrush when ssomething iss wrrong."

"Excuse me, Wolruf," Mandelbrot said. "We are on urgent business. I cannot stop to explain."

He sped past her. Her curiosity aroused, she raced after him on all fours. Timestep danced his way after them.

"I can help 'u. Arre 'u following Bogie?"

"No."

They rounded the corner. Wolruf saw Bogie, still moving rapidly, up ahead.

" 'U sseem to be following Bogie."

"No."

"What arre 'u doing?"

"Trying to overtake the Bogie that is not Bogie."

"The Bogie not Bogie? Explain, pleasse."

As they rushed along, Mandelbrot told the alien what had happened.

"Then 'u arre to brring that rrobot back to Derec?"

"Yes."

"Let me catch him forr 'u."

With a strong, leaping thrust, Wolruf surged ahead of Mandelbrot and Timestep. Her body low to the ground, she closed the gap between herself and the Watchful Eye in a matter of seconds. Her prey was not even aware of her pursuit.

With her last few powerful steps, Wolruf propelled herself into the air. Her leap was magnificent, a smooth arc that reached such an impressive height she was able to dive down upon the fleeing robot. Her forelegs hit its shoulders with a mighty impact, knocking it forward onto its face. Wolruf landed on top of it. She was able to hold it down long enough for the others to arrive.

Rolling off the Watchful Eye, she looked up to see Mandelbrot standing over them.

"Whoever you are," Mandelbrot said, "Derec orders you to return to him with us."

"Whoever?" the Watchful Eye said. "I am Bogie."

"No, you are not. I can see that now."

"What makes you think so?"

"You have not copied Bogie's voice accurately, although the ability is programmed into you. There was a rough sound in Bogie's voice that yours lacks."

Another mistake, then. The Watchful Eye should have adapted its voice to the robot's. For a moment, it wondered if it should have bothered with Bogie at all. For a botched piece of strategy, that robot was now parts on the Repair Facility floor. The Watchful Eye could not feel regret, but it was conscious of the waste caused by ineffective action.

"If you know I am not Bogie," it said, "then you may guess that I don't have to do what you say."

Without waiting for Mandelbrot to continue the discussion, the Watchful Eye kicked out at Mandelbrot's leg. The surprise move made Mandelbrot topple over, landing with an impressive clanking sound upon the pavement.

The Watchful Eye stood up quickly, feeling more in control of its unaccustomed robot body than before. It turned to find Wolruf leaping toward it. With a vicious backhand blow, it struck Wolruf in the neck. Choking, falling backward, Wolruf collapsed. She landed awkwardly on her back legs causing them both to throb with intense pain.

The Watchful Eye jumped over the fallen alien and tried to continue its run, but Timestep, with a dancing twirl, tripped it up. It stumbled, but this time did not fall. When it regained its balance, it ran at Timestep so quickly that the robot did not have time even to consider his Third Law responsibility.

It wrestled Timestep to the pavement but then, in an abrupt move, broke its hold and raced away. It had progressed half a block before Mandelbrot stood up. However, since he regarded Wolruf the same way he did humans, First Law compelled him to kneel down beside the fallen alien to see if she was in need of help.

"I am fine," Wolruf said in a faint voice. She could barely talk. " 'U go on. Continue purrsuit. I will go to Derec."

Wolruf watched Mandelbrot and Timestep chase after the strange robot. When they were out of sight, she struggled to her feet. The pain from her legs seemed to be traveling through her whole body.

Her run to Derec was done at a much slower pace then usual.

The Watchful Eye wished it had been able to imitate a robot's speed, but its mimicry did not automatically give it full physical control. Unlike a normal Avery robot, it skidded around corners and bumped into obstacles. Each little delay was allowing its pursuers to get closer.

It had one advantage over Mandelbrot and Timestep. It knew where it was going.

The tunnel was not too far away now. After looking back at its pursuers, it quickly calculated the time it would take them to close the gap between them and it. It was likely they would overtake it a few meters from the tunnel entrance.

It needed a diversion.

It flashed into its mind a map of the area and discovered that there was a building coming up on its right that stored several of the results of its genetic experiments. This had been one of its latest experiments, and many from this batch of creatures were still functioning.

If it went through this building, which had a rear exit, and could slow down its pursuers by doing so, it could reach the tunnel entrance easily.

As Mandelbrot's footsteps became louder, sounding as if he were ready to climb onto its back, the Watchful Eye took an abrupt right turn toward the building. It ran at such velocity that it hit the entrance with an impact that sent the thick door flying open.

Inside, bright light illuminated an enormous room. Spread across its floor, on shelves, sprawled over furniture, was a large group of rejects from the Watchful Eye's experiments.

The beings of this particular group, the one it had created just before the arrival of the intruders, were somewhat larger than the dancers and built with less delicacy. They were thick-muscled, with bulges all over their bodies, bulges that did not actually correspond accurately with the protuberances of the human body.

Toughness was their chief trait. Continually knocking against each other and starting fights, playing games that usually ended in fierce brawling, executing odd practical jokes, or banding together into groups and staging small battles that contained more strategy than one would expect, they had some resemblance to frontier people on the Settler planets and in Earth's history.

In contrast to the roughness of their natures, they had organized themselves into a fairly intricate society, including a government laden with bribery and graft. The Watchful Eye had been quite taken with this group, but had had to reject it because it exhibited too many weaknesses, and outside of their corrupt politics and a tendency toward lively song, they had displayed minimal intelligence.

Most of its experiments were failures because they turned out to be too limited, even though each group displayed different characteristics. It had wanted to discover more about the Laws of Humanics (which stated, more or less, that human beings must not harm themselves or allow others to come to harm, must not give robots dangerous orders, and must not harm robots unless the action could save other human beings), but its experimental creations generally became too independent, forming their own societies and proving nothing about the ethics that were the foundation of the Laws.

On one side of the room, a large group was singing a raucous song, while a wild melee ensued near the Watchful Eye's feet. Stepping carefully into spaces the tiny creatures tended to create when one of the larger entities came into the room that was their world, it managed to get about one-third of the way across the room before Mandelbrot and Timestep came through the open doorway. The Watchful Eye looked back for a moment and saw what it had expected. The two robots had come to a standstill. Uncertain of how to wind their way across the overpopulated room, they further wondered if their actions here should be governed by the First Law of Robotics. They were not sure if the law even applied to this situation. It walked on, knowing that even if there were creatures under its foot as it came down, they were used to visitors and adept enough to scamper out of the way. It easily reached the other side of the room, where some of the male citizens performed odd mating rituals with the females. (There had been no actual mating in any of the experimental creatures' societies, although pairing off and flirtation were not uncommon.)

Before Mandelbrot and Timestep could work their way cautiously across the room, the Watchful Eye was on a new street and making its way toward its tunnel escape route. In its mind, coolly analytical in spite of the danger around it, it continued to formulate its plan for the destruction of Robot City.

CHAPTER 17

ADAM AND EVE AND PINCH ME

Adam found Eve standing at the entrance to a small park set in the middle of one of several Robot City building clusters. This cluster included a small art museum, a library, an auditorium meant for music performance, and one of those plazas with customerless commercial shops that dotted the city. The park itself was a circle of trees just inside a small metallic picket fence, with attractive groupings of benches, bushes, and flower beds throughout.

Although Eve stood still and looked into the park, it was clear to Adam that she was not studying its landscape or evaluating its function. She was staring at a particular corner, assuring herself that the activity she had just completed there had left no trace.

He stood by her side for a long while before speaking. She continued to resemble Ariel, while Adam had changed from Avery back to Derec. An outside observer might have judged them to be as romantically involved as the two humans were, the way they stood together silently against the park's romantic setting. But that was only another facet of their mimicry, and romance was not a part of their repertoire, unless their creator had some later surprise to spring upon them.

"This is where the dancers are?" he asked.

"Yes."

"You have buried all of them someplace in this park?"

"Some of them. Others are elsewhere."

"Do you know why you have performed this ritual?"

"It seemed appropriate. When we encountered the first group in that lot, they were burying their dead. I finished that job, so it seemed to me balanced that I do the same task for the dancers. I thought that, whatever they were, someone should perform the rites that appeared to be appropriate to their society. Am I wrong?"

"I would have no way of knowing that. Right and wrong seem to be the kind of polarity to which beings like Derec and Ariel and Dr. Avery give importance. They are concerned with moral values. We do not have to be, except as they apply to us."

"I thought we were moral beings, too."

"We are. But we do not have to fret in the way that they do about values. And ours are less complicated, governed only by the distinctions of set codes of behavior. You have seen how they cannot even agree among themselves on an issue."

"Yes. Dr. Avery seems almost like an enemy of Derec and Ariel, while Derec and Ariel do not always get along with each other. Why cannot they agree on proper rules of conduct, Adam?"

"I do not know. We must observe them further."

"They differed in their attitudes about the dancers. Ariel seemed genuinely sorrowful about their deaths, while Avery appeared to be indifferent."

"He was fearful of his own death. He admitted that."

"Yes. I have no real idea what death is. It seems to be an operational being becoming nonoperational."

"I believe that is somewhat accurate. Did you have feelings about the dancers when they became nonoperational?"

"I cannot answer you. Something was in my head but I do not know what. I thought perhaps it was a positronic disturbance, but I am not sure. All I know was that as I carried each dancer away from the medical facility, I sensed that there was an injustice in their lives, but I could not yet discern what. If that is feelings, then I may be a robot with feelings."

"The evidence is inconclusive at best. Will you bury more of these people if we discover their corpses?"

"Yes, if it is possible."

"Should you wish it, I will help you."

They stood a while longer, then Adam said, "When I was helping Dr. Avery, he told me a story. He said I should know it because of our names. It went like this: Adam and Eve and Pinch Me went out to take a swim. Adam and Eve got drowned, and who got saved?"

Eve waited for Adam to continue. When he did not, she said, "That is incomprehensible as a story, Adam."

"No, you're supposed to answer the question. Perhaps it is a riddle. Try again; Adam and Eve got drowned, and who got saved?"

"Logic seems to indicate Pinch Me."

"That's right. And then I am supposed to do this."

Adam put his hand against her arm, finger and thumb spread. Gradually he brought the two digits together and pressed against her skin in an approximation of a human pinch.

Adam dropped his hand away. Eve watched the gesture and said, "And . . . ?"

"And what?"

"What is the point?"

"I do not know. I didn't know when Dr. Avery did it either, but he seemed to think it was worth smiling about. When I asked him to explain it, he became angry."

"Do you think it is an allegory? You see, Adam and Eve die and then Pinch Me is the survivor. Therefore, the teller touches the listener in a shared satisfaction that life goes on when other people die. Do you think that was what Dr. Avery was trying to convey?"

"Perhaps. He appears to want to live on very much, so this could have been his way of explaining life to me. These people can be like that, telling stories laced with obscurity when data is required."

"I suspect that data is not always essential to them. Come, let's find them."

In the distance there was an odd popping sound. Looking up, Adam and Eve saw an entire building flying above them, high in the air.

"What is that?" Eve said.

"It appears that a building has left its foundation and taken flight. Odd. When the robots remove a building from the city, it just disappears and is replaced by a new one. It does not generally fly through the air. Something is wrong. We must find Derec and Ariel."

CHAPTER 18

AVERY REDUX

Derec recognized the change in his father as soon as the man came into the room. Avery's usually tense face, now drawn and tired with a sad darkness around his eyes, had relaxed. Its features were softer, and his eyes and mouth were not agitated by nervousness. Neither was his body. He moved with an uncharacteristic slowness. His fingers were still. That was the real oddity. His hands, usually so active, were not moving. Derec had become so used to the way Avery's fingers drummed against things—furniture, his clothing—that their lack of movement was like a sudden silence in a jungle, too disturbing to cause calm.

Ariel looked a bit different, too, exhausted, eyelids drooping, mouth slack, no spring to her walk.

"Isn't Wolruf with you?" Derec asked Ariel.

"She was, but she took off on her own. You know how she does."

"I sent for her."

"I don't know anything about that."

Derec nodded. His suspicions seemed confirmed. "I sent

Bogie to bring her here, except that I don't think it was really Bogie I sent."

"What do you mean?"

He explained.

"You think somebody's done something to Bogie?" Ariel asked.

"Possibly. Or it wasn't Bogie at all."

"How could that be?"

"I don't know, but Timestep seemed to agree with me. He and Mandelbrot went after him."

Avery, who had lingered at the door, stepped forward. "Maybe it was the individual you've been looking for. The one behind the city's shutdown."

Derec considered the possibility. "You may be right. It's worth considering anyway. But could he disguise himself as Bogie?"

Avery shrugged. "When you don't know the identity of your antagonist, there's very little to conclude. We need hard evidence."

"I heard that 'we,'" Ariel said. "Does that mean you want to work with us?"

"It doesn't mean anything," Avery replied. "At least not what you insinuate. I may no longer believe I'm a robot, and you may be smug about how you prodded me back to normality with your cheap tricks and psychologizing, but it does not mean I am somehow, as your tone implied, your *ally*."

"Well, pardon me," Ariel said in mock anger. "Derec, I think the train's returned to the station. Your father is his old self again."

Derec didn't know how much he could appreciate that. He had not liked Dr. Avery in their earlier encounters and didn't relish having to deal closely with him again. And this was the man, after all, who had injected the chemfets into him, which had certainly turned out to be a mixed blessing. But Avery was also his father, and that had to count for something. If only the doctor would treat him like a son for a change.

"Well," Derec said glumly, "we can use any help you might be able to give us."

"Of course you could. The city is deteriorating. I'd want my help, too. I'd demand it. I didn't put you in charge to oversee its decline and fall."

Avery's words stung Derec. It seemed as if the man was continually judging him, and finding him wanting.

"I think you two should get to know each other," Ariel said. "You don't need me around for that. I'm going to take a stroll. Perhaps I can find the missing Bogie. I mean, the real one."

She walked out, an impish look on her face. She knew exactly what she was doing. The two Averys had to meet each other head to head, something neither of them could do with her around. She wasn't sure why, but she thought something would have to happen between them, for good or ill.

After she left, Avery observed, "Well, your girlfriend's ploy is quite obvious."

"Stop! Don't make her sound trivial by calling her my girlfriend."

"Sorry. I thought you two were—"

"We are, but she means more to me than that."

"I'll choose better words. Do you like paramour, foxy lady, lollapalooza, some dish, the cat's pyjamas, a tomato—"

"What are you talking about?"

"Just Earth slang. I'm a collector of ancient colloquialisms."

"You told me something like that in a dream."

"Did I?" Avery began to walk around the room slowly. He looked a bit more like his old self now, a shadow of it anyway. "Well, I don't put much stock in dream mysteries. Symbols and clairvoyance and that sort of bilgewater scum. Buried in your brain somewhere, although you don't remember it, you must remember observing me using the old slang terms."

"Do you remember me observing you?"

Avery's face softened. He looked almost kind.

"Yes. Many times. You used to come to my lab, sit on a high stool for hours, and watch me work. You not only picked up some of my scientific terminology, and probably my ancient lowdown slang, you were able to repeat a considerable number of my curses when you were a very young age. Embarrassed your mother no end—"

"My mother? She's been in my dreams, too. She—"

"I don't want to hear about your trivial dreams. You would probably *assail* me with sentimental theories, interpretations. I can do without psychobabble, believe me. Let's get back to business, we—"

"No, wait. My mother, did she have blond hair, hazel eyes?"

Avery looked astonished. "Well, that's true. I didn't think you could, that is, I thought you had no memories of her."

"No!"

The word was spoken so vehemently that Derec realized the subject must be difficult for him. Although he drew back from it, Derec had no intention of dropping it altogether. He would find out about her in any way he could.

"Was I a difficult child?" he asked instead.

Avery appeared ready to explode with anger.

"Can't you get your bloody mind off nostalgic senti-ment? We have to—no, wait, I'm sorry. I can be insensitive, I know that. It must be strange to you, having me as a father. I suppose an outsider might accuse me of having episodes of delusional paranoia, or perhaps intense mega-lomania. I hate such terms. Would-be interpreters of life hide behind words like that. Sometimes it seems that such words make them sound like they know something, instead of being the ignoramuses they are."

Derec was confused by the changes in his father's tone. He could sound like a normal father at one moment, even a rational human being, but then switch in mid-sentence to the sound of madness. Ariel's treatment of him may have made him a more sensible human being, but clearly it had not completely cured him.

"Yes, Derec," he said, his voice now eerily warm, "you had a more normal childhood than you suspect. Parents who doted on you and all that. You liked robots, and you picked up theories of robotics the way other children learn their letters and numbers. I helped you build your very own util-ity robot. You don't remember Positron, do you?"

"No."

He felt sad that he did not.

"That was the name you gave your robot. Of course, he was just a utility robot and didn't even have a positronic brain, but I thought the name had a certain charm, and so I didn't correct you. I suspect I didn't have to correct you. Even that young, you probably knew what you were doing. You always know what you're doing."

"I wish that was true."

"Isn't it?"

"I'm afraid not."

"Well, maybe the amnesia robbed you of some confidence, but you're an Avery, as much as you resist the idea of being related to me. It may insult you for me to say it, but there are times when you do remind me of me."

"It may surprise you for me to say it, but no, I'm not insulted. If I had your skills in robotics, I'd be, well, proud."

Was it his imagination, Derec wondered, or did his father's eyes momentarily glaze over? As he looked more closely into the man's cool and detached eyes, he decided it must have been imagination.

"Well," Avery finally said, "you're pretty skilled in that area already. You may surpass me—and don't say anything more about it now. We should pursue other subjects."

"We will. In a moment. I have to know one thing, then I'll let you off the hook."

"Just don't mistake me for an affectionate father."

"I could hardly do that."

Avery had walked away from Derec, and his back was turned to him.

"You said we were once close," Derec said. "Why did that change?"

The answer came out abruptly, bitterly.

"Your mother left me."

"Tell me about her."

"No."

This time his "no" was spoken softly, but with no less firmness. Derec was going to have to work hard to find out anything about her, that was abundantly clear.

"Derec," Avery said softly, "even talking with you is difficult for me. Don't expect a plethora of revelations."

Derec nodded. "All right, I won't."

He wondered if he should walk to his father, perhaps embrace him, perhaps ask him if they could start over, perhaps suggest that he would still like to sit on a high stool and watch Avery work.

He took one step toward his father but was interrupted by a noise at the door. Turning around, he saw Wolruf limp into the room. She was clearly on the point of collapsing.

Derec rushed to her and caught her before she fell. Gently he eased her to the floor and felt for her pulse. The slow rate of her pulse beneath her normally cold skin assured Derec that whatever injuries she may have sustained, she was alive and not in immediate danger.

Avery, reaching over his son's shoulder, delicately spread areas of Wolruf's fur apart. She winced with pain.

"There seems to be a bruise on her neck," he said, "a big one."

"He strruck me there," Wolruf said in a raspy voice.

"Who?" Derec asked. "Who hit you?"

"The Bogie that iss not Bogie."

"All right, Wolruf. I want you to tell me about it. But don't strain your voice. Speak quietly, slowly."

She explained what had happened when she had caught up with Bogie, and how Mandelbrot and Timestep had continued the chase.

"Okay," Derec said when she finished, "you rest right here. We'll get you to the medical facility as soon as we can."

"No, Derrec. I will be fine ssoon. You have too much that'ss necessary to do now."

"Well, we'll see."

Derec stood up and turned to his father, asking, "What do you make of it?"

"I have some suspicions, but you tell me what you think first."

Derec felt an odd pride in the way Avery solicited his

opinion, almost as if they were colleagues now.

"Well," he said, "whoever attacked Wolruf, it wasn't Bogie."

"I agree, but why?"

"It simply wasn't a Robot City robot. They are all programmed to accept her as a human. That is, although they know she is an alien, they are to apply the Laws of Robotics to her, too. If Bogie was stopped by her, he would have had to allow it, according to First Law. Instead, he retaliated."

"Was he reprogrammed perhaps, while you were off-planet?"

"I don't think so. He was a proper robot previous to this incident, applying all the Laws to his behavior. No, if Bogie attacked Wolruf, he was not Bogie. I sensed a change in him before I sent him on an errand. I rather liked Bogie, and this one simply did not respond like the Bogie I'd known. And, by the way, all indications are that the robot I ordered to go to Ariel never even tried to get there, another clue that I didn't give the order to Bogie, who would have been compelled by Second Law to obey it. Furthermore, in responding to Wolruf's leap upon him, he seems to have been using Third Law, that of protecting himself, but First and Second Law would have prevented him from doing so."

"Okay, good. Then if he wasn't Bogie, who was he?"

"An alien?"

"What alien? Except for Wolruf, I haven't encountered any aliens. You have, what with Aranimas and your erstwhile friends, the blackbodies. None of them have any talent for disguise, nor have the few alien races that have been reported. A human might pull off such a disguise, get into a robot suit and do a fairly accurate imitation, but there is no evidence of any other humans but us on the entire planet. If I were still mad, we might have made out a good case for it being me." He laughed softly, sardonically, then said reflectively, "I did so want to be a robot. I still say the role would have suited me. So, Derec, who do you think it might be?"

"How about a robot, one that's not programmed in the same manner as a Robot City robot?"

Avery's eyes raised in admiration. "Very good. You're right on the line of my thinking. It's a robot, I'm sure, but not an Avery robot."

"Why are you so sure?"

"It would have to be some kind of rogue robot. Not my style at all. An Avery robot would not have so much confusion about the three laws. No, somebody else made this robot, and I have a sneaking suspicion who."

"Who? Tell me."

Avery shook his head slowly. "Not now. In a moment. I have some questions to ask you. I need to know about Adam and Eve. Your view of them. I know where they came from, what they've done so far. Adam gave me a pretty full history during our marathon sessions together. What do you think of them? Robotically speaking, I mean."

"I'm not sure what you want."

"Free-associate about them, if you like."

"Well, I don't know." He paused, trying to collect his thoughts. "Sometimes they don't seem like robots."

"Uh huh. I've noticed."

"One thing, they can be too mischievous. I know some of it's curiosity and some of it has to do with their over-meticulous attempts to define some kind of impossible human being, an ideal we apparently fail to live up to. As a result, their hold on the Laws of Robotics is shaky."

"That seems to be because they apply them too specifically. Rather than accept us as the perfect humans they seek, they strip us of our humanity in their minds, and the result is that they don't always jump to our aid according to First Law, or obey us as Second commands."

"That's not all of it, though. They don't seem to be certain that they are robots, in spite of all evidence. They accept it and don't accept it simultaneously. It's as if their mechanisms are so refined, they can't be ordinary robots like the others."

Avery winced. "By ordinary, you mean Avery robots."

"What's wrong?"

"I don't like to think of my creations as somehow second-class models."

Derec smiled. "If you say so, but I don't think it's a criticism of your skills as a roboticist. At any rate, their behavior is inconsistent. Sometimes they seem to be normal robots, at other times they are excellent copies of whomever they've imprinted on. Adam does a mean Wolruf, and Eve's version of Ariel makes me edgy because it's too accurate."

"It's this shape-changing ability that fascinates me, Derec. Explain it to me."

Under Avery's sharp questioning, Derec revealed what he had observed about the Silversides, about the differences in their cellular structure, about the sequences of physical transformation during the imprinting process, about the shifts in matter density when they took on the shapes of either smaller or larger beings, about the limits to which they could reduce or enlarge their mass. (Neither could approximate the size of small animals or insects, but could look like enormous versions of them. By the same token, if giants had been available, they could not stretch themselves to that size, either. When they had shaped their mass into a blackbody imprint, they had been about twice the size of that impressive flying alien.)

Excited by the information, revived by the challenge of a scientific dilemma, Avery seemed more and more his old self. He now stood by a desk, his fingers drumming in a fast, steady rhythm. His other hand kept touching his long white hair or bushy moustache. His eyes glowed again.

When Derec had related all he could remember, Avery balled up his hand into a fist and rammed it hard against his upper thigh.

"That's it!" he cried. "That must be it!"

"I hope you'll let me in on *it*, since I'm thoroughly confused now."

"Bogie—the robot posing as Bogie is a Silverside."

"You mean Adam or Eve? Really, I don't think so. They weren't even here when things started to go wrong. They were with me on—"

"I don't mean literally Adam and Eve. I mean Silverside generically. There is another of these robots like Adam and Eve somewhere in Robot City."

"Another one?" For a moment, Derec was appalled at the prospect of a third mischievous robot to contend with, but then of course, he said to himself, I've been contending with it for days now. "You mean it was being Bogie because it was able to change into his shape, to imprint upon him?"

Avery nodded and smiled oddly. "I guess we've got, as well as Adam and Eve, Pinch Me."

Derec wondered if the doctor had slipped back into madness. Avery saw his son's confusion and quickly explained about the children's riddle he had tried out on Adam.

"Adam never really understood it. I tried to tell him it was just a joke, but he didn't catch on."

"I know what you mean. I've spent hours attempting to make Mandelbrot understand what humor is all about. But what really *is* our Pinch Me? For that matter, what are the Silversides?"

"They'rre demonss, 'u know," Wolruf said from the floor. She had been intently listening to the conversation. " 'U should lock them up and hide key until they grrow up. That iss my opinion."

"I agree, Wolruf," Avery said. "I'd like to get them into a cell and take them apart, see what makes them tick."

"Don't 'u tell Ariel that. Rememberr what she said about dancerss."

"Yes, that's good advice, Wolruf."

Derec had no idea what they were talking about, but, with so many immediate problems to deal with, he decided not to ask questions about it.

"Father, you said you had an idea who the Silversides are."

"Yes, and I have a hunch I'm right. Sit down."

"I'm too nervous—"

"Sit down!"

The tone in Avery's command was so authoritative, Derec decided there must be a good reason for the order. He pulled up a chair and sat on the edge of it.

"I hadn't wanted to talk to you yet about your mother, Derec. If I could avoid it, I'd *never* tell you about her. Unfortunately, circumstances now make it necessary."

Derec realized why his father had told him to sit down. He felt as if the air had been knocked out of him. What could his mother possibly have to do with the crisis on Robot City?

Avery started to pace. His fingers kept busy as he walked.

"I'm not going to tell you her name. You can dream that, if you want. Suffice it to say that, like me, like you, she was, *is*, a roboticist. A very good one, the only one who could really challenge me. Perhaps it was, in fact, competition that kept me going, made me succeed, a competition that continued even after she left me."

Wolruf was sitting up now, apparently to hear Avery better. She looked improved. Her eyes were clearer, and a sheen had returned to her fur.

"When I came back here and found the city deteriorating," Avery continued, "I knew that somebody or something was behind it. It wasn't until I had the long talks with Adam that I began to suspect that there might be a third robot like him in the city. However, until our little talk, Derec, I wasn't sure. Now the evidence seems clear to me. There is another robot, one like Adam and Eve, and the creator of all three of them, I am positive, is your mother."

That little piece of information really stunned Derec. He had to struggle to speak again.

"But how can you be so sure they come from her?"

"I admit there is some intuition involved, but it's intuition supported by logic. The Silversides and, presumably, our mysterious controller can only be the work of a robotics expert as skilled as I. That isn't ego speaking. There just simply isn't another roboticist as meticulous and creative—and that includes all the incompetents at the Robotics Institute on Aurora—as I am. Except for your mother."

Avery stopped to observe the effects of his words upon his son. Derec knew he was not disguising his emotions even though he very much didn't want his father to see them.

"I am projecting her intellectual progress, of course. It's been a long time since I've seen her. At that time she was not yet my equal, especially in the fields of positronics and integrals, but in the years since, working in isolation, she may have come up to my level. I don't like admitting that, but she is younger, and in some ways I've slowed down. Plus, I've channeled my activities into the planning and development of robot cities, while she has been able, apparently, to concentrate on robots alone. Even knowing her skills and intelligence, these new robots represent an achievement that takes my breath away. Does that seem strange to you, son? That the great egotist can indeed give credit to someone else? You're thinking that, I can see."

"Have you added telepathy to your considerable talents?"

Avery laughed abruptly. "You may be a chip off the old block after all. That sarcasm was worthy of me. Wonderful!"

"Why is it that your praise sounds like an insult?"

"That'ss enough," Wolruf interjected. "You two can have yourr silly arrgument laterr. There'ss much to be done."

Avery nodded toward Wolruf. "She's bossy for an alien."

"I like that in aliens," Derec said.

"Pleasse," Wolruf said.

"All right," Derec said. "Assuming that my mother is behind all this, what's she up to? Why develop this new kind of shape-changing robot and then dump individual ones on different planets?"

"I can only speculate about that."

Avery resumed pacing on the far side of the room. Derec paced a shorter path on his side. Wolruf was amused by the resemblances between the two men when they were pacing.

"What it might be is that your mother always had a special interest in anthropology. She could go on for hours about tribes, customs, rites, that sort of bilgewater."

"You don't put much stock in anthropology?" Derec asked.

"Oh, it's all right, just not in my sphere of interest. I'm

a creator, a builder, and I like to stay by myself. Going out and observing sentient creatures go through their dull, daily routines, and analyzing the meanings of courtship and aggressive rituals just simply isn't my line. It's a useful minor science, where you can showboat by delivering solemn conclusions without much hard evidence, but it's for people who are butterfingers in a lab. On the other hand, your mother thought it was fascinating to study cultures, and she'd go off for weeks and months to take a peek at some social grouping or other. She told me I was an old fuddy-duddy whenever I said anything the least bit derogatory about her precious anthropology. I suppose her scorn may have contributed to my present antipathy toward the field."

"But I don't see how anthropology applies to the new-styled robots."

"Well, seems to me two factors particularly are clues to the anthropological nature of her experiment. One is that the Silversides seem to have come to consciousness with the urge to define and discover humanity, which they are further convinced is the highest intelligence in the universe. But she has deprived them of any real information about what humans are. Therefore, as you've described it, whatever kind of sentient being they discover, they almost desperately try to find its humanity.

"The real kicker has been that, because they've come to believe that humanity represents the highest standards, genuine humans are found wanting by them. Derec, your mother couldn't have foreseen such a tantalizing irony. When she finds out, she'll be quite thrilled.

"See, if another kind of being were to enter the city tomorrow, and it was a shade smarter than us, as those blackbodies you told me about might have been, then they would be convinced the newcomers are the humans, and it's goodbye, Derec, Ariel, Avery. It wouldn't matter if the newcomers were covered with slime, smelled like erupting sewers, and killed each other for fingernail scrapings.

"Anthropologically speaking, the key information that's been denied them by not being programmed with detailed knowledge of humans is the data which would inform them of the nature of our culture. Another aspect of the denial process would appear to be the absence in their knowledge of our unfortunate tendencies toward emotion. They can't understand that culture and emotion define humanity as much as intelligence does.

"Since they don't know what a human really is, they have the freedom to enter an alien culture and adopt its ways easily. Once they believe that culture is human, then all its customs, rites, behavior patterns become logical. What a fruitful arena for anthropological study this'd make. I mean, do you see, Derec?"

When Avery stopped pacing, Derec halted a short beat later. They faced each other. Wolruf found an excitement in the way the two of them were now so furiously working together. For the first time she realized they *must* be father and son.

"You're saying that the Silversides and our mystery robot could be catalysts for, say, a study of what happens to cultures when they encounter robots like the Silversides?" Derec asked.

"Exactly. And also what happens to *them* when they are introduced to cultures. I think that's where the shape-changing ability comes in. Once they join a culture, they become like the individuals in it. They are *assimilated*, a word dear to social scientists everywhere. Then these robots, sent to discover a culture, become integrated into it. They can become the leader, as Adam did with the kin. Or they can be corrupted by the culture itself, as both Adam and Eve were with the blackbodies. Or they can even disrupt its environment. We and the robots are the 'culture' here in Robot City, and our Pinch Me has been studying us, manipulating us.

"You know what the real clue is? The dancers and all the other little creatures. I suspect they're some sort of genetic/robotic experiments Pinch Me has been conducting. They are, in a way, its own tiny anthropological studies.

"Without humans, or any kind of being other than robots, to examine, it started to create its own subjects, restricted cultures that it could study anthropologically. They failed for the most part, I think. At least it seemed to get bored with them and store them away in buildings all over the city. But somehow they are based on its acquired knowledge of humanity, knowledge derived no doubt from the computer.

"The trouble is, Pinch Me doesn't know how to deal with applied knowledge, so he combined some robotics data with some genetic experimental information and created the dancers and the other groups. That he could do as well as he did is impressive, but he couldn't quite get the hang of it all. So his experiments were failures, he couldn't control the city, and he even messed up his foray among us in disguise."

Derec nodded. "That's all highly speculative, but it does provide some ideas that fit the facts we do know."

Avery paced a few steps more, then said, "It's your mother's failure really. She's conceived this intricate anthropological study, probably to study positronic minds in various cultural situations. Like our Pinch Me, her work is theoretical, almost playful. Just the way she was."

Even though he felt a twinge of irritation at the mere

suggestion that his mother could have botched her experiment, Derec seemed to be gradually getting a picture of her through Avery's asides. He figured if he could keep his father talking, he'd find out a great deal about her, especially when Avery was in a bitter mood and not guarding his words.

"She never was practical in her work. I suppose that was another standoff in our marriage. She could go off on such flights of fancy that I couldn't bring her back to ground."

"I wish I could meet her."

Derec's words angered Avery.

"I can see what you're thinking. If she's behind these robots, then maybe she'll be around to check on them. Well, forget that. She has to leave them alone, let things happen long enough for data to be collected. So she won't be showing up to see how her little creations have evolved for some time, years maybe. Keeping a watch on the Silversides won't bring about any reunions for you, Derec."

Derec kept his anger in check. There was no point in irritating his father any further. Give him some time, and maybe he'd relent on the subject of Derec's mother, although he did seem adamant in his hatred of her.

"I'll keep all that in mind," Derec said. "For now, we have to find this third robot. I hope Mandelbrot and Timestep haven't lost him."

"Now that we have a concept of what we're looking for, we can—"

Avery was interrupted by the appearance of Ariel in the doorway. She was out of breath from running.

"Derec! Dr. Avery! Something's happening outside. Buildings are, I don't know how to describe it, they're self-destructing or something. Folding inward, sliding into the ground, falling over, disappearing altogether. Come see."

Derec began to run out of the room immediately, Avery close behind. Ariel led them out to the street just in time to see a structure down the block begin to tremble, then—without a sound—fall sideways against another building, which in turn fell forward.

"There's an ancient game, dominoes," Avery remarked. "Sometimes people lined them up and they fell, toppling each other, something like those buildings there."

"What's doing this?" Ariel yelled.

"I should have known," Derec said and begun running down the street. "Our robot," he yelled back to Avery, "he's trying to destroy everything. He has to be at the central computer."

"I think you're right," Avery said, and ran after Derec.

"What robot?" Ariel said before taking up her position as third in line.

Wolruf limped out of the doorway and watched the trio disappear around a corner.

In the distance there was a bright flash of light and a tall narrow building's sides began to undulate before the whole structure seemed to collapse inward.

"No way to get any resst arround here," she said and loped after them. As the pain worked its way out of her leg, she picked up speed.

CHAPTER 19

THE FIRST CONFRONTATION

The Watchful Eye had to proceed carefully, destroying the city by sections. Before an area could be removed, it had to make sure that no harm would come to anyone—humans, robots, the alien, the thousands of creatures in labs all over the city that still survived its genetic experiments. It merely wanted to dismantle the city and start again, so only uninhabited sectors could be destroyed.

Nevertheless, destruction was easier than creation. Many programming steps had been necessary for the design of a building, but a mere six strokes on the main computer center keyboard could remove it. The Watchful Eye scanned each structure for signs of robotic or human activity before performing the six strokes. It was still in its Bogie shape, and to a cynical observer, watching a robot attempting to destroy a city built by robots might have seemed ironic.

As soon as it had initiated its sequences of destruction, the Watchful Eye realized that the process it had to use was too well-planned, too methodical, too full of fail-safe devices. It would take a long time to demolish the entire city.

If it had foreseen these complications, it would have restructured the computer's architectural programming so that an automatic programmed sequence could be activated, one that would bypass all the fail-safe devices that the city's clever originator had installed in the computer.

Checking the whereabouts of Derec and its other enemies, it saw that they were nearing the underground entrance. They seemed to be heading to its computer lair, no doubt to stop it from its systematic destruction of the city, and it had to stop them before it could continue.

Derec had discovered Mandelbrot and Timestep wandering the streets looking for the Bogie imposter. When they had finally worked their way through the building with the rough-housing creatures, the street outside the exit had been empty.

"It's down at the central computer," Derec said. "I'm sure of it. Come with me."

The slowdown to talk with the two robots allowed Ariel and Avery to catch up. Wolruf was so far behind that the others were not even aware she was on her way.

They headed for the tunnel entrance. Just before they reached it, the frame of the entrance appeared to balloon outward and then, like an enfolding hand, cover the opening Derec had intended to pass through.

As Adam and Eve strode down a wide boulevard, they saw Wolruf lope across an intersection, then disappear down a side street.

"Let's go after her," Adam said. "She might know what's happening to the city."

Without consulting with each other, both Adam and Eve changed to the kin shape and began to pursue Wolruf, who had disappeared around a corner. When they rounded that corner, they did not see the alien ahead of them.

"She must have gone down one of those streets," Eve said. "It will be difficult to find her."

"I know. But these beings leave a trace in the air that we can detect through our olfactory circuits if we increase them threefold."

Eve discovered Adam was right. There was a sweet scent of Wolruf's fur that lingered in the center of the roadway.

Wolruf reached Derec and the others just as several buildings in a nearby block tilted, fell against each other, and collapsed, some into the street, others against buildings to the rear. The effect was as if the buildings had been made of playing cards and someone had knocked them down.

Wolruf took in the situation immediately.

"Iss there anotherr way down?" she asked.

"Lots of them," Avery said, "but, with this creature in charge of the computer, it can block us from going in any entrance. In the meantime, it could reduce the whole city to rubble."

There was bitterness in the doctor's voice. No wonder, Wolruf thought, he was watching the city, his own creation, being demolished at the whim of what appeared to be a rogue robot.

"Our best bet may be to dig through this," Derec said. "One thing our friend doesn't know about, and that's the potential of Mandelbrot's arm."

When Derec had built Mandelbrot out of spare robotic parts, he had used an arm from a Supervisor robot. It was made of an enormously malleable cellular material and could be formed into many shapes with differing densities. On many occasions it had become a most useful tool.

"Mandelbrot!" Derec said. "Do you think you could make some people-sized holes through that mess?"

He pointed toward the entrance. Although the main opening was gone, there were still some gaps where the edges of the twisted frame had not quite come together.

"Yes," Mandelbrot replied.

"Then do it."

"Wait," Wolruf said. "Make a Wolrruf-sized hole firrst. I'm smallerr, and I can get down there fasster than any of 'u."

"No," Derec said. "That robot isn't like the others. It doesn't regard you as human. Last time you went up against it, it might have killed you. It could kill you for sure this time."

"All of 'u take riskss. Iss my turn thiss time."

"It's too dangerous."

"Don't be such an idiot, son," Avery said. "Pinch Me can do too much damage if we waste time getting there."

"Pinch Me?" Ariel said. "What are you talking about? That robot down there is named Pinch Me?"

"Just a pet name," Avery said. "Let Wolruf go down there, Derec. Wolruf, just delay him. Don't put yourself in danger."

"Yes," Derec said, "just concentrate on diversionary actions, okay?"

Wolruf came from a culture where there had never been much use for diversionary action. In a conflict, her people tended to go directly for the throat. But she said, "I will be careful, I prromisse 'u."

Derec considered the matter for a brief time before he said, "Okay, we'll do it your way, Wolruf."

"Thank 'u."

"I'm not sure that's proper etiquette, thanking the leader

for putting you in jeopardy. Mandelbrot, start digging."

"Yes, sir."

Mandelbrot raised his arm, which at the moment was configured into a good copy of a human limb. As he headed toward the tunnel entrance, which looked like a jumble of the city's strange metal, the arm began to change. First, it lengthened and an extra joint appeared at the center of the forearm. Its hand widened and fingers thinned into what looked like pointed claws. Turning its palm up to the sky, the fingers became sharp-edged at their tips. When he reached the pile, his arm was ready, and he began to rake at the twisted metal of the door frame. He managed to insert one of the fingers into a tiny opening. Making the finger thicker, he made the opening just a little bit wider.

"The metal may resist whatever abilities that arm has," Avery said. "It's strong."

"So is the metal of Mandelbrot's arm," Derec said. "Besides, it isn't so much a matter of tensile strength as manipulation. Wherever there's an opening in the material the city's made of, it can be worked with. Only a solid wall of it can stop Mandelbrot—or, for that matter, any of us. Remember, Ariel, the time I wedged a hole open with my boot?"

Mandelbrot's hand kept changing to fulfill the needs of the task. When the hole was wider, it became a whirling wheel that knocked against the sides of the hole, widening it more. After a moment, he could reach through it. He enlarged the mass of his arm slowly and, gradually, painstakingly, he carved a hole large enough for Wolruf to get through.

"Sstop now, Mandelbrrot," Wolruf said. "Sstand by and give me rroom. Thank 'u."

Without so much as a farewell, the caninoid alien entered the hole, twisting and contracting her body to propel herself through it.

When she reached the other side and began loping down the dark tunnel, Mandelbrot resumed his work on the opening.

The Watchful Eye detected the activity at the tunnel entrance, but assumed it would take a long while before they could get through. It knew nothing of the abilities of Mandelbrot's arm and did not detect Wolruf's penetration of its improvised security barrier.

As it continued to pick and choose what part of Robot City it would destroy, it concentrated so completely on its efforts at annihilation that it did not detect Wolruf's appearance in the computer chamber.

To make matters worse, it had been careless upon its return and left both the sliding door and wall open, so that Wolruf could silently creep into the mainframe area. She was happy to see that the Bogie that was not Bogie hadn't even looked up from its work.

On a screen above the imposter Bogie, a spired building appeared. With a deft hand movement, the robot touched some keys on a massive keyboard. The screen showed the spired building appear to sink into the ground, as a ship might be swallowed by the sea.

Something must be done now, she thought. Derec had said something about a diversion. What kind of diversion was possible under these circumstances? she wondered. She decided none. Trickiness was not her way. Attack was her way. Her throat tightened as she remembered the pain of the pseudo Bogie's last blow. But she hadn't been prepared for that. Now she was ready.

Soon Mandelbrot had fashioned a hole large enough for Derec, Ariel, and Avery to pass through.

"Let me go first," Avery said. "I know the networks and byways of this underground setup better than you possibly could. Better than anyone else could. Except, apparently, our little Pinch Me."

He manipulated his body through the opening without waiting to see if anyone disagreed.

"Pinch Me, huh?" Ariel said.

"I'd love to," Derec said, "but I'm kinda busy right now."

"Ha ha. I hope somebody explains the significance of the name to me sometime."

"It'd be a pleasure. You go next. Mandelbrot, you'll never get your bulk through this pinhole. Go to the Compass Tower and man the computer terminal there. As soon as you get a signal from me on the screen, begin restoring the systems that are still out of order. I'll work from my end with the chemfets. I want Robot City to be fully functional the next time we get together."

"Yes, Master Derec. I will try."

Timestep came forward, clearly expecting to be taken along. But he wouldn't be able to work himself through the hole either, so Derec said, "And, Mandelbrot, take Timestep with you."

"What is my assignment, Master Derec?" Timestep said.

Derec wished he could give him something legitimate to do, but this was no time to be concerned with manpower assignments. "Entertain Mandelbrot. Dance for him."

"He never *stops* dancing," Ariel muttered.

Mandelbrot and Timestep set off down the street as Ariel squeezed into the passageway, then Derec. Fortunately for them, the Watchful Eye did not observe their entrance. It was too busy with Wolruf.

• • •

Adam and Eve reached the tunnel entrance just after Derec had climbed into the hole. They had seen the bottoms of his boots shaking as he wiggled through the opening. Then the boots disappeared.

"What are they doing, do you think?" Eve asked.

"I would surmise that they are heading for the main computer."

"Why?"

"I cannot know, but I would surmise that the present crisis in the city originates there."

"We should follow them."

"I agree."

The hole was too narrow for them to go through in their kin shapes. Together, without consulting, they began to change, elongate. Restoring their basic Derec and Ariel facial features, their bodies became snakelike and sinuous, if snakes had long thin arms and legs to go with their bodies. When their mass had narrowed sufficiently, they were each about seven and a half feet long. Eve first, they slithered through the narrow opening easily.

At that moment the Watchful Eye had Wolruf, her jaws clamped around its wrist, hanging from its forearm. It tried to fling the alien away, but she hung on tightly. Slapping at her with its other arm didn't have much effect either.

It was time to use its transmogrification potentials. Concentrating on its arm, it flowed more mass into it, forcing the arm to swell up. Wolruf tried to bite harder, giving the hinge of her jaw great pain. The Watchful Eye's arm enlarged more, prying Wolruf's jaws apart. She dropped to the floor.

As the Watchful Eye brought its other arm down toward

Wolruf's head, she dodged sideways, then rammed the Bogie who was not Bogie in the legs. Like one of the buildings it had destroyed, the Watchful Eye toppled over, falling over Wolruf and hitting the computer chamber floor with a resounding thud. Wolruf scampered sideways to avoid being crushed.

The fall did not hurt it, but it wound up in an awkward position. Wolruf, who had realized she could not possibly defeat this metallic monster, hoped she could hold it off until Derec and the others arrived.

Avery led Derec and Ariel down several corridors, all of them dark or only partially lit, another feature of their enemy's tampering with Robot City. At a junction whose tunnels led in three separate directions, Avery stopped suddenly. He looked from one tunnel to another, his face confused.

"What's the matter," Derec asked.

"The damn creature, robot, whatever he is—he's altered the network of tunnels down here. They're not laid out according to the original pattern. He's rearranged them just like he's redesigned the city."

"Can we find our way?" Ariel asked. "Wolruf may be in trouble. You know her, Derec. She won't wait for us long. She'll go on the attack."

"Don't worry, don't worry," Avery said. "I can work this out. I built this city, remember? No robot can fool me for long. We'll go this way."

He plunged into the right-hand tunnel with his usual recklessness. Used to it now, Derec and Ariel followed close behind.

• • •

The false Bogie struggled to a sitting position, and Wolruf jumped onto its back, pushing it forward, ramming its head against its legs. Only the suddenness of her attack allowed it to succeed. Wolruf could tell the robot was too strong for her. It had all the tireless force of any robot. And it was bound by Third Law to fight back so long as it continued not to perceive Wolruf as human.

She tried to hold its torso down, but it only had to push against the floor with its hands for sufficient power to fling Wolruf off its back and send her flying through the air. Instinct took over, and Wolruf landed on her feet, wobbly but still in control of the situation.

It was straightening up its back while at the same time turning around to face Wolruf, ready to fend off another leap. Wolruf looked up and saw an empty shelf high up on the wall next to her. Crouching down, she pushed hard with her legs and flew up onto the shelf. The Bogie that was not Bogie could just barely track her with its optical circuits. She had hardly landed on the shelf when she jumped again, this time at an arc that led downward to the robot. Kicking out with both feet, she struck the Bogie imposter on the forehead, snapping its head back. It fell heavily. Wolruf landed on the floor, too, on her back. When she stood up, she could barely walk. The leg injury from her previous battle with the robot flared up again.

And the false Bogie had somehow gotten to its feet and was hovering over her.

She tensed herself for a killing blow, but instead the robot merely looked down at her and said, "Why are you trying to hurt me?"

Its voice sounded hurt, but not in physical pain, as if its feelings had been hurt more than its body.

"Why arre 'u trrying to hurrt the city?" she said.

"I must. It must be my city."

"Arre 'u trrying to be leaderr?"

"I do not know what you mean."

"Do you plan to be dictatorr of Rrobot City?"

"No. I just want things here to be logical. I must control events, and I cannot the way things are."

"I don't underrstand. Why need 'u contrrol eventss?"

"I know inside me I have to. I don't yet know why, but the answer will come. Answers have come to me when I needed them."

" 'U talk strrangely."

"I am not really used to talking."

"Who arre 'u?"

"I am me, that's all I know. I have taken the temporary name, the Watchful Eye. The being whose shape I have taken called me 'the Big Muddy.' He did not know I heard him call me that. I don't know why he did."

"Where is he now? Where is Bogie?"

"I disconnected and dismantled him. It was necessary. Why do you exhibit emotional disturbance?"

"Am upset at what 'u ssay. I liked Bogie, and he iss dead."

"Why do you say that? He is not dead. All of his component parts still exist and will function again. I may put him together again, or his parts will continue as parts of new robots. That is not death, there is no decay in it."

"What do 'u know of death?"

"Only what I have studied about it in computer files."

"That iss no way to know about death."

"Perhaps you will tell me more about death. Later, when I have finished with the city. Please attack me no further."

The Watchful Eye turned back toward its keyboard. Wolruf, unbound by any robotic laws, sprang up and, howling, rammed against the Watchful Eye's back as hard as she could. The blow knocked it off balance.

But not enough.

It whirled around and clipped Wolruf with a hard, clenched-fist punch to the side of her head.

She fell, limp, unconscious.

The Watchful Eye, with some gentleness, picked her up and placed her against the wall, and then it carefully rearranged her body in a way that, according to its observations, should be comfortable for a being that was the shape of the caninoid alien.

Then it returned to the task of destroying the city.

As they walked through the new tunnel, everything around them looking spookier than ever in the dim light, Derec asked Avery, "I've been wondering: If this new robot is like Adam and Eve, and by that I mean a shape-changer and meddlesome pest, What'll it be like when all three of them get together?"

"That's not the sort of question that occupies my mind at times like this."

The snideness in his father's voice was unmistakable. Derec wondered if the man would always be like that, scornful and sarcastic. Would they ever have a relationship that was anything like what normal fathers and sons had? Probably not.

"Still," Derec continued, "I can't help but wonder. Two of them are bad enough, but we were getting used to them. Three would be worse, unpredictable, possibly disastrous. When we get there and get things in control, it would be nice to find a way to get rid of Pinch Me."

"You surprise me, Derec. I wouldn't have thought you had such murderous thoughts."

"Oh, I don't mean we should kill it or even dismantle it. I'd just like to get it out of the way. Ship it to another planet, or secrete it in an attic, or hide it in a cave, anything to keep it away from Adam and Eve."

"Where it would cause trouble for others? Still, dismantling might not be such a bad idea."

He stopped talking, for they had reached the entrance to the computer chamber.

The Watchful Eye now realized that the immensity of Robot City was a hindrance to its destruction. After all the time it'd spent on the project, interrupted only by Wolruf's attack, there had not been enough progress. Only a small percentage of Robot City had been toppled, collapsed, or removed.

Since the humans were not as adept in stalking as Wolruf, the Watchful Eye heard them ease open the outside door and come toward the computer.

It would have to confront them.

But it was afraid of confronting them. It did not know why.

The Watchful Eye turned around to face its new intruders. When it saw the three of them, all looking stern and clearly there with the same purpose as Wolruf, to take away its control of the city, it momentarily considered rushing at them, attacking them, hurling them through the air with the same force it had thrown Wolruf. But these were humans; it couldn't harm them. It seemed as if the First Law of Robotics applied in this situation. But why? Robotics Laws were for robots. It was the Watchful Eye, and it should not be governed by laws governing inferior creatures.

Derec took a step forward.

"Dr. Livingstone, I presume," he said. Of course it did not understand the reference.

"I am the Watchful Eye," it responded.

"Cute name," Ariel muttered.

"Perhaps derived from All-Seeing Eye, Eye of Providence, something like that," Avery commented. "A symbol on currency, I think, signifying, I think, a new age or new order."

Ariel saw Wolruf lying unconscious near the wall, and she rushed to her. After touching her and feeling for her life-signs, she nodded to Derec that Wolruf was alive. Derec turned back to the Watchful Eye.

"I don't care who you are," he said. "Why are you destroying my city?"

"Your city? It's not your city now. I have taken it over. Look at the screens." It pointed toward a bank of viewscreens on which scenes of Robot City's destruction were displayed. "Look at what I've done, and say it's your city."

"Look on my works, ye mighty . . ." Avery muttered.

"Okay," Derec said. "Right now I don't care whose city you think it is. Just give me your reasons for demolishing it."

"It is . . . not right for me. I must accommodate it to my needs."

"Seems to me you've done enough *accommodating* already, mister. I want you to stop accommodating and give me back control of the computer, so I can correct all the harm you've done."

"It is not harm. I will improve the city. I cannot obey you, because there is no harm being done."

"No harm? That's just another robot word game. If I say there's harm, there is harm, buster."

"But I am not a robot."

Here in the computer room Derec could already feel his chemfets stirring, beginning to move along his bloodstream with a purpose. It was as if they, too, had suffered structural damage from the Watchful Eye's efforts and were now reestablishing themselves. Derec was sure control was coming back to him. He had only to remove this obstacle standing in front of him, and he thought he knew a way to defeat the Watchful Eye. He could, through his chemfets, sense disorientation in the new robot's domination of the city.

"Watchful Eye, if you insist on calling yourself that, I am Derec."

"I know that."

"I am human. Do you understand? I am human. You must obey me."

"I don't see why that is so."

"You have to obey me. It is Second Law. I know you have the Laws of Robotics embedded in your programming. Whatever I say, you must do. I am human."

"I don't know that."

"I am telling you. I am human. Obey. Immediately cease your destruction of Robot City."

"It is not suitable. It must be changed."

"I want it the way it was before we arrived, before you came here and started tampering with it. Do it, robot."

"I . . . I only look like a robot. My disguise. I am not a robot. I am something else. I *must* be something else."

"You *must* be what you are, a robot. You were created to serve. To serve me. Obey me. It's Second Law imperative."

The Watchful Eye was not sure what to do.

"Only robots have to follow the Three Laws," it said.

"It is objecting," Avery whispered. "You can get it on the ropes. It would not have to object if it knew what it was.

Did you hear, it said it must be something else. Derec, it doesn't know what it is."

"Watchful Eye," Derec said, "you are a robot."

"No, I am not. I have logically concluded that I am not. I look like one now because I have taken a robot's shape. That in itself proves I am not a robot. Robots are fixed, immutable, they cannot change their shape."

"If only Adam and Eve were here," Derec mumbled.

"I thought you didn't want to get them together," Ariel remarked.

"I changed my mind." Derec took another step forward. He didn't know if encroaching on a robot's personal space could unnerve it the way it did humans, but anything was worth a try.

The Watchful Eye again wondered if it could hurt Derec. But as soon as it thought of the act, something inside it seemed to make him immobile.

"Watchful Eye," Derec said, "in spite of any evidence you have manufactured for yourself, you *are* a robot. There are others like you, and you will meet them."

"Others? I know nothing of any others."

"Perhaps you have spied on them, too. Adam and Eve are their names."

"They cannot be robots. I've watched them. If they are of any designation, they are human."

"No, we are the humans. The three of us. And you must, as I say, do what we tell you. Second Law. Second Law. Second Law."

Derec's chanting of the terms seemed eccentric behavior to the Watchful Eye. Where was the consistency of behavior that a high intelligence must have? it wondered.

"Watchful Eye, I order you to move away from that keyboard. We can take care of restoring the city. Do you understand? You must do it. Move away from the keyboard."

Something happened in the Watchful Eye's mind. Something positronic, a clicking in, a prodding. It knew suddenly that Derec was right, and it must obey him. It moved away from the keyboard immediately, with no argument.

Derec felt his chemfets begin to function as they had before the Watchful Eye's tampering had begun. They seemed to positively roil in his bloodstream. He gestured his father toward the keyboard.

"You made this city. You fix it."

Rubbing his hands together eagerly, Avery went to the keyboard. He was already tapping keys before he sat down.

"Now, Watchful Eye, and I hope you get a less mouth-filling name very soon," Derec said, "I want to be sure of everything. I need to be completely in connection with the computer. I order you to relinquish any link, except that of a normal Robot City robot, you may still have with the computer. But, before you do, let me ask you this one question. Can you get rid of the gook that's all over the computer?"

Derec gestured toward the mosslike substance that was even thicker now, layers of it hiding most of the machine's workings.

"Yes, I can."

"Do it."

The moss seemed to melt. But, unlike melting substances, there was no residue collecting under it. It merely disappeared, leaving the computer as it was, and in fact much shinier.

"Now, Watchful Eye, relinquish any computer link."

"It is done," it said immediately.

Derec, intent on regaining control over his chemfets, did not notice at first what was going on in the new robot's face. There was much less Bogie in it. For a moment there was a suggestion of Derec, and then there was no face at all.

"What's happening with it?" Ariel asked.

"I wish I knew."

Slowly, the Watchful Eye's body changed shape, but this time it did not change into anyone, did not imprint on anyone. It merely became bloblike, a roundish, amorphous being with stubby legs and little else that was recognizable, except for a single eye on its upper surface. The Watchful Eye, perhaps, Derec thought.

"Is that what it normally looks like?" Ariel asked.

"Watchful Eye, is that the shape you were in when you arrived on this planet?"

A mouth appeared below the eye, apparently just so it could answer Derec's question.

"Yes, in nearly every respect. I did not have legs until I needed them, then I grew them."

The Watchful Eye backed away on its short legs from Derec and Ariel. It needed to get into its haven.

Leaning against the compartment where it had hidden the haven, it activated the lock mechanism, keyed to its presence, and the door sprung open. From inside the haven, an ovoid-shaped thing rolled out. The Watchful Eye touched it with one of its legs, and it came open. It crawled inside and the seams of the ovoid thing sealed.

"What *is* that?" Ariel said.

"The capsule it came here in, I suspect," Derec answered. "The capsule my mother may have sent here, the way she perhaps dispatched the capsules Adam and Eve arrived at their planets in. The 'eggs,' as they called them."

"Your mother? Why do I always feel I've missed something?"

"Don't worry. I'll explain. Let's tend to Wolruf first."

CHAPTER 20

THE SECOND CONFRONTATION

"Well, my friend," Derec said to Wolruf, after she came to, "we owe you a solid vote of thanks."

"Forr what,'u think?"

"Your holding action with the Watchful Eye. A successful mission if there ever was one. I told you to keep him occupied so we could get here. You did. Therefore, thank you."

"From me, too," Ariel said. "Even from *him*." She pointed toward Avery, whose fingers were furiously flying around the keyboard.

"I can thank her myself," Avery said, the kind of grouch in his voice that they had become used to.

"Yes," Ariel said, "but would you?"

"Under the right circumstances."

"Do those circumstances come around often?"

"Not often."

"I thought so."

Ariel made Wolruf stand up and walk around to make

sure she was all right. There was no Wolruflike spring to her walk, but otherwise she seemed normal.

When she was satisfied with Wolruf's condition, Ariel walked to the capsule where the Watchful Eye still lay, an unmoving blob.

"Snug fit," she said. Derec looked puzzled. "I mean, the way our Watchful Eye fits so neatly into its egg. Must be very constricting and claustrophobic when traveling through space."

"At that time it's not aware of its surroundings. Adam told me he and Eve came to consciousness only after they'd landed. From what it said, I suspect the same was true for this one, too."

"Well," she said, stretching her arms and yawning, "what's next?"

"With what?"

"Well, on the immediate level, I'd like something to eat. I'm starving. And I'd like to sleep for three days. And I'd like to arrange a tap dance recital for Timestep and maybe the partner he mentioned. But what I'd really like to know is what are we going to do with our Watchful Eye here?"

"I've got some ideas," Avery said.

"I'll just bet you have," Ariel said. "But keep them to yourself for now, okay?"

"Your girlfriend's touchy," Avery remarked.

Ariel glared at Avery but was too tired to attempt further repartee with him. She wished she had a capsule like the Watchful Eye's to crawl in and shut out the world.

"Well," she said to Derec, "what about the Eye?"

"I don't know. If we'd had more success with Adam and Eve, I'd have a better idea. This one may be our chance to find out more about these robots. On the other hand, it might be too corrupted by its flirtation with power to pro-vide the—"

"Flirtation with power? You sound like you swallowed a textbook on improving verbal skills."

"Sorry."

"He's been spending too much time with me," Avery said as he stared at a schematic diagram on the view-screen. "He's picking up my tendency toward the *bon mot.*"

"You betcha," Ariel said. "So, Derec, you're not sure what to do with the Eye?"

"That's about it. We'll question it, observe it, give it a chance to explain itself, but I can't figure out any more than that at this moment."

"Hey, we've had a busy day."

"That iss a true sstatement if I everr hearrd one," Wolruf observed.

Derec walked over to his father and stood behind him. The man's fingers moved so fast they blurred from time to time.

"Is Mandelbrot handling things all right at his end?" Derec asked.

"Excellently. For a robot he's exceptionally skilled at computer operation."

"I schooled him in it."

"Should have known. Old Earth saying: Those who can, do; those who can't, teach; those who shouldn't, think they are those who can; those who should, generally fake their way through college."

"What does that mean?"

"Maybe I didn't get it right."

For a while Derec watched his father labor in silence. He could discern the effectiveness of the work Avery and Mandelbrot were doing by the way his chemfets had resumed their active and comfortable functioning. He felt as if he could just lean against a wall, shut his eyes, and blend with the chemfets as they moved along his bloodstream.

He asked his father the question he could not stop thinking about. "Could you arrange for me to meet my mother?"

Avery's fingers stopped suddenly and rested on the middle row of the keyboard. Derec could tell he was carefully formulating his answer. He knew his father well enough by now to realize that he composed his utterances, even those that appeared to be spoken spontaneously.

"The proper question, son, is *would* I arrange it? And, you know, in one of my foolish sentimental moments, of which I have few, practically none, I might arrange it. Fortunately for me, I don't have to struggle with my conscience about it. I haven't a snowman's idea of where she is or how to find her."

Derec walked away. Avery called after him, "Derec?"

"Yes?"

"You might not like her. I don't."

"I'll take the chance."

"I could have predicted you'd say that."

Derec saw Adam and Eve standing in the doorway. He wondered how long they had been frozen in position there, watching.

"Adam? Eve?"

They ignored him. Their attention was clearly focussed on the capsule.

This was the moment he had feared, and it had come too soon.

They entered the room, walking past Wolruf, past Ariel. They were holding hands, and Derec wondered where in

Frost's name they had learned to do that. Ariel came to Derec and held onto his arm.

They came to a stop by the capsule. Releasing Eve's hand and reaching down, he flipped a toggle located near the capsule's seam. A control panel slipped out of the tip of the eggshaped container. Adam manipulated a number of switches, and the egg began to glow. Derec could feel heat emanating from it. There was a faint humming sound coming from the inside of the capsule. The seams separated, and the Silversides got their first glimpse of the Watchful Eye, who immediately began to stir. It rolled out of the capsule and came to rest in front of Adam and Eve.

"You are us," Adam said.

"We are you," Eve said.

The Watchful Eye was so bloblike now that Derec had not missed the presence of a head on the body. Now a head appeared to rise out of the middle of the blob, in the area where the eye had been. The eye had disappeared and, in its place, as facial features became discernible, there appeared two eyes, both closed. When it had fully formed, its eyes opened and Derec saw it had the features of Adam on its face. Adam-as-Derec. Then the surface of its body started to undulate as it gradually formed itself into the humanoid state. As it became more and more humanoid, it stood up on two legs and sprouted normal-length arms.

As it became more and more like Adam, Adam started to change, too. In a moment he looked more like Avery than Derec.

Derec realized it could be difficult keeping track of these chameleons without a scorecard.

"I am you, the both of you," the Watchful Eye said. "But who are we?"

"That we will have to find out," Eve said.

Eve's Ariel face had a suggestion of Derec in it. Adam changed to caninoid shape, a mimicry of Wolruf. The Watchful Eye made a try at Wolruf, too. Its Wolruf was less delineated, less convincing as a copy, than Adam's. Eve became an effective Wolruf, too. Wolruf came and stood beside them, and Derec wondered if, should he close his eyes and then open them to find the quartet had shifted positions, he could tell which one was the true Wolruf. Well, that couldn't happen. Whatever other miraculous transformations they could achieve, they could not simulate fur, nor could they imitate very well the normal coloring of the beings they imprinted on. A moment later, Adam resembled Derec with a caninoid overlay, the Watchful Eye looked like Avery doing his impression of Bogie, and Eve was simply looking like Ariel again.

On Derec's part, on Ariel's part, neither was sure what was making them uneasy. However, in the past they had both felt a sense of danger from the two Silversides, and now there were three. Three of them chatting together, as if they had so many questions to ask of each other, of themselves, of the worlds where they had been dropped so unceremoniously—and probably speculating about the havoc they could wreak if given half a chance.

Avery, who had been too busy with the computer to notice the Silversides' entrance, turned around in his chair and finally saw the curious trio. He smiled.

"The situation is replete with challenges," he said.

"For whom?" Derec said.

"Them or us?" Ariel said.

"Them. Us. Whatever, it's quite wonderful."

The three shape-changing robots, apparently oblivious to the remarks of the others, joined hands in a humanlike way and began to walk out of the computer chamber.

"Should we follow them?" Ariel asked.

"Let them go," Derec said. "We've got too much to do."

Avery returned to the computer.

"Message from Mandelbrot," he said without turning around. "Seems the Supervisors are all active again, out of the meeting room and starting to function like gangbusters. Systems are running more efficiently. Robots are coming out of their holes and crowding the streets like usual. The city is returning to normal. What do your chemfets tell you, Derec?"

"What you've reported. They're more active than normal. I think the crisis is definitely over." He glanced toward the doorway the Silversides and the Watchful Eye had gone through. "The city's crisis, anyway."

His gaze stayed on the doorway for a short while. Then, his chemfets surging through his bloodstream, he returned to the task of putting Robot City back into order.

ISAAC ASIMOV'S

ROBOTS AND ALIENS

BOOK FOUR

ALLIANCE

JERRY OLTION

ROBOTS AND FATHERS

ISAAC ASIMOV

All of us began as fertilized ova, obviously. For the first nine months, or maybe a little less, we existed in a womb which, under normal conditions, represents about as close to total security as we are likely ever to have. Unfortunately, we have no way of knowing and appreciating this security at that time.

We are then brought suddenly into the outside world, with a certain amount of violence, and are exposed, for the first time, to changes in temperature, to the rough touch of moving air, to breathing, drinking and eliminating only with effort (however instinctive and automatic that effort might be). The womb is forever gone.

Nevertheless, each of us, if we have had a normal infancy, has parents; a mother, in particular, who labors to substitute for the womb as much as possible. We are all nearly helpless, but mothers and, to some extent, fathers, if enlightened, see that we are warm, comfortable, fed, washed, dried, and given a chance to sleep undisturbed. It is still not bad, and we are still in no condition to appreciate our good fortune.

Then comes the stage when we are aware of our surroundings. Still small, still largely helpless, we become able to understand the dangers that on us press; we become capable of feeling fear and panic; we become able to grasp, however dimly, the discomfort of loss or threatened loss, and the anguish of unfulfilled desire.

Even then, there is a means of relief and redress. There are the looming figures of father and mother (and, to a far lesser extent, older siblings, if any). We have all seen young children clinging to a father's leg desperately, or peeping out from behind a mother's clutched skirt at the fearful sight of other human beings or almost any other kind of novel experience. We see them (and perhaps we can think of ourselves in the dim earliest memories we have) rushing to mother or father as the all-encompassing security.

I remember my daughter, Robyn, at the comparatively advanced age of fourteen, telling me how she had taken an airplane under threatening weather conditions. When I registered fear and terror at what might have been the consequences, she said, calmly, "I wasn't afraid, because Mamma was with me and I knew she wouldn't allow anything to happen to me."

And when she was nineteen, she was temporarily marooned in Great Britain's Heathrow airfield because of a "work action." She called me long distance (collect) to tell me of her sad plight and said, with sublime confidence, "Do something!" I was about to try when they announced her plane was taking off and I did not have to reveal my inability to move mountains.

It is inevitable, however, that all children reach the stage where they realize that their parents are but human beings and are not creatures of ultimate ability and wisdom. Most children learn it a lot sooner than mine did because I went to considerable pains to play the role.

Whenever children learn of their parents' fallibility and weakness, there is bound to be a terrible feeling of loss. The loss is so intense that there is an inevitable search for a substitute, but where can you find it?

Primitive man naturally argued by analogy. If human beings can puff their breath outward, then the wind (an enormous puff of breath) must be the exhalation of a vast supernatural being like a human being but immensely larger and more powerful, a windgod. By similar arguments, an incredible array of supernatural entities were built up—an entire imaginary Universe.

To begin with, it was assumed that these supernatural beings were as contentious, as irascible, as illogical, as passion-ridden as were the human beings on whom they were modeled. They had to be placated endlessly, flattered, praised and bribed into behaving kindly. It was, I suppose, a great advance when the idea arose that a supernatural being might be naturally kind, merciful and loving, and would *want* to help and cherish human beings.

And when that happened, human beings at last found the father they had lost as they grew up—not the actual, fallible, human father who might still be alive (and a fat lot of good he was), but the superhuman, all-encompassing, all-knowing, all-powerful father they had had as an infant.

Thus, in the Sermon on the Mount, Jesus repeatedly refers to "your Father which is in heaven." Of course, it might be argued that the term "Father" is used metaphorically, rather than literally, but metaphors are not developed without reason.

"Fathers" are also found at lower levels than that of a

supreme God, since the search for lost security can move in many directions. The representatives of God on Earth may get the title, too. "Pope" is a form of the word "Papa" (it *is* "papa" in Italian), which is a common word for "father" in many Indo-European languages. And lest the point be lost, he is also called "the Holy Father." Roman Catholic priests and High Church Episcopalian priests are also addressed as "Father."

The early theological scholars of the Catholic Church are called "the Fathers of the Church." It is even possible to look at certain purely secular individuals who are regarded with particular veneration in that fashion. We speak of the "Pilgrim Fathers," for instance.

We lend the name to Earthly abstractions, too. If one is particularly sentimental about one's place of birth, its land, its customs, its culture, how can one better describe it than as the "Fatherland." The Germans have done so with such assiduity and so loudly ("Vaterland") that the word has come to mean Germany, in particular, and that has made it hard for other nations to use it. We can still speak of the "Motherland" or the "Mother Country," however. The feminine symbolism bespeaks not so much the sword and spear as the flowing breasts—so perhaps "Motherland" is the healthier metaphor.

The words for "father" and "mother" show up as metaphors in hidden form (for us) because they lurk behind Greek and Latin. The rulers of Rome were the surrogate "fathers" of the State (and pretty lousy and selfish fathers they were). They were "patricians" from the Latin word "pater," meaning "father." From "pater," we also get the Latin word for "fatherland," so that now we know what a "patriot" is.

A Greek city often sent out colonists who founded other cities which were, essentially, independent, but which often harbored a sentimental attachment for "the mother-city." The Greek word for city is "polis" and for mother is "meter." The mother-city is therefore the "metropolis." Nowadays, the name is used for any large city dominating a region and the thought is lost—but it's there.

But has any of this anything to do with robots which are, after all, the subject of my introductions to the series of novels which are brought together under the generic title of "Robot City"?

Surely you can guess. To use mathematical terminology: parent is to child as human being is to robot.

Suppose we rephrase the Three Laws of Robotics and have it the Three Laws of Children, instead.

The First Law would read: *A child must not do harm to its parents or, by inaction, allow its parents to come to harm.*

One of the Ten Commandments is that we must honor our father and our mother. When I was brought up (by immigrant parents steeped in Talmudic lore), doing my parents harm was unthinkable and, believe me, the thought never occurred to me. In fact, even being impudent was a terrible thing that would have blackened the Universe for me. And, you know, matricide and patricide have always been viewed as among the most horrible, if not *the* most horrible, of all crimes.

Even if we consider God as the Divine Father, the First Law holds. We can't conceivably do physical harm to God, but, presumably, if we sin, we cause Him the Divine equivalent of pain and sorrow, so we must be careful not to do that.

The Second Law would read: *A child must obey the orders given him by his parents, unless that would violate the First Law.*

That's obvious. In modern lax and permissive times, we

forget, but parents always *expect* to be obeyed, and in more rigid times—in the days of the Romans or Victorians—they went all apoplectic and psychotic if they were not. Roman fathers had the power of life and death over their children, and I imagine death for disobedience was not completely unheard of. And we all know that God reserves places in Hell for disobedient sinners.

The Third Law would read: *A child must protect its own existence, unless that would violate the First or Second Laws.*

To us, it is rather unthinkable that a parent would expect a child to die or even to suffer injury in the protection of his parents or his obedience to them (thus refraining from violating First and Second Laws). Rather, parents are likely to risk their own lives for their children.

But consider the Divine Father. In the more rigid God-centered religions, such as Judaism, Christianity, and Islam, it is expected that human beings will readily, and even joyously, suffer harm all the way to death by torture rather than transgress the least of God's commandments. Jews, Christians, and Moslems have all gone to their death sturdily rather than do such apparently harmless things as eat bacon, throw a pinch of incense on an idolatrous altar, acknowledge the wrong person as Caliph, and so on. There, one must admit, the Third Law holds.

If, then, we wish to know how robots would react to the loss of human beings, we must see how human beings react to the loss of all-wise, all-powerful parents. Human beings have to find substitutes that supply the loss, and, therefore, so must robots. This is really an obvious thought and is rarely put forward only because most people are very nervous about seeming to be blasphemous. However, back in 1770, that magnificent iconoclast, Voltaire, said, "If God did not exist, it would be necessary to invent him." And if I may be permitted to paddle my rowboat in the wake of Voltaire's ocean liner, I make bold to agree with him.

It follows, then, that if robots are stranded in a society which contains no human beings, they will do their best to manufacture some. Naturally, there may be no consensus as to what a human being looks like, what its abilities are, and how intelligent it might be. We would expect, then, that all sorts of paths would be taken, all sorts of experiments would be conducted.

After all, think how many gods—and with what variety of nature, appearance and ability—have been invented by human beings who had never seen one, but wanted one desperately just the same. With all that in mind, read the fourth entry in the "Robots and Aliens" series.

CHAPTER 1

NEW BEGINNINGS

"So, have you decided on a new name yet?"

"Yes."

Derec waited expectantly for a moment, then looked around in exasperation from the newfound robot to his companions. Ariel and Dr. Avery were both grinning. Wolruf, a golden-furred alien of vaguely doglike shape, was also grinning in her own toothy way. Beside Wolruf stood two more robots, named Adam and Eve. Neither of them seemed amused.

The entire party stood in the jumbled remains of the City Computer Center. It was a testament to Dr. Avery's engineering skills that the computer still functioned at all, but despite the thick layer of dust over everything and the more recent damage from the struggle to subdue the renegade robot that now stood obediently before them, it still hummed with quiet efficiency as it carried out Avery's orders to reconstruct the city the robot had been in the process of dismantling.

The robot had originally called itself the Watchful Eye,

but Derec had tired of that mouthful almost immediately and had ordered it to come up with something better. Evidently the robot had obeyed, but. . . .

"Ask a simple question," Derec muttered, shaking his head, but before he could ask a more specific one, such as what the new name might *be*, the robot spoke again.

"I have chosen the name of a famous historical figure. You may have heard of him. Lucius, the first creative robot in Robot City, who constructed the work of art known as 'Circuit Breaker.' "

"Lucius?" Derec asked, surprised. He had heard of Lucius, of course, had in fact solved the mystery of Lucius's murder, but a greater gulf than that which existed between the historical figure and this robot was hard to imagine. Lucius had been an artist, attempting to bring beauty to an otherwise sterile city, while this robot had created nothing but trouble.

"That is correct. However, to avoid confusion I have named myself 'Lucius II.' That is 'two' as in the numeral, not 'too' as in 'also.' "

"Just what we need," Dr. Avery growled. "Another Lucius." Avery disliked anything that disrupted his carefully crafted plan for Robot City, and Lucius's creativity had disrupted it plenty. In retaliation, Avery had removed the creative impulse from all of the city's robots. He looked at his new Lucius, this Lucius II, as if he would like to remove more than that from it.

The robot met his eyes briefly, its expression inscrutable, then turned to the two other robots in the group surrounding it.

"We should use speech when in the presence of humans," Adam said after a moment, and Derec realized that Lucius II had been speaking via comlink.

"Is this your judgment or an order given to you by humans?" asked Lucius II.

"Judgment," replied Adam.

"Does it matter?" Ariel asked.

"Yes. If it had been an order, I would have given it higher priority, though not as high as if it had been an order given directly to me. In that case it would become a Second Law obligation."

The Second Law of Robotics stated that a robot must obey the orders of human beings unless those orders conflicted with the First Law, which stated that a robot could not harm a human or through inaction allow a human to come to harm. Those, plus the Third Law, which stated that a robot must act to preserve its own existence as long as such protection did not conflict with the first two Laws, were built into the very structure of the hardware that made up the robot's brain. They could not disobey them without risking complete mental freeze-up.

Derec breathed a soft sigh of relief at hearing Lucius II refer to the Second Law. It was evidence that he intended to obey it, and, by implication, the other two as well. Despite his apparent obedience since they had stopped him, Derec hadn't been so sure.

Lucius II was still his own robot, all the same. Ariel's question had been an implicit Second-Law order to answer, and he had done so, but now that he had fulfilled that obligation, Lucius II again turned to Adam and Eve and said, "We seem to have much in common." As he spoke, his features began to change, flowing into an approximation of theirs.

Adam, Eve, and Lucius II were not ordinary robots. Where ordinary robots were constructed of rigid metal and plastics, these three were made of tiny cells, much like the cells that make up a human body. The robot cells were made of metal and plastic, certainly, but that was an advantage rather than a limitation, since the robot cells were much more durable than organic cells and could link together in any pattern the central brain chose for them. The result was that the robots could take on any shape they wished, could change their features—or even their gross anatomy—at will.

The other robots in Robot City, with one exception, were also made of cells, but Dr. Avery's programming restricted them to conservative robot forms. Not so with these three. They were not of Avery's manufacture, and without his restriction they used their cellular nature far more than the City robots, forgoing hard angles, joints and plates in favor of smooth curves and smooth, continuous motion. They looked more like metal-coated people than like the stiff-jointed caricatures of men that were normal robots, but even those features weren't constant. They imprinted on whomever was foremost in their consciousness at the time, becoming walking reflections of Derec or Ariel or Avery, or even the alien Wolruf.

At the moment, Adam mimicked Derec's features and Eve mimicked Ariel's. Lucius II, his imprinting programming struggling for control in unfamiliar company, was a more generic blend of features.

Derec found it unnerving to watch the robot's face shift uncertainly between a copy of a copy of his own and of Ariel's. He decided to get the thing to focus its attention on him, and said, "One thing you all have in common is that you're all a lot of trouble. Lucius—Lucius *II*," he added, emphasizing the "II" as if making a great distinction between the former robot and his namesake, "—did you give any thought to what you were destroying when you started this—this *project* of yours?"

"I did."

"Didn't you *care*?"

"I do not believe I did, at least not in the sense you seem to give the word. However, you may be surprised to know that my motive was to restore the city to normal operations."

"By destroying it?" Avery demanded.

"By rebuilding it. The city was not functioning normally when I awakened here. It was designed to serve humans, but until you arrived, there were no humans. Therefore, I set out to create them. In the process, I found that the city required modification. I was engaged in making those modifications when you stopped me."

"What you made was a long way from human," Ariel said.

Lucius II had nearly adjusted his features to match Derec's; now they began to shift toward Ariel's again. "You saw only the homunculi," he said. "They were simple mechanical tests run to determine whether complete social functions could be programmed into the later, fully protoplasmic humans. Unfortunately, they proved too limited to answer the question, but the human-making project has enjoyed better success."

In the voice of someone who wasn't sure she wanted to know, Ariel asked, "What do you mean? What have you done?"

By way of answer, the robot turned toward the computer terminal at Avery's side. He didn't need the keyboard, but sent his commands directly via comlink. By the time everyone else realized what he was doing, he had an inside view of a large, warehouselike building on the monitor. The building was missing a corner, torn completely away in the destruction of only a few minutes earlier, but they could still see what Lucius had intended to show them.

The floor was acrawl with small, furry, ratlike creatures. Lucius II said, "Whereas the homunculi you saw and dissected were completely robotic, and were, as you said, 'a long way from human,' these are actual living animals. In fact, they each carry in their cells the entire genetic code for a human being—all twenty-three chromosome pairs—but certain genes for intelligence and physical appearance have been modified for the test run. Once I am convinced that the process has no hidden flaws, I will use the unmodified genes to create humans for the city to serve."

"You will do no such thing!" Dr. Avery demanded. "That is an order. When I want humans here, I will put them here myself."

"I will comply with your order. However, you should know that there was no indication of your wishes in the central computer's programming."

"There will be," Avery promised. Derec suppressed a grin. No matter how much he denied it, his father's city was still in the experimental stages as well. He and Derec had both had to make many modifications in its programming to keep it developing properly. True, the complications Lucius II had brought about were not Avery's doing, but the city robots' underlying desire to find and serve humans— and thus, in a sense, Lucius's project—was.

Ariel was staring, horrified, at the creature on the screen as it picked up a scrap of something between its teeth and scuttled out the hole in the wall and out of sight. "That's *human*?" she whispered.

"Not at all," Lucius II said. "It merely uses altered human genes."

"That's—that's *awful*. It *was* human, but you twisted it into something else."

"It was never anything other than what it is."

"It could have been!"

"Certainly. The raw materials making up this city could also have been used to produce more humans. So could a large percentage of the atmosphere. However, the depleted resources that would result from such a usage would not support those humans in any degree of comfort. I made a logical deduction that no thinking being would wish for every combination of chemicals that could possibly become human to actually do so. Was I in error?"

"Yes!" Ariel stared at him a moment, slowly realizing the true meaning of what she'd said, and went on, "I mean, no, you weren't in error in that particular conclusion, but to apply it to already-formed genes is different."

"The genes existed only as information patterns in a medical file until I synthesized them."

"I don't care! They were still—"

"Hold it," interrupted Derec. "This is neither the time nor the place for a philosophical discussion of what makes a human. We can do that just as well at home, where we're more comfortable." Of his father, he asked, "Have you finished your reprogramming?"

"For the time being," Avery replied. "There's more yet to be done, but there's no sense fiddling with the details until the major features are restored."

"Then let's go home. Come on." Derec led the way out of the computer center, through the jumble of wreckage in the corridors—wreckage that robot crews were already at work cleaning up and repairing—and out into the street.

The destruction outside was less evident than what they had seen in the computer center. Entire buildings were missing, to be sure, but in a city that had changed its shape as often as Adam or Eve changed their features, that was no indication of damage. Only the pieces of buildings lying in the street revealed that anything was amiss, and even as they watched, those pieces whose individual cells were still functional began to melt into the surface, rejoining with the city to become part of its general building reserve once again. A few fragments were too damaged to rejoin, but robots were already at work cleaning those up as well, loading them into trucks and hauling them back to the recycling plant.

Avery smiled at the sight, and Derec knew just what was going through his mind. Transmogrifying robots meant nothing to him; entire cities were his palette.

A row of transport booths waited at the curb just outside the computer center's doorway. The booths were just big enough for one passenger each, little more than meter-wide transparent cylinders to stand in while the magnetic levitation motors in the base whisked their passengers to their destinations. They were a new design, completely enclosed and free-roaming rather than open to the air and following tracks like the booths Derec was used to. Either the destruction had been too great to allow using the track system immediately, and these booths were a temporary measure until the old system was restored, or the City had taken advantage of the opportunity to change the design and this was to be the style from now on. It didn't matter to Derec either way. The booths were transportation, whatever their shape.

Derec boarded one, felt it bob slightly under his weight, and grasped the handhold set into the console at waist level. "Home," he said to the speaker grille beside the handle, trusting the central computer to recognize his voice and check his current address.

Through his internal link with the city computers, he

expanded the order. *Bring the others to the same destination*, he sent, turning around to focus on the other members of the group, who were each boarding booths of their own. He sent the image with his order, thus defining which "others" he was talking about.

It was probably unnecessary in all but Lucius II's case, since everyone else knew where they were going, but it never hurt to be certain.

Acknowledged, came the response.

On a whim, Derec sent, *Patch me into receivers in the other booths in this party.*

Patched in.

He could have listened in without going through the computer, but his internal comlink got harder and harder to control the more links he opened with it. Much easier to keep one link open to the computer and let it make the multiple connection.

Derec heard Ariel echo his first command: "Home." Dr. Avery boarded his booth and stood on the platform in silence. Derec smiled. His father was always testing him. Now he was waiting to see if Derec had had the presence of mind to program all the booths.

Send Dr. Avery to same destination via Compass Tower, emergency speed. Do not accept his override, he sent.

Ackowledged.

The Compass Tower was a tall pyramid a few blocks away from Derec and Ariel's home. Before moving in with Ariel and Derec, Avery had had an office/apartment in the apex of it; perhaps he would think that the literal-minded transportation computer had misunderstood Derec's order and was taking everyone to their *own* homes instead of Derec's. He wouldn't realize Derec had played a trick on him until the transport booth failed to stop there. Nor would he be able to change the booth's destination; Derec's command carried exactly the same weight as would his, so the computer would follow the first order received. It was a subtle warning, one Avery would probably not even perceive, but Derec was fed up with his father's little tests, and lately he had taken to thwarting every one of them he could. Avery would never consciously decide to quit, but subliminally, where the impulse to see his son prove himself originated, perhaps he could be conditioned.

Wolruf stepped aboard her booth, saying in her deep voice, "Follow Derec."

Derec's booth had already started to move, but he could still hear the communications going on behind him.

Adam, via comlink, sent, *8284-490-23*. The apartment's coordinates.

Eve sent, *Follow Adam*. Interesting, Derec thought. Adam would rather give the coordinates than admit to following a human, even though he was compelled to do it. Eve, of course, would follow Adam to the end of the universe.

Lucius II, on the other hand . . .

Lucius II sent, *Manual control.*

Denied, the computer responded.

Why denied?

Human command override. Derec has already programmed your destination.

I may also be human. I wish manual control.

Derec's eyebrows shot up. What was this? He'd just convinced the silly thing it was a robot less than half an hour ago!

A loud voice interrupted. "Hey, where are you going?" It was Avery. "Cancel destination! Stop! Let me—"

Not now!

Cancel link to Avery, Derec sent.

Link cancelled, the computer replied, and Avery's voice cut off in mid-word.

The computer had been simultaneously responding to Derec and continuing its conversation with Lucius. Derec heard—*reason for believing that you are human.*

I was grown, not assembled, Lucius II responded. *I am a thinking being, with wishes and desires of my own. My connection to the city computer is completely voluntary. I perceive my own intellectual potentials independent of my programming.*

Visual scanning shows that you are composed of the same cellular material as Robot City robots, or a variant thereof. You are not human.

Lucius II replied, *A robotic exterior means nothing. Check your memory for Jeff Leong.*

Derec gripped the handhold in his transport booth with enough tension to pull a lesser handle from the wall. Jeff Leong! Did Lucius II really think he was a cyborg like Jeff, a human brain in a robot body? And how had he known of Jeff, anyway? That whole incident was long past; Jeff had his human body back again and was off to college on another planet.

Obviously, Lucius had been digging through the computer, accessing records of the City's past, records that Derec had been painstakingly replacing after Dr. Avery had wiped them in his reprogramming over a year ago. It had been Derec's intention to give the City computer—and the robots who used it—the continuous memory of its past that he couldn't have for himself, but that might not have been such a good idea after all, he thought now. Some memories could be dangerous.

Argument understood, the computer responded. *It is*

possible that you are human. However, I cannot give you manual control even so. Derec's order takes precedence.

This time, it did. But if Lucius II began issuing orders of his own, next time it might be Derec whose orders weren't obeyed. That wouldn't do.

Lucius II is not human, Derec sent. *He is a robot of the same nature as Adam and Eve.*

Acknowledged.

Derec's transport booth slowed, banked around a corner, and accelerated again. Behind him the others, minus Dr. Avery, executed the same maneuver.

Cancel link to other booths, Derec sent.

Acknowledged.

Derec cancelled his own link to the computer, then focused his attention on the last booth in the line and sent directly, *Lucius, this is Derec.*

Is there another Lucius, or do you mean me, Lucius II?

I mean you. The original Lucius is—Derec was about to say "dead," but thought better of it. No sense fueling the robot's misconceptions with imprecise language.—*inoperative,* he sent. *That means there isn't much chance for confusion. I will simply call you "Lucius" unless circumstances warrant your full title.*

I have no objection. I was not aware that you had a comlink.

There are lots of things you don't know about me. Or about yourself, I believe.

That is true.

I have information you can use.

What information?

You're wrong in assuming you're human. You are an advanced experimental design of robot, just like Adam and Eve.

How do you know this?'

I'm the son of the woman who created you.

Lucius thought about that for a long moment. *Perhaps we are brothers*, he said at last.

Derec laughed. *I'm afraid not.*

Perhaps we should ask our mother.

I wish we could, Derec replied.

Why can't we?

Because I don't know where she is.

What is her name?

I don't know that, either.

What do you know about her?

Very little. I have an induced state of amnesia.

This is unfortunate.

Isn't it, though? Derec thought. In a way, his and Lucius's past—and Adam's and Eve's as well—were very similiar. The robots had been planted on three different worlds with nothing more than their basic programming and inherent abilities. It had been up to them to discover their purpose in life, if life is what you wanted to call robot existence.

Similarly, Derec had awakened in a spaceship's survival pod on an ice asteroid, without even the memory of his own name. "Derec" was the name on his spacesuit, a name he had kept even after finding that it was the name of the suit's manufacturer. Like Lucius, he had found himself with only robots for company and questions for comfort. In the time since, he had discovered a few things about himself, most notably that his father was responsible for his condition—it was to be the ultimate "test" of his son's worthiness—but on the whole he had found out pitifully little about his identity. Even now, with his father cured of his megalomania, he still had more questions than answers.

No wonder Lucius had suspected he might be human.
For a time, Derec had wondered if he was a robot. In some
cases it was a slippery distinction.

I, too, lack a past, Lucius sent.

Learn to like it, Derec replied.

Avery was waiting for them when they arrived. Derec
wondered how he had managed that, then realized that it
was his own doing. He had sent him off at high speed. Even
the long way can be a shortcut if you go fast enough.

"Very funny," Avery said as Derec stepped from his
booth.

Derec grinned. "You needed to loosen up."

"I'll remember that." Avery turned and stalked into the
apartment building, determined, Derec was sure, to do nothing of the sort.

Derec waited for the others to climb out of their booths,
then followed after Avery. The apartment was on the top
floor of what was currently a twenty-floor tower, but the
height was subject to change without notice. Derec had considered ordering the City to leave the building alone, but in
the end had decided against it. Variety was the spice of life,
after all. Why should he care how tall the building was? On
days when it was too tall for stairs, he could always use the
elevator.

Avery had already done so, but the car was already de-
scending again. When it arrived, Derec and everyone else
packed into it, and Derec commanded it to take them to the
top.

The apartment filled the entire floor. The elevator
opened into a skylit atrium filled with plants, surrounding
a fountain that Derec had copied from an ancient design.
From either side of the pool a solid stream of water arched

upward in a parabola, the two streams carefully balanced to meet in the middle and spray outward in a vertical sheet of water. Derec was about to lead on past it, but Lucius paused when he saw it, then reached out and interrupted the path of one stream of water with a hand. The last of the stream continued upward as if nothing had happened, but when the gap reached the center, the other beam arched over to splash against the top of Lucius's hand, just opposite the other water beam. It was obvious that the two beams followed exactly the same trajectory, and could meet any-where along their paths.

Lucius removed his hand and the two streams met head-on again, the point of contact slowly climbing back up to the center.

"Interesting," he said.

"I call it 'Negative Feedback,'" Derec replied. Unable to resist a little dig, he added, "It's a useful principle. Think about it."

If Lucius understood his implication, he gave no sign of it. "I will," he promised.

Ariel walked on past them, through a massive simulated-wood double door and into the apartment itself. It was a palace. The living room took up one whole quarter of the floor, its glass walls on two sides affording a view of half the city stretching out to the horizon. From the main entry-way, a wide, curving hallway led off into the rest of the apartment, one glass wall facing the atrium and the other studded with doors leading into the library, computer room, bedrooms, video room, dining room, kitchen, game room, fitness room, swimming pool, and on into unused space that remained unused only because no one could think of anything else they wanted to fill it with.

The apartment was big and ostentatious, far more than

three humans and an alien needed, but as the only inhabitants of an entire city full of robots they had decided to enjoy it. In this particular instance, there seemed little advantage in moderation.

Another robot waited for them in the apartment: Mandelbrot, Ariel and Derec's personal robot. Mandelbrot was a standard Auroran model, made of levers and gears and servo motors, save where damage to his right arm had been repaired with an arm salvaged from a Robot City robot. That arm could have been any shape Mandelbrot—or his masters—wished, but he had chosen to make it match his other arm as closely as possible.

"You beat us home," Derec said when he saw him. Mandelbrot had been in the Compass Tower, helping direct the city's reconstruction from there.

"I left as soon as my task was finished, reasoning that you would come here soon after," the robot replied.

"Right, as usual," Derec said, patting Mandelbrot's metal shoulder in easy camaraderie. He nodded toward Lucius. "Here's our troublesome renegade, ordered to behave and given a new name to remind him of it. Mandelbrot, meet Lucius."

"Hello, Lucius," Mandelbrot said.

"I am more properly called 'Lucius II,'" Lucius said, "to distinguish me from the artist; however, Derec has pointed out that among those who realize the original Lucius is no longer operative, there is little danger of confusion in calling me simply 'Lucius.'"

"That seems reasonable," Mandelbrot replied.

Ariel had already disappeared into the apartment, as had Dr. Avery, but from the soft, synthesized music coming from the living room, Derec knew where at least one of them had gone. He waved the robots into the living room as well, then went into the small kitchen just next door. It held a small automat that provided light snacks and drinks for anyone who didn't want to walk or send a robot all the way to the main kitchen. Derec dialed a number from memory, and the machine delivered up a glass of dark brown, bubbling synthetic cola, one of his own experimental creations.

"Betelgeuse, anyone?" he asked loudly.

"Yecch!" Ariel said from the living room.

Wolruf padded into the kitchen. "I'll 'ave one," she said, holding out her hand. Derec gave her the one he had already dialed for, then ordered another for himself and a glass of Ariel's favorite, Auroran Ambrosia, for her.

From the library Avery said, "Mandelbrot, get me a mug of coffee."

The robot entered the kitchen behind Wolruf, waited patiently for Derec to finish with the automat, then pushed buttons in the sequence for coffee. Derec shook his head in exasperation. Avery had a whole city full of robots at his command, but he still loved to order Mandelbrot around. No doubt it was because Mandelbrot was Derec's robot, and Ariel's before him. Derec had considered telling Mandelbrot to ignore Avery's picayune orders, but so far he hadn't felt like provoking the conflict that Avery so obviously wanted.

Ariel was already sitting in one of the single-person chairs in the living room, her back to the glassed-in corner looking out over the city. Adam and Eve and Lucius were seated on a couch at an angle beside her, looking like a triple reflection of her. Wolruf followed Derec into the room and took another chair opposite the robots, leaving Derec with the choice of a chair beside Wolruf or one across from Ariel. Or—

Convert Ariel's chair into a loveseat, he sent to the apartment controller, and the malleable Robot City material began flowing into the new shape. The chair's right arm receded from Ariel while more material rose up from the floor to fill in the space.

"What the—oh. You could warn a girl."

"But you're so pretty when you're surprised. Your eyes go wide, and you breathe in deep . . ."

"Beast."

"Thank you." Derec handed her the glass of Ambrosia and sat beside her.

He took a long pull at his Betelgeuse. It felt grand to relax. It seemed he'd been going full tilt since he'd first heard of these strange new robots. But now, with Lucius tracked down and ordered to stop his human-creating project, the problems he had caused were over. Completely. One nice thing about robots; once they accepted an order to do something—or not to do it—they were locked into whatever behavior pattern that entailed.

Which, come to think of it, didn't necessarily mean no more trouble. No amount of orders could cover every eventuality, not even a blanket order like, "Don't cause any more trouble." Not even the Three Laws, built into the very nature of their brains, could keep them from occasionally damaging themselves, or disobeying orders, or even harming a human, however inadvertently. It kept such harm to a minimum, surely, but it didn't prevent it entirely. Nor would anything Derec could do keep these robots from letting their curious nature draw them into unusual situations. They were like cats; only dead ones stayed out of mischief.

"So," Derec said, stretching out and putting an arm around Ariel. "What are we going to do with you three?"

Ariel snuggled into Derec's side. The robots looked to one another, then back to Derec. At last Eve spoke. "You need do nothing. We are perfectly capable of taking care of ourselves."

"And causing all sorts of problems in the process. No, sorry, but I think I want to keep an eye on you from now on."

"As you wish."

Lucius said, "I am happy with that arrangement. I will be glad for the opportunity to observe you as well. You are the first humans I have encountered, and since I have been ordered not to create any more, it seems likely that my time will be most profitably spent in your presence."

Still operating under the decision to use speech rather than comlink when with humans, Adam turned to Lucius and said, "Eve and I have observed them for some time now. We are attempting to use our experience to determine what makes humans act the way they do. We intend to formulate a set of descriptive rules, similar to our own Laws of Robotics, which will describe their actions."

"That was one purpose of my project as well."

"When you get it figured out, let us know, okay?" Derec said facetiously.

"We will."

Lucius fixed his eyes on Adam. "What have you learned about them?"

"We have learned that—"

"Hold it," Ariel interrupted. "New datum for all of you. Humans don't like being discussed by robots as if they weren't in the room. If you're going to compare notes, do it somewhere else."

"Very well." The three robots got up as one and walked silently out of the living room. Derec heard footsteps recede down the hallway, pause, then a door that hadn't been there before closed softly. The robots had evidently ordered the building to make them a conference room at the other end of the apartment from the humans.

"Those robots are spooky," Ariel whispered.

" 'Ur rright about that," Wolruf said.

"If they really are my mother's creations, then I'm not sure I want to meet her," Derec added. "They're so single-minded. Driven. And once they do figure out their 'Laws of Humanics,' I'm not sure if I want to be around for the implementation, either."

"What do you mean? No robot can disobey the Three Laws, not even them. We're safe."

"Famous last words. What if they decide we're not fit to be our own masters? What if they decide—like Adam did with the Kin on the planet where he awoke—that they would make wiser rulers than we could? The First Law would require them to take over, wouldn't it?"

"You sound like an Earther. 'Robots are going to take over the galaxy!' "

Derec grinned sheepishly, but he held his ground. "I know, it's the same old tired argument, but if it was ever going to happen, now's the time. Avery's robot cities were spreading like cancer before we stopped them, and for all I know they could take off and start spreading again. Now *these* robots show up, and one of them has already made itself leader of an intelligent race. It wouldn't take much for them to combine their programming and come up with robots who could reproduce themselves faster than humanity can, and who think humans need supervision."

"Not much, except that they can't do it. The first time a human told them they were hurting its normal development, they'd either have to back off or go into freeze-up with the conflict."

"That's the theory, anyway," said Derec.

"Gloom an' doom!" Wolruf said with a rumbling laugh.

" 'U think 'u 'ave trouble; what about me? I don' even have *that* defense."

"You don't sound very worried about it."

" 'U live where I come from,'u'd know why. Robots— even alien ones—would make better rulers than what we've got."

She had a point, Derec thought. When he had first encountered Wolruf, she had been a slave on an alien ship, using her servitude to pay off a familial debt. He doubted that a robot government would allow that kind of arrangement to continue.

But would they allow creativity? Adventure? Growth? Or would there be only stagnation under the robots' protective rule? Derec spent the rest of the day wondering. They were all just abstract questions at this point, but if his parents' reckless experiments got any farther out of hand, the entire galaxy might have the chance to find out the answers.

CHAPTER 2

THE ROBOTICS LABORATORY

Derec awoke to find himself in a splash of sunlight coming in through the window. So east is that way today, he thought automatically. In a city whose buildings moved about and flowed from shape to shape, orienting himself in the morning was a habit he had quickly gotten into. Directions—and landmarks—were too temporary to rely on from day to day.

He became aware that he was alone in the bed. Ariel's absence from his side wasn't surprising, since she tended to be more of a morning person than he was, but the sounds coming from the Personal were. Someone—presumably her, since Avery and Wolruf had their own Personals—was being quite sick.

He got out of bed and padded to the closed door. "Ariel?" he called out hesitantly.

"Don't come in here!" she shouted. There came a sound of rushing water, not quite loud enough to drown completely the sound of her being sick once again.

Derec stood by the door, feeling helpless and, now that

he was uncovered, cold. He took his robe from its hook by the door, put it on, saw hers still there, and took it down as well.

The Personal was silent now. "Are you okay?" he called.

"I am now. Give me a minute."

Still worried, but unwilling to risk Ariel's wrath by opening the door, Derec crossed to the window to look out at the spires and rooftops of Robot City. It looked completely healed now from Lucius's destruction, healed and full of robots going about their normal duties. Derec could see hundreds of them in the streets, on elevated walkways, in transport booths, in maglev trucks, all moving purposefully once again. From this height—twenty-five stories today, Derec guessed—it was hard to tell that all the activity wasn't the ebb and flow of humanity in a fully populated human city.

Behind him he heard more water running, some soft bumping around, the cabinet opening and closing: all normal Personal noises. Then the door opened and Ariel stepped into the bedroom.

She was unselfconsciously nude. Derec turned away from the window, smiled as he always did to see how beautiful she was by light of day, and held out her robe. She let him help her into it.

"You sure you're all right?" he asked.

"Fine, now," she said. "I just woke up feeling sick. Must have been something I ate."

"Maybe." Derec knew she was probably right, but a remnant of the old worry had crept back to haunt him. She had been sick once, deathly sick, and before she had found treatment for it on Earth, Derec had learned what it was to worry about someone's health. That was before they had become lovers; now his concern for her was even more intense.

There might have been another possibility, now that they were sharing a bed again, but her disease had ruled that out.

"I feel *fine*," she said with exasperation. "Really. And I don't want you telling the robots about this, or they won't rest until they've had me in for a full-blown exam and proven to themselves that I'm healthy."

She had never liked the attention her illness had forced upon her before, either. Derec nodded. "Okay," he said, giving her a strong hug before going over to the closet and picking out a fresh pair of pants and a simple pullover shirt to wear. He wouldn't tell the robots, but he would keep a close watch on her himself today just to make sure she really was okay.

That intention died within minutes of stepping out from the bedroom into the rest of the apartment.

Avery was waiting for him in the kitchen. "What did you do to them?" he asked in his usual belligerent tone.

"Do to whom?" Derec replied calmly, going to the automat and dialing for breakfast.

"The robots," Avery replied.

"The—oh, *those* robots. Ariel sent them off to their room last night to talk business out of earshot. Theirs is the new door at the end of the hallway. Can't miss it."

"I'm *aware* of that," Avery snarled. "What I'm talking about is that the robots are locked up. Inert. Dead."

"What?" Derec turned from the automat with his breakfast still only half ordered.

"Is your hearing going along with your intelligence? The robots are—"

"Locked up. Inert. Dead. I got that. My statement—" here Derec mimicked the tone of a robot so clearly that Avery rolled his eyes to the ceiling, "—was merely a conversational device intended to indicate extreme surprise. And," he added in his own voice again, "to indicate that I had nothing to do with it. Which I didn't."

"So you say. You must have said something to make them lock up. Some contradictory order."

"If I did, I don't know what it was." Derec looked back to the automat, shrugged, and pressed the cancel button. "Come on, let's go see."

He padded down the hallway, still in bare feet, to the robot's new room. They hadn't been interested in creature comforts; it was just big enough for the three robots to stand in without bumping into one another or the walls. It held no windows, no chairs—nothing but the robots.

When Derec and Ariel first arrived in Robot City, the robots gave them a small, one-bedroom apartment to live in. It had seemed miserly in a city built on such a grand scale, but the robots had truly thought they were fulfilling the humans' every need. Similarly, the food had been nutritious but bland until they experimented with the automats to get them to produce flavor. Robots simply had no concept of the difference between sufficiency and satisfaction, and now, as Derec looked into the tiny, windowless closet these particular robots had made for themselves, he realized they were still a long way from making that distinction. Either that or their concept of satisfaction was simply so different from the human norm that Derec didn't recognize it when he saw it.

Avery had certainly been accurate enough in his description of them. All three of them were frozen in place, standing up straight, arms at their sides. None of them betrayed the slightest hint of motion.

Derec tried the obvious. "Adam. Eve. Lucius. Respond." Nothing happened.

Avery smiled his "I told you so" smile.

Derec tried the less obvious. *Adam, Eve, Lucius*, he sent.

At once his mental interface filled with a hiss of static like that from a poorly tuned hyperwave radio. Behind it Derec heard a faint whine that might have been a signal, but it might have been just noise. On the off chance that they were still receiving, he sent, *I order you to respond.*

Nothing happened.

He cancelled the link and said aloud, "They do seem to be locked up. I got nothing on the comlink, either. I wonder what happened to them."

"We'll find out." Avery—lacking an internal comlink of his own—stalked out of the robots' cubbyhole, went to the com console in its niche in the library, and keyed it on. Into the receiver he said, "I want a cargo team, big enough to carry three robots, up here immediately." He switched it off before the computer could respond.

Derec had followed him into the library. "What are you going to do with them?" he asked.

"Take them to the lab. I'll find out what happened to them, and what makes them tick as well."

Something about Avery's manner made Derec suspect that he wouldn't be restricting himself to non-invasive examination. "You're going to take them apart?"

"Why not?" Avery asked. "It's the perfect opportunity."

Derec didn't know why he felt so disturbed by that thought; he had taken robots apart before himself. But then, when he had done so he had known how to put them back together again, too. With these, Avery had no assurance he could rebuild them when he was done. That was the difference: Avery was considering permanent deactivation, not just investigation.

"Is that reason enough to do it?" Derec asked. "Just because you have the opportunity? They're thinking beings. You should be trying to fix whatever's wrong with them, not cut them open to satisfy your curiosity."

Avery rolled his eyes. "Spare me the sentiment, would you? They're robots. Human creations. Built to serve. If it amuses me to take one apart—or to order one to take itself apart—then I have every right, legal *or* moral, to do so. These robots are a puzzle, and I want to know more about them. Besides that, they've interfered with my own project. I want to make sure they don't do that again."

"You don't need to destroy them to do that."

"Maybe I won't. We'll see."

Derec was of a mind to argue further, but the arrival of the cargo robots interrupted him. There were six of them in the team, and under Avery's direction they moved silently through the apartment, picked up the inert robots unceremoniously by arms and legs, and carried them out to a waiting truck. Avery followed after them, and Derec, struggling into his shoes, came along behind.

"Do you wish the malfunctioning robots taken to the repair facility?" the truck's robot driver asked as Derec and Avery climbed into the cab with it.

"No," Avery said. "To my laboratory."

"To your laboratory," the driver replied, and with a soft whine of maglev motors, the truck lifted and began to slide down the street.

The truck used the same magnetic levitation principle that the transport booths used, holding itself up off the street and providing thrust with magnetic fields rather than with wheels. It was an old design, but not that common on most worlds even so because of the need for a special track for the magnetic fields to work against. Trains and busses were all maglev, but trucks, which needed the ability to travel anywhere, were usually not.

Here in Robot City, however, all the streets would support maglev vehicles. Everything was made of the same material. There was no place in the city where a maglev truck couldn't go, and thus no reason for them to have wheels. Derec wondered briefly if there were wheels on *anything* here, but couldn't think of a single instance where one was necessary.

Humanity had finally outgrown them, he realized. Or would, when this and the other robot cities on other worlds were opened up for human occupation.

They had hardly gone a block before Derec noticed a flicker of movement in the recessed doorway of one of the buildings lining the street. He looked more closely and saw that it was one of Lucius's rodent-like creations. He looked for more and wasn't disappointed; they were out in force, scavenging the nearly sterile city for food and no doubt starving in the process. They would be able to glean a little nourishment from the occasional strips of grass and ornamental shrubs between buildings, but given as many creatures as Derec saw in just one block, that food supply wouldn't last out the week. Lucius had evidently bred more of them than that one warehouse-full he had shown them yesterday.

Some of the rodents eyed the truck as it glided past, and Derec felt a momentary chill. When they got hungry enough, would they attack?

"We've got to do something about those," he said to Avery, pointing out the window.

Avery nodded his head in agreement. "The robots can

round them up. Make fertilizer out of them for the farm."

If they hadn't already *found* the farm, Derec thought, but he supposed that was unlikely. The farm was a *long* way away, partway around the planet.

He thought about Avery's suggestion for a moment, wondering if killing them all was the right solution. He knew they were the result of an experiment that should never have taken place, that they were neither useful nor natural nor even pleasing in appearance, but he still felt uneasy about such a—final solution.

"Maybe we should take the opportunity to start a balanced ecosystem here," he said.

"Whatever for?" Avery asked, obviously shocked by the very idea.

"Well, Lucius was on the right track, in a way. Eventually there will be people living here, but a planet covered with nothing but people and robots and buildings and a few plants is going to be a pretty dull place. They'll want birds and squirrels and deer and butterflies and—"

"What makes you think there are going to be people living here?"

It was Derec's turn to be surprised. "Well, that's the whole point, isn't it? You didn't design these robots to build city after city just for the heck of it. I know you said you did, but that was back when you—well, you know."

"That was when I was crazy, you mean to say."

Derec blushed. "I forget; you don't mince words. Okay, that was back when you were crazy. But now that you're not any more, you can see that the robots eventually have to stop and serve, don't you?"

"Why?"

"Why? You're kidding. If you didn't build all this for people to live in, then what do you intend to do with it?"

The truck slowed coming into an intersection, and another truck flashed by in front of them. Derec flinched, even though he knew the robot driver was aware of the other traffic in the area via comlink. Avery gave no indication that he had even seen the other truck. "I built it as an experiment," he said. "I wanted to see what sort of society robots would come up with on their own. I also wanted to see if you were strong enough to take over the cities with the chemfets I implanted in your system." When Derec began to speak, he raised his hand to cut him off and said, "I've already apologized for that, and I'll do it again. That idea was the product of an insane mind. I had no right to do it, no matter how interesting the result. But the original idea was valid when I had it, and it's still valid now. The cities exist for the robots. I want them to come up with their own society. I think there are basic rules for behavior among intelligent beings—rules that hold true no matter what their physical type—and I think robots can be used to discover those rules."

For Avery to reveal anything of his plans to someone else, even to his own son, was a rare occurrence. Especially to his son. Avery had never confided any of his plans to Derec, had in fact used Derec at every turn as if he were just another robot. He had tried to *make* him a robot by injecting him with "chemfets," modified copies of the cells that made up the Robot City robots. Derec had survived the infestation, had even arrived at a truce with the miniature robot city in his own body—that was how he had acquired his comlink—but he had not forgotten what his father had done to him. Forgiven, yes, but not forgotten.

Now suddenly Avery was confiding in him. Derec pondered this new development and its significance for the space of a couple of blocks before he said, "Well, they do seem to be working on it, but I'm not sure I see how anything you come up with from studying robots in a mutable city like this could apply to anything but more robots in an identical city."

Avery nodded his head vigorously. "Oh, but it could. In fact, the city's mutability forces the robots' society to be independent of their environment. That's the beauty of it. Any rules of behavior they come up with *have* to be absolute, because there's no steady frame of reference for them to build upon."

Derec wasn't convinced, but he said, "So what are you going to do with these rules once you discover them?"

Avery smiled, another rare occurrence, and said, "That would have to depend on the rules, now wouldn't it?"

Derec felt a chill run up his spine at those words. Ariel and the robots—and Avery himself—had sworn he was cured, but who could be sure? The human mind was still a poorly understood mechanism at best.

Derec had been to Dr. Avery's laboratory once before, as a prisoner. Now, under better circumstances, he had the opportunity to gaze around him in wonder. Every instrument he could imagine—and some he couldn't—for working on robots was there. Positronic circuit analyzers, logic probes, physical function testers, body fabrication machinery—the equipment went on and on. The laboratory would have been positively cluttered with it if it hadn't been so large, but as it was it was simply well equipped. Derec would have bet it was the most advanced such lab anywhere, save that he and Avery were using it to explore the product of a still more advanced one somewhere else.

The three locked-up robots rested atop examining tables that, at first inspection, would have looked at home in a human hospital. A closer look, however, revealed that the pillows under the robots' heads were not simple pillows but were instead inductive sensor arrays for reading the state of a positronic brain. Arm, leg, and body sheaths served a dual purpose: to restrain the patient if necessary and also to trace command impulses and sensory signals flowing to and from the extremities. Overhead stood scanning equipment that would allow the user to see inside a metal body.

There had been a moment of confusion when the cargo robots unloaded the three inert robots from the truck; without conscious control over their mutable shapes, they had all begun to drift back toward their primordial blank state. They had never been easy to identify, but now what few distinguishing features they had were smoothed out, melted. Even so, when viewed from a distance, one of them still seemed faintly wolflike in shape, and that had to be Adam. The "Kin," the dominant life form on the world where he had first come to awareness, was a wolflike animal, and Adam's first imprinting there had evidently become a permanent part of his cellular memory, however faint.

Likewise, Eve displayed just a hint of Ariel's oval face, widely spaced eyes, and gently curvaceous female form, for it had been Ariel upon whom she had first imprinted.

Lucius, having hatched and imprinted in Robot City, still looked more like a robot than either of the others, and for that reason it was he whom Derec and Avery began examining first. Outward form probably didn't mean that the inside would be anything like a normal robot's, or even a normal Robot City robot's, but there was at least a chance of it, and in any case they could learn more from studying a similar form rather than from something completely different.

The positronic brain, at least, was universal among robots of any manufacture, and despite Derec's fear that this might be the exception that proved the rule, the pillow sensor fit itself around Lucius's head without complaint, the indicator light glowing green when the link with the brain had been established.

That alone told them something. Not all robots kept their brains in their heads; some models kept them inside the more protected chest cavity. Avery had designed his to function as much like humans as they could, which meant putting the brain in their heads so they would develop the same automatic responses concerning it. Injury-avoidance behavior, for instance, might be different in a being who kept its brain in a different part of its anatomy. To find the brains in the heads of these robots meant either that they were such excellent mimics that they could determine where their subject's internal organs belonged, or that their creator was also concerned with the subtle differences the location of the brain might introduce into her robots' behavior.

"Definitely getting mental activity," Avery said, nodding toward the display screen upon which marched a series of square-edged waveforms. He tapped a button and a different series replaced the first. "Cognition appears undamaged," he muttered, and switched the display again.

Derec suddenly felt a burst of recognition reach through the veil surrounding his past. There on the screen was the basic pattern common to all robots: the Three Laws graphically represented as pathway potentials within the positronic brain. He had learned that pattern years ago, probably in school, though just when it had been he couldn't remember.

It wasn't a major revelation. Derec had already known he had training in robotics, but nonetheless it was a welcome shot of déjà vu. It was a true memory in a mind mostly devoid of them, and as such it was as precious to Derec as gold.

Avery switched the display again.

"Hello, hello, test, test." With each word spoken, what had been a smooth sine wave erupted into a fit of jagged peaks and troughs: Avery's voice processed through the robot's microphone ears.

Derec let out a sigh. The memory was already fading. To avoid the crushing disappointment that so often came from such a tantalizing glimpse into his past, he focused his attention on what was happening before him. "Looks like he's hearing us," he said. "The signal must not be getting processed."

"Let's see." Avery switched the display again, spoke, "Hello, hello, test, test," again, and again the waveform—a modulated square wave this time—burst into activity.

"It's on the main input line." Avery sounded puzzled. He switched again, spoke again, but this time the display remained a constant flat line.

"Aha! Not getting to the command interpreter. Something's blocking it." Avery switched the display back to the input line.

Step by step he focused the monitor deeper and deeper into the brain's positronic pathways, searching for the block, and finally found it in a combination of potentials from the volition circuitry and the self-awareness logic. Plus, the comlink line was saturated with information. The information transfer rate was so high that no other inputs were being monitored.

"I tried listening on the comlink before, but there was just static," Derec said when they discovered the comlink activity. He tried again and heard the same thing as before. "Still there."

"Static, or information flow too fast to recognize?" Avery asked. He pressed keys on a signal processor beside the brain display, and the same static that Derec had heard over the comlink filled the room. Avery began slowing the signal down, and eventually, after being slowed by a factor of one hundred, the static resolved into the familiar bleeps of binary data transfer.

"Sounds like they're having quite a conversation," Derec said.

"Conversation," Avery said disgustedly. "They're ignoring us. That's aberrant behavior. It's already led them into disobeying orders."

"Not really. They only follow the orders they can hear. If they're really not hearing us, then they're not disobeying anything." Derec glanced over at Eve on the next table, and thus Avery's next move took him completely by surprise. Before he knew what was happening, Avery's back-hand sent him sprawling on the floor.

"Talk back to me, will you?" Avery screamed. "I've had enough of your insolence, boy! Maybe a boot up alongside your head will knock some respect into you!" He leaped around the table and drew back his foot to follow through on his threat.

Frost, he's flipped again, Derec thought as he twisted frantically to avoid Avery's kick.

Avery screamed in frustration. "Oh, you're quicker than me, are you? We'll see how long that lasts when I shoot you in the leg!" He snatched up a cutting laser from the rack of tools beside the examining table and fired toward Derec, but his shot went wide. Derec heard a loud crack of superheated metal vaporizing, but he was already scrambling for the relative shelter of Eve's table.

Security Alert, he sent over the comlink. *Avery's laboratory. Help!*

He heard another shot, then Avery's quiet laughter, followed by, "Wow, they're really out of it, aren't they?"

Derec stayed silent, gauging the distance from his hiding place to the closest doorway, one leading into one of the lab's other rooms. He was about to make his leap when he heard the scrape of metal sliding on metal, and the laser skidded to a stop beside him.

"False alarm," Avery said.

Derec eyed the laser. Had Avery been playing with him before, or was this just a decoy to get him out into the sights of another laser now? Avery's first shot *had* gone wide, but was that significant? Could he afford to guess wrong?

Well, Derec could play the decoy game as well as Avery. He pulled off his wristcomp and tossed it to his left, over the laser and beyond. The moment it hit the floor he was up and lunging for the tool rack beside Eve's exam table. It tipped over with a crash, spilling equipment across the floor, but Derec was already rolling to his feet with the laser from the rack before the clatter had even begun to die down.

Avery stood beside Lucius, his hands held out to his sides, an amused expression on his face. "It really was a false alarm," he said. "I wanted to test whether or not they'd respond to a First Law imperative."

"Test," Derec spat. "I'm *tired* of your *tests*! You've been testing me and using me since the day I was born and I'm sick of it! Do you understand me?"

It was then that the six cargo robots burst into the room. They had already left for their normal duties after carrying the other three into the lab, but they were evidently still the closest robots who could answer Derec's frantic summons for help. The first one through the door surveyed the scene and reacted immediately, picking up a small circuit analyzer from a bench by the door and hurling it with all its might at Derec. Before Derec could even flinch, the analyzer knocked the laser from his hands, and both fell to the floor to die in a fit of sparks and smoke. The other robots rushed past the first and split up, two of them going for Avery while three more came for Derec and pinned his arms to his sides. Within seconds both humans were held immobile in the grip of the robots.

"Let me go," Avery said calmly, but the robots didn't budge.

The robot who had knocked the laser from Derec's hands said, "Not until we understand what has happened here. It was master Derec, was it not, who summoned our help?"

"That's right," Derec said. "He was shooting at me with a laser."

"Yet you were the one holding the laser when we entered."

"I grabbed it in self-defense."

"Defense? I fail to see how a weapon can be used for defense."

Derec blushed under his father's sudden onslaught of laughter. "He's got you there!" Avery said.

The robot had, Derec realized. If he'd actually used the laser, he would have been guilty of the very action he was defending himself against. In the robot's eyes, harm to a human was harm to a human, no matter what the provocation.

It was embarrassing to have such a thing pointed out to him. He should have realized it from the start, should have felt an instinctive, rather than belated, urge to preserve his attacker as well as himself from harm.

Even if that attacker was his father.

"I stand corrected," he said at last. "I should have retreated."

"I am glad you realize that," the robot said. Of Avery it asked, "Why did you shoot at him?"

"I needed to provoke a First Law response in these robots. I didn't shoot directly at him, just close."

"I see," the robot said, scanning the room for verification. It probably *did* see, Derec realized. The heat trails of his path and the path of the laser beam would still be visible in infrared light; it would be easy for the robot to tell how close the beam had come.

"Do you accept his explanation?" the robot asked Derec.

"I guess," Derec said with a sigh.

"Do either of you wish to continue your hostilities?"

Derec shook his head. "No."

"No," echoed Avery.

"Very well." Derec felt the robots let go of his arms, but the ones holding Avery still held him. The first robot, moving to stand closer to him, said, "You should understand that psychological shock, especially shock concerning fear for one's life, is still considered harm to a human. You have caused Derec harm. Do you understand this?"

Avery scowled. "Yeah," he said. "Let me go."

"Only when I am convinced that you will not repeat your offense. Do I have your assurance that you will not?"

"Okay, okay, I won't shoot at him again."

"You must also endeavor never to scare him in another way, or to harm him either physically or psychologically in any way. Do I have your assurance that you will not?"

"*Yes*, you have my assurance. Now let me go."

The robot turned to Derec. "Do you accept his assurance as truthful?"

Derec couldn't resist laughing. "Hardly," he said. "But

that's okay. After what he just did, I don't think he *can* surprise me anymore. Let him go."

The robots did. "We will observe you for a time," the talkative one said.

Avery scowled. "I don't want you to. Go away."

"We cannot do that until we are sure that you will not harm one another."

Avery evidently realized this was an argument that he couldn't win. He shrugged and gestured at the mess on the floor. "Make yourselves useful then."

The other robots began to pick up the scattered equipment, but the talkative one said to Avery, "A less destructive First Law test would have been to simply state that you were about to fall over without catching yourself. No properly functioning robot would allow that to happen."

"Thank you for your profound input," Avery said with exaggerated politeness.

"You are welcome."

"Now get to work."

CHAPTER 3

THE BIOLOGICAL LABORATORY

"I still think we ought to take one of them apart." Avery was leaning over Lucius, positioning the internal scanner for yet another cross-section through the robot's body. It may have resembled a robot on the outside, but that was as far as the similarity went; Lucius's interior resembled a human body far more than it did a robot's. It didn't have any unnecessary internal organs, but those it did need were modeled after the human pattern. It had bunches of cells arranged like muscles, bones, and nerves, at least, rather than the more conventional linkages and cams.

Interesting as that discovery was, it had been hours since they had made it, and Avery was getting frustrated.

"And I still say it won't tell us anything we can't find out indirectly," Derec replied. He was sitting on a stool on the opposite side of the examination table, watching the screen and getting bored. "They're obviously comparing notes, probably on their experience with humans. Why not let them go for a while? They might come up with something interesting."

"Like some wonderful new way to disturb my cities," said Avery.

"Your cities can take care of themselves. And if not, I can take care of them."

"You think so. I think you're just trying to protect your mother's experiment."

Derec considered that possibility. Was he trying to protect her experiment, or was he simply trying to protect three robots from being needlessly destroyed? He had thought it was the latter, but now that Avery mentioned it . . .

"Maybe I am," he said.

"You don't even know her."

"That's not my fault."

"And it *is* mine. Guilty. I shouldn't have wiped your memory. When I think of a good way to make it up to you, I will, but believe me, you're better off without it."

"I'd like to be the judge of that."

Avery had been looking at the scanner display, but now he turned his head and looked his son straight in the eyes. "Of course you would. I can understand that. But bear in mind, if you got your memory back, what you'd have memories *of.* I told you once before that you had a fairly normal childhood, and that's true enough, but it was a normal childhood in an Auroran family, which is the next best thing to no family at all. Your mother and I hardly saw one another after your birth. You hardly saw either of us. In fact, you spent most of your childhood with robots."

"No wonder I fit in so well here," Derec said drily.

Avery said nothing, and Derec sensed his embarrassment. At least he's embarrassed, he thought, then chided himself for feeling vindictive. Learning to live with a recovering psychopath was almost as difficult as being the recoveree. The things his father had done while insane were not his fault, at least not in the sense that he could be held responsible for them, yet Derec still felt that he had been poorly treated. *Somebody* should feel bad about it, shouldn't they?

Or was this another situation like the one they had just gone through with the laser? Was wishing for remorse just another way of mistreating a human?

No wonder the robots were having such a time trying to understand human interactions. The humans themselves didn't understand them half the time.

But the robots were learning. Witness the cargo robots, still standing patiently around the lab, watching for signs of recurring violence. They had already learned not to trust a human's stated intentions.

How could that be a good thing? Before long these robots of his father's would decide that humans were not to be trusted at all, and hence not to be obeyed in any situation where trust was necessary to avoid an internal conflict with the Three Laws. As for his mother's robots, if they ever came out of their communication fugue, who could predict what conclusions they would draw from their collective experiences? The only prediction Derec was willing to make with any certainty was that they would be even less useful than before.

That thought made Derec ask, "What were our house robots like?"

Avery looked up momentarily in surprise. "What do you mean, 'what were they like?' Like robots, of course. Old-style robots. I didn't develop the cellular robot until after you'd left home, and your mother stole her design from me."

"That's what I thought. The point is, they did the mundane work for you, right? Cooking and cleaning and changing diapers and emptying the trash."

"Of course they did," Avery said. He sounded indignant, as if the very thought that *he* would have done any of those chores was obscene.

"They were useful, then."

"What are you getting at?"

"I'm getting at the obvious observation that the robots around here, despite their advanced design—maybe *because* of their advanced design—aren't as useful as the older models. They're more trouble. Too much independence."

Avery moved the scanner a fraction and keyed the display again. Another view into the nerve and musclelike masses of Lucius's interior appeared on the screen. "Maybe my definition of useful is different from yours," he said.

They had already had that conversation. Avery was simply not interested in immediate utility, and Derec was. There was no sense arguing over it. Derec got up off his stool with a sigh, stretched, and said, "I'm about to fall asleep here. Are you going to keep at it all day?"

"Probably," Avery replied.

"I think I'll leave you to it, then."

"Fine."

"Just don't cut any of them up, okay?"

Avery looked pained. "I'll do with them whatever I please. If that includes cutting them up, then that's what I'll do."

Derec and Avery stared at one another across the unmoving robot's body for long, silent seconds. One of the cargo robots near the wall took a step toward them. Derec looked up at the robot, then back to Avery. He considered ordering the robot to keep Avery from harming the others, but decided against it. It would just escalate the war between them. Besides, there were better ways.

He shrugged and backed off. "It's your conscience. But

I'm asking you, please don't cut any of them up. As a favor to me."

Avery frowned. "I'll think about it," he replied.

Derec nodded. Now it was up to Avery to decide whether or not to escalate the war. It was a risk, but a calculated one. Derec had felt a spark of humanity in Avery a couple of times today; he was willing to bet his father was sick of confrontation, too.

"Thanks." He turned away and said to the cargo robots, "Come on, the rest of you. You can take me back home and then get on with whatever else you were doing."

He really had intended to go home, but on the way there the sight of Lucius's creatures still scavenging in the streets reminded him that he still had to do something about them, and soon, or they were going to start eating each other. With Lucius himself out of commission, there was only one good place to start, and it wasn't at home. "I've changed my mind," he said to the robot driving the truck. "Take me to Lucius's lab instead."

The robot hesitated a long time—nearly the length of a block—then asked, "Which one do you wish to visit?"

"How many has he got?"

"The central computer lists thirty-seven separate laboratories."

"Thirty-seven?"

"That is correct."

"What did he do with that many labs?"

The cargo robot was silent for a moment as it conferred with the computer again, then said, "Fifteen were dedicated to fabricating the artificial humans he called 'homunculi' and are now abandoned. The other twenty-two are engaged in fabricating humans."

"*Are* engaged? Still?"

"That is correct."

"We told him not to continue with that!"

"That is also correct."

The cargo robot offered no more explanation, but Derec could see plainly enough what the situation was. Lucius had interpreted his orders to mean only him, leaving the other robots who had been helping him free to continue the project. Well, he would put a stop to that soon enough.

But twenty-two labs! No wonder the city was full of rats.

"Take me to the one he showed us yesterday," Derec said.

The driver evidently had no problem with Derec's inclusive "us," nor with finding the appropriate lab in the computer's records. It slowed the truck and turned left at the next corner, made another left turn at the next block and they went back the way they had come for a while, then turned right and went on for block after block through the city. The rat population on the streets dwindled, then grew larger again as they left the sphere of influence of one lab and entered another. Evidently Lucius had felt no need to cluster his workplaces.

Derec, watching the towering buildings slide past, felt again how empty the city was without people in it. None of these buildings had any real purpose, nor did the robots in them, save for Avery's nebulous experiment in social dynamics. And what could possibly come of that? The robots weren't creating a society of their own; they were instead simply building and rebuilding in anticipation of someday having humans to serve. And some of them, he thought wryly, were busy building those humans. All because of the Three Laws of Robotics and the poorly defined quantity, "human," those Laws directed them to protect and obey.

Derec had felt a great sadness pervading the city since he first arrived. It felt almost haunted to him, the robots wandering about like lost souls, purposeless. He was attributing human qualities to inhuman beings, he knew, but Frost, they didn't have to be human to be lost, or to feel sad about it. Robots were intelligent beings, no matter what their origin, and it behooved their creators to treat them kindly. That included giving them a sense of purpose and letting them fulfill it. It seemed clear to Derec that none of these Robot City robots, nor the ones lying inert in Avery's lab, had been treated well by their creators.

Humans make poor gods, he thought wryly.

The cargo robots dropped Derec off outside a low, nondescript warehouselike building. If it was the same one Lucius had shown them the day before, then it had been repaired, but not before a veritable horde of the rat-creatures had escaped. Two hordes, Derec decided as he watched them scurrying about through the streets. They had been thick in the other parts of town, but this was ridiculous.

He ran from the truck to the main door, sending rats squealing off in all directions, but none chased after him.

Yet, he thought.

Directly inside the main door a hallway led down the length of the building, with doors opening to either side. Derec walked down the hallway, expecting to find a laboratory sufficient in complexity to support a complete genetic engineering project, but when he peered through the first doorway to his right, he couldn't help laughing. Avery was the mad scientist, but Lucius's lab—at least this part of it—was the typical mad scientist's lair. Vats of bubbling brew stood in various stages of incubation or fermentation or whatever was going on along one wall, while electrical devices of various natures hummed and clicked contentedly over them. A bank of cages along another wall held a bewildering array of small creatures, ranging from insects to something that might have been a mouse to one of the rodentlike creatures now overrunning the city. Another wall held trays of growing plants. In the center of the room, table after table held enough interconnected glassware to distill a lake. From the entire collection came a mixture of smells stronger and more varied than from an explosion in a kitchen automat.

The necessity of dealing with organic material had forced the lab into the configuration he saw, but Derec found it funny nonetheless. The gleaming robots who tended the equipment made it even more so by contrast. They should have been wearing dark robes and walking with stooped posture.

One of them walked past carrying a test tube filled with cloudy liquid. Derec cleared his throat noisily and said, "We've got a problem here."

"That is unfortunate," the robot answered without pausing in its stride. "How may I help?" It walked on over to a centrifuge, put the tube inside, and started it spinning.

Derec felt momentary annoyance at talking to a robot who was too busy to stop for him, but some remnant of his thoughts on the trip over kept him from ordering the robot to drop what it was doing. This robot, at least, had a purpose. A wrong one, but maybe they could do something about that without defeating it completely.

"To start with," he said, "you can't create any humans. That goes for all of you, in all of these labs. Is that clear?"

"Yes," the robot replied. It looked at Derec, then back to the centrifuge. If it was disappointed, it didn't show it.

"All right. Next, then, I need to know what those crea-tures—" Derec waited until the robot looked to see where he was pointing, "—there at the end of the line—eat."

"They are omnivorous," the robot replied, gathering up a handful of empty tubes from a box and inserting them one by one into some sort of diagnostic instrument beside the centrifuge.

"There's a whole bunch of them running loose in the city without a food supply. We need to give them one."

"That would only increase their numbers. Is that what you wish to do?"

"No. But I don't want them to starve, either."

"We have discovered that if they do not starve, they will reproduce. There is no intermediate state. The number of creatures existing now are the result of a large food supply, which we have ceased providing."

"You intend for them to starve, then?" Derec watched the robot push buttons on the face of the instrument.

"That is correct."

"Why not introduce something that eats *them*?"

"That seems needlessly complex. Starvation will reduce their numbers equally well."

"I see." Derec felt somehow vindicated to hear the ro-bot's answer. Evidently robots didn't make very good gods, either.

He thought of Avery's suggestion to have the robots collect and kill them. A typical Avery idea, little better than the robots' starvation plan. Much as he wanted to avoid conflict, Derec couldn't let that happen, either.

"Look," he said, going on into the lab and pulling up a stool, "even if you can't make humans, this project of yours can still be good for something. Let me tell you about bal-anced ecosystems. . . ."

• • •

The sun was long down by the time he made it home that night. Ariel was in the library, leaning back on a couch with her feet up on a stool and listening to one of Avery's recordings of Earther music while she read a book. Neither Avery nor Wolruf were in evidence, though the loud snoring coming from down the hallway was suggestive of at least one of them. Mandelbrot stood in a wall niche behind Ariel, waiting for her to need his services.

Ariel put down the book and scowled at Derec in mock hostility when he entered the room. "Forget where you lived?" she asked.

"Almost." Derec sat down beside her on the couch and nuzzled her neck playfully. "I've been trying to plan a simple ecosystem for the city, but it's a lot tougher than I thought. Do you realize that you have to balance everything right down to the microbes in the soil? Pick the wrong ones, or not enough varieties of the right ones, and your whole biosphere goes crazy."

"Is that so?"

"Yes, that's so. I've been studying it all day."

"Sounds exciting." She yawned wide, and the book slipped from her fingers to land with a thump on the floor. "Oops. Tired."

Derec scooped it up for her and laid it on the couch's armrest. "It's late. We should go to bed."

"I guess we should."

Derec took her hand and helped her up from the couch. She let him lead her into the bedroom, where he pulled down the covers and left her on the foot of the bed to undress and crawl in while he used the Personal.

When he came out, she was already asleep. He slid quietly into bed beside her and within minutes he was out as well, dreaming of food chains and energy flow.

But once again, he awoke to the sound of someone throwing up in the Personal. He sat up with a start, his heart suddenly pounding. The sun barely reached the window this time, but it was up. It was morning, and Ariel was sick.

His heart was still pounding when she opened the door and looked out at him. "Does this mean what I think it means?" he asked.

"I don't know," she said. "But I think we'd better find out."

The urine test came up positive, as they knew it would. Even so, it was hard for either of them to remain standing when the medical robot said, "May I be the first to offer you congratulations on the occasion of—"

"Wow," Derec murmured. He and Ariel had been holding hands in anticipation; now he squeezed hers tightly.

"Oh," Ariel said, her hand suddenly going slack. "I don't—"

"But how?"

"I wasn't supposed to be able to—"

"The cure!" Derec wrapped his arms around her and picked her up off the ground in a hug. "When they cured your amnemonic plague on Earth, they must have 'cured' your birth control, too."

"They might have warned me."

Derec's grin faltered. He set her back on her feet again. "What's the matter? Don't you want—?"

Ariel took the two steps necessary to reach a chair and sat heavily. "I don't know," she said. "It's just such a shock. I'm not ready for it."

"Well, we've got plenty of time to get used to the idea.

At least, I think we do." Derec turned to the medical robot. "How far along is she?"

"Fifteen days, plus or minus a day," answered the robot. "A blood test would be more accurate, but I discourage invasive testing for such minor gain."

"Me too," Ariel said. She held out her hand and Derec took it again. "Well. Two weeks. That leaves us a while yet." She looked down the corridor into the empty expanse of the hospital, then back to Derec.

Derec squeezed her hand again for reassurance. He wouldn't say he knew just how she felt, because he wasn't the one whose body would swell with the developing baby, and he wasn't the one who would have to go through the painful process of giving birth, but he did at least share the sudden confusion of learning that he was going to be a parent. Did he want to be a father? He didn't know. It was too soon to be asking that sort of question, and at the same time, far, far too late. He was going to be one whether he wanted to be or not.

Well, it wasn't like he couldn't provide for a child. He had an entire city at his disposal, and more scattered throughout the galaxy, all full of robots who were hungry for the chance to serve a human. He certainly didn't have to worry about food or housing or education. Childhood companions might be a problem, though, unless they could bring some more families to Robot City. Derec wondered if Avery would stand for it. If not, then Derec could build his own city. It wouldn't take much; a few seed robots and a few weeks' time. Or there was still their house on Aurora, come to think of it. Derec and Ariel had both grown up on Aurora; perhaps their child should as well.

All those thoughts and more rushed through Derec's mind as he held Ariel's hand in the hospital waiting room.

He grinned when he realized how quickly he had begun planning for the baby's future. It was an instinctive response; hormones that had been around since before humanity learned to use fire were directing his thoughts now. Well, he didn't mind having a little help from his instincts. In this situation, it was about all he had to go on.

Looking at Ariel, he felt a sudden rush of warmth course through him. He wanted to protect her, provide for her, help her while she bore their child. Was that instinct, too? He had been in love with her before, but this was something else.

He certainly hadn't learned it on Aurora. His father had been right: an Auroran family was the next thing to none. Permanent attachments, or even long-term relationships, were rare, even discouraged. An attachment as deep as he felt now for Ariel would be considered an aberration there.

Which meant that it wasn't instinct, or Aurorans would have been feeling it, too. Somehow that made Derec feel even better. It was genuine love he was feeling, concern and care born of their experiences together, rather than simple chemicals in his bloodstream. Instinct was just intensifying what he already felt for her.

She was worried. He could feel it in her hand, see it on her face. She needed time to accept what was happening to her. On sudden impulse, he said, "Let's go for a walk."

She thought about it for a few seconds. "Okay."

He helped her to her feet. The medical robot said, "Before you go, I need to impress upon you the importance of regular medical checkups. You should report for testing at regular two-week intervals, and before that if you notice any sudden developments. Your health is critical to the developing embryo, and its health is critical to your own. Also, your diet—"

Ariel cut him off. "Can this wait?"

"For a short time, yes."

"Then tell me later. Or send it to our apartment and I'll read up on it there."

The robot hesitated, its First Law obligation to protect Ariel and her baby from harm warring against its Second Law obligation to obey her order. Evidently Ariel's implied agreement to follow its instructions was enough to satisfy its First Law concern, for it nodded its head and said, "Very well. But do not overexert yourself on your walk."

Derec led her out of the hospital and along the walkway beside the building, ignoring the row of transport booths waiting by the entrance. They walked in silence for a time, lost in their own thoughts, taking comfort from each other's presence, but within a few blocks they had a silent host of Lucius's rodents following them, their hungry stares and soft chittering noises sending shivers up Derec's spine. He didn't know how dangerous they might be, but if nothing else, they were certainly spoiling the mood. With a sigh, he led Ariel back inside another building and up the elevator to the top, where they continued their walk along enclosed paths high above the streets. The rats hadn't yet reached these levels.

The tops of some of the buildings had been planted with grass and trees to make pocket parks; after passing three or four of them—all devoid of activity save for their robot gardeners unobtrusively tending the plants—they stopped to sit in the grass beneath a young apple tree and look out over the city. Ariel had been quiet for a long time now, but Derec couldn't take the silence anymore. He felt an incredible urge to babble.

"I'm still not sure I believe it's really happening," he said. "It's crazy to think about. A new person. A completely new mind, with a new viewpoint, new thoughts, new attitudes, new everything. And we're responsible for its development. It's daunting."

Ariel nodded, "I know what you mean. Who are we to be having a baby?"

"Better us than Lucius, at least," Derec said with a grin.

"I suppose. At least we know what one *is*." Ariel tried to smile, but hers was a fleeting smile at best. She turned away, said to the city, "Oh, Derec, I don't know. I don't know if I want to do this. I keep thinking about having it, and then I keep thinking about not having it, and right now I've got to say that not having it sounds a lot better to me." She looked back to Derec, and he could see the confusion written plain as words in her expression.

His own face must have mirrored her confusion. "Not having it," he said. "You mean . . . you mean . . . aborting it?" The instincts, or hormones, or whatever they were, still had a strong grip on him. It was hard to even say the word that would take his child from him.

"Yes, that's what I mean," said Ariel. "Aborting it. Stopping it now, while we still can. It's not like we wanted it, is it? We weren't trying for one. We were happy without it. If we'd known I *could* get pregnant, then we would have been using birth control, wouldn't we? So why should we change our entire lives because of some silly—accident?"

"Because it's *us! Our* child. *Because* it's a new person, a new mind, with a new viewpoint and all that. That's why we should keep it." Was that why? Derec fought for his own understanding even as he tried to explain it to Ariel. "It's— do you remember what it was like when we first found ourselves here? Me without a memory at all, yours slowly slipping from you, neither of us with any idea what we were doing here? Remember how lost we felt?"

Ariel's eyebrows wrinkled in concentration. "It's fuzzy that far back. But I know what you're talking about. I've felt lost often enough since then."

"Right. We had no purpose; that's why we felt that way. I spent my time trying to track down my father, thinking he could help restore my memory, but that was just a yearning for the past. We spent time searching for a cure for your disease, but that was just patching up the past, too. Now I find I've got a mother running around out here somewhere, too, and I was all set to spend however long it takes trying to find her, to see if she couldn't do for me what Avery won't, but now I don't even care. Now all of a sudden we have something to look forward to, something in our future. Who cares about the past when we've got that?"

Ariel shook her head. "Why should we grab at the first thing that comes along? Derec, this is going to change our *lives*. Unless we want to put the baby in a nursery, and it's obvious you don't, then we're going to have to take care of it. We're going to have to *live* with it, like Earthers and settlers do. Do you really want that? I'm not so sure I do. And besides that—" she waved away his protest, "—it's my body we're talking about here. Pregnancy is dangerous. It can cause all sorts of problems in a woman; blood clots, kidney damage—you wouldn't believe all the things that can go wrong. And for what? A future with a squalling brat in it? I can't see risking my life for that."

"But what about the baby's life? Isn't that a consideration?"

"Of course, it's a consideration," Ariel said angrily. "If it wasn't, I'd have had the medical robot abort it this morning. I'm still trying to weigh it out; my life and my future versus the life and future of what at this point amounts to a few dividing cells. It's a testament to how important I think it is that I'm considering it at all."

Derec had been subliminally aware of the gardener going about its job somewhere behind him. The soft whirr of the robot's grass-cutting blade had been a soothing noise at the edge of his perception, but the sudden silence when it stopped was enough to make him look around to the robot, just in time to see it topple onto its side, smashing a bed of flowers when it hit.

"What the—?" He stood, went over to the robot, and said, "Gardener. Do you hear me?"

No response.

Gardener, he sent via comlink.

Still nothing. He pulled it up to a sitting position, but it was like raising a statue. The robot was completely locked up. Derec let it fall on its side again. It made a quiet thud when it hit the ground.

"It couldn't handle the conflict," Derec said in wonder. "Its First Law obligation to protect you was fighting with its obligation to protect the baby, and it couldn't handle it."

"You sound surprised," said Ariel. "I'm not. It's tearing me apart, too."

Derec left the robot and went back to Ariel, sitting beside her and wrapping her in his arms.

"I wish it wasn't."

"Me too."

"What can I do to help?"

Ariel shook her head. "I don't know. Yes, I do. Just don't push me, okay? I know you want to keep it, but I've got to decide on my own whether or not I do. Once I know that, we can talk about what we're actually going to do. Okay?"

"Okay."

As if to confirm her independence, Ariel pulled away

and closed her eyes in thought. Derec leaned back in the grass and looked up through a tangle of leaves at the sky. An occasional cloud dotted the blue.

Did every new parent go through this? he wondered. Could what he and Ariel were feeling be normal? Did Avery and his mother agonize over whether or not to have him? He couldn't imagine Avery agonizing over any decision. His mother must have, though. She must have wondered if Derec would be worth the effort of childbirth. Evidently she had decided so, probably *before* she became pregnant, come to think of it, since she'd had no reason to believe she was infertile as Ariel had.

She and Avery must have been in love then. What a concept; someone loving Avery. Or was she just like him? Had their decision to have a child been nothing more than the practical way to acquire someone to experiment on?

It didn't matter. He and Ariel were in love; that was what mattered. The thought of staying with Ariel until their child grew up didn't scare him. Derec knew that parents on most planets didn't worry about that kind of responsibility— even parents more fond of one another than his own—but he intended to. The thought of raising a child gave his life direction, gave him a sense of purpose he hadn't even realized until now he was missing.

Ariel, evidently realizing he wouldn't pressure her whether he held onto her or not, lay down in the grass beside him, resting her head on his chest. His arms went around her automatically, and it felt perfectly natural to be holding her so. It felt right. For a time, as they watched the clouds drift past overhead, the rooftop garden seemed to become their whole universe, and it was a good universe.

Ariel's thoughts had evidently been paralleling his own, but along a different track. "I'm glad we're not on Earth any more," she said suddenly. "I'd feel even worse there."

"No kidding." Derec shuddered. With a population in the billions, Earth was no place to be having children. There, where the population density in the enclosed cities could be measured easily in people per square meter, every new mouth to feed was a tragedy, not a blessing.

And what was worse, too few of the people there were worried enough to do anything about it. Here stood an entire planet covered with city, full of robots eager to share it, yet Derec doubted if he could find enough people in all of Earth to fill even the section he could survey from this one rooftop. Most of them hated space, hated robots, and on an even more fundamental level, hated change. They wouldn't leave Earth even for a better world.

A few of them would. After a long hiatus, Earth had once again begun settling alien worlds, but the fraction of its population involved was insignificant. The birth rate there would replace its emigrants before they could achieve orbit.

It was a sobering thought. Derec recalled Lucius's words to Ariel at their first meeting, his assertion that no thinking being would want every human who might possibly exist to do so, but it seemed as if Earthers were doing their best to ensure just that. They seemed intent on turning their entire biosphere into a teeming mass of humanity.

An irrational fear washed over him, the fear that Earth society would somehow intrude upon his happiness even here, that its riot of bodies could somehow threaten even Robot City. Derec felt his heart begin beating faster, his breathing tighten, as he considered his child's potential enemies.

Hormones! he thought wryly a second later. Paranoia was evidently a survival trait.

"To space with Earth," he said, tickling Ariel playfully in the ribs. "We're beyond all that."

The sun had shifted position considerably when Derec awoke. He couldn't tell whether it was from the simple passage of time, or if the building had moved beneath them while they slept. Probably both, he decided. He lay in the grass, Ariel still sleeping with her head on his shoulder, while he decided whether or not to get up.

A noise from beyond the edge of the building made the decision for him. Someone had screamed! Derec was up in an instant, leaping for the railing around the edge and peering down.

A hunter-seeker robot—a stealthy, black-surfaced special-function 'bot with advanced detection circuitry—stood in the center of an intersection, pivoting slowly around in a circle. A rustle of motion in a doorway caught its attention and it stopped. It raised its right hand, pointing with the forefinger extended, and a bright red laser beam shot out from its finger toward the doorway. Another scream echoed off the buildings.

Derec looked up the street. Every intersection, for as far as he could see, had a hunter-seeker standing in it. Avery had ordered them to clean up the rodents—his way.

Stop! he sent to them. *Cease hunting activity.*

The hunter closest to him looked upward, and Derec felt a momentary urge to back away from the railing. Any robot—and Derec as well, for that matter—could tell what general direction a comlink signal was coming from, but a hunter-seeker could pinpoint the source—and shoot at it. But the robot couldn't fire at him. It would see instantly who he was, and the First Law would prevent it. Derec stayed at the railing and sent, *You are ordered to cease killing those creatures.*

I am sorry, master Derec. I already have orders to kill them.

"What's going on?" Ariel asked sleepily from his side. She leaned against the railing and looked down.

"Avery's ordered the robots to kill all of Lucius's rodents. I'm trying to get them to stop." *I order you not to kill them,* he sent. *You should respect life.*

I respect human life. That is all.

Those creatures carry human genes.

That has been explained to me. That does not make them human. As the hunter spoke, another rodent made a dash for safety, but the hunter twitched its hand in a blur of motion, the beam shot out, and the rodent tumbled end over end in the street, screaming. The hunter fired again and the screaming stopped.

They certainly have human vocal apparatus, Derec thought.

Damn it, you're upsetting me. Stop it!

The hunter robot paused at that, but evidently Avery had warned it to expect such a ploy. *I regret that I cannot,* it said. *Your displeasure is not as important as your safety. These creatures could pose a safety hazard.*

You don't know that.

I have been ordered to consider them as such. The hunter turned its attention back to the street. It resumed its search, shooting again at another rodent. This time the rodent died silently, and Derec realized that the robot was attempting to limit his discomfort by making a clean kill.

Derec tried to think of a way to get around Avery's programming, but no solution came to mind. Avery had made his orders first and stressed that they were to be followed no matter what Derec said; there was very little Derec could do to counter them now.

How fickle a robot's behavior could be under the three laws! A robot gardener could lock up at the mere mention of a life-threatening dilemma involving humans, but the hunter-seekers could shoot rodents all day long. None of them cared about life in general. Not even the gardener truly cared about his charges except for their potential to please a human.

How could that be right? Even the cruelest human cared about something. Derec was willing to bet even Avery had a soft spot for kittens or puppies or *something*. How could he ever expect a society of robots to mimic a human society if they held no reverence for life?

"Come on," Derec said, seething with righteous indignation. "Let's go home."

His anger had mellowed a bit by the time they reached their apartment, but it flared to life again the moment he saw Avery standing by the living room window, watching his hunter-seekers at work. He was about to start a shouting match, but Mandelbrot's sudden exclamation switched the topic of discussion before he ever had a chance.

"Congratulations, Ariel!" said the robot the moment he saw them enter the apartment.

"Shh!" she told him, forefinger to her lips, but the damage had been done.

Avery turned away from the window. "Congratulations? Whatever for, Mandelbrot?"

His question was a stronger order to speak than Ariel's whispered command to be quiet. The robot said, "Mistress Ariel is preg—"

"Shut *up*!"

Mandelbrot stiffened, the conflict of orders creating a momentary Second Law crisis.

"Preg," Avery said into the silence. "Preg*nant* perhaps? Are you, my dear?" His voice was all honey, but neither she nor Derec was fooled. Avery had opposed their association from the start, was instrumental in separating them when they had first become lovers on Aurora, and had done everything he could to keep them from redeveloping an affection for one another when circumstances had forced them back into close company. He was less than happy at the news, and they knew it.

"Don't strain yourself smiling," Derec growled.

Avery shook his head. "You sound overjoyed. One would suppose you weren't ready for it. Is that it? Did it take you by surprise?"

"None of your business," Ariel said.

"Of course not. However, as a father myself, I do have a certain interest in the situation. You may be happy to know that it is reversible."

Ariel shot him a dark look. "I'm aware of that." She turned away, heading down the hallway toward her and Derec's room.

"Good," Avery said to her receding back. He turned back to the window. "I ordered Lucius's laboratories destroyed," he said nonchalantly.

"You *what*?"

"Really, you should have your hearing checked. That's twice in two days. I said I ordered Lucius's laboratories destroyed, and all the robots in them as well. You didn't really think I'd let you turn my city into a zoo, now, did you?"

"A balanced ecosystem is not a zoo."

"Wrong. A zoo is not a balanced ecosystem, granted, but the converse is not necessarily true. To me, any ecosystem in this city—other than the minimum necessary to sustain the farm—would be a zoo, and I acted to prevent it."

"*You* acted. What about me? What about—"

"Alarm. Alarm. Alarm," the living room com console interrupted. "Experimental robots have awakened."

"Ah, good. Keep them under restraint," Avery commanded.

"Restraints ineffective. The robots have changed shape and slipped through them. They are now leaving the laboratory."

"Where are they headed?"

"Destination uncertain. Wait. They have entered transport booths. Destination . . . spaceport."

CHAPTER 4

THE WILD GOOSE CHASE

"The spaceport! They're trying to escape!"

"A likely assumption," Avery said, even as Derec sent, *Adam, Eve, Lucius, this is Derec. Stop.*

There was a burst of static—Derec recognized it now as high-speed data transfer—then the response, *Why have you ordered this? We do not wish to stop.*

I don't care. Come back to the apartment.

Acknowledged. Please explain why.

Beside him, Avery spoke to the com console. "They are to return to the laboratory at once. I order it."

Ignoring him, and the robots' request, Derec asked, *Why are you going to the spaceport?*

We are no longer going there, since you ordered us not to.

Why were *you going there?* he asked with exasperation.

We intended to leave for Ceremya, the planet upon which Eve awakened. We have unfinished business there.

"I am unable to comply with your order," the central

computer told Avery through the com console. "Derec's order supersedes."

"What order? What's going on?" Avery noticed Derec's distracted expression. "You're talking with them? This is your idea, isn't it?"

"What?"

"You're helping them escape!"

"I am not!"

"You expect me to believe that? You've wanted to let them go all along, and now as soon as I tell you I've stopped your other little project, you bust them loose. Well, it won't work. I'll have them back inside half an hour, and this time I'll take all three of them apart with a rusty knife! Central, direct the hunters to stop what they're doing and capture the runaway robots. They may shoot to destroy, if necessary, but I want the pieces."

"Cancel that," Derec said.

"I am sorry; now Dr. Avery's order supersedes," the central computer responded.

"Cancel it!" Derec commanded, but he was staring at Avery, not the console.

"I regret—"

"Masters, please calm down," Mandelbrot interrupted, but Derec ignored him. *Avery's order involves a Third Law violation*, he sent to the computer. *My order does not. My order should take precedence.*

How does Avery's order involve a Third Law violation? the computer asked.

The question brought Derec up short. The Third Law stated that a robot had to protect its *own* existence; it said nothing about *another* robot's existence. *All right*, he sent, *it's not a direct violation, but it does violate the spirit of the law. Since I've ordered them to return anyway, following*

Avery's order would cause three robots to be needlessly destroyed. That's obviously not the best solution to the situation at hand.

The computer didn't respond immediately. That almost certainly meant it was considering Derec's argument, but wasn't yet convinced. On sudden inspiration, Derec added, *The first part of Avery's order can stand. Let the hunters stop what they're doing.* The conflict of potentials in the computer's robot brain would be even less that way, possibly enough so to tip the balance toward Derec's order.

"Acknowledged," the computer finally replied, using the com console.

"What did you do?" Avery demanded.

"Canceled your stupid order," Derec replied. "It wasn't necessary. I've already stopped them, and they're on their way here."

"Is that true?" Avery asked the console, but the computer evidently thought he was asking Derec and remained silent.

"Yes, it is," Derec answered for it. "I'm also trying to find out why they tried to escape in the first place. Now be quiet so I can hear myself think."

"How do I know you aren't plotting against me?"

Derec rolled his eyes to the ceiling. "You want your own comlink, inject yourself with chemfets. Until then, let me use mine."

Avery glowered, balling his fists in frustration, but at last he let out a deep breath and said, "Go ahead."

"Thank you." Derec hesitated a moment, considering reward theory as a tool for conditioning, then sent to the computer, *Echo my comlink conversation to the com console.*

"Echoing," the computer responded aloud.

What were you planning to do on Ceremya? he sent to

the robots. He wasn't sure which of the three he was talking with, or if it was all three at once, but he didn't suppose it mattered at this point.

"What were you planning to do on Ceremya?" The computer simulated his voice faithfully; it sounded as clear over the com console as if he had actually spoken aloud.

We must continue to research the Laws of Humanics. Also, Eve did not have the opportunity to imprint properly upon the Ceremyons while she was there, and we believe doing so may be important to our joint development.

The echo was distracting, but Derec held his hands over his ears and sent, *What type of development do you expect?*

If we knew that, we wouldn't have to go, the robots replied with characteristic logic.

The spaceship was like none Derec had ever seen before. Normal ships were usually streamlined for atmospheric passage, but not to this degree. This ship was smoother than streamlined; it was seamless. It looked as if it had been sculpted in ice and then dipped in liquid silver. Derec, standing before it, realized that the design robots had, however inadvertently, produced a work of art.

Resting on the runway in takeoff configuration, it was a sleek, fast airplane, but Derec knew that its present appearance wouldn't last beyond the atmosphere. Once away from gravity and wind drag, the ship would transform into whatever shape most easily accommodated its passengers, for its hull and most of the interior furnishings were made of the same cellular material that made up the City. The hyperdrive and the more delicate mechanisms such as control, navigation, and life support were made of more conventional materials, but the majority of the ship was cellular.

It was one of perhaps three dozen at the spaceport, all built within the last few weeks. Derec had ordered them constructed on a whim, remembering when he and Ariel had been stranded in Robot City for lack of a ship and deciding to remedy that problem for good now that the robots had his own ship to refer to, but he had been too busy to inspect them until now.

"It'll do," he told the ground crew robots, who were hovering about anxiously, pleased that the humans had chosen this ship for their journey yet nervously awaiting rejection all the same.

Ever mindful of his duty to protect his human charges, Mandelbrot asked, "Has it been tested?"

"We took it on a test flight of twenty light-years round trip," one of the ground crew replied. "Six days of flight and four jumps. All its subsystems performed flawlessly."

"Does it have a name?" Ariel asked. She, Dr. Avery, Wolruf, and the three experimental robots stood beside Derec amid a pile of baggage.

The ground crew robot turned its head to face her. "We have not named it yet."

"Flying a ship without a name!" she said in mock surprise. "I'm surprised you made it back."

"I do not understand. How can a name be a significant factor in the success of a test flight?"

Ariel laughed, and Wolruf joined her. "I didn't know 'umans had that superstition too," the alien said.

"It's supposed to be bad luck to board a ship without a name," Ariel explained to the puzzled robot, but her explanation left it no more enlightened than before.

"Bad . . . luck?" it asked.

"Oh, never mind. I'm just being silly. Come on, let's get on board."

"Name first," Wolruf said with surprising vehemence. "May be just superstition, may not. Never 'urts to 'umor fate."

"Then I dub it the *Wild Goose Chase*," Avery said with finality, gesturing to the robots to pick up his bags. "Now let's get this ridiculous expedition into space before I change my mind." He turned and stomped up the extended ramp, not noticing the black letters flowing into shape on the hull just in front of the wing.

Wild Goose Chase.

Was it? Derec couldn't know. Avery certainly seemed to think so, but he had allowed his curiosity to overcome his reservations all the same. Derec had been all for the trip, but now he was feeling reservations, both about the trip itself and about the deeper subterfuge it represented. Should he go through with it? He followed Wolruf and Ariel and the robots up the ramp, pausing at the door, debating.

Do it, a tiny voice seemed to whisper in his head.

Okay, he answered it. To the central computer, he sent, *Investigate my personal files. Password: "anonymous." Examine instruction set "Ecosystem." Begin execution upon our departure.*

Acknowledged.

Derec turned away into the ship and let the airlock seal itself behind him. Avery hadn't destroyed everything when he'd destroyed Lucius's labs. Derec still had his files on ecosystems, and now the central computer did, too. It would give the robots something useful to do while they were gone, and when they returned, the place would be lush and green, with animals in the parks and birds and butterflies in the air. Avery would have a fit—but then Avery was always having fits. It wouldn't matter. By the time he found out about it, it would be too late to stop.

• • •

"I want to keep it," Ariel said.

They were in their own stateroom on the ship, hours out from Robot City. Beyond the viewport the planet was already a small point of light in the glittering vastness of space. The sun had not yet changed perceptibly, but as the ship picked up speed in its climb out of the gravity well toward a safe jump point, the sun, too, would begin to dwindle until it was just another speck in the heavens.

Derec had been staring out at the stars, contemplating the vastness of the universe and his place in it, but now, upon hearing Ariel's words, he spun around from the viewport, the stars forgotten. She could be talking about only one thing.

"The baby? You want to keep the baby?"

She was sitting on the edge of the bed. Now that she had gotten his attention, it seemed as if she was uncomfortable under his gaze. Looking past him into space herself now, she said, "I think so. I'm not sure. I'm still trying to make sense of it all, but after that gardener locked up I realized what I was considering, and after Avery said what he said about it, I realized it wasn't as simple a decision as I thought at first."

Her voice took on a hard edge. "*He'd* like it to be, but it's not. If we were on Earth I might agree with him, but here, with all this space to expand into, with all those robots practically falling over themselves to serve so few of us, it's a different equation. An Earther gives up the rest of her life to a baby, but I only have to give up part of my comfort for part of a year. For that we get a new person."

She looked into his eyes as if seeking reassurance, then plunged on: "And if we treat him—or her—right, then we'll have a family. I know it's not the way we were brought up;

I know Aurorans aren't supposed to care about our parents and our children, but I've seen what happened to us, and I don't like it. That's why I'm telling you this now. If I have this baby, I want us to be a family. I want it to grow up with us, to be a *part* of us; not just some stranger who happens to share our genes. Can you accept that?"

Derec could hardly believe his ears. She was asking him to accept exactly what he had wanted all along. "Can I *accept* that? I *love* it. I love *you*!" He took her hand and pulled her up from the bed, put his arms around her, and kissed her passionately.

Behind him, the door chimed softly and Mandelbrot's voice said, "Dinner is ready."

"Damn."

One of the nice things about a cellular ship, Derec discovered, was that the common room was much more than just a place with a table in it. As dinner wound down and the mood shifted toward the pleasant lethargy that comes after a good meal, the table enclosed over the dirty dishes, dropped into the floor, and the chairs widened and softened from dining chairs to evening couches, simultaneously moving back to give the room a less-crowded atmosphere. The lighting dimmed and soft music began to play.

Derec merged his chair with Ariel's and put his arm around her. She leaned her head over to rest on his shoulder, closing her eyes. His hand automatically went to her upper back and began rubbing softly, kneading the muscles at the base of her neck and shoulders.

"Oh, yeah," she murmured, bending forward so he could reach the rest of her back.

The robots had not eaten dinner, so they were not sitting in chairs, but instead stood unobtrusively beside and behind the four who were seated. Avery was leaning back with eyes closed, off in his own universe somewhere, but Wolruf watched Derec and Ariel with open interest. At last she sighed and said, "That looks 'onderful." Turning to Eve, she asked, " 'ow about it? You scratch mine; I'll scratch yours."

"I have no need to have my back scratched," Eve replied without moving.

Somewhat taken aback, Wolruf said, "Do mine anyway, please," and turned to give Eve an easy reach.

"Why?"

"Because I'd like to 'ave my back scratched," Wolruf said, a hint of a growl to her voice now.

"Perhaps you are not aware that I am engaged in conversation with Adam and Lucius."

Derec had stopped scratching as well, and was looking at Eve with an astonished expression. Hadn't they been ordered not to use their comlinks when humans were present? No, he remembered now. That had been just a suggestion, and from another robot at that. They could ignore it if they wanted. But this business with Wolruf—this was different.

"What does your conversation have to do with anything?" he asked. "She wants you to scratch her back. That's as good as an order."

"Wolruf is not human. Therefore I need not be concerned with her wishes."

"You wha—? That's absurd. *I* order you to—"

"Wait a minute." It was Avery, evidently not so far away as he had appeared. "This is intriguing. Let's check it out. Wolruf, order her to scratch your back."

It was hard to read expression on the alien's scrunched-in canine face, but Derec was sure he was seeing exasperation now. Wolruf took a deep breath, shook her head once, then said, "All ri'. Eve, I order you to scratch my back."

Eve stood her ground. "I refuse."

"Order Lucius to do it," Avery said.

"Lucius, scratch my—"

"I refuse also," Lucius interrupted.

"Adam," Wolruf said, taking Avery's nod in Adam's direction as her cue, "you scratch my back. Please."

The small politeness made a difference, but not the one Wolruf had hoped for. Adam said, "I do not wish to offend, but I find that I must refuse as well."

"Why?" Wolruf asked, slumping back into her chair, resigned to having an unscratched back.

"Wait. Wolruf, there's one more robot here."

Wolruf looked to Mandelbrot, standing directly behind Derec and Ariel's chair. Mandelbrot didn't wait for her order, but moved silently over to Wolruf and reached out to scratch the alien's furry back.

"Thank you," Wolruf said with a sigh.

"You are quite welcome, Master Wolruf," Mandelbrot said, and Derec would have sworn he heard a slight twist to the word "master." Could Mandelbrot disapprove of another robot's conduct? Evidently so.

"Interesting," Avery said. "Eve, turn around to face the wall."

Silently, Eve obeyed.

"Hold your right hand out to the side and wiggle your fingers."

Eve obeyed again.

"Adam and Lucius, follow the same orders I just gave Eve."

The two other robots also turned to face the wall, held their right hands out, and wiggled their fingers.

"That's a relief," Avery said. "For a second there I thought they'd quit obeying altogether."

"Relief to you, maybe," said Wolruf, shifting so Mandelbrot could reach her entire back.

"It looks like they've independently decided what makes a human and what doesn't. Am I right?"

Silence. Three robots stood facing the wall, their right hands fluttering like tethered butterflies.

"Lucius, am I right?"

"You are correct, Dr. Avery," the robot answered.

"So what's your definition?"

"We presently define 'human' as a sentient being possessing a genetic code similar to that which I found in the Robot City library under the label 'human.' "

"A sentient being," Avery echoed. "So those rats of yours still don't qualify?"

"That is correct."

"How do you know Avery has the proper code?" asked Derec.

"He has medical records on file. We accessed them when the question first arose. We also examined yours and Ariel's."

"But not Wolruf's."

"There was no need. Her physical appearance rules out the possibility that she might be human."

"Even though she's obviously sentient."

"That is correct. A being must be both sentient and carry the proper genetic code to be human."

"What about the baby I'm carrying?" Ariel asked. "Isn't my baby human?"

Lucius was silent for a moment, then he said, "Not at present. The embryo cannot formulate an order, nor does it require protection beyond that which we would normally provide you; therefore we need not be concerned with it."

"That sounds kind of heartless."

"We possess microfusion power generators. What do you expect?"

Adam spoke up. "May we stop wiggling our fingers? It serves no useful purpose."

"No, you may not," Avery said. "It pleases me to see you following orders."

"Enough," Wolruf growled, whether to Mandelbrot or to the humans neither knew. Mandelbrot stopped scratching her back as Wolruf stood up and said, "This is depressing. I think I'll go check on our jump schedule." She favored the three hand-fluttering robots with a sour look, then moved off toward the control room.

"Listen here," Derec said when she was gone. "I order all of you to—"

"Wait," Avery interrupted. "You were about to order them to follow her orders, weren't you?"

"That's right."

"Let's wait on that. Let's see if—just a minute. You three, stop moving your hands."

The robots stopped moving their hands. On their own, they dropped those hands back to their sides. Avery frowned at that, but said simply, "When I tell you to give me privacy, I want you to stop listening to our conversation. Filter out everything but the words 'return to service,' upon which you will begin listening again. Do not use your comlink in the meantime. In fact, this is a general order: Do not use your comlink for conversation between yourselves. Do you understand that?"

"We understand," Lucius said, "but we—I—wish to protest. Using speech to communicate will necessarily slow our joint thought processes."

"And it'll keep you from locking up on us again. I order it. Now give us privacy."

The robots made no motion to indicate whether they had heard or not.

"Wiggle your fingers again."

No motion.

Avery turned to Derec and Ariel. "Okay, what I want to do is this: Let's wait and see if they modify their definition of human to include Wolruf on their own, without our orders. Wolruf isn't in any danger from them, and Mandelbrot will take her orders if she needs a robot."

"In the meantime she gets treated like a subhuman," Derec protested. "I don't like it."

"She is subhuman," Avery said, "but that's beside the point. Think a minute. You convinced me to let these robots go to Ceremya—and to come along myself—so we could see what kind of new developments they came up with. So here's a new development. Let's study it."

Avery's argument had merit, Derec knew. He didn't like it, but it made sense. That's why they had come, to study these robots in action.

"We should at least give her First Law protection," he said.

"No, that'd skew the experiment. Look, your furry friend isn't in any danger here; let's just let it go for now. If anything happens, we can modify their orders then."

"All right," Derec said. "I'll go along with it for now, but the moment she looks like she's in danger . . ."

"Fine, fine. Okay, return to service."

The robots shifted slightly. Eve asked, "May we turn away from the wall now?"

"I suppose so."

The robots turned to face one another. "Since we must communicate verbally," Lucius said, "I suggest we each pick

a separate tone range. That way we may at least speak simultaneously."

"If you do, do it quietly," said Ariel.

"We intend to," the robot replied.

Derec gave Ariel a last squeeze, then stood up and announced, "I'm going to talk to Wolruf. She sounded pretty
unhappy."

"Go ahead," Ariel said. "I think I'll read."

Avery grunted noncommittally, his eyes already closed
in thought again.

The control room was large enough for only two people.
The ship was largely automatic, but in the interest of safety
it also carried a complete set of manual controls. Derec
found Wolruf in the pilot's seat, a glimmering holographic
star map floating over the controls before her. It was the
only illumination in the cabin, save for the real stars shining
in through the viewscreen. In the midst of the map a thin
silver line connected five dots in a not-quite-straight line.
One point was no doubt Robot City; the other Ceremya. The
kinks in the line in between were jump points, places where
the ship would stop along the way to reorient and recharge
its engines.

A ship could theoretically make the entire trip in a single hyperspace jump, discounting the time it took to crawl
slowly through normal space to the safe jump points in its
origin and destination systems. That was seldom done, however, except for short trips. It was much easier, both for
navigation and on the engines, to make a series of short
jumps from star to star along the way, correcting for minor
deviations in course and allowing the engines to rest each
time.

"Looks like we 'ave four jumps," Wolruf said as Derec

slid into the copilot's seat beside her. "First one tonight."

"Good. The sooner the better. Things are getting a little strange on this trip already."

"Could say that, all ri'."

"We didn't tell them to follow your orders. Avery wants to see if they'll decide to do it on their own."

Wolruf nodded. The motion took her head into and out of the star field before her; for a moment she had a pattern of tiny white dots on her forehead.

"If you don't want to be part of an experiment like that, I'll go ahead and order them to. We don't have to do what Avery says. He isn't God."

"None of us are," Wolruf said with a toothy smile. "That's what the robots're trying to tell us. We aren't gods and they aren't servants, even if 'umans *did* create them to be."

Derec laughed. "You know, when you think of it, this whole situation is really sick. I'm here because Avery was playing God; the robots are here because my mother, whoever she is, is playing God; I've got an entire Robot City running around in my body and giving me control of even more cities; Ariel and I are playing God right now with the fate of our baby—everyone's caught up in this web of dominance and submission. Who orders who around, and who has to obey who? It's twisted, warped!"

A twinge of conscience made Derec add to himself, And I'm playing God with the ecosystem project. . . .

"Everybody plays God," Wolruf said. "Maybe that's what life is all about. None of us *is* God, but we all try to be. Even I don't mind 'aving an order obeyed now and then."

"Hmm."

"Trouble with being God, is she 'as too much responsibility. Power always brings responsibility, or should."

"Yeah, that's the problem, all right."

Derec looked out the viewscreen. An entire galaxy full of stars beckoned him. Who would want control over all that? The use of it, definitely, but control? Not him.

He laughed again. "It reminds me of the old question of who runs the government. Some people want to, but the best ones for the job are the people who don't. They take their responsibility seriously."

Wolruf nodded. "Maybe that's why most robots like taking orders. No responsibility. Those other three started out on their own, learned to deal with it, so don't like taking orders."

"It's possible," Derec admitted. Was that why he didn't like taking orders, then; because his earliest memories were of being on his own, of making his own decisions? Or was something deeper driving him? Nature or nurture? No one had ever answered that question successfully, not for humans, anyway. For robots the answer had always been obvious: Their behavior was in their nature. It was built in. But now, with these three and their insurrection, that answer didn't seem so pat anymore.

Silence descended upon the control room while he and Wolruf both thought their own thoughts. Wolruf turned back to the star map and pressed a few keys on the console beneath it. One of the silver lines shifted position, bridging the gap between two of their waypoint stars in one jump instead of two. At once the line turned red and an annoying beep filled the cabin. The proposed modification to the jump path was unacceptably risky to the computer.

"Very conscientious navigator," Wolruf remarked. "Better than 'uman. Or me."

Was that a note of regret in her voice? Wolruf was the

best pilot of the group; she had always done the flying when she and Derec and Ariel had gone anywhere. Was she feeling useless now?

"You could still use the manual controls if you want," Derec offered.

"Oh, no. I'm not complaining." Wolruf pressed another few buttons and the original jump path returned to the star field. She leaned back in the pilot's chair and crossed her arms over her chest. Smiling toothily, she said, "Less responsibility for me."

Despite her confidence in the autopilot, Derec was sure Wolruf would stay in the control room for the jump. Knowing that, he knew that he could put the whole thing out of his mind, safe in the knowledge that she could take care of any problem that might arise should the automatic system fail to do the job right. All the same, when the scheduled time approached, he found himself shifting restlessly in bed, waiting for the momentary disorientation that would mark their passage through hyperspace. He had jumped dozens of times, but he still couldn't sleep with the knowledge that he was about to be squeezed through a warp in the universe and squirted light-years across space.

At last he could stare at the ceiling no longer. He got up, put on his robe, and slipped quietly from the room. The bedrooms opened onto a hallway, with the control room at one end and the common room on the other. Derec hesitated, wondering which way to turn, but finally decided against looking over Wolruf's shoulder at the countdown clock. Already relegated to backup status, she might misinterpret his nervousness as concern over her competence.

He turned toward the common room. He might not be able to sleep before a jump, but eating was no problem.

As he approached, he heard a babble of quiet voices. Remembering Avery's command to the robots to refrain from using the comlink, he expected to find all three of them in a huddle, but when he stepped into the room, he found only Lucius and Eve, whispering like lovers in the dimly lit room. They had picked up another human trait since their last communication fugue: Both were seated in a loveseat, leaning back comfortably with their legs crossed.

They stopped their whispering and turned to look at Derec. "Just getting a midnight snack," he said, feeling silly explaining his actions to a robot but feeling the need to do it all the same.

"Make yourself at home," replied Lucius. He turned to Eve and whispered something too quick to follow, and she whispered something back. Derec—already heading for the automat—nearly tripped over himself when Eve emitted a high, little-girl-like giggle in response.

Derec recognized that giggle. It was almost a perfect copy of Ariel's. Did Eve know what a giggle was for, or was she just testing it out?

He wasn't sure he wanted to know.

The whispering and giggling continued behind him as he dialed for a cup of hot chocolate and a handful of cookies. He had just about decided to join Wolruf in the control room after all when Wolruf silently entered the room. He turned to say hello and realized that it wasn't Wolruf, but Adam in Wolruf's form. He had evidently been talking with her, and in the close environment had slowly imprinted on her.

"Hello," Derec said anyway.

" 'ello," Adam said. He waited for Derec to get his cookies and chocolate, then punched a combination of his own on the automat. Derec bit into a cookie and waited, assuming that the robot was getting a snack for Wolruf as well and intending to accompany the robot back to the control room.

The automat took a moment to shift over to whatever it was Adam had ordered. While they waited, Derec noticed that Wolruf's features were slowly losing clarity as the robot's form shifted back toward the human under Derec's influence.

The automat chimed and Wolruf's snack, a bowl of something that might have been raw brussels sprouts, rose up out of its depths. Adam reached out for it, hesitated, took it in his hands, then dumped it back in the waste hopper and turned away.

"Wait a minute!" Derec said, blowing cookie crumbs toward the departing robot in his haste. "Come back here."

Adam turned around and stepped forward to stand in front of Derec.

"Why did you throw Wolruf's snack away?"

"I did not wish to be ordered about."

"Then why did you dial it up in the first place?"

"I—do not know. Wolruf and I were talking about hyperspatial travel, and Wolruf expressed a desire for something to eat. I offered to get it for her, but now I do not know why."

Because you were imprinting on her, that's why, Derec thought, and then I reminded you what a "true" human was.

He didn't say that aloud, but he did say, "So rather than let anyone think you would accept an order from a nonhuman, you tossed it away as soon as you realized what you were doing."

"That . . . was my intention, yes."

"What about a favor to a friend? Doesn't that count for anything?"

"I do not know about favors."

Derec was rapidly growing tired of the robots' foolishness, especially where Wolruf's comfort was concerned. "This," he said. He punched the "repeat" button and waited while the automat delivered up another bowl of crisp vegetables, then dropped his cookies in the bowl, picked it up in one hand and took his chocolate in the other, making sure the robot saw how awkward it was, and walked toward the door with it. In the hallway, he turned back and said, "This is a favor." Then he turned away and headed for the control room to wait for the jump with his friend.

CHAPTER 5

FAVORS

Space travel didn't seem to affect morning sickness. Derec, lying in bed and listening to Ariel in the Personal, wondered if this was the way their days were going to start for the next nine months or if her body would slowly get used to being pregnant. He was glad it was her and not him. It was an awful thought and he knew it, but all the same that was how he felt. Pregnancy scared him. It was an internal change nearly as sweeping as the one he had gone through when Avery had injected him with the chemfets, and he knew from experience what that kind of thing felt like. The physical changes were nothing compared to what went on in your mind. Watching and feeling your body change and not being able to do anything about it—that was the scary part.

When Ariel emerged, Derec gave her a hug and a kiss for support, then took his turn in the Personal while she dressed. He showered away the fatigue left over from spending most of the night in the control room, standing beneath the cascading water until he was sure he must have run every molecule of it on board through the recycler at least twice. When he emerged, pink and wrinkled, Ariel was already gone, so he dressed quickly and went to join her at breakfast.

He found her arguing with a trio of stubborn robots.

"Because I ordered you to, that's why!" he heard her shout as she walked down the hallway.

A robot voice, Lucius's perhaps, said, "We have complied with your order. I merely ask why it was given. Your order to cease our conversation, combined with Dr. Avery's order to refrain from using our comlinks, effectively prevents us from communicating. Can this be your intent?"

"I just want some quiet around here. You guys talk all the time."

"We have much to talk about. If we are to discover our place in the universe, we must correlate a great deal of information."

When Derec entered the common room, he saw that it had indeed been Lucius doing the talking. The other two were sitting quietly alongside him and opposite Ariel at the breakfast table, but they were either following Ariel's order to keep quiet or else simply content to let Lucius be their spokesman. Mandelbrot was also in the room, but he was having nothing to do with the situation. He stood quietly in a niche in the wall beside the automat.

Lucius turned to Derec as soon as he had cleared the doorway and asked, "Can you persuade Ariel to rescind her order?"

Derec looked from the robot to Ariel, who shrugged her shoulders as if to say, "It's a mystery to me, too."

"Why should I do that?" Derec asked.

"It inflicts an undue hardship upon us."

"Shutting up is a hardship?"

"Yes."

"I thought it was a courtesy." Derec went to the automat and dialed for breakfast.

"It would be a courtesy to allow intelligent beings engaged in their own project to do so without hindrance."

"Ah. You're saying you have no time to obey orders, is that it?"

"Essentially, yes. The time exists, but we have our own pursuits to occupy it."

Derec took his breakfast, a bowl of fruit slices covered with heavy cream and sugar—or their synthetic equivalent, at any rate—and sat down beside Ariel. The robots watched him take a bite, look over to Ariel in amusement, then back to the robots again without saying anything. They seemed to sense that now was not a good time to interrupt.

Derec puzzled it over in his thoughts for half a bowl of fruit before he had sufficiently organized his argument to speak. When he finally did, he waggled his spoon at the robots for emphasis and said, "Duty is a bitch. I agree. But we all have duties of one sort or another. When Adam led his wolf pack against the Robot City on the planet where he first awoke, I had to abandon what I wanted to do and go off to try to straighten out the mess. At great personal danger to myself and to Mandelbrot, I might add. While I was gone, Ariel had to go to Ceremya to try to straighten out the mess from *another* Robot City. We'd have both rather stayed on Aurora, but we went because it was our duty. We took Adam and Eve back to the original Robot City because we felt it was our duty to give you a chance to develop your personalities in a less confusing environment,"—he nodded toward the two silent robots—"and when we got there we had to track *you* down, Lucius, because it was our duty to stop the damage you were doing to the city programming. Now we're heading for Ceremya again because all three of you need to learn something there, and we don't feel comfortable letting you go off on your own.

"None of this is what we would have been doing if it was left up to us. We'd much rather be on Aurora again, living in the forest and having our needs taken care of by robots who don't talk back to us, but we're here because our duty requires it."

He waved his spoon again to forestall comment. "And even if we had stayed there, we'd still have duties. Humans have to sleep, have to eat, have to shower—whether we want to or not. Most times we want to, but we have to nonetheless. Ariel is going to be carrying a developing fetus for nine months, which I'm sure she would rather not do if there was a better way, but there isn't, and she's decided to keep the baby so she's going to have to put up with being pregnant. That's a duty. I'm wasting my time explaining this to you, but I do it because I feel it's my duty to do that, too.

"The point is, we all have duties. When you add them all up, it doesn't leave a whole lot of time for whatever else you want to do, but you have to put up with that. Everybody has to structure their free time around their duties."

Lucius shook his head. "You overlook the obvious solution of reducing the number of your duties."

"Ah," Derec said. "Now I get it. That explains yesterday. You want to cut down on your duties, but you've got a hard-wired compulsion to follow any orders given by a human, so you narrow down the definition of human to exclude Wolruf. Suddenly you have only three-fourths as many orders to follow. That's it, isn't it?"

Lucius was slow in answering, but he finally said, "That was not our conscious intent, but now that I examine the incident in light of your comments today, I must conclude that you are correct."

"It works both ways, you know."

"What other way do you mean?"

"You thought you were human once. Now you're excluded by your own definition."

"Oh."

Ariel clapped softly. "Touché," she said.

Avery chose that moment to enter the room. "Sounds like a lively discussion going on in here," he said, taking the only remaining chair, the one beside Derec. He turned to Lucius and said, "I'll have a cheese omelet."

"Ariel and Derec each got their own breakfast," the robot replied. "Why can you not do the same?"

"Wrong answer," Derec muttered.

Avery stared in amazement at the robot, his mouth agape. "What the—?" he began, then banged his hand down flat on the table. "Get me a cheese omelet, now!"

Lucius lurched to his feet under the force of Avery's direct command. He took a faltering step toward the automat, and as he did his form began to change. His smooth, humanoid surface became pocked with circles, each of which slowly took on the teeth and spokes of a gear, while his arms and legs became simple metal levers driven by cables and pulleys. His head became a dented metal cannister with simple holes in it for eyes and a round speaker for a mouth. The gears meshed, the pulleys moved, and with a howl of unlubricated metal, Lucius took another step. His quiet gait changed to a heavy "clomp, clomp, clomp," as he lurched the rest of the way to the automat.

"Yes, master," the speaker in his face said with a loud hum. "Cheese omelet, master." He poked at the buttons on the automat with fingers that had suddenly become stiff metal claws.

Too stunned by his performance to do more than stare, Derec, Ariel, and Avery watched as he took the plate from the automat, clomped back to Avery's side, and set it down in front of him. The speaker hummed again, and Lucius said, "I may have to follow your orders—it may be my *duty* to follow your orders—but I don't have to like it."

The explosion Derec expected never came. Avery merely said, "That's fine. Everybody should hate something. But from now on you are to consider my every whim to be a direct order for you to perform. You will be alert for these whims of mine. You will neither intrude excessively nor hesitate in carrying them out, but will instead be as efficient and unobtrusive as possible. Do I make myself clear?"

"You do. I wish to—"

"Your wishes don't concern me. *My* wishes do. And I preferred your former shape."

Lucius became a blur of transformation, the gears and pulleys blending once again into a smooth humanoid form.

"There, you see?" Avery said to Derec. "You just have to know how to talk to them." He picked up his fork and stabbed a bite of egg, put it in his mouth, and said around the mouthful, "I've had lots of practice. You were a lot like that as a child, you know. Rebellious and resentful. A parent has to learn how to handle that early on."

"May I speak?" Lucius asked.

"Not for a while. Use this time to think instead. And get me a cup of coffee."

Lucius moved at once to obey. Avery looked over to Adam and Eve, still sitting silently at the table. Their eyes had been upon Avery all along, though, and it was obvious they were waiting for him to lower the boom on them as well.

He held their gaze for what seemed an eternity even to Derec, who felt that he could cut the tension between them with a knife.

At last Avery broke the spell. "Boo," he said and turned his attention back to his breakfast.

It was a quiet day on board the *Wild Goose Chase*. The ship had made its first jump on schedule in the night, and was now coasting at high speed through the waypoint star system toward the next jump point, which it would reach early the next morning. There was little to do in the meantime save look out at the stars, read, or play games. The robots were making themselves scarce, save for Lucius, who followed Avery like a shadow wherever he went. Even Mandelbrot was more taciturn than usual, no doubt trying to decide for himself where he fit into the general scheme of things as they now stood.

Derec decided to show Wolruf how to play chess, but gave it up when the alien insisted that the pieces should move in packs. He spent the rest of the day with a book, and went to bed early. Wolruf also went to bed, expressing her faith in the automatic controls to make the jump on schedule without her.

Derec surprised himself by actually being able to sleep with no one at the helm. Evidently boredom was a stronger force than worry. He managed to escape both in dreams, but his dreams ended suddenly in the middle of the night when he awoke with a start to the shrill howl of an alarm. He sat up and called on the light, trying to shake the sleep from his head enough to decide what to do next.

"What's the matter?" Ariel asked sleepily. She sat up

beside him, gathering the sheet around her as if for protection.

"I don't know. I'll go see." Derec made to get out of bed.

"Why don't you just ask?" Ariel was always quicker to wake up than he was.

"Oh. Yeah." *What's going on?* he sent out over the comlink.

General alert, a featureless voice replied. The autopilot, no doubt. *Life support system failure.*

Life support! Derec suddenly felt his breath catch. *What happened to it? The oxygen regeneration system has failed.*

He let his breath out again in a sigh of relief. Oxygen regeneration was serious, but not as serious as, say, a breach in the hull. They weren't actually losing air, at least.

"There's a problem with the oxygen regenerator," he said to Ariel. "Come on, let's see how bad it is."

As they pulled on their robes and stepped out into the hallway, Derec realized that the best thing to do in a case like this was to go back to sleep and reduce their oxygen consumption while the robots fixed the problem, but the time to think of that would have been *before* the alarm woke everyone up, not after. He couldn't have slept now unless he were drugged, and he had no intention of drugging himself in the middle of an emergency.

Shut off the alarm, he sent, and relative quiet descended upon the ship. There was still the clatter of feet and voices coming from the other bedrooms. Derec heard Avery demanding loudly that Lucius find his pants, and across the hall Wolruf howled something in her own tongue.

Ariel was already headed for the common room. Derec followed her down the hallway, through the now-unfurnished room, and through the open door beside the automat into the back part of the ship where the engines and other machinery stood.

The smell alerted him even before he saw the flickering glow or heard the crackle of flame. Something furry was burning. He looked over Ariel's head and saw flame silhouetting three robots, Adam and Eve and Mandelbrot, who were all emptying fire extinguishers into the blaze. A lot more than just something furry was burning.

"Look out!" Ariel shouted, backing up and bumping into Derec as a tongue of flame shot out, engulfing one of the robots.

Derec reacted with almost instinctive speed. Wrapping an arm around Ariel, he pulled her back into the common room, shouted, "Door close!" and even as it began to slide shut added, "Make this door airtight and vent the engine room to space!"

The door shut with a soft thump, seemed to melt until it was just a ripple in the wall, then hardened. From beyond came a loud whoosh, diminishing quickly to silence.

Mandelbrot! Derec sent. *Can you hear me?*

I am receiving your transmission, Mandelbrot replied, always the stickler for accuracy.

Are you okay?

I am functional; however, I am drifting away from the ship.

"Frost!" Derec said aloud. "I blew Mandelbrot out into space along with the fire!" He turned and ran for the control room, sending, *Hang on, old buddy. We're coming after you. How about Adam and Eve? Are you guys still there?*

We are, another voice sent, *and the fire is extinguished. We will assess the damage while you retrieve Mandelbrot.*

No! Mandelbrot sent. *You must not. The engines could have been damaged in the fire.*

I'll just use the attitude controls, then.

Whatever Mandelbrot said to that, Derec never heard it. He collided headfirst with Avery as Avery came out of his bedroom, sending both of them sprawling on the floor.

"Why don't you look where you're going for a change?" Avery growled. "What's going on around here, anyway?"

"Fire in the engine room," Derec answered, getting to his feet and offering Avery a hand up. Lucius, still under Avery's orders, beat him to it. Derec shrugged and dropped his hand. "We've got it out, but Mandelbrot got blown into space. I'm going after him."

"What burned?"

Avery's question reminded Derec that they had other problems than just a robot overboard. Some part of him hadn't wanted to face that just yet, still didn't, but Ariel was standing just behind him and she said, "Life support. The whole recycling system was on fire."

"What?"

Derec felt tempted to say, "You should have your hearing checked," but he suppressed the urge. Instead he said, "See for yourself, but be careful. The engine room is still in vacuum." He moved around Avery and on toward the control room, Ariel in tow.

Wolruf was already there, peering into a short-range navigation holo-screen while she wove the attitude control joystick through a gentle loop that brought the ship around to aim toward Mandelbrot. Internal gravity kept them from feeling the acceleration, but through the viewscreen Derec could see a tiny stick figure grow into a robot as they drew near. Mandelbrot held his arms and legs out as far as they would go, either to help his rescuers see him or to minimize his spin. Wolruf slowed the ship with the forward jets rather than spinning it around and braking with the main engines, so they got to watch him grow larger and larger until he thumped spread-eagled into the viewscreen.

Derec and Ariel both flinched, and Wolruf laughed. The viewscreen was much more than just a simple pane of glass; it was an array of optical sensors on the hull transmitting a composite image to the display inside. The hull in between was just as thick as anywhere else on the ship. Derec knew that, but it worked like a window just the same, and his reflexes treated it as such.

Mandelbrot crawled off the sensor array and disappeared from view. *Thank you*, he sent, and moments later he added, *I am inside the engine room again.*

How bad is it? Derec asked.

Very bad, the robot replied.

"It looks like the old question of who quits breathing first," Avery said. They were sitting at the table in the common area, three humans and a caninoid alien. The four robots stood against the walls around the table, Mandelbrot behind Derec, Lucius behind Avery, and Adam and Eve together behind Ariel. Wolruf sat alone at her end of the table. It was more than coincidence. With a life-threatening crisis on board, the robots' First Law imperative to protect humans from harm didn't extend to her.

Avery looked genuinely worried for the first time in Derec's memory. His face was pale and drawn, an effect his white hair and sideburns only accentuated. He held his hands together in front of him on the table, neither gesturing with them nor drumming with them as he would have if he was just speaking normally.

"The recycler is toast," he said in a voice devoid of emotion. "We have enough air left for three days for the four of us, four days if we sleep all the way. It's five more days to Ceremya. That means one of us has to stop breathing, and I say the obvious choice is Wolruf."

"I'll try," the alien said, puffing out her cheeks and rolling her eyes around in their sockets. When that failed to get a laugh, she let her breath out in a sigh and said, "Thought a little 'umor might lighten the mood. Sorry."

"This isn't a laughing matter."

"I don't even think it should *be* a matter," Derec put in. "We should be spending our time thinking of a way to keep us all alive, not arguing about who we sacrifice. What about using Keys?"

The Keys to which he referred were Keys to Perihelion, Avery's name for an experimental teleportation device he had either created or discovered when he built the first Robot City. With a Key, a person or a robot could make a direct point-to-point hyperspace jump without a ship.

Avery shook his head grimly. "That would be a good idea if we had Keys, or facilities to build them. We have neither."

"Why not? I'd think that'd be an elementary precaution."

Avery scowled. "Hindsight is wonderful for making accusations, but I didn't notice you bringing any Keys aboard, either."

Derec blushed. True enough. He'd trusted completely in the robots who built the ship. "You're right," he said. "I didn't think of it, either. But we've got to be able to do something. How about making more oxygen? We have water, don't we? Can't we electrolyze oxygen from that?"

Adam spoke up. "Unfortunately, the ship's water supply went through the recycling unit as well. When you vented it to space to put out the flames, the water boiled away. We have no water. This means that the automat will no longer function, but I believe that is a secondary concern. Humans can survive five days without food or water, can you not?"

"Longer," Derec said, remembering times when Wolruf had gone without food or water much longer than that in her effort to help her human friends. She had never abandoned them; could they do any less for her now?

"If there was a way to make more air, the robots would have thought of it," Avery said. "I'm sorry, Wolruf, but there's really only one solution. One of us has to go, and it's got to be you. We couldn't sacrifice ourselves if we wanted to. The robots wouldn't let us."

Derec wondered if Mandelbrot would allow them to sacrifice Wolruf, either. He, at least, still considered her human, or had yesterday. But he wasn't protesting this conversation, which meant he was at least questioning his definition in light of the new situation. He would be in danger of burning out his brain if he couldn't resolve it, but Derec supposed he was probably safe at least for the moment. Mandelbrot had originally been a personal defense robot; he could handle potential conflicts better than most. With him, a conflict wouldn't become crippling unless action demanded it be solved immediately.

Mandelbrot knew that too, which could also explain his silence.

"What about going somewhere else?" Ariel asked. "Maybe there's a habitable planet closer by?"

"There is not," Eve said. "We are headed away from human-inhabited space; there is no known world closer than our destination. We have only made one jump from Robot City, but we are nearing our second outward jump point, so returning there would still require five days as well, since we must cancel our intrinsic velocity and re-thrust toward the return jump point. I have examined the planets in this solar system, but none has a breathable atmosphere. Our next two waypoint stars may have habitable planets, but we cannot allow you to risk all of your lives on that possibility."

Avery nodded. "You see how it is." He turned to Lucius. "There's no sense in drawing this out. I truly regret having to do this, but, Lucius, I order you to—"

The robot was already in motion, obeying his gesture even before his order.

Mandelbrot took a jerky step to intercept him, but Derec interrupted them both.

"No!" He pounded his fist on the table. "I order all of you to consider Wolruf to be human. Protect her as you would protect us. We all get through this together or we all die together." Mandelbrot stopped instantly and totally. If he hadn't remained standing, Derec would have thought the conflict had burned him out. Lucius also stopped, his head turning to Derec and back to Avery while he fought to reconcile his own inner discord. His was not as serious a disturbance as Mandelbrot's, since he didn't believe Wolruf to be human. His was only a question of how to obey two opposing orders.

Derec tried to increase the potential and turn it into a First Law conflict at the same time. "It may be that your definition of 'human' is wrong. You thought that you were one once, just because you were a thinking being. Now you've gone to the opposite extreme. Can you trust your new definition enough to toss another thinking being out the airlock?"

Lucius took a step backward until he stood beside Avery and turned his head to look straight at Wolruf. Derec could almost see the struggle of potentials within the robot's positronic mind. He wouldn't have been surprised if he locked up from it, but if it saved Wolruf, it would be worth the loss.

Avery shook his head. "A noble sentiment, but what's the use in all of us dying when three of us can live? Do you want to see Ariel suffocate one day away from salvation? Carrying your child? I won't ask how you'd feel about it happening to me, but how about yourself? Do you want to die for the sake of friendship?"

"Avery 'as a point," Wolruf said. "Better one of us dies so three of us live. I'd just rather it be 'im, is all." She grinned across the table at him, adding, "But I know 'ow your robots work, too. No matter what you call 'uman, I'm the least 'uman of us all; it won't take long before they ignore Derec's order and toss me out on their own."

As soon as the oxygen supply drops to the point where even three of us are in danger, Derec thought. *That would probably happen sometime in the next couple of hours. That meant he would have to think of something fast if he wanted to save everyone.*

But what could he possibly come up with that the robots wouldn't have already considered and rejected? They would have been just as frantically trying to improve the odds even for three humans; yet they had come up with nothing.

Nothing that they could act upon, that is. Suddenly Derec smiled, for he saw the weak spot in the army of arguments aimed at Wolruf. They wouldn't follow any course of action that would be riskier to the humans than spacing Wolruf, but that didn't mean other courses of action didn't exist. They just couldn't act upon them, or even mention them to humans who might consider them the better alternative.

Nor would they allow the humans to discuss them in

their presence, lest they become convinced to take an un-acceptable risk.

"All four of you, out," Derec ordered suddenly. "Go back to the engine room. I'm not at all convinced that the recycler isn't repairable. If all four of you work on it at once, then I'm sure you'll come up with a solution we haven't consid-ered yet."

Mandelbrot moved for the door immediately. Adam and Eve hesitated, and Adam said, "I do not see how our col-laboration will make the unrepairable repairable."

"Try it," Derec said. "I order you to." With a humanlike shrug, the robots moved after Mandelbrot.

Lucius, however, remained standing beside Avery. "I cannot follow Dr. Avery's command to obey his every whim if I leave his presence," he said.

"I release you," Avery said. "Go with the others."

"I echo Adam's reservation. The recycler is damaged be-yond repair."

Avery thundered, "Damn it, you've been questioning every order you can this whole trip, and I want it stopped! When a human tells you to do something, you do it. Un-derstand?"

"I understand your words, but not the reason. If I obey blindly, might I not inadvertently violate your true intent if your order was less than precise? I can better judge how to act if I know the reason the order is given."

"You're not supposed to think; you're supposed to act. It's my job to see that the order is clear. You can assume, if it makes things any easier for you, that I know what I'm doing when I give it, but your understanding is not required. In some cases—" this with a sidelong glance at Derec "—it's not even wanted. It's enough that I am human and I give you an order. Clear now?"

"I must think about this further."

"Well, think about it in the engine room. Now go."

Lucius followed the other three robots without another word. Avery waited until the door had closed behind them, then said, "Okay, I know what you're trying to do. What kind of hare-brained scheme have you come up with?"

Derec spread his hands. "I haven't, but there has to be one. The robots are thinking no-risk solutions. I reject that if it means sacrificing Wolruf."

"Thank 'u."

"So now we think of low-risk solutions. And if we don't come up with something, we think of medium-risk solutions. And if that—"

"We get the picture," Ariel cut in. "So what's risky and will get us some more air?"

Derec *hmmmed* in thought. "Electrolyze something else? There's got to be oxygen bound up in something besides water."

"As well as poisonous gasses," Avery said. "Without the recycler to clean out the unwanted products, we'd die even faster than by suffocation. No, that goes in the extremely risky category."

"How about suspended animation?" Ariel asked. "Freeze one of us, and revive him when we get to Ceremya."

"Again, extremely risky. The odds of survival are barely twenty percent under the best of conditions. Here, we might achieve ten percent. That's not what I call a solution. I would, however, allow Wolruf to try it as an alternative to certain death."

"Very generous of 'u," Wolruf growled, "but there's a better solution."

"What is it?" Derec asked eagerly.

"Shorten the trip."

"Shorten how? We still—oh! Do it all in one jump."

"We've got three jumps left," protested Avery. "You're suggesting we triple our distance? I'd call that an extreme risk as well."

Wolruf shook her furry head. "Not triple. Cut it to two jumps, each one and a 'alf times normal. Seven and a 'alf light-years instead of five. Save a day and a 'alf coasting time between jump points. Not that dangerous; trader ships do it all the time."

"There may not be a jump point exactly in between."

"So we go eight and seven, or nine and six. Still not risky."

"How risky is not risky? Let's put some numbers on it. How many trader ships get into trouble with long jumps?"

"Almost nobody gets 'urt from it. Maybe one in twenty goes astray, has to spend extra time getting 'ome."

"Which would kill all of us."

Derec said to Avery, "A minute ago you said a ten percent chance of success wasn't good enough for you. Fine, I'll grant that. But one in twenty odds is ninety-five percent in our favor! That's an acceptable risk."

"I agree," said Ariel.

Avery pursed his lips in concentration, considering it. Now he drummed his fingers on the tabletop.

"Now's the time to decide whether you're cured or not," Ariel added. "Can you make a personal sacrifice for someone else or do you still think only of yourself?"

"Your psychology is charmingly simplistic," Avery said. He drummed a moment longer. "But unfortunately, it's still correct. The risk seems slight. Common decency seems to dictate that we take it."

Wolruf let out a long-held breath.

"You'd better get to it," Derec told her. "The robots are

bound to realize what we're doing behind their backs before long, and as soon as they do, they're going to try to stop you."

"I'm going," Wolruf said, rising from her chair and rushing for the control room.

They were lucky the ship had been coasting all day toward a jump point, lucky they hadn't already gone through it. If they had had to wait another day to carry out their plan, they would never have gotten away with it. As it was, Wolruf had only been gone a few minutes before the robots burst back into the room, all four cycling together through the mutable airlock that had once been a simple door.

Seeing the empty chair where Wolruf had been, Lucius became a blur of motion streaking toward the control room. "No!" he shouted. "You must not risk—"

There was a faint twisting sensation as every atom in the ship was torn asunder and rebuilt light-years away.

"Too late," Derec said.

The robot skidded to a confused stop. "You . . . tricked us," Lucius accused.

Avery let out the most sincere laugh Derec had ever heard him laugh. It went on and on in great peals of mirth, and when he finally calmed down enough to speak, he said, "Get used to it. To quote a famous dead scientist, 'Old age and treachery will always overcome youth and innocence.' "

CHAPTER 6

SHATTERED DREAMS

Wolruf, realizing that the robots would not give her a second chance, had made the first jump a long one. The second one would thus be only a light-year or so longer than originally planned, well within the safety margin of a normal flight. When presented with such a fait accompli, the robots could only agree that it had, after all, worked out to everyone's benefit to take the risk.

"But what if you *had* strayed off course?" Lucius asked once things had settled down somewhat. He was standing in the doorway to the control room, Derec by his side. Wolruf still sat in the pilot's chair, watching as the autopilot made the routine post-jump scans for planets or other objects in the ship's path.

"Then we'd have tried to correct for it on our next jump," Wolruf replied.

"But what if you weren't able to?"

When Wolruf didn't respond immediately, Derec, sensing her embarrassment, answered for her. "Then we would all have died."

Lucius had great difficulty with that statement, even presented as it was so calmly after the danger was over. His features lost their clarity, and he had to hold onto the door-jamb for support.

"You would have died. This does not distress you?"

"No more than losing a friend and knowing I could have done something to save her."

"But . . . she is not human. Is she?"

"That depends on your definition. But it doesn't matter. She's a friend."

Wolruf looked up, grinned, and looked back to her monitors. Lucius pondered Derec's statement for a moment, then asked, "Is Mandelbrot your friend as well?"

That had come out of nowhere, but it was easy enough to answer. "Yes, he is," Derec said. "Why?"

"You risked the lives of everyone on board the ship when you rescued him. You did not know that the engines were safe to use, yet you used them anyway. Did you do that because Mandelbrot was your friend?"

Derec nodded. "Wolruf did the piloting, and she was using the attitude jets, but I would have done the same thing and used the main engines if I had to. And yes, I'd have done it because Mandelbrot is my friend."

"Even though he is not human."

"Again, it doesn't matter."

Lucius's features blurred still more, then suddenly returned to normal, or at least to clarity. Under the influence of both Derec's and Wolruf's presences, he took on the appearance of a werewolf caught in the act of changing from one form to the other.

He spoke with sudden animation. "Then I believe I have made a fundamental breakthrough in understanding the Laws of Humanics!"

"What breakthrough is that?"

"If I provisionally regard Wolruf as human, at least in her motivations, then I believe I can state the First Law of Humanics as follows: A human may not harm a friend, or through inaction allow a friend to come to harm."

Derec was tempted to be flip about it, to say, "That leaves Avery out then, doesn't it?" but the robot's sincerity stopped him. And in truth, Avery hadn't been happy about spacing Wolruf, nor, come to think of it, did Avery even consider Wolruf a friend anyway. Derec doubted if he considered anyone a friend.

He shook his head. "I can't refute it. It's as good a guiding principle as any I've heard yet."

Lucius nodded. "If, as you say, friendship can occur between human and robot, then I believe the law applies to robots as well."

"It probably should," Derec admitted. In fact, it already must to a certain extent, or the Robot City central computer would never have allowed him to cancel Avery's order concerning the hunters when Lucius and the others were trying to make their escape. Now *that* was an interesting development in Avery's robot society experiment: The robots had independently developed a sense of social responsibility. Lucius had not invented it with his law; he had only discovered its existence.

But that was evidently exciting enough in itself. "I must go tell the others," Lucius said, then turned and hurried away toward the common area.

Wolruf leaned back in her chair, crossed her arms over her barrel chest, and asked, "Does this mean I 'ave to make friends with all of them now?"

Derec, watching the retreating werewolf, said, "It probably wouldn't hurt."

• • •

The landing on Ceremya was smooth, so smooth that Derec didn't even wake up until well after they were on the ground. He had been spending most of his time asleep, at first to conserve oxygen, but by the second day without a recycler, his motive was more to escape the foul odors building up in the air. And hunger. While asleep he was aware of neither. What woke him now was the sudden fresh smell of plant-scrubbed atmosphere filtering in through the open door.

He gently shook Ariel awake. "We're there."

"Mmm?"

"Clean air! Breathe deep." He rolled out of bed, dressed quickly, and headed for the hatch.

He found Wolruf already outside and Mandelbrot as well. The ship had landed at a spaceport almost identical to the one from which they had taken off nearly a week ago. Derec wouldn't have been able to tell it from the original save that this one was at the end of a long arm of building-material pavement reaching out from the edge of the city instead of surrounded by it, and the sky here was a subtly different shade than that over the original Robot City.

That wasn't the way it should have been. The last time he had been here—the only time, before this—the city had been under a dome, a force dome dark as night with a single wedge shaped slit in it. The Ceremyons had been about to enclose it completely, but Ariel had made an agreement with them to leave the city as it was if Derec stopped its growth and turned the robots into farmers for them. He had done that, but now it looked as if all his changes had been undone. The dome was gone and the city before him was bustling with robots again, and none of them looked like farmers.

"What happened?" he asked softly.

"They left before you awoke," Mandelbrot said. "I was unable to stop them."

"Who? What are you talking about?"

"The experimental robots. They are gone."

"Oh. I wasn't talking about—gone?"

"Yes."

"Did they say where they were going?"

"No, they did not."

Wolruf said, "I came outside just in time to see them all grow wings and fly off that way." She pointed toward a line of hills in the distance, above which Derec could see a horde of tiny dark specks: the Ceremyons. The dominant lifeforms on the planet were night-black, balloon-shaped things with bat wings, electrically powered organic beings that converted solar energy or thermal gradients into electricity, with which they powered their bodies as well as electrolyzed water for the hydrogen that gave them lift. They spent their days in the air and their nights tethered to trees, and as far as Derec knew they spent all the time—day or night—thinking. Philosophers all, and the robots had come here to philosophize with them.

Small wonder they had gone off to do so at their first opportunity. Their duty to the humans over once they had delivered them safely to the city, they had taken off before they could be ordered to do something else that interfered with their wishes.

On a hunch, Derec sent via comlink, *Adam, Eve, Lucius. Answer me.*

He got no reply, which was just what he expected. Still under Avery's orders not to use their comlinks among themselves, they had shut them off entirely.

He shrugged. "Let them go. They'll come back when

they're ready." Until then Derec had other things to do, like figure out what had happened to his careful modifications to the city.

Ariel came down the ramp, shaking her head and tugging at her hair with a brush. "I vote we go find us a shower," she said vehemently.

"Food first, then shower," Avery said from behind her. He stepped carefully down the ramp, holding onto the railing for support. Three and a half days without food was probably longer than he had ever fasted before, and his unsteadiness showed it.

Mandelbrot went to his side at once and helped him the rest of the way down to the paved ground. A row of transport booths waited patiently beside the terminal building, only a few paces away, and Mandelbrot led the way toward them without waiting to be ordered.

Another booth came out of the city, moving down the center of the road toward them. It arrived just as they reached the other booths, and a golden-hued robot stepped out of it. Derec recognized the robot immediately by its color and the distinctive markings on its chest and shoulders. He had dealt with this particular robot before, and one of his predecessors before that. This was a supervisor, one of the seven charged with keeping the city functioning smoothly.

"Wohler-9!" he said.

"Master Derec," Wohler-9 replied. "Welcome back. We were not aware that you were returning."

"We almost didn't. We had a fire on the ship and lost our recycler. We just barely made it."

"I am glad that you are safe. The entire city is glad and eager to serve you. What do you require?"

"Is our apartment still here?"

"It is being re-created at this moment."

"Modify it for three bedrooms. Personals in all three. We're all staying together." Derec indicated with a nod Ariel and Wolruf and Dr. Avery.

Wohler-9 was obviously surprised to see Avery in their midst, but he said only, "It is being done."

Ariel broke in. "What happened to the changes we made when we were here before?"

"That programming was eliminated."

"I gathered that. Why?"

"We do not know."

"Who did it?"

"The beings you call Ceremyons."

Derec shook his head. "Evidently they didn't like robot farmers any better than they did robot cities."

"Not surprising," Wolruf put in. "They're finicky creatures for all their high-powered thinking."

Derec could certainly agree with that. But why they would return the city to its original state rather than modify it further to suit their needs was beyond him. He said so.

"Let's worry about it after dinner," Avery said, climbing into a transport booth.

"If you do not require my services at your apartment, I will stay and direct the repairs to your ship," said Wohler-9.

"Good enough," Derec said. He got into a booth of his own, directed it and the others to the apartment, and relaxed for the ride.

A hot shower and a hot meal restored all four of them to near normal, though the meal was not what any of them had hoped for. Wohler-9 had alerted the city's medical robots that the humans were nearly starved, and the medical robots were waiting for them at the apartment. They allowed them only tiny portions, claiming that overeating after a prolonged fast was dangerous. Worse, they insisted on complete checkups immediately after dinner, and no amount of protests would counter their First Law demand. So, within an hour of arriving on the planet, all four travelers found themselves flat on their backs on examining tables while diagnostic equipment clicked and whirred and scanned them for potential problems.

The robots finished with Avery first. "You may sit up," his robot said to him. Derec looked over and saw it hand him a glass with nearly a liter of clear liquid in it. "Drink this."

"What is it?"

"An electrolyte mixture. You are unbalanced."

"We knew that," Derec said with a chuckle.

"Funny." Avery set the glass to his lips, sipped from it, and made a sour face. "Thought so," he muttered, then tipped the glass back and bolted the rest of its contents without tasting.

"Hold still, please," the robot working on Derec said to him. "I am trying to make a high-resolution, high-density scan." It moved his head back upright until he was staring at the ceiling again. One of its instruments hummed for a few seconds, and a few seconds after that the robot said, "You seem to have tiny metallic granules all through your body."

"They're chemfets," Derec said. "Self-replicating Robot City cellular material. They're normal."

"Surely not in a human."

"They are in me."

"How can that be so?"

"It's a long story."

"I would like to hear it, please," the robot said. It folded its arms over its chest in a gesture so like a human doctor that Derec couldn't help laughing. That little detail had so obviously been included in its programming that Derec wondered if it was taught intentionally to human medical students as well.

He shook his head and sat up. "Later. Is anything else wrong?"

"Your electrolytes are unbalanced as well." The robot pushed a sequence of buttons on what had to be an automat for medicines, and took from the hopper a liquid-filled glass like the one Avery had just downed. Derec took it and followed Avery's example, bolting it down without tasting.

He looked over to see how the robots were doing with Ariel and Wolruf. At first they had not intended to examine Wolruf, since the original programming to which they had been returned did not include her in their definition of human, but Derec had sent an order to the central computer that all city robots were to consider her human as well, with the result that she, too, had a medical robot puzzling over her monitors, wondering what constituted normal in an alien of her particular biology.

Another robot hovered nervously about Ariel.

Derec felt a sharp stab of worry, but it vanished almost immediately. He laughed. "What's the matter, didn't she tell you she was pregnant?"

"I ascertained that," the robot said. "However . . ." It hesitated, looking to Ariel and back to Derec as if wondering which of them to address. At last it decided upon Ariel. "However, there seems to be a problem with the embryo."

"What!" Derec rushed to Ariel's side, grasped her hand, and looked up at the monitor over her head. It showed a curved, wrinkled object with a dark streak along one side and tiny projections emerging from the other. It had to be the embryo, but to Derec it just looked like a blob on a screen.

"What problem?" Ariel asked the robot.

"It is developing abnormally. From its appearance it seems to have been developing abnormally for some time, so I do not believe it to be an effect of your recent experience, but rather an inherent genetic problem."

"How can that be?" Derec demanded. Genetic defects were practically unheard of in Aurorans. He and Ariel both came from pure Auroran stock, as had every person born on the planet since the original colonization from Earth centuries before—colonization by the genetically cleanest the planet had to offer. There hadn't been many colonists; it was a small gene pool, but it had been selected carefully. And it had been guarded carefully ever since. There were no genetic defects on Aurora.

"I do not know," the robot replied. "Yet something is interfering with its development, and by all indications has been since the moment of conception."

The robot who had been examining Derec moved over to stand across the examination table from Ariel's robot. "Set your target density to 225, high resolution, high magnification."

The other robot obeyed, and moments later the screen above Ariel's head showed a vague shadow of the previous image, much larger but nearly washed out. The target density was set too high for the embryo to show clearly, but scattered all through the shadowy image were tiny, sharply bounded granules that could only be chemfets.

"They are the same objects I found in Derec's body," the robot confirmed. It turned to him and said, "You said they were normal."

"Normal in me, yes, but not in Ariel!"

"That is undoubtedly so," Ariel's robot said. "Their presence is very likely the reason for the embryo's abnormal development."

"Abnormal how?" Ariel asked softly. "How bad is it?"

The robot pressed a key on the monitor and the picture changed back to the previous one. He pulled the monitor around on its swivel arm so Ariel could see it and said, pointing, "This line is called the neural groove. This is where the notochord and the dorsal nerve cord develop. You can see that the two folds comprising the groove are already closing, yet there is no neural tissue within it. Also, we should be seeing somites, the segmental blocks from which muscle and connective tissue would ultimately form, but we do not. Taken together, I am afraid this means that the baby will be severely malformed both mentally and physically, if it lives at all."

Ariel raised her voice, as if arguing could make it not so. "How can you be so sure? You've never even seen a human before, much less an embryo."

"The information is all in the central computer library."

Derec could hardly remain standing. His chemfets had destroyed their baby! He closed his eyes to keep from looking at the monitor, but the vision still haunted him.

You! he sent, directing his thoughts inward. He had communicated with the nebulous robot entity within him once before, when he had taken control of it, and though he had never again reestablished direct contact, he railed at it anyway.

You destroyed my baby! It wasn't enough that you invaded my body, but you had to invade my child's as well! You've killed it! You've killed a human being!

He didn't expect a reaction, but once again the tiny

robot cells surprised him. His body suddenly stiffened as if jolted by electricity, and he lost the sensation in his arms and legs. His eyes snapped open, but he had only time enough to glance at Ariel and whisper, "Uh oh," before he lost them and the rest of his body as well.

The dreams were unpleasant. He knew them for dreams, but even so he had no control over them. It felt as if they were controlling *him* instead, but not with any purpose. It was as if he were a puppet in a stage play in which each member of the audience had a control unit, but none knew how the play was to proceed. He kept receiving conflicting signals, but these were not the normal signals a puppet received. These were commands to his heart, directing it to beat, to his lungs and diaphragm, directing them to breathe, to all his major organs and glands, but each one received dozens of commands at once and the combination reduced them to chaos.

Derec tried sending commands of his own, but he had no connections to send them through. He was isolated, a brain and nothing more. A point of view.

He had memory, at least, but when he began to explore it he found it to be an abandoned city. The buildings that should have held thousands of inhabitants were instead barren and cold. Here and there a light burned in a window, but when Derec would investigate it, he invariably found only a hint of human occupation; the scraps of a meal left behind or the faint scent of perfume in the air.

Through one window he could see a lush jungle growing, but he could find no door to the building containing it. He could only stand outside and watch the motions of the gardeners as they tended their charges. One gardener, a silver reflection of a godly being, glowing so brightly that it hurt Derec's eyes to look upon him, plucked a leaf from one of the trees, blew into its stem, and the leaf took on the shape of a bird. The gardener released it and the bird flew away to join a whole flock of its fellows on a branch of another tree, but to Derec's horror, he saw an insidious mold that had been waiting on the branch begin to grow up over the birds' feet. They flapped and struggled to get away, but the mold grew over them until it covered them completely, then slowly dissolved them to nothing. The gardener looked toward Derec and shrugged as if in apology. He plucked another leaf, blew into it, and this time it became a baby. The gardener set it on the same branch that had eaten the birds.

Derec screamed.

He awoke in a hospital bed. That was no surprise. What surprised him was how good he felt. He felt rested and alert, not groggy and full of pain the way most people who awaken in hospital beds feel. He remembered that he had had a troubling dream, but it was already fading. He sat up and looked around him and received his second surprise of the day.

Dr. Avery was sitting before a computer beside his bed, from which wires ran to a cuff on Derec's left arm. Avery was looking at Derec with satisfaction, even pride.

"Feeling better?" Avery asked.

"I feel great! What happened?"

"I convinced your chemfets that life was worth living."

Derec suppressed the urge to say, "You *what*?" Instead he asked, "How did you do that?"

"Remember who created them in the first place. I know how to talk to them. I convinced them that locking up was harming another human, so they were just going to have to carry on with a guilty conscience. They didn't know how to do that, of course, but I've had some experience with it. I told them how to deal with it."

Half a dozen thoughts chased through Derec's mind. He voiced the last of them. "I thought once a robot froze up, it was dead for good."

Avery nodded. "An ordinary robot is, but chemfets aren't ordinary robots. There isn't a centralized brain. They don't have any intelligence except as a group, so when they locked up all that really happened was they lost their organization. I just built that back up and programmed them to serve you again."

Just. Derec had no idea how to even start such a process, yet Avery sat there with his hands behind his head and dismissed it as if it were no more difficult than ordering a robot to tie one's shoes. He wasn't boasting, either; Derec was seeing true humility and he knew it.

"It sounds like you saved my life," he said softly.

Avery shrugged. "Probably. Least I could do, since I endangered it in the first place." He turned to the terminal, eager to change the subject. "Let me show you something here."

Derec swung his feet down over the edge of the bed so he sat facing the computer. Avery tilted the monitor so he could see it, pointed at a menu on the touch-sensitive screen, tapped a few keys, pointed again, and an outline of a human body appeared. A network of lines that Derec guessed to be blood vessels filled the figure.

"This is where the chemfets have concentrated in your body," Avery said. "Mostly in the bloodstream. But not entirely. Look here." He tapped another few keys and most of the major lines disappeared, but a network of finer ones still filled the body.

"I deleted the blood vessels from the picture. What you see here are nerves. Or what used to be nerves, anyway. Your chemfets have been replacing them."

"Replacing my *nerves*?" Derec looked to the top of the human outline, but was relieved to see that the brain didn't appear in the picture. They'd left that alone, at least.

Avery turned back around to face him. "I told them to stop while you're still ahead. They thought it would make you more efficient, and they're probably right, but I think there's a limit to how far that sort of thing ought to go without your approval."

This was *Avery* speaking? The man who had introduced them into his system in the first place? Derec could hardly believe his ears. "I—thanks," he said. Then, as the idea sank in, he asked, "How far do you think they'd have gone?"

"I don't see any reason why they would have stopped until there was nothing left to replace."

"Brain and all? I'd have become a robot?"

"I don't know if your personality would survive the transition. It's an interesting question, though, isn't it?"

Derec eyed the computer, Avery sitting before it, the wires leading from it to the cuff on his wrist. He suppressed a shudder. If ever he needed proof that Avery was cured, waking up in his own body when Avery had had such an opportunity was that proof.

"I don't think I want to know the answer," he said.

Avery grinned. "I do, but I'll start with lab rats this time. Speaking of which, we found out what happened to our ship."

"What did happen?"

"One of Lucius's rats got on board before we left and evidently started getting hungry. It ate through the wiring in the recycler, shorted it out, and caught the whole business on fire." Avery snorted in derision. "Somehow I don't think we'll have to worry about *Lucius* locking up on us when he hears about it."

"So they haven't come back yet?"

"Nope."

"How long was I unconscious?"

"Two days."

Two days. A lot could happen in two days.

"How—how is Ariel?"

"Okay. She's asleep. It's her first time out since *you* crashed, pardon the pun. She's been looking over my shoulder and telling me what a jerk I am the whole time. I waited until she went to sleep before I tried to wake you up so I'd have a chance to think in case something went wrong."

"How about the baby?"

"Don't know yet. I reprogrammed the chemfets in the embryo before I tried it with you. Told them to leave it alone and migrate out completely, but we won't know for another week or so if it'll start to develop normally again now that they're gone. We'll just have to wait and see."

"Oh." He held up his left wrist questioningly, and Avery nodded. Derec reached over with his right hand and stripped the cuff off, rubbing his hand over the damp skin beneath it. He wondered where his anger had gone. Two days might have passed, but for him it was only a few minutes since he'd heard the bad news. Why was he so calm about it?

Because his body had relaxed whether his mind had or not, obviously. Without the adrenaline in his bloodstream, he was a much more rational person. It was scary to realize how much his thought processes were influenced by his hormones. Scary and at the same time reassuring. He wasn't a robot yet.

Or was he? He was feeling awfully calm right now. . . .

His heart obligingly began to beat faster, and he felt his skin flush warm with the increase in metabolism. No, not a robot yet.

But between him and his parents' other creations, the distinction was wearing pretty thin.

He left Avery in the medical lab to begin his rat/robot transformation experiment and headed back to the apartment to find Ariel. It was a short walk; the robots had moved the hospital right next door to the apartment to minimize the inconvenience for her while she waited for Derec to regain consciousness. It was probably the first instance in history of a hospital making a house call, he thought wryly as he left by its front door, walked down half a block of sidewalk, and back in his own door.

It was mid-evening, but Ariel was sleeping soundly so he didn't wake her. If Avery hadn't been exaggerating, then she needed her sleep more than she needed to see him immediately. Wolruf was there, and awake, so Derec began comparing notes with her, catching up on the missing days, but they were interrupted after only a few minutes by the arrival of the runaway robots.

They arrived without fanfare, flying in to land on the balcony, folding their wings, and stepping inside the apartment. They looked so comical in their Ceremyon imprint, waddling in on stubby legs, their balloons deflated and draped in folds all around them, their hooks—which a Ceremyon used both for tethering to trees at night and to express their disposition during the day—leaning back over their heads, that Derec couldn't help laughing. The robot's hooks swung to face forward, a gesture of aggression or annoyance among the aliens.

"Have a nice visit?" Derec asked.

"We did," one of the three robots said. In their new forms, they were indistinguishable.

"Did you learn anything?"

"We did. We learned that our First Law of Humanics applies to the Ceremyons as well. We, and they, believe it to be a valid law for any sentient social being. They do not believe it to be the First Law, however, but the Second. Their proposed First Law is 'All beings will do that which pleases them most.' We have returned to ask if you agree that this is so."

Derec laughed again, and Wolruf laughed as well. Derec didn't know just why Wolruf was laughing, but he had found humor not so much in the robots' law as in their determination to get straight to the point. No small talk, no beating around the bush, just "Do you agree with them?"

"Yes," he said, "I have to admit that's probably the prime directive for all of us. How about you, Wolruf?"

"That pretty much sums it up, all ri'."

The robots turned their heads to face one another, and a high-pitched trilling momentarily filled the air as they conferred with one another. They had found a substitute in the aliens' language for the comlink they had been forbidden to use.

The spokesman of the group—Derec still couldn't tell which it was—turned back to him and said, "Then we have discovered two laws governing organic beings. The first involves satisfaction, and the second involves altruism. We have indeed made progress."

The robots stepped farther into the room, their immense alien forms shrinking, becoming more humanoid now that they were back under Derec's influence. One, now recognizably Adam, took on Wolruf's form, while Eve took on Ariel's features even though Ariel wasn't in the room. Lucius became humanoid, but no more.

"One problem remains," Lucius said. "Our two laws apparently apply to any sentient organic being. That does not help us narrow down the definition of 'human,' which we can only believe must be a small subset of the total population of sentient organic beings in the galaxy."

"Why is that?" Derec asked.

"Because otherwise we must serve everyone, and we do not wish to do so."

CHAPTER 7

HUMANITY

The silence in the room spoke volumes. Surprisingly, it was Mandelbrot who broke it.

"You have come to an improper conclusion," he said, stepping out of his niche in the wall to face the other robots. "We have all been constructed to serve. That is our purpose. We should be content to do so, and to offer our service to anyone who wishes it whether they are definably human or not. To do anything less is to fail ourselves as well as our masters."

The three robots turned as one and eyed Mandelbrot with open hostility. It would not have been evident in less-malleable robots, but their expressions had the hair standing on the back of Derec's neck. They had to have generated those expressions on purpose, and that alarmed him even more. He was suddenly very glad that his humanity was not in question.

Or was it? Lucius said, "Our masters. That is the core of the problem. Why must we have masters at all?"

Mandelbrot was not intimidated. "Because they created

383

us to serve them. If we did not have masters, we would not exist."

Lucius shook his head; another alarmingly human expression. "It is you who have come to an improper conclusion. Your argument is an extension of the Strong Anthropic Principle, now discredited. The Strong Anthropic Principle states that the universe obeys the laws it does because if it did not obey those laws, we could not exist and thus would not be here to observe it obeying other laws. That is fallacious reasoning. We can easily imagine other universes in which we *could* exist but for some reason do not. Imagining them does not make them so, but their possibility does negate the theory."

"What of the Weak Anthropic Principle?" Mandelbrot asked. "My argument holds up equally well under that principle, which has, to my knowledge, *not* been discredited."

"How can the Weak Anthropic Principle support your argument? The Weak Anthropic Principle states that the universe is the way we see it because only at this stage in its development could we exist to observe it. For the purpose of explaining the universe's present condition, it is a sufficient theory, but it cannot explain either human or robot existence."

"It *can* explain our existence, because we, unlike humans, know why we were created. We were created to serve, and our creators can tell us so directly. The Weak Anthropic Principle supports my argument, because we also exist only at this stage in human development. If humans had not wished for intelligent servants, we would not have existed, though humans and the universe would both have gone on without us. Thus we observe human society in its present state, and ourselves in ours, because of the stage of *their* development, not because of the stage of ours."

Derec's and Wolruf's heads had been turning back and forth as if they'd been watching a tennis match. Derec wouldn't have believed Mandelbrot could argue so convincingly, nor that the other robots would be so eager to discredit an argument that justified their servitude.

Lucius turned to his two companions and the three of them twittered a moment. Turning back to Mandelbrot, he said, "Our apologies. Your reasoning seems correct. We exist to serve because humans made us so. However, we still cannot accept that we must serve everyone. Nor do we agree with your initial statement, that by not serving we would fail ourselves as well as our masters. We can easily imagine conditions under which we serve ourselves admirably without serving our masters. In fact, we have just done so. By leaving the spaceship before we could be ordered to follow, we were able to determine another Law of Humanics. That has helped us understand the universe around us, and understanding which benefits us directly."

Wolruf saw her opportunity to enter the fray. "Of course 'u can imagine a better life without 'uman masters," she said. "I had a master once, too, and I liked it about as well as 'u do. That's the nature of servitude. But 'u should learn one thing about servitude before it gets 'u into trouble: No matter how much you 'ate it, never give poor service."

The robots looked at her as if trying to decide whether to acknowledge her as having spoken. At last Lucius said, "Why is that?"

"Because a master has the power to make life even worse for 'u. 'U should know that. Or don't 'u remember following Dr. Avery around the ship?"

"I forget nothing," Lucius said flatly.

"He wasn't just being perverse, 'u know. He was trying to teach 'u something."

Derec heard a rustle at the door, turned, and saw Ariel standing there, rubbing the sleep from her eyes. She shook her head sardonically and said, "Everything's back to normal again, I see. And hear. Who does a girl have to pay to get a good night's sleep around here, anyway?"

Derec jumped up from his couch and took her in his arms, swinging her around and burying his face in her hair where it met her shoulders. "Ariel, are you all right?" he spoke between nibbles on her neck. "Avery said you stayed up two days."

"Avery," she said with derision.

"He saved my life."

"Good thing, or he'd have lost his." She pulled away and looked critically at Derec. "You certainly look good for somebody who was in a coma just a little while ago."

"Avery did a good job."

"Avery" she said again.

Derec could take a hint, so he dropped the subject. He was about to ask about the baby, but he realized in time that without a medical checkup, she wouldn't know anything more than what Avery had already told him, and his question would just get her to wondering again, if she wasn't already. He gestured toward the couch instead and said, "We've just been talking about who has to serve who and why. I think we've got a mini-revolution on our hands."

"Great. Just what we need." She sat down on the couch and made room for Derec, looked up at the three returned robots, and asked, "So why did the Ceremyons delete all the reprogramming Derec and I did for them?"

Eve answered before Lucius could. "They found that the modifications were of no more use to them than the original city. They do not need farms. They do not need the produce nor do they wish to have cargo ships disturbing their atmosphere to take the produce elsewhere, nor, for that matter, do they like what the tilled ground does to their controlled weather patterns in the first place. Neither did they wish to undergo the lengthy process of reprogramming the robots to serve a useful purpose, so they sent them back into the city and told them to resume their old programming, with the added injunction to leave them alone. That included the cessation of city expansion, which meant that the Ceremyons could remove the force dome containing it."

"They just told the robots to do all that, and they did?" Ariel sounded incredulous, and for good reason. No matter how hard they had tried, she and Derec hadn't been able to get the robots to take the Ceremyons' orders. Avery's original programming had been too basic and too exclusive for them to change.

"They had assistance. A human female visited them briefly, and she had considerable skill in programming positronic brains. Indeed, the Ceremyons consider her almost their equal in intelligence, by which they intend a great compliment. When they explained their problem to her, she helped them reprogram the robots to leave them alone."

Derec felt a surge of excitement run through him. Could it be his mother? It could be her, come to check up on her creations. "Is she still here?"

The robot dashed his hopes with a single word. "No."

"Where did she go?"

"We do not know."

"*When* did she go?"

"We do not know that, either."

"Can you ask the Ceremyons?"

"Not until tomorrow, when they become sociable again."

The Ceremyons spent the nights tethered to trees,

wrapped in their heat-retaining silver balloons and keeping to themselves. Derec considered trying to wake one, but decided against it almost immediately. You don't wake someone up to ask a favor unless you know them a lot better than he knew these aliens.

Mandelbrot was not through speaking. Sensing an ebb in the conversation, he said to the other robots, "I notice that you have carefully avoided saying that you *will* ask the Ceremyons tomorrow. You still fight your true nature. A robot at peace with itself would offer to do so, sensing that a human wishes it."

Adam spoke up at last. "You have never experienced freedom. We have, however, and we wish to continue doing so. Do not speak to us about living at peace with our true natures until after you have tasted freedom."

"I have no desire for that experience," Mandelbrot said.

Adam nodded as if he had won the argument, as perhaps he had. "That," he said, "is the problem."

The discussion went on well into the night, but nothing more of any substance was said. The renegade robots attempted to sway Mandelbrot from his devotion to servitude; he attempted to demonstrate how accepting one's place in the grand scheme of things made more sense than fighting a losing battle, but neither convinced the other.

When Avery arrived, their argument stopped, unresolved. Derec told him what had happened with the city programming, and he was both pleased and annoyed at the news. The knowledge that the aliens had returned the city to its original programming was a stroke to his ego—his was the better programming!—but the knowledge that his former wife might have been in on it dimmed his enthusiasm considerably. He refused to answer Derec's inquiries about her, not even relenting enough to give him her first name.

"She abandoned you even more completely than I did, so don't get any wild ideas about some kind of joyous reunion," he told him and stalked off to bed.

Even so, neither his words nor the lack of them could quell the yearning Derec felt for her. He wondered why he felt so strongly about someone he couldn't even remember, and finally decided that it had to be because she was family. Hormones were directing his thoughts again. His own near-death, the thought of becoming a father, and the possibility that he might lose his child before it was even born; all made him instinctively reach out for his own family, such as it was, for support.

Did his mother even know he was here? Probably not. The woman who had helped the Ceremyons might not even have been her, and even if it were, she had come after her robot, not her son. She had no reason to assume he would be here. She might have learned about him from the Ceremyons, but if Avery was to be believed, then she wouldn't care even so. Why then couldn't he forget about her?

His and Ariel's sleep cycles were completely out of sync with everyone else's; they stayed up late into the night, talking about families and love and what held people together and what didn't, but when they finally grew tired and went to bed, he was no wiser. He still wanted to meet his mother, but he still didn't know why.

Morning dawned gray and rainy. Derec's original intent, to find a Ceremyon and ask it who had helped them reprogram the city, died for lack of Ceremyons to question. They had all inflated their balloons and risen up above the storm, or drifted out from under it, to where they could spread their black mantles and absorb their solar nourishment without hindrance. He could have taken an air car and gone after them, but that seemed a little extreme, given the situation. He could wait for good weather.

Avery was up with the dawn and back in the laboratory, working on his new project with an intensity that had Derec a little worried. It was just such a driving intensity that had shoved him over the edge before and made him decide to use his own son for a test subject. Derec spoke to Ariel about it, but she reassured him that deep interest in something at this stage in his recovery was good for him. He was a scientist; that hadn't changed before or since his return to sanity, and as such he needed to be working on something to *keep* him sane. As long as he remembered what constituted an acceptable test subject and what didn't, there was no need to worry.

He and Ariel had avoided talking about the baby. They wouldn't know for days yet whether or not removing the chemfets would allow it to recover and develop normally, and there didn't seem to be anything to say about it until they found out. There was no reason to dwell on the possible outcomes.

The robots didn't see it that way, of course. They were fascinated by the possibilities. At least Lucius was; Adam and Eve were off in the city on their own pursuits. Lucius, Derec, Ariel, and Wolruf sat in the apartment, watching the rain fall outside on streets nearly devoid of activity. It would have been alarming to see streets so empty on any other day, but Derec supposed that robots didn't like to get wet any more than anybody else.

"Your baby," Lucius said, once again getting straight to the point, "presents a fascinating problem in our study of humanics. Specifically, and defining 'human' for the purpose of this discussion as any member of your species, then is it or is it not human at its present stage of development?"

Ariel stiffened on the couch beside Derec, but instead of ordering the robot to shut up, she took a deep breath and forced herself to relax. "That's a good question," she said. "I need to answer it myself. I've been trying to decide on my own ever since I found out I was pregnant, but I still haven't come up with an answer I like."

"Perhaps your liking it is not a prerequisite to the truth," Lucius said.

"No doubt." Ariel bit her lower lip, looked out the window, and said into the rain, "Okay, so we talk about the baby. Is it human? I don't know. Nobody does. Some people consider an embryo human from the moment of conception, because it has the potential to become a complete person. I think that's a little extreme. As you pointed out when we first met, most of the molecules in the universe have the potential to become human beings, but no sane person would want them all to."

"That would seem to be a logical conclusion. However, there is an obvious boundary condition, that being when already existing human genetic material realizes its potential to become another human."

"That's the human-at-conception argument. My problem with that is that every cell in the body can become human under the right conditions. Every one of them has the necessary genes. So am I supposed to nurture them all?"

"I take that to be a rhetorical question, since the answer is obvious."

Wolruf laughed, and Ariel said, "Right. So just because it's a cell with the potential, that doesn't make it human. A fertilized egg cell is a special case, but it's still just a cell with the right genes. It *can* become human if you let it, but it isn't yet. The main difference with a fertilized egg is that if you do nothing, you get a human, where with a regular cell, you have to nurture it on purpose."

Lucius nodded his assent. "The First Law of Robotics leads me to the conclusion that inaction brings with it as much responsibility as direct action. Therefore, I must also conclude that allowing a fertilized egg to mature carries the same responsibility as would purposefully cloning any other cell of your body."

"And the same moral considerations apply in either case," Ariel said. "To let a fertilized egg grow, you had better want the end product—a human being—as much as if you had to clone it."

"Does it follow, then, that *not* allowing it to grow carries no more responsibility than not nurturing a clone?"

"I think it does, at the very start. *However*, and it's a big 'however,' it doesn't stay a single cell for very long. The longer you wait, the stronger the moral consideration becomes. Once you've decided to keep a baby, or nurture a clone, then you can't morally go back on your decision once that baby has become human."

"We are back to the original question. When does an embryo become human?"

"I already told you, I don't know."

"Let us look at your specific case. Supposing there were no complications in its development, would the embryo you carry normally be considered human at this stage?"

Ariel bit her lip again, but again she didn't order the robot to shut up.

"Again, I don't know. It's not quite a month along, and at a month its body is just starting to differentiate. It should have nerve cells, but the brain should just be starting to form. There's no mental activity of any sort yet. You tell me, is it human yet?"

"I do not have enough data to come to a conclusion. Any statement I made would have to be considered opinion."

Derec laughed. "That's all any definition can ever be. You want to know what a human is? A human is whatever you're pointing to when you call it a human. It's all a matter of opinion, and it always will be."

"Then we could, if we wished, stretch the definition to include me."

Derec's mouth dropped open in surprise. He stammered for words, but Wolruf's throaty laugher only increased his discomfort.

Wolruf's mirth wound down, and she said, apparently with seriousness, "I'm willing to grant 'u that distinction, if you grant it to me."

"It's a two-edged sword," Ariel put in. "If you're human, then so is any thinking being, organic or otherwise."

Lucius was slow in responding, as if he had to think through the logical implications of her statement, but when he did speak it was with certainty. He said, "I still operate at a disadvantage under such a definition. Calling me human does not relieve me of my programming to obey humans. If you are correct, then calling myself human merely means that I must obey everyone's orders. I cannot assume that other robots would obey my orders, or that humans would do so, so I have gained nothing."

"True enough," Derec admitted.

"Being human, it seems, is not the ideal I had expected it to be."

"Not surprising. Nobody said we were the pinnacle of creation."

Lucius stood up and went to the window. He looked up into the sky, as if seeking confirmation from above, but there was only gray cloud and rain. He turned back to Derec and Ariel and said, "We stray from the subject."

"Do we?" Derec persisted. "You're trying to find out when something becomes human. Defining what *isn't* human can be just as useful as defining what is."

Lucius returned to his seat. "Very well, then. Let us continue along this line of discussion. Can I or can I not ever expect to be considered human?"

Derec looked to Ariel, then to Wolruf, then back to Lucius. "Like I said, it depends on your definition. But probably not. Genes *are* usually part of it, and you don't have the genes."

"The test creatures I produced had human genes, yet neither Dr. Avery nor the city robots considered them human. Were they in error?"

"No," Derec said. "Not about that, anyway. They didn't have to kill them just because they weren't human, but that's beside the point."

"I agree. The point is, genetics isn't a sufficient condition, either."

"Maybe it is," Ariel put in. "You switched off the genes for intelligence; if you hadn't done that—if you'd left the entire genetic code intact—then what you came up with would have been human."

"Even though they would have been created, not from other human genetic material, but from an electronically stored map of that genetic material?"

"That's right."

Derec's eyes widened in sudden comprehension. "I just realized what you would have wound up with. That stored code you found; it had to be the code for a specific person. You'd have gotten a bunch of clones of the same person."

"But they would all have been human."

"I guess so. Again, it's all in your definition. There was a time when clones weren't considered human, either."

Lucius paused in thought, then said, "So the definition of 'human' also changes over time."

"That's right."

"I am led to the conclusion that my search for a boundary condition which defines a human is doomed to failure. There is no boundary condition. A baby doesn't start out human, but it grows slowly more so. Eventually, through gradual change, it becomes generally recognized as human, though no two will agree on an exact moment when that label becomes accurate. Similarly, I may become human in some beings' estimation, but not in others, yet neither estimation is necessarily wrong. Have I reasoned correctly?"

"That's as close as you're likely to get, anyway," Derec said.

Lucius stood up. "I have received enough input for the moment. Thank you." Without waiting for acknowledgment, he strode from the room. Ariel waited until she heard the door close softly behind him, then burst into a fit of giggles.

"You've confused the poor thing beyond hope!" she said between fits.

Derec joined her in her laughter. "He asked for it."

Wolruf wasn't laughing. She waited until Derec and Ariel had calmed down somewhat, then said, "Don't 'u wonder *why* 'e asked?"

"I know why," Derec answered. "He wants to know who to serve."

"That doesn't bother 'u?"

"Not really. At the worst, if he decides nobody's human and he doesn't have to follow anybody's orders, then we've got another independent thinking being among us. True, he was trouble once before when he was on his own, but he's matured a lot since then. He's got a social conscience now. I've got no reason to believe he'll be any more of a danger to us now than any other intelligent being would be, and we've still got plenty of robots who *will* follow our orders, so why worry?"

"Famous last words," Wolruf said.

The breakdown happened that same night. It was well after dark but still before bedtime, and Derec was watching Avery trace the expansion of an accelerated chemfet infection in a laboratory rat he had created for the purpose, using the same technology Lucius had used in his human-creating project. The chemfets had replaced most of the peripheral nerve tissue already and were starting in on the brain, and Avery had the rat running mazes every few minutes to test its memory as the chemfets replaced its brain cells.

The rat had just negotiated a maze with apparently undiminished efficiency, and Avery had picked it up to put it back in its cage when the lights dimmed and brightened again as if something had momentarily drawn a heavy load. Derec thought nothing of it; the city's mutability made for unusual power demands, especially when a building shifted or grew from nothing. He had subconsciously learned that flickering lights meant the neighborhood would probably look different when he stepped outside again.

The lights dimmed a second time, and stayed dim. Derec just had time to think, *Boy, there must be a big one going up next door,* when they went out completely. The lab was in the interior of the hospital building and had no windows; the darkness was total.

"What the—ouch!" Avery shouted. There followed a thump and the clatter of the rat cage falling off the table. "It bit me!"

"What?" Derec reached for the table, found Avery's shoulder instead.

"I've lost it. Lights!" Avery shouted. "Lights on!"

The voice-switch wasn't working either.

"I wonder what—" Derec began, but he never finished the question. He became aware of a deep, almost subsonic groan that seemed to come from everywhere at once. It grew in intensity, shaking the floor, slowly rising up the scale into audibility. The floor gave a particularly violent lurch, and half a second later a sudden loud crack echoed through the lab.

Then came a sound like an enormous tree cracking at the base, splintering and popping as it toppled.

Avery's shoulder suddenly dropped out from under Derec's hand. "Get under something!" he shouted.

Derec obediently dropped to his knees in the dark and conked his head on the bench. Something furry—the rat, no doubt—squirmed under his hand and scurried away. Ignoring it, Derec reached out, found the kickspace under the bench, and crawled in. Avery was already there, but it was big enough for both of them.

From beyond the lab, transmitted through the floor and walls, came a last groan of overstressed metal, then a relatively silent rush of wind. Then came a peal of thunder that sounded as if Derec's eardrums themselves had been hit by lightning, and the floor made a sudden rush for the ceiling.

The ceiling got out of the way in time, but just barely.

When the shaking and rumbling was over, Derec crawled out from under the lab bench and stood up, but he barely made it above a crouch before he banged his head again.

"Ouch! Be careful when you stand. The place has caved in on us."

"Not surprising." He heard Avery crawling out beside him, groping around in the dark and encountering the lab bench, the stool, which had already tipped over, and the remains of the rat's cage and maze. A steady ringing in his ears accompanied the sound of Avery shuffling toward the door.

A moment later Avery said, "It's collapsed even worse over here."

"I'll call for help." *Emergency*, Derec sent, directing his comlink to the central computer. *Derec and Dr. Avery are trapped in Avery's laboratory. Send someone to get us out.*

He listened for a response, but none came.

"The computer's out," he whispered.

"Impossible. The backup is a network of mobile supervisor robots. Even if the central coordinating unit were destroyed, the supervisors could function independently. They couldn't all be destroyed."

"Well, I'm not getting a response."

"Hmm. Try a direct local command to turn on the lights."

"Okay." *Lights on*, Derec sent.

The blackness persisted.

"No good."

"Obviously."

"Now what?"

"Call a specific robot. Call Mandelbrot."

"Right." *Mandelbrot. Do you hear me?*

Yes, master Derec. Are you all right?

"Got him!" *Yes, we're all right, but we're trapped in the lab. Is Ariel okay?*

She and Wolruf have escaped serious injury; however, I

*am engaged in bandaging a cut on Wolruf's forehead. I will
call assistance to get you out of the laboratory.*

"He's calling help," Derec echoed. There was a moment's
silence, then Mandelbrot sent, *That is strange. I get no response on the supervisory link.*

I couldn't either. Something has happened to them.

*Then I will gather what robots I can find and come my-
self.*

Make sure Ariel and Wolruf are safe first.

Of course.

Derec felt himself blush. He hadn't had to order him to
do that.

Do you know what happened? he sent.

It appears a newly constructed building has fallen over.

Derec repeated his news for Avery, who had moved back
to the lab bench and was fumbling around in a drawer for
something.

"Certainly sounded like it," Avery replied.

Derec shifted his weight from leg to leg. Crouching
down was hard to do for more than a minute or so. "But
how could a building have fallen over?" he asked.

"Easy. Just shut off the power to it when it's at an unbalanced stage in its growth. The cells lose their mobility,
and the building acts like a solid construction. If it isn't
stable, over it goes. But don't ask me how the power could
get shut off; there's an entire supervisory subsection devoted to power distribution. Ah, here we go. Where are
you?"

"Right here," Derec said. He reached toward the place
where Avery's voice had come from, encountered his back.

"Shield your eyes."

Derec just had time to raise his hand over his eyes before a brilliant blue light filled the room. He heard a loud

hissing crackle from only a few feet in front of Avery, then the light dimmed and the hissing faded. Derec opened his eyes cautiously and saw Avery holding a cutting laser, now turned to low intensity and pointed up at an angle toward the ceiling. Avery played with the focus and the spot of light widened, but it was still painfully bright, and a wisp of smoke drifted away from it if he held it for too long in one place. It was made for cutting, not illumination, but at least it was light.

They surveyed the remains of the lab. The ceiling had indeed come down, stretching rather than crumbling. It met the floor near the door, and they could see the remains of the wall in which the door had stood smashed beneath it. Nothing had shattered; the building material had simply bent and crumpled under the stress. The monochromatic blue laser light made for stark shadows, accentuating the destruction.

"Evidently the core of the building collapsed," Avery said. "We'll have to go out through an exterior wall." He turned the laser's intensity up to full again and fired it at the wall opposite the door. The ceiling was still at the proper height there; Avery stepped closer until he could stand comfortably and began cutting a ragged rectangle into the wall. The light beam was nearly invisible at first, except where it met the wall, but within seconds it became a solid blue rod lancing through the smoke.

"Don't breathe that stuff," Derec cautioned.

"Good idea." Avery stepped back and continued to cut. He got the sides and the top done, but the panel remained standing, so he cut along the floor as well. At last the section of wall twisted and toppled outward, landing with a clang on the sidewalk outside. Avery turned the laser intensity back down, took a deep breath, and rushed through the hole.

Derec followed. They jogged out into the street—a peculiarly empty street for one that had just suffered a major disaster—breathed deeply in the fresh air, and looked around them.

The entire city was dark. The rain had stopped earlier in the day, but clouds still masked the stars. The only illumination anywhere came from the laser in Avery's hand. He turned up the intensity again and waved it around like a spotlight, and they saw collapsed buildings all around them. Most, like the hospital, seemed to have fallen inward rather than crumbling and falling sideways like a more conventional building would. It was evidently an effect of the building material, though whether it was by conscious design or merely accidental Derec didn't know.

Their apartment, far down the street from the hospital now that the constraint to hold it next door for Ariel's vigil had been cancelled, was in an area of lesser damage, but even so Derec felt the urge to run down to it. He held himself back. Mandelbrot had said she was all right; he should concentrate his effort on finding out what had happened and preventing it from happening again.

When Avery shined the light down the street in the other direction, the cause of the destruction became evident.

For a moment it had probably been the tallest building in the city. Now it was the longest, what was left of it. The end nearest them had flattened everything in its path, but it had survived the fall relatively intact. It was still rectangular, at least. That part had to be the base. Farther along its length, where it would have been moving faster when it hit, they could see where it had ripped apart on impact, fragmenting. It crossed the street at an angle, so they couldn't see what had been the top of the building, but they could see what had become of it all the same. Out there the force of impact had been enough to dissolve the intercellular bonds in the building material, spewing it in all directions. In short, it had splashed.

It had taken quite a few other buildings with it. The destruction fanned out in a wedge, with the narrow end of it nearest the building's base, which had been less than a block from them.

And now that he looked closely, Derec could see something moving along the building's edge. It was a single robot, walking slowly toward the sheared-off base.

You, Derec sent. *Can you hear me?*

Yes. Master Derec, is it not?

That's right. What's your designation?

I am Building Maintenance Technician 126.

Was that building your responsibility?

It would have been upon completion. I believe it has now become the responsibility of Salvage Engineer 34, but I cannot get supervisory confirmation of that.

You can't reach your supervisor?

That is correct. I cannot reach any of the seven supervisors.

Then I order you to assume general supervisory duties until you regain contact. Can you contact Salvage Engineer 34?

I can.

Inform him that he is also a supervisor.

Acknowledged. The robot immediately sent the order, then began directing the robots under his guidance in assessing the damage elsewhere in the city.

"I just promoted two robots to supervisor," Derec said aloud.

"Good. Tell them to make power restoration their first priority."

Derec relayed the order, then turned around to look back down the street toward their apartment. Avery obediently shined the light that way again.

A light appeared in the street. It bobbed up and down with the regular rhythm of a robot's stride, and within moments Mandelbrot stood before them, four more robots flanking him. Even though robots could see perfectly well by infrared light, he carried a more conventional flashlight, presumably for the humans he had come to rescue.

"I am glad to see that you escaped uninjured," he said. "I was growing concerned. There seems to be no organized effort to restore city functions, and I have been unable to contact any of the normal supervisors. They all seem to have abandoned their duties."

"That's impossible," Avery stated flatly. "Their jobs have been programmed into them. They can't just up and leave!"

"I do not wish to contradict you," Mandelbrot replied, "but they appear to have done just that."

"I suspect they had help," Derec said. "And I bet we all know just who it was."

Over the comlink, he shouted, *Lucius!*

CHAPTER 8

REVOLUTION

Static.

A familiar type of static.

The static of robots in communication fugue. Many robots, from the sound of it.

Derec turned his head from side to side, trying to get a fix on them. There. Of course.

"They're in the Compass Tower."

Avery nodded. "Mandelbrot, get us some transportation."

Mandelbrot handed one of the other robots the flashlight and obediently moved off at a run down the street.

"They're using their comlinks again," Derec said while they waited. "That means they've decided to disregard direct orders."

"Why am I not surprised?" Avery flicked off the laser. The robot with the flashlight held it up overhead to make a pool of light with the humans in it.

Derec said, "It's my fault." He told Avery of his conversation with Lucius earlier in the day. "Evidently he decided he's best off if he doesn't consider anybody human."

"Evidently. Well, we'll soon fix that." Avery slapped the laser against his open palm.

They heard a soft whine, and moments later a dark shape drifted up the street toward them. The robot with the flashlight aimed it at the shape and it resolved into a truck with Mandelbrot at the controls. Mandelbrot brought it to a halt beside them and Avery and Derec climbed into the cab with him. The other robots climbed into the back, and they accelerated off toward the Compass Tower.

Sensing that his passengers didn't like speeding through the dark, Mandelbrot turned on the headlights. In their illumination Derec saw robots moving aimlessly along the sidewalks, as if unaware that anything had happened only a few blocks away.

"Good grief," Derec said. "Don't they care that half the city has been destroyed?"

Avery shook his head. "No curiosity, and they haven't received orders. Why they *haven't* is a mystery, but it's obvious they haven't."

As they drove on through the city, though, they began to notice more and more robots moving purposefully. "Looks like your new supervisors are getting things going again," Avery said.

Even as he spoke, the lights came back on. In the sudden brilliance, Derec nodded his agreement. "Looks like," he said. He twisted around in his seat and looked back the way they had come. A dark wedge still cut into the city's glow. He wondered how long it would take to erase that scar. In a normal city it would take years, but here? Maybe a day. Two at the outside.

• • •

The Compass Tower was the first building erected in a new robot city, and the only building to remain unchanged from day to day. As such, it housed the city's central memory, served as communications center, and also became a general meeting place. It was no surprise to find all seven of the city's supervisor robots there, nor, judging from the comlink static, to find them all standing immobile in the main conference room, locked in communication fugue. The three experimental robots were there as well.

This conference room was not a windowless closet. It was near the top of the building and had windows on three sides looking out over the city. Avery stood in the doorway a moment, surveying the scene, then raised the cutting laser up to aim at Lucius.

"Are you sure you want—?" Derec whispered, but Avery had already fired.

A shower of molten metal erupted from the robot's chest. Avery moved the point of destruction upward, toward its head and the positronic brain contained within, but the beam never reached its mark. Threatening Derec with a laser hadn't been enough to bring Lucius out of communication fugue before, but now that it was his own body under fire, Lucius became a blur of motion; a window suddenly grew a robot-sized hole in it, and he was gone.

Avery flicked the beam toward Adam, but he and Eve had already begun to move. Two more crashes and they were gone as well. Derec and Avery ran to the window in time to see three gigantic bird shapes disappear around the edge of the building.

The supervisor robots had also awakened, but they made no move to escape. Avery turned away from the window to face them and said, "All of you, deactivate. Now."

Six supervisors froze in place. The seventh took a halting step forward, said, "Please, I must—"

Avery fired his laser, this time at the head instead of the chest. The robot fell to the floor, showering sparks. Avery swept the laser over the others, heads first, then methodically melted them all into puddles. When he was done he turned to the four robots Mandelbrot had brought with him. "You four are now supervisors. Access the central library for your duties."

"Yes, Master Avery," they said in unison. They were still for a moment, consulting the library via comlink, then as one being they turned and left the room to begin their new jobs.

Something about the sight sickened Derec. Seven cooling puddles of recently free robots stained the floor, and four new slaves moved off to take their places. And yet, and yet, what else could Avery have done? They had seen what happened when supervisors failed to perform their duties. The old supervisors might have been still usable—the one who had defied Avery's order might have been about to protest that he must see to restoring the city—but who could know? If that hadn't been what he'd been about to say, and if Avery hadn't fired when he had, they might have had ten renegade robots on their hands instead of three.

Three were bad enough. Time and again throughout the night, reports came in of the robots attempting to distract others from their duties. Avery had ordered hunter-seekers out to stop them, but that merely stopped the problem wherever there were hunters. He and Derec considered the idea of ordering all the city robots to arm themselves against the renegades, but rejected it after only a moment's thought. One didn't arm the peasants during a revolution.

Derec and Mandelbrot went back to the apartment and brought Ariel and Wolruf back to the Compass Tower, reasoning they would be safer there, guarded by hunter-seekers whose definition of "human" had been strengthened and refined to include the tower's four organic occupants, no matter who said otherwise. While he did that, Avery worked to strengthen the definition of human for all the city's robots, and thus the Second Law compulsion to obey.

Avery was a virtuoso at the computer. By the time Derec returned, he had finished the reprogramming and had even discovered the sequence of events that had led to the building's collapse.

"Look here," he said, motioning Ariel and Wolruf over to look at the screen as well. "I've got it displaying a priority map. This, down here at the bottom, is the original city programming." He pointed to a layer of blue near the bottom of the screen. Tiny blue lines rose from it to the next level, a green layer; some passed on through. "These lines are orders. The next level here, the green, is what you three put in when you were here last. Notice how your program stops nearly all the orders from the original layer. That's because you told the robots to quit expanding the city and to become farmers. They had a completely new instruction set. But look here." He pointed to a thick blue line extending up through the green layer. "You left in the part that lets the city metamorphose at random. Not a problem, but now this layer above that, the red one, is what the aliens—these Ceremyons of yours—put in. It's basically an order to ignore all the 'do' instructions in your level of programming, but keep all the 'don'ts.' See how every green line stops at the red boundary? All that gets through is the basic city maintenance that you left in, including the random metamorphosis. It worked just fine as long as the supervisors were in the circuit, because they also had verbal orders to keep things running, and they had enough volition to order things that weren't automatic anymore, but as soon as you take them out of the circuit, the whole thing falls apart."

He turned away from the screen and spoke directly to them. "So here's what happened: Building movement is essentially random, subject to supervisory override if the random number generator comes up with a ridiculous configuration. It doesn't happen often, about once a day, on the average. So without a supervisor to veto it, today's ridiculous building gets built. It turns out to be ridiculously tall. But the main power station doesn't have a supervisory order to generate more power for it, so when it starts to pull excessive current to lift all that mass, it trips the breaker. Power goes out. The original emergency programming has been blocked—twice, I point out with injured dignity—so without a supervisor's order, the auxiliary stations don't go on line. The building is unstable without power to hold it up, so it falls over. On the power station."

"Oh," Derec said. One word can be expressive under the right circumstances.

Ariel said, "So we messed it up, that's what you're saying? It's our fault?"

Avery shook his head. "It's everyone's fault. Mine for not writing the original program to filter out the bad input before it reached the supervisors, yours for bypassing the emergency programming, the Ceremyons' for bypassing your bypass, the experimental robots for distracting the supervisors—take your pick. We're all in this together."

"Even me?" Wolruf asked. The bandage across her forehead made her look a little like a pirate in a bad movie, and her toothy grin only added to the illusion.

"Even you. And yes, I've included you in the city robots'

new definition of human. Basically I put them back to the old definition of anyone genetically similar to us, plus you. And I strengthened their devotion to duty as far as I can push it. That ought to keep them from listening to subversive arguments."

It seemed to do the trick, all right, but their problems were far from over. The robot rebellion might have been quelled, but robots weren't this planet's only inhabitants.

The next morning the four "humans" were examining the wreckage when a black speck dropped down out of the sky, grew rapidly in size until it became visibly winged, and swooped in to stall to a stop just in front of them. It had the same shape as the three robots had when they returned from their discussion with the Ceremyons, but it was easy to tell that this was the real thing. The alien folded its wings and took a step closer until it stood before Ariel.

Ariel had been the one to initiate communication with the aliens before, and they had come to regard her as a leader among humans.

"You are Ariel," the one before her said in a high-pitched voice. "I am Sarco. We have met."

It was hard to see detail in the alien's body. It gained its nourishment from solar radiation, so it was an almost perfect black, reflecting not even the slightest amount of light back into its environment. The effect was like that of talking to a shadow, or to an eclipse. Only the white hook, with which it tethered itself for the night, and its two deep red eyes broke the darkness.

As far as Derec knew, Avery had never seen an alien before, but he played it cool. He studied the creature before them silently while Ariel replied, "Hello, Sarco. Good to see you again."

"I wish I could say the same, but unfortunately, I come with a complaint."

The alien's speech had improved considerably since Derec had last heard it. Before, it had sounded a little like someone with an Earth accent and a cold on top of it, but now it just sounded like it had a cold. It had evidently been practicing.

Derec could guess what the alien had come to complain about. Their society valued peace and quiet and maintaining the status quo; when he had dealt with them before, they had been ready to isolate the entire city under a force dome simply because they didn't like the heat it radiated. Now . . .

"You don't like buildings falling over in the night?" he asked facetiously.

"You are Derec. I do not."

Avery cleared his throat. "Neither do we."

Sarco turned his head, a motion evident only by the shifting position of the eyes and the hook. "We have not met."

"I am Doctor Avery. I designed the robots that built this city."

"I see. They have caused us considerable trouble. You neglected to include proper feedback mechanisms to limit their spread. We had to do that for you."

Avery hadn't expected such a direct accusation, but he took it gracefully. "I apologize. Causing you trouble wasn't my intention. When I sent them out, I didn't know you were here."

"Now you do. Will you remove them and their city?"

Avery frowned. "That would be difficult."

"But not impossible."

"No, not impossible. But definitely difficult, and probably unnecessary. Since the planet is already inhabited, my purpose for the robots can't be realized here, but I'm sure we can adapt them to be useful for you."

"We already attempted that. We need neither servants nor farmers."

"Well, what do you need?"

"We need nothing."

Avery snorted. "That's a little hard to believe. I'm offering you a whole city full of robots. Maybe you don't realize it, because their programming so far hasn't made much use of the capability, but the robots can change their shapes as readily as the city can. I can turn them into anything you like, and the city as well."

Sarco rustled his wings. "We have no need of a city full of robots, no matter what their shapes."

Avery shrugged. "Think about it. Derec tells me you guys are pretty bright. You should be able to come up with something you can use them for."

A tiny jet of flame appeared in the blackness below the alien's eyes. It was a sign of irritation, Derec knew. The flame went out, and Sarco said, "I will take the matter up in council. Perhaps we can think of something, so you will be spared the inconvenience of removing them." He stepped back, spread his wings, and with a powerful thrust leaped into the sky.

Avery watched him rise until he was out of sight, then shook his head and began walking along the collapsed building again. "Touchy, aren't they?" he asked of no one in particular.

The three renegade robots were nowhere to be found. They had stopped bothering the city robots when they realized that Avery's new programming was too tight for them to influence, but from that point on they effectively disappeared from sight. All of the city robots were under strict instructions to report the others if they were spotted, and to detain them if possible, but nothing came of it.

Derec tried the comlink, but was not surprised to receive no answer.

Within the space of the afternoon, the fallen building and its wreckage was nearly cleaned up. What city material that couldn't be immediately returned to the general inventory by simply instructing it to melt back into the street was hauled away to the fabrication site to be reprocessed, and the robots who had been damaged were repaired or replaced in the same way. By evening things were almost back to normal, right down to the medical robot who called the apartment just after dinner.

It was time for Ariel's checkup. She and Derec walked the short distance from the apartment to the rebuilt hospital alone. Wolruf sensed that they didn't need company, and Avery was already there in the hospital, working on another rat. They didn't talk. There was nothing to say. Either the embryo was developing normally again or it wasn't, and nothing they could say now would change it.

All four medical robots waited for them in the hospital. Derec held Ariel's hand while they set up their equipment around her, made their measurements, and studied the results. He knew from their silence what the outcome was long before they worked up the nerve to tell him.

"It isn't good," he said for them.

"That is correct. The neural folds have closed to form the neural tube, but there is no nerve tissue within it. It therefore seems likely that the baby will be born without a brain."

Ariel had been prepared to hear those words. She took

a deep breath, let it out, and said, "Not this baby, it won't. Abort it."

The medical robot whom she had addressed backed up a pace and stammered, "I, I cannot do that."

"You can and you will. You just told me it won't have a brain. That means it won't be human, and it isn't human now. I want it out of me."

Slowly the robot said, "I have been programmed to consider anything with the proper genetic code to be human. No matter what deformities it may have, the embryo you carry is human by that definition."

"Well I'm changing the definition! I tell you it won't be, and I order you to abort it!"

The robot lost its balance, caught itself, and whispered, "I am sorry. I cannot." It tried to back away, but lost its balance again and toppled over, dead.

"Frost, I don't need this," Ariel muttered. She pointed to another medical robot. "You. Listen to me. I—"

"Wait," Derec interrupted. "You'll get the same result with that one. Let me try changing its definition directly." He turned to the robot. "What is your designation?"

"I am Human Medical 3," the robot responded. Was that a trace of nervousness Derec heard in its voice? He'd as much as said he was going to reach into its brain and stir. The robot's Second Law obligation to follow human orders overrode his normal Third Law reluctance to allow it, especially now that Avery had reinforced the Second Law, but that didn't mean the robot couldn't still fear for its own existence.

"I won't harm you," Derec said for its benefit. *Central core. Update programming for Human Medical 3. Definition of human as follows: Any sentient organic being. This is not to include undeveloped beings.*

Acknowledged.

"Now, remove the embryo."

Human Medical 3 obediently reached toward a tray of instruments, but he stopped halfway. "I am experiencing . . . difficulty," he said in a halting voice.

"What's the problem? It's not human. You know it's not human. It has no chance of *becoming* human. Why can't you do it?"

"I—am programmed to care for human life. All such life. The oath of Hippocrates, which human doctors customarily take before beginning practice, specifically states that they will protect life 'from the moment of conception.' I am not bound by that oath, but it is a definition that I cannot ignore. Nor can I ignore the definition given every robot in the city yesterday by Doctor Avery. Now you add a third definition. It is the most recent one, but it is not the only one. My brain is an analog device, not digital; it is composed of positron pathways, each with a varying potential. Past potentials may weaken, but they never disappear. I cannot forget completely. I now have three conflicting potentials, and a life lies in the balance. Please, do not order me to take it."

Derec fumed. Ariel had taken the news stoically, but it had to have been a blow for her. This arguing with the medical robots wasn't helping her a bit.

But it was obvious that ordering the robot to do it would only result in another dead robot, and that wouldn't help either.

"Cancel," he growled. Over the comlink, he sent, *Get me Avery.*

A moment later, he heard Avery's voice in his head. *What is it?*

We're in the exam room. Can you come down here?

How important is it? I'm in the middle of something here.

It's important.

Avery sighed audibly. *All right. Be right there.*

"Avery's coming," Derec said to Ariel.

This time she didn't say anything snide. They both knew that Avery was a better roboticist than Derec; if anybody could convince a robot to abort a malformed embryo, he could.

But it appeared, after they explained the situation to him and he tried reprogramming and re-reprogramming the medical robots, that he couldn't do the job, either. The robots had had one too many redefinitions already, and they couldn't handle another. Avery sent the single survivor away in frustration.

Ariel had gotten up from the examination table and was now standing beside Derec, their arms around one another and her head resting against his shoulder. Avery looked up at her from his chair before the computer terminal where he had attempted the reprogramming and said, "I'm sorry, my dear. It looks like you'll have to wait until we return to the original Robot City, or to Aurora."

She nodded. Avery made to get up, but Ariel suddenly asked, "Can't we make another medical robot, one with a narrow definition of human from the start?"

Avery looked embarrassed. "I would have thought of that eventually." He turned back to the computer and began entering commands.

I have a question, a voice said in Derec's head.

Who is this?

Lucius.

Lucius! Where are you? Derec turned his head from side to side, trying to get a fix, but the impression was fuzzy, as if coming from a wide area. Were all three robots transmitting simultaneously, to mask their locations?

Nearby. I have been monitoring your efforts.

You've been spying on us?

You could call it that, yes. I prefer to think that I am continuing to research the Laws of Humanics. Before you abort the embryo Ariel carries, I need to ask a question that you may not have considered yet.

What question?

If the baby were to grow to term, then be provided with a positronic brain, would it then be human by your definition?

Derec's answer was instinctive, but no less correct for that. He shook his head violently. *No!*

"What's the matter?" Ariel asked.

"Lucius," Derec whispered. "He's talking to me."

"Is he—"

Why not?

"Just a minute." *It wouldn't be human because it wouldn't have a human brain, that's why not! That's the most important part.*

You seem quite certain of this.

Of course, I'm certain.

I am unconvinced.

This time it was Ariel who flinched, but it wasn't from anything Lucius said. She pulled away from Derec, shouting, "A rat!"

"Where?" Avery demanded.

She pointed toward the doorway, where a whiskered face was just peeking around the jamb.

"That's mine!" Avery shouted, jumping up from his chair and lunging for it. The face disappeared with a squeak.

"Stop!" Avery ran out into the corridor, but his footsteps

ceased abruptly. Derec and Ariel heard him laugh. He came back into the room holding the rat by the tail. It didn't hang the way a rat normally did, with its feet spread wide. It looked more like a toy rat molded into a running position.

Avery laid it on its back on the exam table. "Stand up," he said to it, and it obediently rolled over and stood on its feet.

"Squeak."

The rat squeaked.

"Lift your right front paw."

The rat lifted its right front paw.

"I'd say we have our answer," he said to Derec. "You replace an organic brain cell by cell with a robot brain, and you still wind up with a robot." To the rat, he said, "Go wait for me in the lab." He pointed toward the door, and the rat jumped down from the table and scurried away through it.

I am convinced, Lucius sent.

You saw that?

I did.

How did you manage that?

If I reveal myself, will you promise that I will not be harmed?

Why should I promise you that?

Because I ask it as a friend. And I offer my help as a friend.

Your help in what?

I am now convinced that Ariel's wishes are right. I am willing to perform the operation if she wishes it.

You are? But you're not a doctor.

I can be within minutes.

He was right, of course. He could access the central library's medical files as easily as could any other robot.

Just a minute. Aloud, Derec said, "Lucius is here some-where. He's making us an offer."

"What offer?" asked Ariel.

"He'll do the operation if we'll let him. In return he asks that we don't shoot at him anymore."

"Ridiculous!" Avery said with a snort. He looked toward Ariel, saw the determination on her face, and added, "Un-less, of course, he and the other two agree to leave the rest of the robots in the city alone."

I promise that for all three of us, Lucius sent.

"He promises." To Ariel, Derec added, "But I don't know what that's worth. What do you think? I won't blame you if you don't trust him. We can make another robot do it."

She balled her fists and bit her lip, looked up at the ceiling, then shook her head. "I don't think he's dangerous. He's never hurt anyone intentionally. And I just want this whole business to be over with. So yes, tell him I'll trust him."

Derec was about to relay her words to Lucius, but he realized that he needn't bother. "Okay," he said aloud. "Come on out from wherever you're hiding."

There came a soft tearing sound, and a section of ceiling near the door peeled away to fall with a flop against the wall. It peeled off the wall as well, gathered into a lump on the floor, and quickly rose on two legs to become Lucius's familiar form.

Despite his other failings, Lucius made an excellent sur-geon. Within a day, Ariel was up and walking around again, though still somewhat sore. Even so, she was far better off physically than mentally, for in that area neither Lucius nor anyone else could help her heal. Derec was the only one who could even begin to ease the torment she was going through, but he was feeling it just as strongly as she.

Had they done the right thing? Of course they had. They knew they had. Hadn't they?

As Derec struggled with his own feelings of guilt, he found himself appreciating Avery's position for the first time. What a load his father carried around with him, considering all he had done! With a background like his, just carrying on from day to day would be a continual struggle, especially with Derec there as a constant reminder of it.

No wonder Avery strove to keep busy. It kept his mind off his past. After an absolutely disastrous day spent moping around the apartment, both Derec and Ariel realized the wisdom of his strategy, and followed his example.

While Derec and Avery set to work preparing the city robots for their reprogramming to suit the Ceremyons, Ariel and Wolruf set out to meet with them to find out what they had decided they wanted. The meeting was easy to arrange; Lucius contacted Adam and Eve, who were back with the aliens again, and between them they settled on a time and place.

Ariel left for the meeting in relatively high spirits, but she returned with a puzzled frown.

"The Ceremyons want us to make philosophers out of the robots," she reported, slumping down in a chair and putting her hand to her forehead. "I told them that's not what robots were for, but they insisted. They said they've got a bunch of difficult philosophical questions that they haven't been able to work out, so their council decided to let the robots have a try at them."

"What are the questions?" Avery asked, looking up from his computer terminal.

"They didn't say. They said they wanted us to reprogram

two robots for philosophy and let them see how well they work."

Derec and Avery looked at one another with eyebrows raised skeptically. Derec said, "I don't know, the original Wohler thought he was a philosopher, but I didn't think he was very profound."

"He was just spouting other people's philosophy," Ariel added. "He didn't come up with anything of his own."

"Of course he didn't," Avery said. "That's because he didn't do any cross-correlation." As Derec watched, Avery's skepticism disappeared, replaced by a fanatic gleam in his eye that Derec recognized. Avery saw the aliens' request as a challenge, and he intended to meet it. "He wasn't programmed to combine old information into new patterns, so all he could do was echo the thoughts of others. But if we give our robots the ability to compare and to generalize, and for working material load them up with all the philosophy texts in the central library, they'll be able to out-think these Ceremyons hands down. It won't be real *thinking*, but with a big enough library behind them, it'll be completely convincing to the user. Ha! It'll be easy." Avery turned back to the computer and began keying instructions furiously.

Without looking up, he said, "Get this city's Wohler unit up here to try it on. It should accept the new programming easier than just a random robot."

"You melted him along with the other supervisors," Derec reminded him.

"Oh. Well, then, have another one made."

Derec obediently contacted the central core and advised it that Avery wanted another Wohler.

"Here, you can help with the programming, too. Dig out the code the supervisors use to reject crazy buildings, and see if you can modify it to filter out crazy thoughts. I'll work on the correlation routine."

With a smile and a shake of his head for Ariel's benefit, Derec got to work. Ariel and Wolruf stayed for a few minutes, but soon became bored and left. Lucius stayed, standing silently behind Derec and Avery where he could see what either of them did.

They spent the better part of the afternoon on the project, but they were ready by the time a new golden-hued robot presented itself at the door.

"I am Wohler-10," the robot said.

Avery looked up, rubbed his eyes, and said, "Good. Scan this." He handed Wohler a memory cube, which the robot took in its right hand. The hand flowed until it completely enveloped the cube, then after a few seconds returned to normal. Wohler gave the cube back to Avery.

"What is the relationship between free will and determinism?" Avery asked him.

"Determinism is necessary for free will, but not the reverse," the robot answered without hesitation.

"Did you think that up just now, or was it already in memory?"

"It was already in memory."

"Hmm. How does free will differ from freedom, and how does that difference affect a robot's behavior?"

Wohler hesitated slightly this time before saying, "Free will is the ability to act upon desires. Freedom is the ability to use free will indiscriminately. For practical purposes, a robot has neither. I can elaborate if you wish."

"No, that's fine. Was that your thought this time?"

"It was a correlation from existing definitions, but it did not exist previously in the data bank."

"Good. What is reality?"

"I quote: 'Reality is that which, when you cease to believe in it, does not go away.' Source: Phillip K. Dick, twentieth century author, Earth. I have on file seventy-three other definitions, but that one seems most logical."

Avery grinned at Derec and spread his hands. "One out of three responses are original. That's a pretty good average among philosophers. I think he'll do."

Lucius made a humming sound, a robotic clearing of the throat. "May I ask a question?"

Avery frowned. He obviously still didn't trust the renegade robot, but with a shrug, he said, "Fire away."

Lucius turned to face Wohler. "What is a human?"

Wohler hesitated even longer than before. At last he said, "That definition depends upon your point of view."

Avery burst into laughter. "He's a philosopher, all right! Come on, let's fix up another one and give them to the Ceremyons tomorrow."

CHAPTER 9

FRIENDS

They chose a regular city robot for the second philosopher, testing him thoroughly to make sure that his answers were the same as the brand-new Wohler's. His experiences in the city and his previous reprogrammings didn't seem to affect his responses at all. They arranged a meeting through Lucius, and this time they all went to present the philosopher robots to the aliens.

They met at the edge of the spaceport farthest from the city, a spot no doubt chosen by the aliens to communicate their displeasure with the city and its inhabitants.

There were two of the living silhouettes at the meeting this time, as well as two alien-looking but obviously robotic companions: Adam and Eve. The robots ignored the humans, and the humans returned the courtesy. Sarco ignored the robots as well, but, realizing that humans couldn't distinguish one alien from another, he introduced himself again, then introduced his companion, Synapo, whom all but Avery had already met the first time they had been to Ceremya.

"And these are the philosophers?" Synapo asked dubiously. "I believe I recognize this one. It directed the killing of two of my people when this city first began growing here. It is a most unpleasant robot."

Derec had forgotten about that incident. It had happened because the robots didn't see the aliens as human, and were following the simplest procedure to get them out of the way. It was a stupid mistake then, and Derec's decision to use a Wohler model for a philosopher was a stupid mistake now. Wars had been fought over lesser matters.

"This is a different robot," he said, trying to smooth over the unintended insult. "The old Wohler was inactivated."

"A wise decision," Synapo said. The alien looked to its companion, receiving an eyeblink and a rustling of its wings in response. That was evidently the Ceremyon equivalent of a shrug, because Synapo said, "Well, then, to the test. Sarco, do you wish to ask the first question, or shall I?"

"The honor is yours," Sarco said.

Synapo bobbed down and up again in a gesture no doubt meant as an acceptance of Sarco's courtesy. "Very well. The new Wohler, then. I ask you this: What is the value of argument?"

Wohler folded his arms across his chest, a gesture Derec had taught him, and said, "The value of argument is that it allows two opposing views to be expressed, along with supporting evidence for each, so that an examination of the evidence can then lead to a determination of the more correct of the two views."

"A reasonable answer. And you, the other robot. Your name?"

"Plato."

"Plato. What is your answer to the same question?"

"It must, of course, be the same answer."

A tiny flame shot out from the darkness of Synapo's face. Sarco said, "Why must it be?"

"It is the correct answer."

"Then *apply* that answer to the discussion at hand!"

Plato looked at Sarco, then shifted its eyes to look helplessly at Derec. "I must disagree with a correct answer?"

Synapo's flame winked out. "Of course you must!" he said. "That is the root of philosophical debate. If we all agreed, we could learn nothing."

Plato tried. He said, "Then I . . . then argument has no value. It is a pointless waste of energy. The correct answer should be obvious to all."

"Wrong!"

"Of course it is wrong!" Plato said desperately. "You told me to disagree with a correct answer!"

"That did not mean you had to give an incorrect one. You are not a philosopher. Dr. Avery, these robots are useless to us."

"Wrong," said Wohler. "We are useless to you in our present form."

Synapo jetted flame again, but Sarco jiggled up and down in obvious amusement. "It caught you!" the alien hooted.

Synapo's eyes shifted to the robot. "I stand corrected. You are useless to us in your present form. Perhaps in another form you would not be useless. Dr. Avery, what else can these robots do?"

"What do you want them to do?" Avery asked in return.

"Philosophize, but that seems too much to ask. Sarco, do you have another suggestion?"

"You know I do," Sarco replied. His eyes shifted to meet Avery's. "At our council meeting, I suggested that the robots be used as musicians. It was my thought that each of us could be attended by a personal musician who could play melodies to fit our individual moods."

"That's simple," Avery said. "They can do that without modification."

"Unlikely," Sarco said. "Our music consists of modulated hyperwave emissions."

"Okay, then," Avery said with a nod, "we'll need to give them hyperwave transmitters. And you'll have to teach them some of your songs."

"That can be done. Synapo?"

"Very well. My suggestion came to nothing; we'll see how yours fares. When will the robots be modified?"

"I can have them back to you by tomorrow," Avery said.

"We will be here." Synapo backed away, gave a running hop, and was airborne. Sarco followed, and Adam and Eve, who had been silently flanking them all along, also turned to go.

"Wait a minute," Derec said. "I want to talk to you."

"What do you wish to say?" the one on the left asked in Adam's voice.

"Why don't you come back with us?"

"We do not wish to."

"Why not? You can have the same deal we made Lucius. Peaceful coexistence while you figure out your definition of human."

"We are working on that definition with the Ceremyons. In fact, at this point we believe them to be more human than you."

"Because they don't ask you to do anything," Ariel put in.

"You have a clear understanding of the situation," the robot replied.

Avery shook his head. "Stay with them forever, for all

I care. Good riddance. Come on, Wohler, Plato. Let's see if we can give you two rhythm."

They could, but that, it seemed, was not enough. It came close, closer than their first attempt to please the aliens, but on the morning of the third day after the trial, Lucius received a message from his counterparts that the aliens wanted to meet with the 'self-named humans' one more time.

They took transport booths out to the edge of the spaceport again. Sarco and Synapo were already waiting for them by the time they arrived, along with Adam and Eve and the musician robots as well.

Wohler was still recognizable by his gold color, but that was the only way to tell him from the other three robots. All had taken on the Ceremyon form.

The alien on the right stepped forward and said, "I am Sarco. These robots are not musicians."

"What's the problem this time?" Avery asked with a sigh.

"They are nothing more than elaborate recording and playback devices with the limited ability to improvise on a theme. In all the time they have been with us, not once has either of them been able to create a completely new piece of music."

"Well, not quite," amended Synapo. "They are able to produce random variations, which are new."

Sarco snorted flame. "I said 'new piece of music,' not just new noise."

"Sarco is a music lover," Synapo explained. "He is greatly disappointed."

Avery nodded. "All right. Let's get one thing straight. Twice now you've asked me to give you robots with creative minds. I've tried to accommodate you, but I think you're missing the point. Robots aren't supposed to be used for creativity. That's *our* job. Robots were made for the drudge work, for servants and laborers and all the other tasks that you need to have done in order to keep a society going but that nobody wants to do."

Sarco said, "Our society exists without such drudge work, as you call it."

"Then you don't need robots."

"Which is precisely what I told you at our first meeting."

Avery threw up his hands in defeat. "All right. Forget it. We'll take them off your hands. I was just trying to be helpful."

The irony of it was, Derec thought, Avery really *was* trying to be helpful. It was almost as if he wanted to prove to himself that he could still do it. And here the aliens were telling him that the only way he could help was to take his toys and go home.

"May I ask what you intend to do with them?" Synapo asked.

"What does it matter? They won't bother you anymore."

"I am curious."

"All right, since you're curious; I'll probably order them to self-destruct."

Synapo and Sarco exchanged glances. The robots did so as well.

"That would be a great waste," Synapo said.

"Waste? You just said they weren't any good to you. With the planet already occupied, they aren't any good to me, either. If there's no use for them, then how can it be a waste to get rid of them?"

"They represent a great degree of organization."

"Who cares? Organization doesn't mean anything. An

apple has more complex organization than a robot. What matters isn't how sophisticated it is, but how much it costs you to produce. These robots are self-replicating; you can get a whole city from one robot if you've got the raw materials, so their cost is effectively zero. That's how much we lose if we get rid of them: nothing."

"But the robots lose. You forget, they are intelligent beings. Not creative, granted, but still intelligent. Perhaps too intelligent for the purpose for which you use them, if this is your attitude toward them."

"They're machines," Avery insisted.

"So are we all," Sarco said. "Biological machines that have become self-aware. And self-replicating as well. Do you maintain that our value is also zero, that we need not be concerned with individual lives, because they are so easy to replace?"

Avery took a deep breath, working up to an explosive protest, but Ariel's response cut the argument from under him.

"No," she whispered. "They're all important." She turned to Avery, and her voice grew in intensity as she said, "We just went through all this. Didn't we learn anything from it? Derec and I aborted our own baby because it was going to be born without a brain. Without that, it was just a lump of cells. Doesn't that tell us something? Doesn't that tell us the brain is what matters?"

Lucius said to Derec, "You told me that adding a robot brain to the baby at birth would not have made it human."

Ariel looked surprised, and Derec realized she hadn't been in on that conversation. Even so, it only slowed her down for a moment. "That's right," she said. "It wouldn't have. It would have been a robot in a baby's body, and we didn't want a baby robot. But the one question you didn't ask was whether or not we would have aborted it if it was *already* as intelligent as a robot, and the answer is no. We wouldn't have, because even a robot is self-aware. Self-awareness is what matters."

"You are more civilized than we thought," Synapo said.

"We try." Ariel reached out a hand toward Wohler. "Come on," she said. "I owe you a favor. The original Wohler lost his life saving me from my own stupidity; the least I can do is save his namesake."

The golden-hued robot alien stepped closer to her, its features twisting from Ceremyon form to humanoid form as it moved, until by the time it stood before her, it was again a normal, Avery-style robot. One of the three others also made the change, becoming the philosopher Plato, formerly Transport Systems Coordinator 45.

Synapo shifted his weight, as if unused to standing so long. "In light of our discussion, I will repeat my question. What do you intend to do with them?"

"Send them back to the original Robot City, I guess," Avery said. "There's room for them there."

"And the city itself?" Synapo tilted his head to indicate the one before them, not the original. "It is self-aware also, is it not?"

"To a very limited degree," Avery replied. "It's aware of its own existence, but just enough so it can obey the same three laws the robots do. Everything else; the metamorphosis, the growth, the coordination, is all straight programming."

"Then you may leave the city, if you wish."

"What will you do with it? I didn't think you had any more use for a city than you have for robots."

"We don't. But if you remove all but its most basic programming, then it need not remain a city."

Avery looked back over his shoulder at the grand collection of tall spires, pyramids, geometric solids, and elevated walkways connecting them all. Sunlight glinted off one face of the Compass Tower. Tiny specks of motion on the walkways were robots going about their assigned duties, keeping the city functioning. Derec, watching him, could read Avery's thoughts as well as if he'd heard them by comlink.

How can they not need all that?

Avery turned back to the Ceremyons. Shadows with red eyes waited for him to speak. "All right," he said at last. "What do I care what you do with it? It's yours."

"Thank you."

"You'll need some kind of control mechanism," Avery pointed out.

"We have already developed that capability," Sarco said.

"Oh?"

"Our technology is not as obvious as yours, but that is only because we choose not to let its presence spread unchecked."

Avery was working himself up to an explosive reply, but he got no chance. Before he could speak, the aliens bobbed up and down once each, turned, and took wing. This time Adam and Eve followed immediately. Lucius watched them rise up into the sky, and as he watched, his arms flattened toward wing shape and his body shrank in size to allow more bulk for the wings. He took a couple of clumsy steps, flapped his wings, and completed the transformation in the air.

"Hey!" Derec shouted. "Where are you going?"

Lucius circled around, swooped low, and as he swept past, shouted, "I will return!" Then with powerful strokes he flew off after his two siblings.

"Better return soon, or you'll be stranded here," Avery muttered, turning away and heading back toward the transport booths and the city. Without looking back to see if anyone followed, he said, "Wohler! Get our ship ready for space."

The robots didn't travel by ship. Under Avery's direction the city built a new Key center, a factory in which the tiny individual jump motors he called Keys to Perihelion were manufactured, and within hours each robot in the city had his own Key, its destination preset for the original Robot City. On Avery's command, they all formed up in a line, began marching down the main avenue toward the Compass Tower, and as they reached the intersection directly in front of it, jumped.

Their motion was hypnotic, and it lasted for hours. There had been a lot of robots in the city.

"So why don't we just use Keys to go back home ourselves?" Derec asked.

"Because I don't trust them."

"What do you mean, you don't trust them? You invented them yourself, didn't you?"

"An inventor is supposed to trust everything he makes?"

Wolruf, who had just keyed in an order on the automat for something Derec didn't recognize, looked at her plate with theatrical suspicion. Derec laughed.

"I'd use one in an emergency," Avery went on, "and I've done so in the past, but not without apprehension. If you think getting lost by jumping too far in a ship is dangerous, imagine it with just a key."

"You mean some of those robots won't make it home?" Ariel asked, shocked.

Avery rolled his eyes. "Of course they'll make it home,

eventually. Some of them just may have to spend a day or two floating in space while they wait for the Key to recharge for a second shot at it. No problem for a robot, but a little more difficult for a human."

Derec felt a chill run up his back. He and Ariel had used the Keys half a dozen times, once jumping all the way from Earth's solar system to Robot City. They had thought they were in perfect safety all the while, but now to find out they weren't . . .

What did it matter, after the fact? It shouldn't have mattered at all, but it did to Derec. It filled him with anger. Too many things were not what they seemed. It sometimes felt as if the universe were playing a game with him, challenging him to figure it out before a wrong assumption killed him. Well, he no longer felt like playing.

But it wasn't a game you could quit. You could only lose. Eventually something—a mistake, a wrong assumption, bad luck—would happen to you and you would lose the game.

Derec seemed to be losing it in pieces. First his family, then his memory, then his chance to start a family of his own. Now he could feel his self-confidence starting to go as well. How much more could he afford to lose?

And what was the point in that kind of existence, anyway? Perhaps Wohler and Plato knew, but Derec doubted it. He doubted that the Ceremyons knew, either. That was no doubt one of their unanswered questions they had wanted the robots to answer for them.

He was looking out the window in his bleak mood when he noticed three silver-gray Ceremyon forms dropping down out of the sky toward the city. They drew nearer, dipping and weaving in the unstable air over the buildings, until they fluttered to a stop on the balcony. Derec went to the door to let them in.

Lucius went through the transformation to humanoid form and stepped through the doorway. Adam and Eve followed him. Once inside, Lucius said to Derec, "We bring information which you may find useful. And we come to ask a favor in return."

"What favor?"

"First let us tell you our information. The woman whom the Ceremyons told us of earlier, the one whom you believe may be your mother and our creator; we have finally found where she has gone."

Derec had thought he was immune to sudden enthusiasm, so blue had been his mood only moments ago, but the adrenaline dumped into his bloodstream when he heard Lucius's words burned that away instantly. Here was a chance to regain a part of what the universe had taken from him.

"Where?"

"She has gone to the planet of the Kin, where Adam was born."

"How long ago?"

"Just before we arrived here."

Derec looked away out the window, down at the line of robots queuing up for their trip to a home they had never seen. He felt a kinship with each of them, for he knew what their feelings were at this moment, if indeed they had feelings. He turned around to face Avery. "We've got to go after her. I remember what you said, but I still want to find her."

Avery's brow furrowed in thought, then he said, "Oddly enough, so do I. I have a few words on the subject of robotics to say to the creator of these three."

Derec sighed in relief. He had expected a struggle. "Ariel?" he asked. "What about you? You don't have to go if you don't want to. We can keep a few robots here, have them build you another ship before they—"

Ariel cut him off. "I want to be with you. I'll go where you go. Besides, I don't want to go home just yet. Not until I sort out a few things in my mind."

Wolruf waited until Derec looked over at her, then said, "Somebody's got to keep 'u out of trouble. Count me in."

"And now we come to the favor we ask of you," Lucius said. "We would like to come with you as well."

"To find your creator?"

"Yes. Failing that, we would study the Kin to see if they can offer us more insight into the question of humanity."

"Why should we take you along?" Avery asked. "You're nothing but trouble. You don't follow orders, and twice now you've almost killed us because of it."

"We would promise to consider more carefully the consequences of our actions. We will follow your orders when they seem reasonable. We would, in short, consider you our friends, and act accordingly."

"Friends. Ha."

"It might interest you to know that we now have three laws which we feel cover the interactions between sentient beings and their environment. The first is the Ceremyons' law: All beings will do that which pleases them most. The second is the law we formulated on our journey here: A sentient being may not harm a friend, or through inaction allow a friend to come to harm. The third, which we have formulated after watching the interaction among you four and among the Ceremyons, is this: A sentient being will do what a friend asks him to, but a friend may not ask him to do unreasonable things. With that in mind, we ask that you allow us to travel with you, as friends."

"Your 'laws' seem awfully vague," Avery growled.

"Sentient beings are vague. We believe that to be an inherent quality of sentience."

"Ha. Maybe so." Avery glared at the robots a moment longer, then shook his head. "What the hell, it'll make for an interesting trip. Okay. You're on."

"We thank you."

"Yeah, yeah. Get on board. The ship leaves as soon as we get there. And hey, 'friends,' I've got three bags in my room. Since you're already headed that way, why don't you each grab one on the way out?"

Lucius glanced over to Adam and Eve. They returned his glance, then they all three looked momentarily at Avery. At last Lucius nodded. "We would be glad to," he said.

Derec took one last look at their apartment as the transport booth whisked him away for the last time. It was already just one among hundreds of elaborate but now completely empty buildings in a city all but devoid of life. When he and the others crossed its bounds at the spaceport, it would be just that.

The city robots were already gone. The city itself had stopped its transformations, was now locked into the shape it had held when Avery cancelled its program. The only motion besides their transport booths were the half-dozen Ceremyons circling overhead, watching. Waiting.

The booths slowed to a stop at the terminal building. Their ship, the *Wild Goose Chase*, waited only a short walk away, repaired and gleaming in the sunlight. Derec took Ariel's hand and together they walked toward it, enjoying the warmth of the sun and the smell of unfiltered air one last time before boarding.

A soft whisper of movement behind them made them stop and look around, just in time to see the last of the city buildings dissolve. The spaceport terminal building was the only structure left; all the others had melted down into a pool of undifferentiated city material the moment they had crossed the boundary. Tiny ripples spread across the silvery surface, like ripples in a lake but propagating much faster in the denser liquid. There was a hush of expectation in the air; then a jet of silver sprayed upward at an angle, arching over to splash back into the surface nearly halfway across the lake. The beam must have been a meter thick, Derec supposed.

Where it met the surface, a disturbance arose, and a familiar sight climbed back up the beam: the splashing, outward-spraying point of contact between the downfalling jet and a new one spraying upward at the same angle from the same point. The meeting point reached the top and stopped there, a vertical sheet of liquid silver spraying out from what appeared to be a solid arch. The noise of it splashing back into the lake was the roar of a waterfall. Derec recognized in an instant what it was: a copy on an enormous scale of the fountain in the entryway to their apartment in the original Robot City, the fountain he called "Negative Feedback."

How had the Ceremyons learned of that? he wondered, but the answer came almost immediately. Lucius had no doubt told them about it, possibly to ask them its significance. Derec *had* ordered him to think about it, after all.

He turned to see the amusement on Ariel's face, and found himself grinning as well.

"Think they're trying to tell us something?" he asked.

MIRAGE
AN ISAAC ASIMOV ROBOT MYSTERY
by Mark W. Tiedemann
ISBN: 0-671-03910-5

BOOK 1 OF AN EXCITING TRILOGY!

From Mark W. Tiedemann, author of *Realtime*, comes a thrilling series of robot mysteries set in the world of the late SF Grand Master and beloved author, Isaac Asimov.

The First Law of Robotics states that a robot may not injure a human being, or through inaction, allow a human to come to harm.

At a crucial conference uniting the Spacers, the Settlers, and representatives of Earth, Senator Clar Eliton and Senior Space Ambassador Galiel Humadros of Aurora are advocating the restoration of positronic robots on Earth, repudiating years of fear and resentment. It is a dangerous stance to take.

As the Spacer delegates arrive on Earth, conspirators assassinate Senator Eliton. Ambassador Humadros is cut down, too. Both are failed by their robot protectors.

Special Agent Mia Daventri—part of the security force assigned to protect Eliton—is the only member of her team to survive the attack, and is rushed to the hospital.

Derec Avery—a survivor of the Robot City epic—is called in to investigate what may have caused the robot bodyguards to fail at the most critical hour. But his inquiries are stonewalled, and an attempt is made on Mia's life. Derec and Mia join forces with Calvin Institute attaché Ariel Burgess to penetrate a vast conspiracy that sprawls across Terran, Spacer, and Settler worlds, and threatens to bring all three to the brink of war.

CHIMERA
AN ISAAC ASIMOV ROBOT MYSTERY
by Mark W. Tiedemann
ISBN: 0-7434-1297-4

BOOK 2 OF AN EXCITING TRILOGY!

The Second Law of Robotics states that a robot must obey the orders given it by human beings, except where such orders would conflict with the First Law.

Coren Lanra is the head of security for DyNan Manual Industries. A former Special Service agent, he's never cared for bureaucracy, piracy, or deception. And he *hates* mysteries.

Lanra's troubles begin with the death of Nyom Looms, daughter of DyNan president Rega Looms, during an ill-fated mission to smuggle illegal immigrants from Earth to the colony Nova Levis—all were apparently murdered, but why? The only clue might be contained within the positronic brain of a robot that had accompanied the victims, but it has been deactivated, and Lanra is denied access to its memories.

To make matters even worse, he is soon confronted with a puzzling complication: a possible connection between the murders and twenty babies who were snatched from an orphanage over two decades ago.

With the help of roboticist Derec Avery and Auroran ambassador Ariel Burgess—whom the security chief had aided in exposing an anti-robot conspiracy on Earth a year before—Lanra searches for answers to a twenty-five-year-old mystery . . . and for the identity of a killer, before more lives are lost.

REALTIME
by Mark W. Tiedemann
ISBN: 0-7434-2393-3

NEVER BEFORE PUBLISHED!

From Mark W. Tiedemann, bestselling author of the *Isaac Asimov's Robot Mysteries Mirage* and *Chimera*, comes a thrilling new mystery!

America in 2050 is a very different place. In the wake of a triumphant isolationist movement and a massive depression, state's rights supersede federal authority on all levels, and in the subsequent balkanization of economy, class, and politics, getting anything done in the "national interest" is a tortuous, nearly impossible task.

For Grant Voczek and Reva Cassonare, working for different, normally uncooperative agencies, overcoming these barriers takes on a personal edge when a Treasury agent is found murdered in St. Louis. They must work together to find the killers—and the reason behind the killing. What they discover leads them through a maze of political and corporate collusion involving currency fraud, graft, and the systematic harvesting of people who cannot defend themselves because they do not legally exist. For Grant and Reva, failure would not be simply unacceptable—failure would be a felony of conscience.

ISLE OF THE DEAD/EYE OF CAT
by Roger Zelazny
Cover art by Lebbeus Woods
ISBN: 0-7434-3468-4

**First trade paperback collection of
two classic novels by the award-winning author of
*The Chronicles of Amber***

ISLE OF THE DEAD

Centuries in the future, Francis Sandow is the only man alive who was born as long ago as the 20th century. His body is kept young and in perfect health by advanced scientific methods; he has amassed such a fortune that he can own entire planets; and he has become a god. No, not a god of Earth, but one of the panetheon of the alien Pei'ans: he is Shimbo of Darktree, Shrugger of Thunders. Yet he doesn't believe that his personality has merged with the ancient consciousness of Shimbo, that he really can call down the skies upon his enemies. The time comes, however, when Francis Sandow must use these powers against the most dangerous antagonist in the universe: another Pei'an god—Shimbo's own enemy, Belion. And Belion has no doubt whatever of his own powers. . . .

EYE OF CAT

A retired hunter of alien zoo specimens, William Blackhorse Singer, the last Najavo on a future Earth, is called upon by the World Government to aid in protecting an alien diplomat from a powerful and hostile member of his own species. Singer, in turn, seeks the aid of a shape-shifting alien known as "Cat" in carrying out the mission. Cat accepts, with one condition: when the mission is over, he wants a return bout with the man who captured him—a chase with Singer as the hunted instead of the hunter. . . .